MALICIOUS
INTENT

Books by Lynn H. Blackburn

DIVE TEAM INVESTIGATIONS

Beneath the Surface

In Too Deep

One Final Breath

DEFEND AND PROTECT

Unknown Threat

Malicious Intent

Praise for *Unknown Threat*

"Blackburn's Defend and Protect series is off with a bang in *Unknown Threat*. This heart-racing romantic suspense is one for the keeper shelf! Don your tactical vests and get ready to engage a compelling story that will forbid you from abandoning its pages. Do. Not. Miss. This. One!"

Ronie Kendig, bestselling, award-winning author of The Tox Files

"*Unknown Threat* is a fantastic read! An action-packed opening and sharply drawn characters drew me right in and held me captive. Blackburn has an exceptional gift for weaving twisting plots with characters that walk right off the page. I absolutely adore Faith, the bright and stalwart FBI special agent. I love the attention to detail regarding Secret Service operations. The swoon-worthy romance between Faith and Luke is the perfect slow burn. *Unknown Threat* is an exciting start to a thrilling new romantic-suspense series!"

Elizabeth Goddard, award-winning author of the Uncommon Justice series

"In *Unknown Threat*, Lynn Blackburn has created a page-turning novel with all the elements I've come to love in her books. The hero and heroine are unique and compelling, while surrounded by a rich cast that adds depth to the story. The suspense thread is intense and pulses with energy and pressure. And the romance? It's perfection, with tension to keep me rooting for the characters. It's a perfect read for those who love engaging stories that are threaded with hope."

Cara Putman, award-wining author of *Flight Risk* and *Imperfect Justice*

"By far the best romantic suspense book I have read this year! Fans of Blackburn will not want to miss this fantastic read!"

Write-Read-Life

"*Unknown Threat* by Lynn H. Blackburn is a fast-paced romantic suspense read. I loved the action-packed scenes."

Urban Lit Magazine

"Wow, talk about an intense and riveting read. This series started with a bang and kept up a thrilling pace. I think this is my favorite book by Blackburn to date."

Relz Reviewz

DEFEND
AND
PROTECT
2

MALICIOUS
INTENT

LYNN H.
BLACKBURN

Revell

a division of Baker Publishing Group
Grand Rapids, Michigan

© 2022 by Lynn Huggins Blackburn

Published by Revell
a division of Baker Publishing Group
PO Box 6287, Grand Rapids, MI 49516-6287
www.revellbooks.com

Printed in the United States of America

Library of Congress Cataloging-in-Publication Data
Names: Blackburn, Lynn Huggins, author.
Title: Malicious intent / Lynn H. Blackburn.
Description: Grand Rapids, MI : Revell, a division of Baker Publishing Group, [2022] | Series: Defend and protect ; 2
Identifiers: LCCN 2021035557 | ISBN 9780800741099 (casebound) | ISBN 9780800737962 (paperback) | ISBN 9781493434190 (ebook)
Subjects: LCGFT: Thrillers (Fiction) | Romance fiction. | Spy fiction.
Classification: LCC PS3602.L325285 M35 2022 | DDC 813/.6—dc23
LC record available at https://lccn.loc.gov/2021035557

For Jane B. Huggins, aka Granny,
for a lifetime of memories and a legacy of grit.
We don't make wimpy women in our family,
and I suspect that's because of you.

And in memory of Houston Huggins, aka Pa,
who I adored, who adored me,
and who I suspect would have been my biggest fan.

— 1 —

THE STACK OF CASH on his desk was as close to genuine currency as squeeze cheese was to Brie.

US Secret Service Special Agent Gil Dixon turned one of the fraudulent twenties over and studied the back. There were a few similarities to the real thing, but not enough to confuse anyone paying attention.

"Free money?" Special Agent Zane Thacker asked as he passed Gil's cubicle for his own.

"Hardly enough to fool with." Gil glanced back at the file. Two hundred dollars in twenties. Even if the person who deposited it had been trying to do something illegal, no prosecutor would touch the case. It simply wasn't worth it.

"Where did it come from?" Zane asked the question, but his tone indicated he was making conversation to pass the time, not because he cared about the answer.

"Hedera, Inc."

Zane's head appeared over the top of the cubicle wall they shared. "You're kidding."

"Nope.

"Why would she have counterfeit bills?"

"No idea."

"When are you going to see her?"

"This afternoon. I thought I'd swing by her office first since the cash came from a business deposit."

"What's a company like Hedera doing depositing cash anyway?" Zane's question was the same one Gil had been pondering since the case hit his desk.

"Beats me." Hedera's accounts should have been almost entirely digital. The deposit had been for a little over two thousand dollars in cash, only two hundred of which were fake bills. "That's the reason I want to talk to Dr. Collins."

One reason, but not the only reason.

Everyone in the office knew that Hedera, Inc. was owned by Dr. Ivy Collins. But no one knew that Ivy Collins was *his* Ivy.

No. Not his anymore. And she hadn't been in a long time.

The Ivy from his memory had grown into a delicately boned woman with intense eyes that sparkled from the home page of Hedera, Inc., the company she'd founded four years earlier.

She'd been his best friend. They'd had their whole life planned. School, college, marriage. It was all so simple. Next to Emily, Gil's twin sister, Ivy was his favorite person in the world, so it only made sense that he would spend the rest of his life with her.

It never occurred to either of them that anything could tear them apart . . . until the day she said goodbye and climbed into her mom's sedan. He scampered up a tree and watched until the car disappeared from view, his nine-year-old heart broken.

When he saw her again, she was sixteen. He was seventeen. And that summer, she stole his heart.

And then . . . she was gone.

He'd thought before about confronting her, but he'd never

followed through. What would he say if he ran into her? "Why did you cut me out of your life?" or "What is wrong with you?" or "I missed you." He had no idea what might fly out of his mouth. Their reunion was fifteen years overdue, but this certainly wasn't how he'd expected it to happen. Would she be surprised? Did she even know he was in town? Did she ever think of him?

Not that it mattered. Or it shouldn't matter.

Who was he kidding?

Ivy Collins was the girl who got away. The woman who had haunted him for years. The mystery he needed to solve.

It was time. He was going to get answers. Today.

SIX HOURS LATER, Gil and Zane pulled into an empty Hedera parking lot. Zane waved a hand to indicate the vacant spaces. "It's only four thirty. Why isn't anyone here?"

Gil parked in a visitor space and dialed the Hedera number. A recorded feminine voice with the barest hint of a Southern drawl told him Hedera's business hours were 7:00 a.m. to 4:00 p.m. and encouraged him to leave a message, assuring him he would be contacted during normal business hours.

"These people work seven to four? I wonder if they're hiring." Zane glanced at his watch. "What now?"

Gil wasn't ready to let this go. Not yet. "Do you have time to swing by her house?"

"What else do I have to do?" Zane laughed, but there was a bite to his words. Zane was usually a fun guy, but he'd grown somber and withdrawn over the last few months. Most people assumed it was because of the trauma they'd all been through in the spring. Zane had been shot, then he'd lost his car, his home, and almost everything he owned. And if that wasn't bad enough, his transition to the protective detail had been delayed indefinitely. All solid reasons for a guy to be in a funk.

But Luke Powell, another fellow agent, was convinced it had more to do with Zane's tense relationship with the only female agent in the office, Tessa Reed, and Gil was increasingly sure he was right. This wasn't the time to pry, but the time was coming. For now, he let it go. "She lives about five minutes from here. Let's see if she's home."

Gil slowed as he approached Ivy's house but didn't stop. The house was in an older part of Raleigh, where the lots were large and the subdivision delineations weren't clear. Two stories. Probably with a basement. Sitting on a wooded acre of land.

He drove past five more houses, turned around, and came back. He pulled into Ivy's driveway and parked near the walkway to the front porch. Gil and Zane exited the car and walked to the front door.

Should he warn Zane about his history with Ivy? As far as Zane was concerned, there was no reason to think this would be anything other than a friendly chat.

If the roles were reversed, he would want to know. He paused on the step. "Zane—"

Zane reached around him and hit the doorbell. "What?"

He couldn't very well start this conversation now. "It'll keep." He hoped.

They waited, but there was no sound of footsteps. Gil stepped to the door and knocked. The door swung open as soon as his knuckles made contact.

Not normal.

Was it possible that Ivy had left her front door open? Sure. Was he going to assume that was the case? Absolutely not. Gil pulled his weapon from his hip.

Zane was already dialing for backup. Good. Better safe than sorry. He put his phone back in his pocket and gave Gil a quick nod.

Gil pushed the door all the way open. It swung silently. He concentrated all his senses on this new environment. The foyer was small, with a hexagon-shaped library/office to his left. To his right sat a formal dining room. Both were empty. Straight ahead was a living area with sofas, a large TV, and comfortable chairs. The room was tidy, and there were no apparent signs of a struggle.

But two distinct and wildly contrasting odors battered his senses. Cinnamon and charred flesh.

Zane lifted his chin in a quick up-and-to-the-left. Gil followed, and they cleared two bedrooms and a small bathroom. Then Gil took the lead, and they prowled through the living area. A door to the left was probably another bedroom. If the house plan made any sense at all, then the archway to the right would lead to the kitchen area, but he couldn't get a good sense of the space from where he stood. A door opened from somewhere at the back of the house and feet pounded down steps. But someone was moving in the space on the other side of that wall.

Was a drawer being opened?

After another quick glance at Zane, Gil swung into the next room. A breakfast nook was on his left with a door that he assumed led to the outside, and on his right was the kitchen.

Across the large island stood Ivy Collins.

His Ivy.

It was as if no time had passed. No years of silence. Something strong and true pulled him to her. His body tried to close the gap between them, but his mind resisted. Years of training forced Gil to scan the room.

"Hold here." Zane's voice vibrated with rage as his footsteps retreated. "I'll clear the bedroom."

2

THE MAN'S BODY JERKED BACKWARD. He crashed into the wall and slid down, landing hard.

His right hand reached toward his left shoulder, a reflexive action as he tried to stop the blood gushing from the gunshot wound. Self-preservation appeared to overrule all other instincts, including the one he should have called up—the instinct to flee.

Because if he thought he was in danger from her and her weapon, he clearly didn't have a clue how lethal the man who now stood in front of him was.

Ivy wasn't sure how she knew, but she knew. Gil could kill him. He might even want to. For that matter, she might want him to. She shouldn't, but in that moment, she couldn't dredge up any sympathy for the injured man.

Father, forgive me.

Gil kept his gaze focused on the bleeding man on the floor, but he didn't rush to offer aid *or* arrest him.

"Zane?" Gil spoke in a conversational tone, like he was going to ask if he could grab him a drink or something. "We're clear in here."

A man eased out of her den and into the kitchen area. "You

15

okay?" The man Gil had called Zane did a top-to-toe scan of Gil, then repeated the process on her. His mouth tight, his eyes burning with fury as his gaze paused at her arm, her hand. "Get her. I'll get him."

Gil didn't turn his back on the man on the floor. He backed away. Every step brought him closer to her but kept him where he could rush to Zane's aid if it became necessary. Zane patted the man down, removed two guns—one from a shoulder holster, one from his ankle—then dashed to her hall bathroom. He returned seconds later with two bath towels. He tossed one to Gil. The other he tossed to the man on the floor.

Zane knelt before the bleeding man and applied pressure to the wound. When the man tried to jerk away, Zane's voice rumbled with disgust. "I'm trying to help you. I don't care one way or the other, but it's more paperwork for me if you die."

Ivy heard all this, but it couldn't hold her attention. She was keenly aware of Gil, moving in slow motion in her direction. Once Zane had the man fully under control, Gil didn't hesitate to come to her.

"Gil." His name came out rough. She tried to clear her throat, but her mouth was completely dry. What else could she say? Nothing would make this less awkward.

"Buttercup."

At the long-unheard nickname, spoken with unfathomable tenderness, Ivy forgot she hadn't spoken to Gil Dixon in fifteen years. Her feet moved. She tried to reach for him, but her arms refused to cooperate. She slammed into him, chest to chest, and his arms caught her. "Gil."

"I've got you, Buttercup."

He was so strong. Solid. And for the first time since her ordeal had begun an hour earlier, she was safe.

FIVE INTERMINABLE HOURS LATER, Ivy stared at the clothing the nurse held out to her. "Where did that come from?"

Her nurse, Juliet, ignored the question. "You're cleared to leave. Would you like some help with the shirt?"

Ivy followed the nurse's gaze. Her right hand throbbed with every beat of her heart. Her ring finger and pinky were broken. The doctor said they should heal fine, with no loss of mobility.

Her right thumb sported two burns, courtesy of a cigarette. One on the tip, one at the base. The thumb contained numerous nerve endings. She knew that better than most. But she'd never experienced each and every one of them screaming in distress at the same time.

Neither the cut on her temple nor her lip had required stitches, but that didn't mean her entire face didn't hurt. Her head throbbed. And then there was the nasty burn on her right shoulder. It had come not from a cigarette but from a very hot object that bore a disturbing resemblance to a curling iron but had never been used for anything so gentle. *Will I ever be able to curl my hair again?*

If they'd wanted to hurt her, those morons who tortured her would have threatened to shave her head. Facing that possibility, she might have at least considered giving them what they wanted. It was a small mercy, still having her hair. But in this moment, she would take it.

They weren't big on mirrors in this emergency department. Probably so people wouldn't freak out when they got a good look at themselves after a trauma. But she could imagine the state she was in. When they fried her shoulder, a few strands of her hair were singed. She couldn't see the damage, but the stench of burnt hair was unmistakable and inescapable. She caught a whiff every time she moved.

And there was no way she didn't have mascara and eyeliner

tracks on her cheeks. She had tried hard not to cry. But when the big guy ripped her shirt, leaving her exposed and trembling, already aching from the broken fingers and burned thumb and two times he'd backhanded her, she expected the worst.

There'd been no time to mentally prepare herself to be toasted like a marshmallow. *Great. No more s'mores for me.*

Juliet tilted her head to one side. "Ma'am. Do you want some help getting dressed?"

"No. I can get it. But where did my clothes come from?" They were definitely her clothes. Black yoga pants and a butter-soft T-shirt. Socks. Tennis shoes. A light sweater. And . . . other things. Someone had brought these clothes to the hospital for her. Was it Gil? As much as she wanted to know where Gil was and why he had walked back into her life, today of all days, she couldn't stop the blush at the thought of Gil Dixon going through her underwear drawer.

Not because of the clothes—although that was cringeworthy—but because of the picture, framed and set in a place where she could see it every day. If he'd been in her room, there was no way he could've missed it.

"I don't know, hon. The unit secretary brought them to me." Juliet turned to the door. "I'll check on you in a few minutes, and we'll get you out of here."

Ivy waited for the door to close before she took the clothes into the tiny bathroom. She wouldn't risk changing in the main room, where any minute someone could walk in on her. She'd shown more than enough skin tonight.

She pulled the tie, curly from an untold number of washings, at the neck of the hospital gown, slipped off the gown, and reached for her clothing. She could figure out how to get her clothes on without the use of two fingers and a thumb. She was an engineer, for crying out loud. Thank goodness those idiots hadn't had the sense to look at her hands, pay attention to the calluses, and discern that she was a leftie.

Ten minutes later, she leaned against the doorframe, proud and exhausted. She'd done it. Now she faced a new dilemma. She'd arrived in an ambulance. An ambulance Gil insisted she ride in after she almost passed out in the kitchen moments after he arrived. The paramedics said it was due to a combination of shock and excruciating pain from the burns, but it was still embarrassing. After she swooned— unfortunately, there was no other word for it—Gil refused to let anyone ask more than the most basic questions.

"What did they want?" Access to her computer at work.

"Why?" No clue.

"Have you ever seen them before?" Never.

"How did they get into your house?" She didn't know. She'd been in the kitchen, removing her leftover pad thai from last night's dinner with her ex-boyfriend (a fact she left out of her narrative) from the microwave. She turned, and they were there.

"You didn't hear them?" No. They could have rolled through her house in a tank, and she wouldn't have heard them. She had her AirPods in her ears. She skirted over the fact that she'd been singing and saw no reason to mention that she'd also been dancing or that she'd spun around and landed in the arms of the man who later tried to barbecue her shoulder.

At that point, Gil intervened. "Enough. She needs medical attention." He glared at the police officer questioning her. The police officer glared back.

Gil didn't flinch. His look was cold. Hard. Furious. "Dr. Collins is a prominent member of the community. Her home is here. Her business is here. She isn't going anywhere. She'll be available to answer questions later."

19

He wasn't wrong. But how did he know all this about her? And why was he here in the first place? Armed? With a partner? She had so many questions.

"Right now, she's going to the hospital." Gil spoke with a finality that brooked no argument.

The police officer backed down, but a few minutes later as the EMTs were strapping her onto the gurney, she overheard him on the phone. "No idea. Never been in a showdown with a Secret Service agent before." A pause. "True." Another pause. "Yeah. She's gorgeous, but—" A longer pause. "Yeah. I'll find out."

Gil walked into the room, and the police officer walked away. Gil stared after him for a moment before turning to her. "Ivy." When he said her name, she could almost see the boy she'd known. Although that boy had grown into a man with jet-black hair, which was currently disheveled because he kept running his hand through it. He leaned close, and his sky-blue eyes captured hers. She couldn't look away. "I wish I could go with you, but I have to stay here. We'll have security for you at the hospital. I'll find you as soon as I can." He reached a hand toward her cheek and tucked her hair behind her ear, a move he'd perfected during their last summer together. Then the paramedics had whisked her away.

She probably should have called someone. But who?

She had employees. Coworkers. Business associates. She could pick up the phone and have a lunch date or coffee chat with any number of prominent Raleigh business leaders.

But she didn't have friends. She had colleagues.

And as of today, she had Gil. But she had no idea what he was.

If anyone had asked her this morning what would happen if she ever ran into Gil Dixon again, she would have offered up several scenarios. One possibility involved them making eye contact, after which she would turn and run away. Very mature, that one. Also, the most likely.

She'd also considered the possibility that she might burst into tears and immediately start babbling and asking for forgiveness. Or she might stand before him, mute and miserable, as he unloaded fifteen years of righteous anger. If he wanted to do that, she would have to let him. She deserved it all.

No matter how many times she'd considered the possible options, not once had she dared to hope that he would look at her the way he had tonight.

And never, not ever, had she expected him to call her Buttercup.

—3—

GIL PACED THE EMERGENCY DEPARTMENT waiting room. How long did it take to set fingers and patch up burns? Ivy needed to rest. She was probably starving. Her dinner had been on the counter. Cold. Uneaten.

She didn't need to be facing this alone. *She might not be alone.*

Gil studied the people in the waiting area. Could any of them be here for Ivy? She'd lived in Raleigh for several years. She had to have friends. Her ring finger was blissfully free of adornment, so he was fairly certain there was no fiancé. No husband. But that didn't mean she didn't have a boyfriend.

He'd kept up with her career, and he knew the outline of what her life had looked like during the fifteen years they'd spent apart. But he had no clue what had colored in the spaces between her education and work. There was so much he didn't know about her, but in the few minutes he'd been with her, he'd been able to confirm three things.

One, she was in big trouble. Those guys weren't there to play, but based on her responses, she didn't know why they were there or what they wanted.

Two, she'd known he was in Raleigh, and she was happy to see him. Although he probably shouldn't read too much into that. Anyone would be happy to see any federal agent walk in while they were being tortured. But he'd expected her to be more surprised than she'd been. If he was right, then he wasn't the only one who'd been keeping tabs.

Third, she was still *his* Ivy. She'd grown up, but the Ivy he'd known was still there. Blonde hair only a few shades darker than when they were kids now fell in loose waves to her shoulders, the same blue eyes he'd looked into thousands of times, the same tiny birthmark at her temple. She was taller than Emily by several inches, probably five-foot-seven without shoes. Her skin was still fair. And she still fit perfectly in his arms.

He would never forget the first time she held his hand, or the hours they spent wandering the pasture at twilight, his arm around her shoulders, her arm around his waist, her cheek resting against him. They were young, but he loved her. He wanted to spend his life with her.

And then she cut him out of her life.

He wasn't sure if they could have survived the betrayal that shocked them all that summer, but she didn't even give them a chance to try.

She probably wouldn't want to try again now. Too much water under the bridge and all that nonsense. Sure, she'd practically collapsed in his arms when he called her Buttercup, but she was injured and in shock. She would pull it together, and when she did, Dr. Collins would leave Buttercup behind and go back to pretending he didn't exist.

"Special Agent Dixon?" The voice pulled Gil from his musing. He turned to find the source—a man in scrubs standing a few feet behind a desk. He was tall, blond, thirtysomething, and either in a very bad mood or not pleased to be talking to him.

Gil walked toward him. "Yes."

The man opened a door located to the side of the desk and indicated that Gil should walk through. "I'm Dr. Steele. The officer providing security for Dr. Collins told me you were waiting. We're releasing Dr. Collins, but she shouldn't be alone tonight."

"She won't be."

Dr. Steele frowned at him. "I want Dr. Collins to be safe, but I don't think spending the night with strangers is the best option for her mental health. Not after what she experienced. She's strong, but no one needs to feel alone after they've been tortured. Have you spoken to her friends? Arranged for someone to stay with her? I'm not sure what the protocol is for this, but—"

"I've known Iv—Dr. Collins since we were kids." At this remark, Dr. Steele lost his frown. "For tonight, I'm here as her friend. Lucky for her, I'm the kind of friend who can keep her safe."

"Will you be taking her back to her home?"

"No."

"Where—"

"Dr. Steele, I appreciate your concern. But part of keeping her safe involves making sure her whereabouts remain unknown until we have a clearer picture of the threat."

"I can understand that." Dr. Steele didn't add anything. His interest in Ivy appeared to be more than what would be typical of an emergency department physician. He'd patched up her physical wounds but clearly wasn't going to let her walk out the door until he made sure her emotional needs would be met.

"My sister, also a childhood friend of Dr. Collins, is on her way. She'll be here in a few hours. Ivy will have support, friendship, and security." Possibly more than she wanted. But despite his best efforts to dissuade his sister, Emily was en route and planned to stay for the weekend.

"Good." Dr. Steele handed him a business card. Gil took it, and Dr. Steele stepped a fraction closer. "Torture," he said, lowering his voice, "can result in unexpected triggers. If she struggles, don't hesitate to call."

Gil studied the card, then slipped it into his pocket. "I'll do that." He meant it. He'd tried all evening not to think about what Ivy had endured before he and Zane arrived at her door. But he was going to know all about it, and soon.

Dr. Steele pointed to a room. "She's in there. Give me a moment." He tapped on the door and entered. Gil leaned against the wall, and he could make out the words as Dr. Steele greeted Ivy but lost them soon after when the door closed. Three minutes that felt like thirty later, the door opened, and Dr. Steele emerged. "She's ready for you."

"Thanks." Gil stepped around Dr. Steele and entered the room. Rather than closing the door behind him, he gave himself five seconds to familiarize himself with the room. It was habit. It was training. That's what he told himself. And it was true.

But it was also true that he loathed hospital rooms and had no desire to spend a second longer in this one than necessary. Also, while he knew Ivy and she knew him, she was in many respects a mystery. A beloved stranger, but a stranger all the same.

"Hi." Her soft voice pulled his gaze from his surroundings to her. She was dressed in the clothes he'd brought. Her skin, translucent and fair under normal circumstances, had a pallor to it that had his gut clenching with a mixture of anxiety and something else . . . something proprietary. As if it was his responsibility to be sure she was protected.

"Hi." He was supposed to say something at this point. Should he ask her if she was okay? Or . . . what?

She dropped her head, a smile ghosting across her features.

"I think this might be the longest we've ever been silent in each other's company."

At her joke, his brain and tongue synced. "Not true. We couldn't speak during church."

"Good point." This time her smile lingered a few seconds before fading.

"Ivy." It was on the tip of his tongue to tell her he'd missed her, but he held it back. No need to freak her out. They would have to talk about what had driven them apart, but not tonight. "What do you need right now? Food? Coffee? I can't offer to take you home because your home is a crime scene. And to be honest, the Raleigh police are great guys, but if I don't show up with you soon, they're going to come find you."

"I'm shocked they aren't already here. It doesn't seem like normal procedure." Ivy's lips twisted to one side in an expression of concentration Gil had forgotten about, and it sent a shock of memory through him.

"I promised you weren't a flight risk and I'd bring you to them as soon as I could."

Ivy's eyes widened. "They waited because you asked them to wait, didn't they?"

"They have plenty to keep them busy at the moment. But I do have to take you over there. I'll stay until you're finished. Then it's up to you. Have you called some friends? Is there somewhere you want me to take you tonight?"

Ivy grimaced. "No. A hotel would be great. I don't . . . I didn't . . . there's no one. I can't risk . . ."

"You don't want to put any of your friends at risk?"

"That's part of it."

"What's the other part?" It was pushy of him, and he wouldn't be surprised if she refused to answer.

"Most of my friends"—she put air quotes around the word *friends*—"are more acquaintances or business associates or employees. I work. I eat. I sleep. I go to church on Sunday. Repeat." She fiddled with the hem of her sweater. "I'll go with you to speak to the police, but you don't have to stay. It's late and it's a Friday night. I'm sure you had plans for this evening and they're already ruined. You've already done too much. I'll Uber to a hotel when I'm done."

Gil fought the urge to roll his eyes. Yep. Still his Ivy. Still stubborn as a mule.

"If you think I'm leaving you alone in a police station, you aren't nearly as smart as everyone thinks you are, Dr. Collins. And when you're done, I'm taking you home with me."

HE WAS TAKING her home with him? Had he lost his mind?

Gil wasn't done talking. "I called Emily. She'll be at the house by the time we're done."

Ivy closed her eyes and took in a slow breath. Images from their tangled past collided with their current status, and the resulting picture was murky and confusing.

Until she was sixteen years old, Gil had been her person. Her other half. Ivy had missed Gil most. His sister, Emily, had been such a girly-girl. Into Barbie dolls, nail polish, and clothes. And boys. Even in elementary school, Emily Dixon had been boy crazy. Ivy had hated Barbie dolls and nail polish, and she'd worn whatever her mom managed to find. And there was only one boy Ivy had ever had any interest in and that was Gil.

But that didn't mean she hadn't missed Emily. Gil and Emily were close as kids, and because Ivy spent a lot of time with Gil, she also spent a lot of time with Emily. When Ivy spent the night with the Dixons, which was often because her mom worked third shift a lot, it was Emily's room she crashed in. Emily would give her the top bunk because she knew how much Ivy preferred it. After the lights were out, Emily would talk until Ivy fell asleep. And despite having almost nothing in common other than Gil, they, too, had become close.

Ivy's insides melted a little at the knowledge that Gil and Emily were still tight as adults. Close enough for him to call Emily tonight, and for her to drop everything and come.

Gil's offer felt more like a command than a request, but she couldn't stay with him. But not because she didn't trust him. Because despite the fact that she didn't know this man standing in front of her, she *did* know him. And it wasn't that she didn't want to be with him, to hear him talk, to catch up on every detail of his life. She'd missed him with an ache that had been intense for years, and while it had dulled some, it had never gone away.

But staying at his house? No. She knew, even years later, that Gil would be a gentleman. He would give her a bed to sleep in. And even though she could see the questions burning behind his eyes, he would give her space. But she couldn't accept his hospitality. Not after what happened, and how she reacted, and what she did. There was too much between them. She'd been a coward for far too long. Gil and Emily deserved an apology and as much of an explanation as she could give them about something she still didn't fully understand herself. But she didn't have it in her to face them. Not tonight.

Gil took a step in her direction. "I'm sorry. I promise I'm not usually so presumptuous. But . . . it's you." His voice cracked on the last word. "I won't lie or pretend that I don't have a million questions. But tonight isn't the time for them. Tonight you need to sleep. You need to feel safe. And if you insist on going to a hotel,

I won't stop you. But if you go to a hotel, I'll spend the night in the hallway."

What? No. "I can't let you do that."

"You can't stop me."

They stared at each other. "Why are you doing this?"

"I told you. It's you."

"That's not an answer."

Gil ran a hand through his hair. "Did you miss me?" The words sounded like they'd been ripped out of him, not like he'd chosen to say them.

In the face of his raw vulnerability, the truth spilled out before she could stop it. "Every day."

Something that looked like pain mixed with relief flashed in his eyes. "I've missed you too. Now you're here. That's why."

He'd missed her? He should have hated her. But before she could think through any more, he must have decided the discussion was over, because he changed the subject. "More about that later. Right now, tell me what you need. Food?"

In response, Ivy's stomach grumbled. "Food would be good." Maybe after she ate something her brain would stop short-circuiting every time Gil looked at her and she'd be able to formulate an argument he couldn't work around. She scanned the room to be sure she wasn't leaving anything behind.

Gil leaned against the wall. "Food first. Police second. Emily third."

As Gil's pronouncement settled, her entire body tensed. She tried to hide her reaction by turning to the small table where the nurse had left her paperwork.

While talking to Gil, she'd forgotten that her shoulder was burning, her fingers were throbbing, and pain was pulsing through her thumb approximately seventy times per minute.

For a few precious moments, she'd blocked out the specter of danger hovering over them. And she still didn't know why Gil or, more specifically, the US Secret Service had paid her a visit. Not that she was complaining. She'd been doing her best to keep up a brave front, but she'd never, ever been as afraid as she'd been today.

And she still didn't know why anyone would want to access her computers enough to attack her. She should ask Gil why he'd been the one coming through her door, but depending on his answer, she might fall apart, and she couldn't do that. Not now.

She struggled to keep her voice light. "Okay." One word. That's all she said, and she thought she'd done a pretty good job of keeping her terror out of it. But as soon as the word left her mouth, Gil's footsteps approached, and he squeezed her left elbow. She kept her back to him. She needed a few more seconds to pull it together.

"Buttercup?"

"I'm okay."

"You aren't." The words were certain. "But you will be."

"How do you know?" Gah. She hated the desperation she couldn't keep from bleeding through.

"It's the only option. I found you. I'll find out what's going on. I'll keep you safe."

She turned at that. Gil had always been intense and unafraid of saying what was on his mind and in his heart. Clearly that hadn't changed. His blue eyes burned with a ferocity that conveyed his fury at what had happened to her and his confidence that he could solve the mystery.

"Okay."

He stepped back, face wrinkling in surprise. "That's it? No argument? No detailed explanation of the obvious logical fallacies in my statements?"

He might be right. He might be wrong. But for tonight, she was prepared to go with it. "I'll argue with you tomorrow. It won't take me long to dismantle your assertions and detail how ridiculous it is for you to think you can swoop in and solve all my problems."

Gil reached for her good hand. He tucked it in the crook of his arm and whispered, "I can't wait."

He led her out of the hospital and to his car, a Ford sedan with government plates, conveniently parked in a space reserved for law enforcement.

"Not what I would have expected." She waved her hand at the car. Gil opened her door, then put one hand on her right elbow, the other behind her, and helped her lower into the seat without one bump to her tender hand or shoulder.

He didn't respond to her remark about his car, and her heart sank at the possibility that he didn't get the joke. He closed her door and jogged to the driver's side. After he buckled up, he flashed her a mischievous grin. "Sorry I don't have the Porsche I promised you."

He *did* remember. Was it possible he remembered all the same things she did? She tried to cover her delight with a dramatic sigh. "I guess this means I shouldn't expect a sprawling ranch with horses, goats, and a helicopter pad."

Gil's laughter filled the space around them, but there was an unexpected edge to it. "That's a no. I live in a fixer-upper in a part of town trying hard to come back from the edge. I also don't have a pool or a bowling alley."

"That *is* disappointing." She gave another overdone sigh.

"For me as well. The good news is, I have great neighbors who seem to like having me around despite the fact that I got shot in my front yard earlier this year and ruined our neighborhood crime statistics."

Ivy couldn't stop the shiver that rippled through her at his words. He'd been shot in his front yard. She'd seen the news reports and then scoured the internet for every scrap of news about his shooting. She hadn't slept well for weeks afterward. She should have reached out to him then. But years of avoidance had built a wall she didn't think they could scale. She'd been terrified to try.

Tonight, for better or worse, they faced that wall. What they would be a day, a week, a month from now, she had no idea. But whatever they wound up as, it wouldn't be what it was yesterday.

Gil pulled into the drive-through of a fast-food joint and they munched on fries, which were blissfully hot and salty, burgers, and milkshakes. Chocolate for him. Vanilla for her.

And for ten minutes, she was a little girl again. A little girl whose future made perfect sense. Then Gil parked the car, and she looked up.

The police station.

Gil cleared his throat. "When we get in there, it's up to you if you want me to stay with you. I'll understand if you don't." Without waiting for her to respond, he grabbed their trash and climbed from the car. He tossed the garbage into a nearby can, then opened her door. He reached in and gently wrapped one hand around her right forearm. He helped her out of the car, taking great care not to allow her to bump her shoulder or hand against anything, and then he waited until she was steady on her feet to release her. But once he closed her door, he didn't touch her again until they reached the door. Then his hand hovered at her lower back, and he directed her to the front desk.

Before he could speak, a booming voice pulled Ivy's attention, and undoubtedly everyone's in the room, to a door to the left. "Dixon. What part of 'as soon as possible' wasn't clear to you?"

Gil muttered something under his breath that sounded a lot like,

"I hate this guy." "Morris, good to see you. Feel free to file your timeliness complaints with Dr. Steele, that's Steele with three *e*'s, at Wake Med. I'm sure he'll be delighted to give you a breakdown of how he spent his evening."

"Stand down, Dixon."

"You're the one who wanted another statement from Dr. Collins tonight. She's had a brutal day, and Dr. Steele made it clear she needs rest. You'll have to pardon me for not being in the mood to spar with you tonight."

"Sheesh. You were a lot more fun before you got shot."

Ivy didn't miss the way Gil bristled beside her, but he didn't respond to the taunt. Morris brought his gaze back to hers. "Dr. Collins, if you'll come with me, we'll get this taken care of as quickly as possible." He gestured toward the door.

But she couldn't get her feet to move. He was a police officer. He wanted to talk to her about her case. But he wanted her to go back there, behind the desk, into the maze of halls and offices, alone, with him?

Earlier today, she would have gone without a second of hesitation. But not tonight. She wasn't going anywhere with a stranger. Not alone. Without conscious thought, she grabbed Gil's arm. His forearm flexed under her grip, and he turned to her with one quirked eyebrow.

He must have read her panic, because his eyes flared with understanding and he pulled her a fraction closer to his side, then tugged her with him toward the door. "Lead the way, Morris. The lady is exhausted."

— 4 —

DETECTIVE MORRIS was an excellent investigator. If he wasn't, Gil wouldn't be able to tolerate him. As it was, he could only stand him in small doses. The interview room he'd brought Ivy into was more comfortable than an interrogation room, but not by much.

Ivy sat in a chair on the left side of a worn rectangular table. Morris sat across from her. "Dr. Collins, would you walk me through your day?" Morris leaned back in his chair, a picture of ease. Almost boredom. What was he playing at?

Gil chose to stand, leaning against the wall opposite the door. He could have taken a seat beside Ivy, but he wanted to be able to see her face as she spoke. Somewhere between the moment she grabbed his arm and the moment Morris opened his mouth, Ivy had recovered from whatever had frightened her. He could see it in the set of her shoulders and the way she studied Detective Morris.

Gil didn't know the adult Ivy, but something told him Detective Morris was on the verge of getting his cue ball of a head bitten off.

"You'll need to be more specific, Detective Morris." Ivy didn't give him a chance to respond. "Where would you like me to start? My day began at 4:30 a.m. It will take us quite a while for me to guide you through every part of it. Is that what you want?"

Gil kept his face passive at Ivy's response, but Morris didn't. He rolled his eyes and muttered something about "academics" before he moved his arms to the table. "Why don't you give me an overview of your day, and then get specific when you reach the part where it went south?" Every word dripped with disdain.

Ivy didn't react to his attitude. She sat even straighter and spoke in clear, precise detail. "I woke at 4:30 a.m. Did yoga. Ate breakfast. Did some reading. Spent some time working on a Bible study and in prayer. I got ready for the day and was in the office at 7:30 a.m. I reviewed internship applications for next year. I also reviewed a paper I'm submitting to a journal. Otherwise, the day was normal."

"What is a normal day at Hedera, Dr. Collins?"

Gil perked up at this question. He knew the basics of what she did but not the specifics.

"Today, I spent four hours working with one of our research teams. We're finalizing a prototype of a prosthetic that, if it works, will give amputees the ability to control the prosthetic hand with their mind. We've been working on this prosthetic since the first days of Hedera. It's an exciting time for us."

Gil locked on to the fact that she was about to launch a product that had been in development for years. If it worked, what kind of financial impact would that have on the company? And conversely, what if it didn't? Could there be a motive for someone to hijack the product? Or was it possible the prosthetic couldn't perform as advertised and someone in her company was covering it up? Ivy was smart, but even smart people could be fooled by people they trusted.

The only acknowledgment Morris gave to Ivy's answer was a low grunt. He waved his hand, and she continued. "I spent an hour and fifteen minutes with one of our researchers who is trying to increase the touch sensitivity on one of our other prosthetics. I spent the rest of the afternoon in my office working on an expense report because my assistant is a tyrant and wanted it yesterday."

Gil chuckled. Morris didn't. Ivy cast Gil an appreciative glance, but then her mouth pinched, and Gil braced for what was coming. The normal part of the day had ended.

"Then the power went out. We called the power company, and they told us a car had rammed into a pole and had taken out a transformer. Power lines had come down around the car and made a mess of everything. They said it would be hours before power was restored."

Ivy wasn't looking at Morris anymore. As far as Gil could tell, she wasn't looking at anything. Her eyes blinked several times, and her chin was pointed down and to the left. She wasn't saying anything, but no doubt a lot of activity was going on inside her head. Gil wouldn't have been surprised if her hair had started smoking.

"Dr. Collins?" Morris spoke like he was chastising an uncooperative three-year-old. Couldn't he tell she was working something out in her head?

Ivy didn't respond.

"Dr. Collins?" This time Morris sounded like he was fussing at a rebellious teenager.

Ivy flicked a few fingers in his direction and said, "Hush. I'm thinking."

Gil wanted to give Ivy a high five. Zane and Luke were going to love this.

Morris turned every shade of red. "Dr. Collins." Now he sounded ticked, and this time he broke through Ivy's concentration.

He also broke through her façade of politeness. She leveled a glacial glare at Morris, and her voice was even colder than her look. "Detective Morris, if you would stop interrupting me, I would be able to solve this in my head and give you something useful."

Gil didn't know if Morris was mad, embarrassed, or confused, but whatever it was, he didn't respond immediately. Ivy must not have expected a response, because she went back to staring at nothing, her head turning from side to side, her face focused and intense.

After another thirty seconds, Ivy relaxed into her seat and turned to Gil. "You haven't said and I haven't asked, but I need to know. Why were you at my house?"

There was no hostility in her question, but Gil got the impression his answer was important to whatever she was working out in her mind. "Hedera made a cash deposit of two thousand dollars and change last week. Two hundred of it was counterfeit."

"Hmm."

Hmm? Most people had a different reaction to learning they'd passed counterfeit money. Usually one that involved more surprise or defensiveness. Or flat-out lying if they knew they'd done it. A twinge of doubt flickered in Gil's mind. Ivy had experience with the kinds of people who ran scams for a living. She might know more than she was letting on, but Gil was willing to wait to see where she was going with this, unlike Morris, who shifted in his seat and spluttered incoherent nonsense.

He caught Morris's eye and frowned at him. "Give her a minute, man. She's a freaking genius. Makes sense to let the smartest person in the room work out what's going on."

Morris rolled his eyes and huffed. What was with this guy and the eye-rolling and sighing? He was at least forty-five. Not fifteen.

Ivy shook her head and refocused—not on Morris but on Gil. "You should have someone investigate the accident that knocked out our power. I don't think it was an accident. I don't know what the endgame is, but for whatever reason, they, whoever they are, wanted me out of the office and at home."

Gil took a moment to consider her theory. "You think someone intentionally hit that pole to knock out your power? How could they have known you wouldn't wait for it to be restored?"

"That would have been a risk, but a small one. It was late Friday afternoon, and we were already planning to be out of the office all weekend. We're having the building and offices painted. They start in the morning. I made sure everyone knew to back up everything by noon today. The plan was to shut down all our systems at the close of business. The painting was supposed to be done by Sunday afternoon, and we were assured we could return to work on Monday."

"I'm not sure how that translates into someone intentionally knocking out the power," Morris said, undoubtedly trying to regain control of his interrogation. "Sounds like bad luck. Not a criminal act."

"I might agree with you had I not been tortured for an hour by people who claimed they wanted nothing other than to get access to my computer at work." Ivy had dropped all pretense of civility. She was looking at Morris like he was an imbecile. "A computer that had, an hour earlier, shut down abruptly without me being able to close sensitive financial and personnel documents that were open on my desktop."

"But why would they want that?" Morris asked.

"I assumed that was where you came in, Detective Morris. I'll be very curious to hear what you discover."

Ivy was about to boil over. She had been easygoing and sweet as a kid, but that didn't mean she was passive. Not by a long shot. Gil had always managed to stay on her good side, but there were a few girls who had teased her mercilessly. Usually about her clothes.

Sometimes about what she packed for lunch. One day, she'd had enough and exploded.

Gil couldn't remember the specifics. What he did remember was that when it was over and she came back to his house, Ivy burst into tears of remorse. Those girls had deserved everything she'd said to them and then some, but she still felt guilty about it.

"Dr. Collins, who exactly do you think is in charge right now?" Morris poured fuel on the fire. The idiot.

Gil jumped in before Ivy could decimate him. "Morris. Dr. Collins is right, and you know it. She's also had a horrific day, and she's not the villain here. How about you take a breath and let her get back to her story so we can all go home, huh?"

Morris glared at Ivy but didn't say anything else.

"Ivy, what time did you go home?" Gil asked the question in hopes that she would talk to him, not Morris, and that would help her maintain her composure and give Morris time to cool off.

"Once we realized it was going to be a while, I told everyone to pack up. We left a little bit before three. I'd planned to go back tonight and check all the computers and systems, maybe run backups again if needed. We have tight cybersecurity on our computer network, and I'm a stickler for backups. It wouldn't have been the end of the world if we didn't run them tonight, but I knew I would feel better if we did."

"When you say your cybersecurity is tight, how tight are we talking?" Morris asked the question, but it was hard to tell if he was being a jerk or was genuinely curious.

"It's not a secret that a lack of cybersecurity is a pet peeve of mine. I've fired people over failing to uphold our computer requirements. What we do isn't classified, but we have developed some technology that has triggered the interest of the Defense Department. It's crucial that our network is secured."

"I wish every company took their cybersecurity seriously." Gil wasn't trying to butter her up. He meant every word. Cyber threats were no joke, and companies the size of Hedera were frequent targets. "I hate to speculate, but given that your attackers wanted access to your computer system, I'd guess they've tried to hack you before and failed."

"That could be. I realize there's no proof at the moment, but it makes sense to me that the same people behind the power outage were behind the attack at my home. It's conjecture, but it's reasonable to think they expected me to give them the information and then they could return to our office and have full access to our system."

If there was any way he could spare her this conversation, he would. But he couldn't. "Can you walk us through what happened after you got home?"

— 5 —

IVY SAT STRAIGHTER in her seat and kept her gaze pinned to a spot on the wall. "I got home around three, changed, and warmed up some leftovers. I still had the bowl in my hand, and when I turned around, they were there."

She wanted to push the memory away. She didn't want to relive it. Not now. Not ever.

"Ivy?" Gil's gentle voice was soothing after Detective Morris's brusqueness. "Do you have any idea how they got inside?"

"No. I have a security system, and I thought it was a good one."

"Are you sure you set it? It's not uncommon for people to forget." Morris, again with a statement that could be gentle and kind coming from anyone else, but coming from him? It set her nerves on edge.

"Yes. I'm certain."

Morris didn't hide his doubt.

"My system is time-stamped. It won't be too difficult to determine when I set it and when it was breached."

Morris made a note.

"There were three of them inside, right?" Gil prompted her. She nodded and he continued. "We have one in custody, and you gave descriptions of the other two to the police earlier. Since you've had time to think about it, do you remember seeing any of them anywhere before? Was there anything memorable about them? A tattoo, a birthmark, a scar?"

Ivy closed her eyes. Did Gil remember how good her memory was? Probably not. When she was a child, few understood she had a memory close to what people thought of as photographic. "They all wore ski masks. The tallest was close to six-four, and he was white with green eyes and freckles. I wouldn't be surprised if he was a redhead. His lashes were red, and he had freckles on his eyelids. He wore gloves, but the skin on his forearm was also heavily freckled, and the hair on his arms may have been red. He's the one who stunned me."

"Stunned you?" Gil spoke like he had something lodged in his throat.

"Yes. I saw it but not in time to react. When I came to, I was tied to a chair in my kitchen. The tall guy never got close to me again. And for what it's worth, I don't think he signed up for torture."

Morris scoffed, but Gil didn't spare him a glance. "Why do you say that?"

"Body language. He was miserable. He left the room, and he may have thrown up when they burned my thumb. I think he expected me to give them what they wanted with no drama."

Ivy refused to look at Morris and spoke directly to Gil, but that didn't mean she didn't notice that Morris picked up his pen and started writing.

"We'll come back to that," Gil said. "Can you describe the other two men?"

"One was around six feet and abnormally skinny. I suspect he's an addict. He scratched his arms a lot, and he was the most fidgety of the trio. He had brown eyes, and they weren't always focused.

He wasn't high, but he may have scrambled too many brain cells to be fully cognizant. With that said, I think he knows more than the tall guy. I think the tall guy was muscle. I don't know what the twitchy guy's purpose was, but my guess is he was promised drugs or money if he participated, because he did whatever he was told."

Ivy was trying to hold it together, but in a minute this retelling was going to get messy.

"Tell me about the third man." Gil didn't phrase it as a question, but she still felt it was a request, not a demand. It was small but also huge. She'd had so many demands today. It was soothing to feel like she had some control over what she shared.

She appreciated that he didn't describe the man as the one she shot, but simply as the third man.

"Was there anything specific you noticed about him?"

They had the man in custody, so Gil didn't need a physical description. But she closed her eyes and focused on her memories. He was the shortest and heaviest of the three. Maybe five-eight and pushing three hundred pounds. Brown eyes, pudgy hands, bushy eyebrows. But they could see all of that for themselves. "He was the oldest, probably by twenty years. Maybe more."

"What specifically did you observe that makes you say that?" Gil asked.

"His voice was gruffer, more mature. And the lines around his eyes were deeper, more wrinkled and furrowed than laugh lines."

Gil nodded at her explanation, and she continued. "He needed the other men because everything he did to me seemed to zap him of his physical energy. He was breathing hard, almost gasping for air. It made me wonder if he used oxygen."

Morris continued to take notes. If it was possible to write angrily, that's how he was doing it. But he must have decided to let Gil ask the questions, because he kept quiet. At least for now.

"That's great, Ivy. Do you need a break?"

Morris muttered, "Oh, for crying out loud."

Ivy was tempted to say she needed a break for no reason other than to annoy Morris further, but the sooner this was over, the sooner she could leave this place, so she resisted. "No."

"Can you tell us what they wanted? As specifically as you can remember it."

"The guy you have in custody, he backhanded me twice before he asked for anything. Then he told me he needed my admin user ID and password, as well as my personal user ID and password. I asked him why. He asked me if I had a death wish. I said no, but I couldn't imagine why anyone would go to all this trouble to get into my computer. He asked me if I thought this was a joke. Did I think someone was pulling an elaborate hoax. I said no."

Ivy stared at her fingers. "He broke my pinky. Just grabbed my hand and broke it."

Morris stopped writing.

Gil swallowed hard.

She tried to remember everything. "I think I screamed. I'm not sure. That part is fuzzy. I was in a lot of pain." Maybe pain blurred memory, even a memory like hers.

Gil's mouth opened, then closed, then he swallowed hard and took a deep breath. "He broke your finger to prove to you he wasn't a joke."

"I believe so. Then he went to the bathroom."

"He did what?" This came from Morris.

"He went to the bathroom. Left me with Fidget and Muscle. I couldn't get away. I was tied to the chair. I think he was gone for fifteen minutes. Maybe longer. When he came back, he asked me for my user ID and password again."

"And you didn't give it to him?" This was also from Morris.

"No. That's when he broke my ring finger. Same way as before. Snapped it like a twig. Then he went onto my back porch and smoked a cigarette. He was gone longer. Maybe thirty minutes. Time started to blur. There are a lot of nerve endings in your fingers, and mine were swelling."

Morris muttered a string of expletives. Gil closed his eyes for a moment before fixing his gaze on hers. "What happened when he came inside?"

"He asked me again. I asked him why he needed to know. He grabbed my thumb and burned the tip and the base with a cigarette."

Ivy couldn't stop her legs from trembling. She didn't want to show any weakness. Not in front of Morris. And not in front of Gil. But if she didn't get the rest of it out and fast, she might collapse or throw up—or both.

"Like I mentioned earlier, some of our work is sensitive. One arm of our research tapped into an area that got a lot of attention from the Defense Department. We aren't actively pursuing it right now, but it's on our servers. I don't know if that's what they wanted or not, but there was no way I was going to hand it over."

"Dr. Collins." Morris pulled in a deep breath. "How did you expect it was going to end? Did you have any reason to believe help was coming?"

"I didn't know. I don't know what to tell you, Detective Morris. All I could do was pray God would send someone. I can't say I was praying with much faith. But I did know if he kept breaking my fingers, I was going to pass out. I'd had nothing to eat, and I was tired, in shock, and in a tremendous amount of pain. The body will shut down in a situation like that."

"I didn't think you were a medical doctor." Morris didn't sound nearly as antagonistic as before, but his words still had an edge.

"I'm not. But I have a PhD in bioengineering, and my professional life is spent working with amputees. In some cases the amputations were done in a hospital with anesthesia. But we have many clients who lost limbs in horrific circumstances. Bombs, accidents, war. Because of that, I've studied the psychological and physiological response to pain. I knew I was going into shock, even before he whipped out his curling iron of misery. When he burned my shoulder, I must have passed out. When I woke up, they'd removed the ropes from my arms and legs and laid me out on the floor. I guess they were trying to get me to come to."

For a few mind-shattering seconds, Ivy was back on the floor. Her burned flesh assaulting her senses. She could see the burning device as it moved toward her arm. Hear it sizzle against her skin. Taste the agony on her tongue as her body recoiled from the intense heat and pain. Then, the smell became overpowering. That was the last thing she remembered until she woke.

"Look who's back." Her tormenter's eyes were dead. Cold. He was going to kill her soon if she didn't give him what he wanted. She prayed but wasn't able to stop the tears that leaked from her eyes and ran across her temples and into her hair.

"I think you might be ready to talk to me now. And if you aren't, you'll learn firsthand what it's like to lose a finger." He turned to the skinny guy. "Get her up and in the chair."

Her entire body shook, and she couldn't stop it. She prayed. And prayed. And prayed. And she was certain God wasn't going to answer her prayers. She was going to die.

"Ivy?" Gil wasn't standing against the wall anymore. He was kneeling beside her. One hand on the back of her chair. One hand on her bouncing knee. Not trying to stop it from bouncing, just squeezing it gently. A reminder that she wasn't alone.

"That's when you came in." The worst was over. Well, almost. She could do this. "They must have heard something. I don't know what, but they disappeared and left me sitting at the table. I didn't know what was happening, but I decided no one was going to tie me down again. I keep a gun in my kitchen. I ran to the drawer, pulled it out, and waited."

"The gun registered?" Morris asked, somehow not sounding like a jerk when he said it.

"It is."

"Thank heaven." He kept writing.

"When I saw you, I thought they had all run away, but then I saw him sneaking behind you. I was afraid if I yelled, he would shoot you before you had a chance to turn. So . . . I shot him."

She shot the man who'd been torturing her. In the heat of the moment, she hadn't felt glee or joy. Only fear for Gil. Because he was definitely her Gil grown up. With a badge at his waist and a gun in his hand. He was the fulfillment of the heady combination of a lifetime of wishing and an intense hour of praying.

"You shot him left-handed?" At those words from Morris, Ivy turned to the detective. She didn't think it was her imagination that he was pale. When had that happened?

"They broke fingers on my right hand, but I'm a lefty. And I'm a very good shot."

GIL STOOD and took a step back. "I thought you were going to shoot me."

Ivy's eyes widened at his remark. "If I hadn't been sure I could make the shot, I wouldn't have taken it. But I couldn't bring myself to aim for his chest. I know that's what you're supposed to do, right? Center mass? But . . ." Ivy closed her eyes.

"You were aiming for his shoulder?"

"Yes."

Gil couldn't stop the chuckle. "Then you're an *excellent* shot."

"Is that going to be a problem?" Ivy turned her attention to Morris. "That I shot him? I did it on purpose, and I didn't give him an opportunity to lay down his weapon."

Gil studied Ivy. The earnestness in her expression and her apparent inability to prevaricate told him she was brave and honest, owning her actions and decisions regardless of the consequences. But her knee was bouncing again, which made him wonder if she was doing what she believed was the right thing, even though she was terrified.

"You'd been tortured in your own home by that man. He was holding a weapon. From where I'm sitting, this is a clear case of self-defense. Not to mention that you may have saved the life of a federal agent. We don't make a habit out of prosecuting people for that kind of stuff." Morris was still gruff, but he'd lost the antagonism and attitude.

"That's a relief." Ivy sagged against her chair.

"Morris." Gil waited until Morris looked up. "Can we wrap it up? She's due for pain meds, and we have to swing by the pharmacy to pick them up and then swing by Hedera so she can check on her computer system."

Morris looked over his notes. "One more thing, Dr. Collins."

"Yes?"

"You never answered the question about whether there was anything familiar about those men."

"I didn't see their faces. Although I wonder if I would recognize them in the future, from the way they talked and moved. Other than that, the tall guy, his voice sounded familiar, but I can't place him."

"If you think of anything else, please contact me immediately." Morris glared at Gil. "Or I guess you could tell Special Agent Dixon. He'll keep me in the loop."

Great. More interaction with Morris. "Yes. Absolutely."

Morris stood. "Dr. Collins, I hope you're able to rest tonight and you heal quickly from your injuries. I assure you, I'll make it my mission to get to the bottom of this." He turned to Gil. "I'm interviewing the assailant in the morning. Wake Med. If you want to listen in, you're welcome to."

No way he would miss the chance to get eyes on this guy. "What time?"

"Around ten, if he's conscious. You got a number where I can reach you?"

Gil gave Morris his number and programmed Morris's number into his phone.

"Pick up her prescriptions first. I'll send some units over to Hedera, so you'll have company when you get there."

The knot in Gil's chest loosened a fraction. He didn't want to worry Ivy, but he hadn't wanted to take her into her office without some backup. Now he didn't have to ask for it.

Morris kept going. "Do what you need to do at Hedera. Take her home. Give her some good drugs so she can sleep. Go."

Morris was like a dog with a bone when he got aggravated about something. Usually, Gil found him annoying and abrasive. But if Morris took all that attitude and applied it to Ivy's case? Gil wouldn't complain.

"Thank you, Detective Morris." Ivy wobbled as she got to her feet, and Gil wrapped a hand around one of her elbows and rested the other on her waist, holding her in front of him.

He didn't release her but simply shifted her to his side and kept her there until they reached his car and he had to pull his keys from his pocket. He helped her into her seat, and a minute later they were both buckled up and headed to the twenty-four-hour pharmacy.

Ivy had her eyes closed, head on the headrest. Her left hand cradled her right. "Gil?"

"Right here, Buttercup."

"What was the deal with Detective Morris? I've never been interviewed by the police before. He was so grouchy at first."

"You won him over."

"He definitely seemed less angry by the end. But also more angry. Know what I mean?"

"I do."

They picked up her prescriptions at the pharmacy and then headed to Hedera. When they pulled in, he flashed his lights at the marked vehicles in the parking lot. "Sit tight for a second."

Gil climbed from his car and met two uniformed officers as they approached him. He didn't know their names, but he recognized them from the drama this spring. "Thanks for coming out." He extended a hand to the officer on his right, then to his left. "Gil Dixon." He nodded to his car. "Dr. Collins needs to check the computers inside. Not sure how long it will take, but I'm hopeful we won't be long."

"Not a problem." The officer gestured to the office. "We've gone around the building. Everything appears to be secure from the outside. Want us to enter first?"

Gil struggled with this. He'd been a uniformed officer, working his way to detective, in Chattanooga. He'd been the first one in more than once, and he hated to ask someone to put themselves on the line for him. But the alternative was leaving Ivy with strangers, standing outside in the dark. After her reaction at the police station, that wasn't an option. "I'd appreciate it."

"The door has a keycard entrance. Does she have the card with her?"

Gil walked to Ivy's door and opened it. "The officers need to go in first. Can you give them the access card?"

Her eyes widened. "Do you think something has happened inside?"

"Just being extra cautious."

She reached down to the floorboard for her purse with her left hand, but when she opened it, she bumped her right hand against the glove compartment and a low hiss escaped.

The sound ripped through Gil's chest. If he could get his hands on that guy . . .

Ivy dug through her bag for a few more seconds before she extricated a lanyard. "They need to use the card first. Then enter the code. Should I give them the code? Or go punch it in for them?"

"What are you most comfortable with?"

"We change the code every month. And the code is useless without the card. I don't mind giving it to them." Gil reached for the lanyard, and she handed it to him. "The current code is 5477464."

"Got it." Gil returned to the officers and gave them the lanyard and the code, then went to the car and stood by Ivy's now-open door.

"Should I get out now?"

Her bravery was killing him. She was trying to hide it, but he could see the fatigue, stress, and pain—a nasty cocktail under any circumstances—working their brutal mischief. "Sit as long as you can. Rest. They'll let us know when we can go in."

She settled into the seat and closed her eyes. The fact that she didn't argue with him told him more than anything she could have said.

"I don't suppose I could convince you to take the pain meds

now?" She'd refused them in the pharmacy parking lot, insisting she needed a clear head.

"Need to be able to think."

"Fine. But as soon as we're done inside, you need to take your meds."

This got him a tiny nod.

They didn't speak again until the officers waved them inside and they entered the building. The entrance was modern—all silver, black, steel, and streamlined. The walls were studded with extraordinary art. Black-and-white photos of men, women, and children. All amputees. All stunning in their strength and bravery. There was no cheesy mission statement in evidence, but a person would have to be a soulless monster not to be moved by the company's clear passion for the people behind the work happening at Hedera.

"Wow." The word escaped him, and Ivy gave him the first genuine smile he'd seen her direct at him in fifteen years.

"Like it?"

"It's brilliant." Brilliant was an understatement, but she didn't seem to mind.

"Thank you. I love it. Whenever I get frustrated about our progress, I bring my laptop and work out here. It doesn't take long for me to adjust my perspective." Her eyes flickered over the images, lingering on a few of them.

"Do you know the people in these photographs?"

"Every single one." She blew out a breath. "Let's do this so these officers can go on about their night."

— 6 —

IT TOOK IVY close to an hour to check all the systems to her satisfaction. When she was done, she and Gil grabbed a bottle of water for her from the break room, thanked the officers who had covered their late-night activities, and returned to the car.

Before they left the parking lot, Ivy took her meds. Before they got to the main road, she was struggling to keep her eyes open. Gil figured he had thirty minutes, forty-five tops, before Ivy couldn't stay upright. He needed to get her home and settled.

They rode in silence, but it wasn't uncomfortable. Gil thought Ivy might have fallen asleep, but then she asked, "Is Emily already there?" Ivy wasn't slurring her words, but she was getting close.

"She is. But she knows you're exhausted. She texted while we were at your office that she has your room ready."

Ivy's only response was a low hum, and when Gil pulled into his driveway ten minutes later, she was asleep.

Emily raced out the front door but hesitated when Gil climbed from the car with a finger to his lips. "Are you okay?" Emily scanned him from head to toe, concern, worry, and love radiating from her.

"I'm fine." Gil pulled Emily into a quick embrace. "Thanks for coming."

"Wild horses couldn't have kept me away." Emily bent to look in the car, then turned wondering eyes to Gil. "She's really here."

"I know." Gil swallowed hard. "Not the way I would have ever imagined this reunion."

"Me neither. Let's get her inside. Then you can tell me what happened."

"Em—"

"The short version. I'll wait until morning for the long version."

"Generous of you." Gil walked around the car and opened Ivy's door. She didn't flinch. He didn't want to risk bumping her hand or shoulder, so he reached for her knee. "Buttercup?"

Ivy blinked, then jolted upright.

"Ivy, you're safe. You're with me. Emily's here. Let's get you inside."

Ivy's eyes drifted past him, and she spoke in an emotion-laced whisper. "Emily."

"Ivy," Emily whispered back.

Emily turned to him. "Get her out of the car and into the house. She needs sleep."

Ten minutes later, after a quick tour of the house, Ivy disappeared behind Gil's bedroom door with Emily to change into pajamas and settle in for the night. For the first time in too many hours, Gil closed his eyes and drew in a deep breath. His phone buzzed, and he pulled it from his pocket with a groan.

Gil, you home yet?

The text was from his fellow agent Luke Powell, on a group text.

He typed out a quick response.

Yes. Need something? If not, I'm crashing.

The response wasn't from Luke, but from Zane.

How's Dr. Collins? How bad was Morris?

Before Gil could respond, another message—this time from Faith Malone, Gil's favorite FBI agent who also happened to be Luke's fiancée.

I'm off this weekend if she needs protection.
Tess will help too. We can be unobtrusive.

Then Tessa Reed, the only female Secret Service agent in their office, chimed in.

Is Emily there?

Gil kept typing.

Ivy has two broken fingers and some nasty burns on her thumb and right shoulder. Minor facial cuts. Em is helping her get settled. They gave her some strong pain meds, and she took them. Hopefully they'll help her sleep. Morris started out as a jerk, but she won him over. He offered to let me come with when he interviews the assailant in the morning at 10. Definitely want some protection for Ivy and Em while I'm gone tomorrow. No other details. We didn't get that far tonight. Going to let her sleep, and then we'll come up with a plan tomorrow. Thanks, y'all.

A flurry of "okays" filled his screen. But then another text came through from Luke, this time on a loop that included Zane and Luke only.

Seriously. You okay, man? We could come hang
out if you need to decompress. Zane told us
what happened. Intense.

Then from Zane.

How secure are you there?

Gil responded.

I'm good. So tired I don't think I'll have trouble
sleeping. House is tight. System armed. I'll be
sure Em has a weapon before she goes to bed.
I'm sleeping on the sofa. We'll figure out the
rest of it tomorrow, or later today.

A few more "okays" and "laters," and finally his phone stopped
buzzing. Emily joined him on the sofa. "I'm glad you're here."

"So you said."

"Is she okay?"

"Already asleep. Will you tell me what happened to her?"

Gil considered his twin for a long moment. "Not the details,
but the big picture, yes. Ivy can tell you as much or as little as she
wants tomorrow. Fair?"

"Fair. Now, spill."

Gil told her everything, from the discovery of the counterfeit
bills to the moment they found Ivy's door open. From there, he
glossed over the details, telling her Ivy had been held hostage and
her injuries were a result of that. Emily was sharp as a tack, and it
took her about three seconds to put two and two together and
realize Ivy had been tortured.

Her eyes filled with tears. "How awful."

Gil closed his eyes and dropped his head back on the sofa. "I
wish we'd gotten there sooner, but I'm thankful we got there at

all. If they'd . . . if I'd found her after . . ." Gil couldn't finish the thought. If they'd violated her, killed her. If that's how he'd found her?

No. He couldn't and wouldn't let his mind go there.

Emily squeezed his arm. "Did she say anything about, well, anything else?"

"Not really. We mostly skated around it. I told her I had questions, but they could wait. You saw her. And trust me, she looked a lot worse when I found her. It was hardly the time or place for an inquisition."

Emily didn't respond for several minutes. When she did, he wasn't surprised that they were on the same wavelength. "Part of me wants to be mad at her. Part of me is so happy to see her again that I don't want to rock the boat by bringing up the past. I've missed her, and I want her back in our lives."

Gil managed a grunt of agreement but didn't open his eyes.

"Gil. Look at me."

He lifted his head and forced his eyelids to cooperate so he could focus on Emily. "What is it?"

"I'm worried about you."

"Me?"

She rolled her eyes. "Yes, you."

"*I'm* not the one who was tortured tonight."

"No. You're the one who's been tortured for years. By the way she left. By her silence. She could have written. Mom and Dad haven't moved. They would have forwarded anything from her straight to you. But she didn't. And now she's asleep in your room, and you're hovering over her like she's a wounded chick when she's actually a ticking bomb."

"Again, she was tortured today. No matter what she did to me, I don't have it in me to treat her badly. And you're one to talk.

You dropped everything and drove down from DC so you could see her."

"I'm not here for her, you idiot. I'm here for you. *She* will recover." Emily's expression went grim. "But if she breaks your heart again, I'm not sure *you* will."

He rested his head on the cushions. "I doubt she's interested in my heart, Em."

"I don't think she ever lost interest in your heart."

"Em, you aren't making any sense. One minute you say she's an emotional bomb set to detonate and destroy me. The next, you're telling me she never stopped loving me. It doesn't work both ways."

"Oh, yes it does."

Gil didn't argue the point. Partly because he was too exhausted to think and partly because Emily might be right.

Ivy had always been his easiest relationship. He was too young to remember when she entered his life, but she'd never been like a sister to him. While he and Emily argued less than the average siblings, when they did fight, it was loud and fierce.

He never fought with Ivy. When they disagreed, they talked it out, even as kids. They didn't lose their tempers or yell. When they were in middle school and high school, their relationship happening mostly in the letters they sent almost weekly, they debated. But they didn't argue.

Even when the letters stopped, they didn't fight.

Maybe that was where he'd gone wrong. "I should have fought for her."

Emily leaned hard against him, and he draped an arm over her shoulder. "If things had been different, you would have. Your world imploded, and our family closed ranks around you. By the time you were in the headspace to fight for her, she'd made it clear that she didn't want to see or hear from us. You can't force someone to accept forgiveness and grace. You can offer it, but they have to take it."

"She didn't do anything wrong."

"She doesn't bear the blame, but she chose to bear the shame. And in her shame, she shut you out. She shut all of us out. She was young, immature, and embarrassed by the duplicity of her own mother. We respected her decision, even though we disagreed with it. But I don't think any of us actually believed she would never come back." Emily pulled in a deep breath. "And I hate to have to point this out, but the truth of it is, she still hasn't come back. You found her. She's here. But that doesn't mean she's back."

"I know."

Emily stood and pulled Gil up with her. She studied his face, her eyes narrowed and assessing. "Do you want her back?"

"What do you think?"

"I think you need to decide. If you don't, then you need to get her sorted, get some closure, and get on with your life."

"And if I do want her?"

"Then I'll have your back. I'll help you fight for her. And when you win her, no one will be happier for you."

He didn't ask what would happen if he failed.

— 7 —

SHE WAS IN THERE.

The neighborhood was okay. The house was small. Older. But new roof. Security system. Probably dead bolts. Shouldn't be a surprise. No federal agent would sleep in a house that wasn't secure.

But if Ivy stayed here much longer, he'd have to find a way to breach the house.

It had been too easy to get into her house. Almost no challenge at all. She was brilliant but predictable. She liked her routine, and she didn't mix things up.

Ever.

Until tonight.

He still couldn't believe she'd refused to give up the access codes to her system. He'd expected her to hand them over with the first broken finger.

How she'd managed to hold out through the torture, he had no idea. Watching it on the video had turned his stomach.

He could quit. Drop it. Leave her to her business and wait for another time. A better time. But there would never be a better time.

He'd waited long enough.

— 8 —

BACON? AND BREAD? Ivy let the aromas waft over her. Whatever this dream was, she didn't want it to end. Then a soft chuckle, all male and rumbly, was joined by a harmonizing feminine laugh.

Gil and Emily.

They weren't part of a dream. They were real. Ivy opened her eyes. Rolled over. The events of the day before crashed through her memories and pinned her under a wave of fear that was followed by the realization that she hurt everywhere. She took a deep breath. Then another.

Gil. The scent of him permeated the sheets and pillows and soothed her jagged nerves. She snuggled under the quilt and forced her mind away from the trauma of yesterday.

Last night, Gil and Emily had taken her in, and it would be so easy to pretend they'd forgiven her. Today would be different. Today she would apologize. Today she would attempt to explain her actions. Today she would go home. Alone.

Twenty minutes later, teeth brushed and dressed in the extra clothes Gil had packed for her the night before, she stepped into the kitchen.

Gil and Emily turned to her in an identical movement that forced a grin Ivy could feel stretching across her face.

Gil tilted his head, assessing her, his eyes holding warmth, compassion, friendship, and something else Ivy didn't know what to do with. "Morning."

Emily's eyes, so like her twin's, sparked with excitement, but when she spoke, her tone was controlled. "Are you a coffee drinker? Tea? Cherry Coke?"

"Coffee, please."

"How do you take it?" This from Gil.

"Black is fine."

Emily grimaced. "Sure, it's fine, but is that how you drink it at home?"

Gil grabbed a mug. "Em, not everyone drinks creamer with a splash of coffee."

Ivy hadn't realized how tense she was until she lowered her shoulders several inches and took a deep breath while her old friends bantered.

Watching them, a deep knowing settled in her mind and heart. She didn't just want to stay in touch or make amends. She didn't want to be alone. She wanted back in. She wanted Emily to drag her on shopping trips. And she wanted Gil to be everything he'd been to her before.

Whoa. Hold up.

For all she knew, he had a girlfriend. A fiancée.

Even if he didn't, she'd had her chance. She'd lost him. She might be able to get him back as a friend, but even that was more than she deserved. Getting him back as more? Not going to happen.

Emily turned her attention back to Ivy. "Seriously, how do you drink it at home?"

No point in lying. "Hazelnut creamer."

Gil dropped his head. Emily crowed in delight. "Me too!"

Gil opened the fridge and waved a hand to the door, where three bottles of hazelnut creamer held a place of prominence. "Lucky for you, Em came prepared."

"You brought three bottles of creamer for the weekend?" Ivy laughed despite herself as she settled onto the barstool beside Emily and across from Gil.

Gil set a bottle of creamer and a cup of coffee in front of her. "Do you put anything else in it?" His voice was something she knew she had not remembered accurately. It was deep and almost musical while still completely masculine.

"No. This is great." She poured a healthy slosh into her mug and took a sip. "Perfect. Thank you."

Gil acknowledged her remark with a wink and turned to the stove. "Buttercup, I hope you aren't vegan."

"Are you kidding? Bacon is my best friend."

He looked at her over his shoulder, then to the ceiling and stage-whispered, "Thank you."

After that, breakfast was easy. Like they'd known each other their whole lives. Which they had. Not like they'd been separated for fifteen years. Which they had.

The bacon was perfect, as were the scrambled eggs, toast made from a loaf of homemade bread, the fresh pineapple and berries, and of course, more coffee. They ate and caught up, skirting the big questions and focusing on safe topics.

Emily, it turned out, was a physical therapist and worked in DC. Her practice was unique in the sense that she and her partners all had security clearances and were the preferred physical therapy provider for high-ranking members of Congress, Cabinet members, and, most recently, a Supreme Court justice. Emily hadn't offered any of that information, but Gil shared it on her behalf and didn't try to hide how proud he was of his sister.

"What made you interested in physical therapy?" Ivy took a bite of toast but almost choked on it when the room crackled with unexpected tension. Emily looked at Gil. He shrugged, and they communicated in the wordless way twins sometimes did.

"I was injured," Gil said. "Fall of my senior year."

Understanding hit her. That's when his letters stopped.

"The PT who worked with me to get my mobility back is now one of my best friends. And he saved my life. In doing that, he made quite an impression on Em."

How did a PT save his life? She wanted to ask, but they were in dangerous territory.

The Gil she knew was an amazing pitcher. The scouts were all over him that summer they were together. Everyone expected him to be drafted straight out of high school.

If Gil sensed her discomfort, he didn't capitalize on it. He kept talking, his voice steady. "Rotator cuff tear, and my career ended before it began. My shoulder was never going to be stable enough for anyone to take a risk on me as a pitcher."

"I'm . . . so sorry." She was. Baseball had been his life. She had to say something, but all she could do was apologize. Again. "I'm so very sorry."

Gil didn't shrug off her consolation. He took it like he was soaking it in. "Thank you. It wasn't a great time to be me. I was lost for a while. All I'd cared about was baseball. It was all I wanted."

That hurt. If anyone had asked her, she would have told them that fifteen years ago Gil Dixon had not one but two loves.

Baseball. And her.

Gil kept going, pouring salt in a gaping wound. "Suddenly, as a senior, I needed to apply to go to college, I couldn't use my

64

right arm, and I had no idea what my future was going to look like. Tim, my PT, was in his late twenties. He was cool. Had his life together. I didn't think I'd ever have anything like what he had—a job he loved, a gorgeous woman in his life who he later married, stability. He was always smiling. Always in a good mood. Naturally, I hated him."

Gil delivered the line in such a matter-of-fact tone that it took a second to register. When it did, Ivy set her mug down hard. "You hated him?"

"Completely. But he grew on me. And while I didn't know it, he prayed for me. Good thing too, because the night I decided life wasn't worth living, I called him, and he talked me off the ledge."

Emily's eyes were shimmering. "You can imagine how that impacted me."

Ivy's breakfast sat like a boulder in her stomach. He'd lost his future with her and his baseball career within a few weeks of each other. And he'd been so shattered, he'd considered ending his life.

Guilt clawed at her and doused the tiny flicker of hope that had burned. She could apologize. She would. But nothing would ever be the same. There was no going back. Some things couldn't be fixed.

Gil gave Emily a shoulder bump. "I've grown up a lot since then." Emily snorted. Gil ignored her. "There are far worse things than losing out on a major league career. I went to college a year later than my friends. Double majored in computer science and criminal justice with a minor in history. Took random electives and discovered things I was good at that had nothing to do with baseball. I was twenty-four by the time I graduated from college.

"Then I graduated from the police academy and joined the Chattanooga Police Department. I enjoyed it, but after four years on the force, I applied for the Secret Service. And that's how I wound up here." Gil finished off a bite of toast. "And as much as I'd love to stay here and chat with you lovely ladies, I'm afraid we need to head to the police station."

"The police station?"

Gil looked at his plate, then back at her. "The man who attacked you died this morning. It wasn't the bullet. He was stable, then he was gone. Possible heart attack. The ME will do an autopsy to confirm, of course. Morris got an ID on him last night. His name was Larry Briscoe. I was going to meet Morris this morning to interview him, but since we can't talk to him, Morris wants you to look at photos of some of Briscoe's known associates. See if any of them look familiar."

Ivy's head spun. Had she killed him? Gil said it wasn't the bullet, but getting shot could have caused him to have so much stress that he had a heart attack.

If Gil noticed her turmoil, he didn't let on. "No one expects you to recognize men who were wearing masks. But it's possible you've seen some of his known associates around. At a coffee shop or a grocery store. A restaurant you frequent or a gym. Anywhere they might have been watching you."

Ivy grimaced. "I'll try, but I don't think it will be much use. I work. I come home. I go to church. I leave. I do most of my shopping online, I order takeout. I'm not likely to recognize anyone."

"What do you do for fun?" Emily asked.

"I don't do fun." Ivy said the words lightly. She didn't want anyone to feel sorry for her. She had her calling. She'd made her choices.

"Why not?"

"I love what I do, Emily. Didn't someone once say that if you love your job, you'll never need a vacation? Or you'll never work a day in your life? I enjoy my work. I'm good at it. We're making a difference. The sooner we bring our prosthetics to the market, the sooner people will have a better quality of life. I've been busy for the past few years, starting the business, growing the business."

Emily frowned. "I don't think it's a secret at this point that we've followed your career. And it's impressive. Not that we're surprised. You were always destined for greatness. But you have to do something other than work."

"I tried that, early on. But I learned that people don't understand when you have to stay late or put in extra hours over the weekend." And by people, she meant people of both the male and female persuasion. "I started the company while I was in grad school. After you turn down enough invitations to parties and events, they stop coming. And I didn't mind. I was busy. Then I moved our operation here, and it's been wide open since. I barely have time to eat and sleep."

As she talked, Emily and Gil alternated between looking at her and looking at each other. She had no doubt there was some serious twin telepathy happening, and it probably didn't bode well for her.

Emily spoke first. "That's not a healthy way to live."

"Maybe not, but I've been living a long time on a one-way street. Relationships don't thrive in that environment."

At that, Gil went from concerned to frustrated, and she braced for his response.

He pointed to himself, then to Emily. "You have a couple of relationships right here that have been lying dormant for way too long. We're going to have to talk about that."

"I know." She both dreaded and longed for it.

"But we don't have time this morning."

"I know." She wasn't sorry to have more time with him, even though she knew when it was all out in the open, they would say goodbye and go their separate ways. It would crush her. But she was prepared to pay the price.

Gil and Emily shared another long look. When Emily spoke, her voice was gentle but firm. "Your one-way street is about to get crowded, and you're going to have to deal. I've been ticked off at you for fifteen years. Partly because of what you did to me. Mostly because of what you did to Gil."

"Em." There was an unmistakable warning in the way Gil grumbled Emily's name, but Ivy couldn't look at either of them at this point, so she stared at the counter.

Emily must have decided to ignore Gil because she kept going. "But none of it was because of what your mother did. None of it. So let's just clear a tiny piece of the air. I know this isn't the time or place. And I don't know how this will be resolved, but it will be resolved. We aren't going anywhere until it is. You can't run away this time, Ivy. So don't bother trying."

"I won't." Ivy looked up and was surprised by what she saw.

Gil glared at Emily. Emily glared right back. Great. Now she had them fighting with each other. Wouldn't that just be the cherry on top of the sundae of destruction that her mom whipped up fifteen years ago. Ivy had been back in their lives for less than twenty-four hours and had already driven a wedge between them.

"Good. We're all on the same page. We deal with Ivy's drama. Then we deal with our drama. In between the two, we get to know each other as adults. We remember that we used to be the best friends in the world and maybe we remember how to do that again. Deal?"

Ivy heard every word Emily said, but her gaze was fixed on Gil. Emily offered hope, but what was Gil prepared to offer?

He swallowed, his Adam's apple bobbing, and he nodded. "Deal."

Well, then. "Deal."

— 9 —

GIL CLEANED THE KITCHEN while Ivy got ready for the day. She'd declined Emily's assistance, and Emily wandered to his back porch, phone in hand. As much as he loved his sister, he was thankful for a few moments of quiet.

Ivy was not what he'd expected. She was brilliant. She was gorgeous. But she was driven to succeed in an unhealthy way. He recognized it. He'd done it himself. He'd planned to be the best pitcher in major league history. And in the process, he'd been so focused on baseball that there might as well not have been anything else in the world. Well, except for Ivy.

But when baseball was gone? And Ivy was gone? He had nothing to hold on to. He'd come close to ending it all. In a bizarre twist, at least it seemed bizarre to Gil, losing baseball hadn't been the end of the world. It had opened the door to a world of possibilities. What would it take for Ivy to see the possibilities of a life that didn't revolve around work?

"I'm ready." Ivy appeared at the end of the counter and pulled him from his thoughts.

Emily joined them, tucking her phone in her back pocket. "How long do you think you'll be?"

"No idea. Hopefully not too long."

"Call me when you're done." Emily squeezed Ivy's left hand. "We'll grab lunch."

"Sounds great," Ivy said. She might have even meant it.

Gil didn't comment. Emily was up to something. He didn't know what it was, but she was scheming—that he knew for sure. He also knew there was nothing he could do but wait to see how it played out.

Despite the weight of all that still had to be said, conversation flowed as he drove them to the police department. They talked about college and Emily, and they avoided anything related to her family or the events of that summer. She was still easy to talk to, soft-spoken, and well-mannered. A Southern lady. Something she'd learned, far better than Emily had, from his mom.

"Can I ask you a question?" Ivy studied him with open curiosity.

"Of course."

"I know the Secret Service does more than protect the president. But can you explain to me what you do? It's not like the president spends a lot of time in Raleigh."

Thank goodness this was a question he could answer without any drama. "We're almost to the station, so I'll have to give you the bare-bones version for now."

"Sounds good."

"The Secret Service has two primary missions, both of which involve protection. We protect key political figures and provide security for major national events. We also protect the economic infrastructure by investigating financial crimes. That can encompass everything from credit card fraud to counterfeit currency."

"Am I right to assume that you are on the economic side of the Secret Service and not the protecting-politicians side?"

"Yes and no. My day-to-day job is focused on financial crimes.

But a few weeks ago when the vice president was in town, everything in our office stopped to support the protective mission." He grinned at her. "And don't ask me for details on that, because I can't tell you."

That earned him a soft laugh. "Fair enough. But can you tell me if you were one of the guys jogging beside the limo while the VP was here?"

He laughed. "No. I was in an office running down potential threats. The president, vice president, and their families have a dedicated protective detail. That's where Zane is headed soon. Luke and I will join him in a few years."

"You'll protect the president?"

Gil winked at her. "Maybe. There are a lot of different careers in the Secret Service, but the path I'm currently on has three phases. Phase 1 is where I am now. Mostly investigative work, supporting the protective mission when needed. Phase 2 comes about five years in. That's when agents are assigned to permanent protective details. Most agents only do that for three to five years. Then it's on to Phase 3, where most agents return to a resident office or a field office, sometimes in management or as a senior investigator."

"So you, Zane, and Luke are all in the first phase?"

"Yes. And Tessa."

"Is there anybody in Phase 3?"

Gil sucked in a breath. The pain hit him out of the blue, but he tried not to let Ivy see it. "Our resident agent in charge, Jacob, is Phase 3. We had three others. Our previous resident agent in charge, a senior investigator, and a computer crimes expert. But we lost them earlier this year."

"Oh." The word escaped. "I didn't think."

He gave her what he hoped was a reassuring smile. "Don't worry about it. We're still adjusting, and it's been a challenge to find anyone who wants to be in this office. Zane should have gone on to Phase 2 by now, but until we can replace a few agents, he's stuck."

Gil pulled into the police department lot. Ivy had relaxed while they were talking, but the tension was back in the set of her shoulders and the tightness of her lips.

He parked the car and waited until she looked at him. "The only way out is through, Buttercup."

She dropped her head but not before he caught her flash of recognition of one of his dad's favorite quotes and the smile that tickled the edges of her lips.

"Ready?"

"Not even a little. Let's go."

AN HOUR LATER, they were back in Gil's car. She'd studied all the photographs as requested, but she hadn't recognized anyone. Gil waited for her to fasten her seat belt, then asked, "Ready for lunch?"

"Sure."

"Any place in particular you want to go?"

"I'm flexible as long as it isn't pizza or Thai."

"What's wrong with pizza and Thai?"

"Normally, nothing." She didn't elaborate.

"How about you tell me what's wrong with them now?"

Ivy stared out the window, and he didn't think she was going to respond. But he heard her whisper, "I was warming up leftover Thai last night." That explained the Thai. "And he smelled like pizza." And that explained the pizza.

He could tell she'd given all she was going to give on that subject, at least for the moment. Time to bring the conversation away from the dark side. "How do you feel about tacos? And I don't want to put any pressure on you, but your answer could impact our entire friendship."

She turned in her seat to face him, and mirroring his mock serious tone stated, "My blood type is salsa."

Gil did a fist pump. "Yes!"

"Shouldn't we call Emily?"

Right. Emily. Yes. They should call Emily. They would call Emily. She would only be here until tomorrow, and then she would go home.

It had been a long time since Gil had wanted Emily to go home. Come to think of it, he couldn't remember a time when he'd ever wanted her to leave. But the time had come. With that thought, he called Emily.

When he pulled into the parking lot of his favorite Mexican restaurant twenty minutes later, he almost couldn't believe what he was seeing.

Almost.

Emily was already there, waving at them from an outdoor table. And she wasn't alone. Zane was there, along with Tessa, Luke, and Faith.

Ivy flicked a glance at him, then returned it to the crowd. "Looks like the gang's all here."

Was she nervous? Unhappy? Gil couldn't get a read on it, but something about the crowded table didn't seem to sit well with Ivy. Not that he could blame her. Emily had ambushed them both. "Sorry about this. I knew she was up to something this morning."

Ivy's smile was tremulous but, as far as he could tell, sincere. "It's fine. I recognize them. Zane was with you last night. And I met Luke and Faith last year. Is the woman talking to Emily another agent? Tessa maybe?"

"You're batting a thousand, Dr. Collins."

Ivy reached across her body with her left hand and rested it on the door handle. "I'm guessing if we don't go, it will only make things worse."

She had no idea.

He would have liked to open her door for her, but she was too quick and had climbed from the car before he had a chance. And it wasn't like they were on a date or anything. Still, he stayed close as they joined the table. There was a flurry of greetings, introductions, handshakes, and hugs. When everyone moved back to their seats, it was clear that Emily had arranged them with the ladies on one end, the men on the other. Gil held Ivy's chair until she was settled, then sat beside her, putting him across from Luke and Zane and nowhere near his sister, which was fine with him. But he took a moment to make eye contact with her. Without exchanging more than a look, he knew Emily knew he was annoyed, she didn't care, and she was still up to something.

Great.

When he looked across the table, Luke and Zane were grinning at him. "She's a force to be reckoned with." Luke spoke in a low voice that wouldn't carry.

Zane studied Ivy for a few moments longer than Gil thought absolutely necessary before he muttered, "She okay?"

Gil gave a small shake of his head while pretending to study his menu. Luke and Zane knew him well enough to interpret the response correctly. He had a lot of thoughts to share, and he would, but not with Ivy sitting a foot away.

After ordering his usual and memorizing Ivy's order for what he hoped would be future reference, Gil listened as his sister did what she'd obviously been planning all along.

Emily was playing matchmaker, although thankfully not in the traditional sense of the word. By the time lunch was over, Ivy Collins had two new best friends in Tessa and Faith. They'd already planned to meet for lunch on Tuesday, and there was talk of going to a movie next weekend. Emily was no longer leading the conversation but instead was sitting back and listening as the women made plans. Plans she wouldn't be a part of.

Gil's hand rested on the back of Ivy's chair, and Emily reached across and gave his arm a squeeze. He looked at her and she mouthed, "You're welcome."

She was going to be insufferable.

In the hours since breakfast, she'd managed to make sure Ivy had people she could have fun with outside of work. She'd also pulled Ivy into his circle, and now he would have lots of opportunities to spend time with her without it being weird or even a real date.

Ivy and Emily pushed back their chairs. "We'll be back." They both had their purses. Probably headed inside to the ladies' room.

"We'll come too." Faith and Tessa rushed to join them, and he noted with relief that both women were armed. Tessa patted his arm as she passed him and whispered, "We've got this, Romeo."

Faith ran a hand across Luke's shoulders as she walked by, then leaned in between Luke and Zane and whispered to Gil, "You'd better spill all and fast. I want details."

Then she followed Tessa inside.

Luke and Zane both burst into laughter. "I told Faith months ago that Ivy was your type. Clearly, I wasn't wrong."

"It's not—"

"We bust in and find her being abused by those guys and the next thing I know, Tessa tells me Emily's driving down from DC and Ivy's staying at your place. That's not fast. That's breaking the sound barrier."

"I've known her my entire life."

"No, you knew her as a kid. You met her as an adult less than twenty-four hours ago." Zane tilted back in his chair. "Be careful."

Luke didn't seem to share Zane's concerns. "Go for it. She's gorgeous. Sweet. Friendly. Faith thinks she's amazing, and she slid right in with her and Tess."

Zane dropped his chair back on all four legs. "Like I said, be careful."

TESSA OPENED THE DOOR and stepped into the restaurant first, followed by Emily. Faith held the door and waved Ivy ahead of her.

"You go ahead. I'll be right behind you."

I bet you will. Ivy wasn't fooled. Faith and Tessa were both carrying. They were both trained agents. They were, undoubtedly, more than capable of taking care of themselves.

And clearly, they didn't think she could.

She wanted to be offended, but the rational side of her brain refused to entertain the concept of her sashaying through a Mexican restaurant and taking down the bad guys if necessary. Sure, she'd taken a few self-defense classes, she had a concealed weapons permit, and she was a very good shot. She even carried her weapon, frequently. Her dad had taught her how to handle a gun and protect herself, and he had begged her to be cautious, especially when she was alone in a city. Which was what she usually was. Alone.

Not being alone was a new experience. One she might grow to like.

Faith was hot on her heels as she entered the restaurant. A sign indicated that the restrooms were at the back, and she headed in that direction. A large group exited the main dining area, and Ivy paused to allow them to pass between her and Emily. As they skirted by, a hand closed over Ivy's left bicep and yanked her in the direction of the restrooms.

She glanced up and caught a flash of brown hair, a stubbled cheek, and a broad back in a green T-shirt. The man had her left arm in a tight grip, and the hand that held her squeezed tight and pulled again, but before she could try to get away, another hand, smaller but still strong, closed around her right wrist. Pain shot through her hand and arm as she was pulled in the opposite direction. Faith's voice boomed into the chaos. "FBI. Let her go."

The hand on her left arm released before Faith had finished speaking, and Ivy stumbled toward Faith.

"Are you okay?" The question came from Tessa, but Tessa didn't stop to give her time to answer. She ran toward the door.

Before Ivy could process what was happening, Gil was there. "I've got her. Go!" He slipped an arm around her waist and pulled her against him. He held her tight as he maneuvered them to the exit, where Emily waited with a man who might be the manager.

"Everything okay, Agent Dixon?" Gil didn't respond verbally, but something made the manager flinch. "How can I help?"

"Do you have cameras in here?"

"We do."

"We'll need the footage. But I have to get these two secured first. I'll call you. Please tell Lucia she's getting double the tip when I get back and settle up." He kept his arm around Ivy's waist and pressed his free hand to Emily's back. "Let's go."

No one spoke as they exited the restaurant. They quick-marched to Emily's car, and Gil held up a hand. "Wait."

His car was parked a few spaces over. He jogged to it, opened the trunk, and returned with what looked to Ivy like a giant selfie stick with a mirror on the end. When he slid it under Emily's car, Ivy understood. "He's looking for a bomb?"

Emily met her eyes. "He does this a lot."

"When your friends nearly get blown up, you learn to be cautious." Gil's tone was devoid of humor. "Emily, go straight to my office. I'll be right behind you. Stay in the car until I get you. Got it?"

"Got it."

Gil waited until Emily was in her car and the car was running before he led Ivy to his sedan. He repeated the procedure with the mirror, then held the passenger-side door open for Ivy, closing it gently once she was inside. He put the mirror back in his trunk and jogged to the driver's side. Gil radiated fury and frustration, and Ivy got another glimpse of Gil Dixon, US Secret Service agent. He was a different Gil than Gil Dixon, childhood best friend or Gil Dixon, her first love.

This Gil Dixon wasn't frightening to her, but he was intense. She liked intense.

She waited until they were on the road to ask, "Are you okay?"

"Am *I* okay? I'm not the one who was nearly abducted in broad daylight in a packed restaurant."

He had a point. But . . . "It didn't feel like I was nearly abducted. It felt like I was in a brief tug-of-war, which Faith won immediately. She's very forceful, isn't she? I almost put my hands up and surrendered, and I hadn't done anything wrong."

Gil's lips twitched, and the grip he had on the steering wheel loosened by maybe a millimeter.

"Then Tessa blew by. If she were chasing me, I would stop on a dime. I wonder if some men surrender on the spot when they see her. She's exquisite."

This remark earned her a tiny head shake from Gil as he pinched his lips.

"Then Zane and Luke took off, and they both look like they

could run a triathlon for kicks and giggles at any moment, so my guess is they will catch the guy in no time."

They came to a stop at a red light, Gil on Emily's bumper, and he turned to look at her. "I need you to promise me you'll repeat everything you just said when you give your statement, because I want it all in the official record." Then he winked.

The tension in the car dissipated. Gil remained alert and focused, but the waves of hostility that had been pouring off of him were gone.

"Thank you." Ivy reached over and squeezed his arm.

"I didn't do anything. Faith's the one—"

"I'll tell Faith thank you later. And Tessa, and Luke, and Zane. But you're the one who's protecting me right now. Thank you."

Gil reached for her hand, and she laced her fingers through his and held on. His fingers flexed on her hand and returned the pressure. "I can't say it's my pleasure, because there's nothing pleasurable about you having broken fingers and a fried shoulder, and now having been almost kidnapped. But I'm glad I'm the one who found you."

"Me too."

Gil pulled his hand away and returned it to the steering wheel as he merged into traffic on the interstate. She wasn't sure what to do with her hand. If she left it where it was, it looked weird. But where could she move it without being obvious? Should she tuck it out of Gil's reach? Before she could come to a decision, Gil reached his hand for hers and laced his fingers through hers again.

Well, that was one problem solved. Unless it was the start of a much bigger problem.

—10—

GIL HAD NO IDEA what was going on with him. All he knew was that the second Ivy slid her delicate hand in his, he realized he could never let her go.

It's too soon. You're moving too fast. You don't even know her. He didn't care.

No, that wasn't true. He cared so much, it could destroy him. All through lunch he'd been wondering what it would be like to have her beside him all the time. She fit right in with Faith and Tess, and of course with Emily. It had been easy. Natural.

Just like holding her hand.

He could turn her loose and pretend it never happened or choose to believe it was only about her seeking comfort after a traumatic experience. Or he could be bold. Hold her hand as if he'd held it every day for the past fifteen years.

If things had been different, she would have been his all this time. To have and to hold. He knew it in his bones. They'd been kids when she moved, but after that summer they spent together as teenagers? The way they'd shifted from best friends to more in the space of a few days? If they'd been able to follow through on their plans? If she hadn't shut him out? They would have been one of those couples that had been together since high school and were still ridiculously happy.

He'd never personally met a couple like that, but he knew they existed.

"Why are we going to your office?" Ivy asked the question with genuine curiosity but no apparent anxiety.

He squeezed her hand. "It's the safest place I could think of."

"Oh." The anxiety was back in her voice. "Do you think they're after me because of something on my computers, or do you think it has something to do with the counterfeit money you found?"

"I don't know, but we're going to find out."

Emily had done as he'd asked and waited in her car until he pulled in beside her. When he got out, Ivy waited, which gave him the opportunity to be a gentleman twice over. He opened Ivy's door, then Emily's, and escorted the two women inside.

The weekend security guard stood at the door, brow furrowed. "Agent Dixon. Wasn't expecting you today."

"Wasn't expecting to be here, Greg, but pretty sure we'll have a few more coming soon."

"I'll be on the lookout."

"Thanks. Greg, this is Dr. Ivy Collins." He nodded his head in Ivy's direction.

She extended her left hand. "Sorry, my right hand is out of commission at the moment."

Greg took it in stride and shook her left hand.

"This is my sister, Emily Dixon." Gil nodded toward Emily.

Greg chuckled as he shook Emily's hand. "Not sure you had to tell me that. Anyone could tell y'all are related. You have the same blue eyes and same black hair, although, thankfully, she is a sight prettier than you."

Emily flushed at Greg's obvious flirting.

"I appreciate you bringing two lovely ladies to the office today, Gil. This Saturday has taken a definite turn for the better."

Gil pointed Emily toward the door that led to their office. "Careful, Greg."

"What?" Greg feigned innocence and Gil ignored him.

"He's cute," Emily said as soon as Gil scanned a card from his wallet and let them into the Secret Service offices. "Is he single?"

Emily wasn't serious, but Gil wasn't in the mood to joke. Not about this. "You aren't interested."

"How do you know?"

"Because you prefer men who prefer to date one woman at a time."

Emily's eyes widened and she grimaced. "That is true. I guess I'll have to keep looking."

"Wise decision."

Emily rolled her eyes and turned to Ivy. "He's very bossy. The problem is, he's rarely wrong. It's *so* annoying. This is why I live in DC. I can only take so much of him before he makes me crazy."

It was Gil's turn to roll his eyes and turn to Ivy. "All lies."

"Even the part about you rarely being wrong?"

"Definitely that."

Gil's phone rang. "It's Zane." He accepted the call. "Dixon."

"We got him." Zane yelped at something. "Fine. Faith and Tessa got him. I thought Luke was going to lose it when we caught up to them. Tessa had the guy's legs, and Faith was sitting on his back in the parking lot. Not what you'd call a clean takedown, but it got the job done."

More muttering Gil couldn't hear. "Tess says I'm not telling it right. She and Faith can give you their version later. Guy's name is Leon something. Tess has it written down. At first he claimed it was all a misunderstanding. That didn't hold up after they found a weapon he didn't have a permit to carry and a picture of Ivy in his wallet."

Gil's enjoyment of Zane's story disappeared. "Picture?"

"Of her walking into her house."

Gil kept his gaze pointed to the floor, but he could feel the weight of Ivy's and Emily's stares.

"They're taking him to the station. Faith and Tessa are going to make statements. Morris is going to want to talk to Ivy. Again. But Tess convinced him Ivy doesn't need to make a third trip to tell them he grabbed her arm and then was gone. Morris said he'll be calling, and when he does, you'd better be answering the phone and handing it off to Ivy."

"I will."

"Where'd y'all go?"

"The office."

"Good call. Luke and I will be there in a few. The manager here stopped us, and he already has a copy of the security footage for you. We're going to get it and cover the bill."

"Sounds good. Make sure Lucia gets—"

"Double. I know. She will."

"Thanks."

Gil ended the call and braced for the expressions he would see when he looked up. He wasn't surprised. Emily was wary. Ivy concerned. Both were curious.

He filled them in on what Zane said, but when he got to the part about the guy having a picture of Ivy, he couldn't stop himself from stepping toward her and reaching for her hand. He was prepared to give it a squeeze and drop it, but she threaded her fingers through his and held on.

Fine by him.

WHY COULDN'T SHE STOP herself from holding on to Gil? What did she think? That if she let go, she might blow away, or fall apart? She wasn't fragile. She was tough. Smart. She knew her own mind, and she knew she didn't know what she was going to do with the feelings Gil Dixon was stirring in her.

She'd dated, although not recently and not often. But none of her previous relationships had prepared her for the overwhelming need she was experiencing to be close to Gil. She barely knew him anymore, and she had no idea what he was thinking. He was probably trying to be nice.

Especially right now. He hadn't meant to hold her hand. She knew he hadn't, because she caught the flash of surprise when she didn't let go. But he was too kind to treat her with anything but gentleness, especially after the day she'd had yesterday.

But in the car, he'd made the first move. Hadn't he? What if it hadn't been a move and she'd jumped on it and now—

"What happens now?" Emily's question brought Ivy's worrying to an end.

"We wait." Gil squeezed her hand.

"He had a picture of me?" Ivy tried to swallow, but her mouth had gone dry.

"I don't like it either." Ivy didn't need to get to know Gil better to recognize his remark was the very definition of an understatement. "But now we have someone to talk to."

She heard what he didn't say. "Without him, we don't have any real leads, do we?"

"No." Gil didn't hesitate with his reply. "There are two things in play. Someone desperately wants to get into your computer system. And then there's the counterfeit money that was deposited into Hedera's accounts."

"We had a community fair a few weeks ago. We gave tours of

the building and our labs and had a few carnival rides outside. The response was fantastic. Lots of cash came in at the different booths. It was a fundraiser for our local wounded warrior group. We deposited the cash and wrote the wounded warriors a check."

"That explains the cash deposit."

"That money could have come from anywhere. The people who used it at the fundraiser might not have known they had counterfeit bills."

"Maybe." He tugged on her hand and put his other hand on Emily's arm. "Come on. I'll give you the grand tour before everyone gets here."

Ivy didn't mind the change of subject or the distraction that came from wandering around Gil's office. Although, the truth was, there wasn't much to see.

He walked them back to the entry and talked about their office manager, Leslie Martin, and the recently promoted resident agent in charge, Jacob Turner. Then he led them down the hall and pointed out the conference room on the way to the main office area where he, Luke, Zane, and Tessa all had cubicles. A quick glance revealed cubicles for eight agents, but only four desks were in regular use.

Gil didn't mention them, but she knew who the empty cubicles had belonged to. Special Agent Thad Baker had died in February in a horrific car bomb that also took the life of one of Ivy's interns. Then Jared Smith had died in April on the same day Luke and Zane were attacked, a few days before Gil was shot in the head.

Gil led them back to the conference room and held a chair for Ivy, then for Emily. "Do you want something to drink?" He opened a dorm-sized refrigerator in the corner of the room and peered inside. "We have water, sparkling water, and Cherry Coke."

"I'll take a water."

"Same," Emily echoed.

Gil handed the water to Ivy and she asked, "What's with the Cherry Coke?"

Emily laughed. "It's for Faith."

Luke walked in the room, Zane right behind him. "Did you offer up Faith's Cherry Coke?" Zane winked at Ivy. "Faith's a nice girl, but that Cherry Coke situation is intense. No matter what you do, never take the last cold Cherry Coke."

"Thanks for the tip." Zane looked so different from Luke and Gil. Where Luke's skin was more olive toned and Gil's still carried a summer tan, Zane was fair complected and had dark-blond hair with a lot of red tones in it, and fierce blue eyes. The look that came with his advice was warm and assessing. "Did Gil fill you in?"

She looked at Gil, then back at Zane. "Yes."

Gil nodded. "Anything new?"

"Besides the part where Luke's having to remember his fiancée is an FBI agent and capable of taking care of herself?"

"I said something new," Gil fired back without pause, and neither he nor Zane made eye contact with the unamused Luke.

"You're both hilarious," Luke said.

"We know," Gil said. Zane laughed. Ivy and Emily exchanged "are they kidding or serious?" looks. Luke muttered nonspecific threats as Gil continued speaking. "But neither your relationship drama nor our comedic skills are news."

Luke frowned. "No, but Leon Parish is."

"Is that the guy who grabbed me in the restaurant?"

"It is." Zane's response was more growl than speech. "Did you get a good look at him?"

"No." Ivy looked at each of the men, then at Emily, then back to Gil. "It all happened so fast. I didn't realize he was a threat until Faith stepped in. When Faith spoke to him, he released me and ran. I looked down at my arm and saw his hand, and a bit of his profile, but not his face."

Luke and Zane exchanged a dark look.

"What's wrong?"

"He's claiming he didn't touch you and the only reason he ran is because Faith chased him. It's his word against hers."

"No it isn't. He had a scar."

"How sure are you about this scar?" Luke asked.

"It's on the middle finger of his right hand. Between the top two knuckles, on the inside facing his index finger. It's about an inch long."

Luke had his phone out before she finished talking. "Hey, baby. Are you still at the station?" A pause. "Check his right hand. Middle finger." Another pause. "Yeah, call me back." Another pause, then Luke's skin flushed from his neck to his cheeks. "Mm-hmm. Yeah. I love you too."

Zane and Gil both grimaced. "It never ends." Zane pointed to Emily. "This is what happens when your buddy falls in love. You get to listen to gushy stuff. There never used to be gushy stuff. We talked about ball games and guns."

"I'm sure you still do," Emily said.

"Not the same." Zane blew out a dramatic sigh. "But at least Faith also talks about ball games and guns. Well, guns. It's something."

Luke gave Emily a "what are you going to do?" shrug. "If Faith can identify this guy based on Ivy's info about his scar, then our next step is to find out who put him up to grabbing her. And why."

"How hard will that be?" Emily asked the question before Ivy could.

"No way to know. Morris may be able to take care of it. If not, we'll talk to him. And he'll give it up as soon as we ask the right questions."

Gil leaned in and spoke in a loud whisper. "By 'we,' he means Tessa and Faith."

"I bet if we borrowed that guy's hot poker from last night, we could get answers faster." Luke's phone rang, and he answered it before anyone could respond to his observations. "Yeah, baby." He looked at his feet, then back at Ivy. "Great. That's exactly how Ivy described it." He paused, then said, "She didn't see his face, but she saw that scar. Should be enough." Another pause. "Will do. Yeah. Love you. Bye."

"Faith says the scar is distinctive. Her description matched yours. She and Tessa are going to stay and see if Morris gets him to roll, and she asked us to hang tight."

Ivy blew out a breath. She could do that. She'd use the time to regroup.

"So, Ivy"—Zane's tone sent a weird vibe through the room— "how do you know Gil?"

— 11 —

THIS COULD NOT BE HAPPENING. "Zane, now's not—"

"Now's as good a time as any. What else are we going to do? Sit here and stare at each other?" Zane was all innocence, but Gil wasn't fooled.

If Ivy was offended by the outright nosiness of the question, she didn't show it. "I can't remember ever not knowing Gil and Emily. But I moved away when I was eight. We stayed in touch, reconnected as teens for a few weeks one summer. And then—"

"We lost touch." As much as Gil wanted her to explain herself, the reason they lost touch was a conversation they would have alone.

"So it had been what, fifteen years since you'd seen each other until we walked in yesterday?" Zane pressed. "What's your story after you moved away from these guys?"

"My mom and I moved to Oregon. My biological father has never been in the picture."

She fiddled with a cup on the table. "My mom wasn't like their mom." She pointed to Gil and Emily. "She could barely keep a job, slept around, and didn't hesitate to pawn me off on others so she could do what she wanted to do. But one thing she did right was she kept her men away from me. I'm not exactly sure when she met my dad, Wade, but by the time she introduced him to me, they had been dating for six months."

Zane gave her a searching look. "Was he nice?"

"He was the best. I wasn't sure about him at first, but he won me over fast."

"How did he do that?" Zane asked.

"He brought a chemistry set to the house and helped me do some experiments. I forgot to be wary of him when we were in the middle of setting off a controlled explosion in the dining room. From then on, I was smitten with him. The day he proposed to Mom, I began calling him Dad."

Gil loved that she'd had that. He wished she still had it. But he already knew this story didn't have a happy ending.

"They got married a year later, and a year after that he adopted me, and we changed my name to Collins."

Ivy shuddered, and the sadness in her eyes had him squeezing the arm of the chair to keep himself from going to her.

"When I was fifteen, Dad was in an industrial accident. He was an engineer and was working on a large piece of equipment. Somehow the safety mechanism failed, and the part he was working on closed over his arm. It was too heavy to lift without hydraulics. His arm was crushed. He almost bled out on the plant floor. When it was all over, he lost his arm below the shoulder."

The room went still.

"That story always sucks the life out of a room. But Dad made the best of it. A minute earlier his head and torso had been inside that equipment. If it had closed with him inside, he wouldn't have survived. He always said he was happy to give that machine his arm so long as he got to go home to his girls."

Ivy sat up straighter. "We had six more years with Dad, and I'm sure you've already concluded that his experience is what drove me into my current work. It still drives me. Even though Dad won't benefit from the prosthetics we design, he's the one I think of when I'm working. He gave me ten beautiful years of unconditional love. I never doubted that he adored me. Some people go their entire lives without that kind of beauty."

Luke cleared his throat. "What happened to your dad?"

Ivy stared at the blank television mounted on the wall. "A woman was having car trouble on the interstate. He stopped, along with a few other people, to help push the car off the road. No one knows for sure what happened. He may have slipped—the roads were wet—but somehow a car sideswiped him and tossed him into traffic." She shuddered again. "He was pronounced dead at the scene."

"Oh, Ivy." This came from Emily, and her wobbly voice matched the tears filling her eyes.

Luke and Zane both dropped their gazes to the floor.

Gil couldn't keep his distance and scooted his chair until his knee pressed against Ivy's, and he draped an arm around the back of her seat. He'd wanted to go to her when they got the news through some mutual friends, but he didn't think showing up at the funeral would be a good idea. "I'm sorry, Buttercup." It was a relief to finally be able to say that to her.

She closed her eyes and her body relaxed, her left arm pressing against his. Then her head dipped until it lay on his shoulder. "Me too."

GET A GRIP! Sit up. Stop leaning on Gil like a wimp.

But Ivy didn't move. No amount of self-recrimination could force her to lift her head. In fact, if they hadn't had an audience, she would have been all the way in his arms.

Idiot. Way to mess up everything before it even starts.

"Ivy." She stiffened at the tentative way Zane said her name. Gil's arm tightened around her, and his face pressed harder against her hair. She relaxed deeper into his arm but made eye contact with Zane. "I'm being nosy, but I couldn't help but notice when you're talking about your life, once Wade came onto the scene, you don't mention your mom much."

"That's because my mom is a horrible person. She's a user. Not of drugs, but of people. I'm not sure if she ever loved Dad, but she wasn't going to walk away from a husband who provided for her. After he died, she didn't waste time finding someone new. I have no valid reason to dislike her new husband, Preston, other than the fact that he married my mom. He's tried to mend things between me and Mom but has never understood why I'm so resistant. He even went so far as to make friends with a guy I was dating in an effort to put more pressure on me to patch things up with Mom. They bonded over sports and got along great. Still do. I think they talk a couple times a month." She gave a small shrug. "It's hard to explain. The little bit I've been around him, Preston seems like a smart guy. I never understood the attraction, and I still don't."

"Is he ugly?" Emily asked.

"Not at all. He's hot."

Gil stiffened against her, but Emily grinned. "So . . .?"

"I know exactly what *she* sees in *him*. I have no idea what *he* sees in *her*."

Luke's phone rang, and Ivy could have shouted for joy. This conversation couldn't end soon enough. Talking about her dad had been hard. Talking about her mom in front of Gil and Emily? The worst. She just wanted to crawl in a hole and never come out.

"Yeah, baby." Luke's entire face softened, and even without the endearment, Ivy would have known who he was talking to. She had no doubt that all three of the men in this room were formidable. She'd done her research and knew what it took to become a Secret Service agent. Wimps need not apply. But listening to her tale of woe, they'd all shown a softer side that she doubted they made a habit of putting on display.

Except for Luke with Faith. Apparently, that was on display all the time. It was so sweet, it hurt to watch. But at the same time, she couldn't pull her eyes away. She was still staring at him, so she didn't miss the moment his lips flattened into a tight line. His eyes cut to hers, and there was nothing sweet about the look he gave her.

"I'll find out. Yeah. Come to the office. Love you too." Luke set his phone and both arms on the table. "Ivy?"

Here we go again. "Yes?"

"Why would that guy think you have access to millions of dollars?"

She sat up straight, and Gil didn't try to stop her. He also didn't remove his knee from where it pressed into hers. And while his arm dropped from her shoulders, it only went as far as the back of her chair. His fingers rested lightly on the outside of her arm. "No one knows about that money."

Luke's expression was unyielding. "Morris must have taken a liking to you, because Faith says he did not go easy on ol' Leon. And Leon says you're worth millions. Millions only you can access. He claims he doesn't know more, but he was promised a hefty paycheck after you turn loose of the cash."

"But no one knows—"

"Ivy, you're too smart for this," Zane said. "I believe that until now you didn't know anyone else knew, but obviously someone does. And contrary to what some people will lead you to believe, I don't enjoy being a jerk, so please know I'm not trying to be one now. But you're going to have to tell us the entire truth about the millions of dollars you have access to. If you don't, you're tying our hands, and either you wind up being tortured again or one of us winds up dead. I'm sure, given what happened last spring, you can appreciate the fact that none of us is too keen on option number two."

"Zane." Gil's voice held a sharp edge, and based on the way Emily, Luke, and Zane looked, it wasn't an edge he made a habit of using. "Enough."

"She has to—"

"She will. She probably already would have if you'd give her half a second to pull her thoughts together."

Emily and Luke both pursed their lips together in a way that made Ivy think they were amused. Zane glowered but didn't say anything else.

"Buttercup." Gil's lips brushed against her ear, and he whispered, "You need to tell us everything."

She never talked about the money. Rarely thought about it. She had no plans to ever touch it until she needed it for the prosthetic. But Zane had laid it out for her. And Gil's soft request confirmed that Zane wasn't being overly dramatic or nosy. So what else could she do? "After the accident, Dad received a huge settlement. He didn't sue, but the company paid out big-time. Between the company he worked for and the manufacturer of the equipment that the safety failed on, he got close to twenty million dollars. And he spent very little of it."

"How little?" Gil's question was probing, but he asked it in a soft voice, and it didn't feel as intrusive as it might have if anyone else had asked.

"Less than five hundred thousand."

"Estate taxes would have taken a huge chunk."

"Close to half."

"You have access to over nine million dollars?"

"No. I have access to a little over twenty million. I invested it, it grew, and I haven't touched it."

The room went still for a few moments. Then Gil asked, "Is there a reason you didn't mention it earlier?"

"It's blood money. It's not the kind of thing I would use for a vacation or a new house or a new car. That would be reprehensible. The only thing I would ever use it for is to bring a new prosthetic to the market."

No one said anything, and when the silence became oppressive, Ivy shifted in her seat so she could see Gil's face. He wasn't looking at her. He was looking at Luke and Zane, and a lot was being communicated. "Gentlemen, I speak three languages, and that doesn't count my Latin, which isn't shabby. Unfortunately, I don't speak US Secret Service agent. Would you care to fill me in?"

Neither Luke nor Zane spoke, but with simultaneous chin lifts, they handed off the responsibility to Gil to answer her question. He rolled his head, first in one direction, then the other before he took her hand.

"This changes everything."

"Why?"

"Have you ever heard of ransomware?"

"Of course, but my computer system is state-of-the-art. I've invested a lot of money in cybersecurity, and my system is as impenetrable as I can make it."

"Who set up your system?" Zane asked.

"A colleague." Ivy didn't miss the wary looks they shared. They weren't impressed, but she could fix that. "My guess is you've heard of her. She works with a lot of law enforcement agencies in this area. Her name is Sabrina." Three sets of eyes reflected relief.

"Sabrina Campbell?" Gil didn't try to hide his delight. And

his use of her married name told her he knew her in more than a casual way.

"The same."

"How do you know Dr. Campbell?"

"We have mutual professional contacts. I lectured at the university in Carrington. We struck up an acquaintance. If you know her at all, you can imagine how blunt she was with me about the importance of my computer systems having top-of-the-line security."

That earned her a few chuckles. Yeah. They knew her.

"She revamped my system two years ago, and she runs random checks. She gets a kick out of trying to hack into her own systems."

"Sounds right." Zane looked at Emily. "Dr. Campbell is a genius. Scary smart like Dr. Collins here, but in a different way. Sabrina is a cybersecurity and computer forensics professor at the University of North Carolina in Carrington, but she consults all over the country. We've used her skills more than once. She's married to a Carrington investigator who is also on their dive team, and we dive with them sometimes. Great people. Sabrina has a bit of a reputation for not always catching appropriate social cues. She can come across as abrasive, but she has a heart of gold."

Emily nodded. "That's great, but can y'all explain ransomware and why it matters?"

Ivy had a bad feeling that even though she already knew the answer, she wasn't going to like the explanation.

Gil cleared his throat. "I'll tell you in a minute, but first, we need a list of everyone who knows about the money."

"I don't mind telling you, but I don't understand why that's significant."

"Because the people on that list are now our number one suspects."

—12—

IVY CLEARLY DID NOT LIKE the direction this was going. "I don't want to believe it could be any of them."

"It's possible that they aren't responsible, but we have to start there. Twenty million can make people do things no one would have ever dreamed they would do." Gil's tone was gentle but firm as he asked, "Who knows about the money?"

She didn't look at him. Instead, she focused on Luke when she answered. "To my knowledge, the only people who know are the attorney who handled the will, his secretary, Preston, my mom, and my ex."

Gil had so many questions, he had to fight to keep his expression neutral. "Maybe you should explain how you came to have the money in the first place? When your dad died, wouldn't the money have gone to your mom?"

Ivy blew out a long breath and finally looked at him. There was so much pain in her expression. Grief and resignation and shame. He wished he could take it all away. Or that she would let him help her carry it. "I've had to piece some of this together. Some of this he explained in a letter to me that he left with the attorney. After Mom went to jail, Dad wouldn't file for divorce, but he also knew that unless she repented and changed, truly changed, there was no way he could ever trust her again. That applied to all areas of their lives, but especially when it came to money."

"Would you like to explain that further, in particular the part about your mom going to jail?" Luke asked the question, and Gil made a mental note to thank him later for being gentle when he did.

"After Dad's accident, Mom and Dad fought all the time. Always about money. Then one summer, she took me on a trip across the US and stopped at places she'd lived before. She billed the trip as a way to see old friends. I know now that it was part of her preparing to leave him. I was headed to college that fall on a full scholarship, so even though I was only sixteen, she had decided she was done with parenting. And also done being a wife. She was going to stash money and"—she stumbled over the next words—"other items of value. Once she had her nest egg, she was going to bolt."

Zane paced around the room. "Where was she going to get these items of value?"

Ivy stared at the floor again. "My mom stole from everyone we saw that summer. She waited to start fencing the jewelry and collectibles until we got back to Oregon. But . . ."

Gil heard her swallow, and he knew what was coming.

"She had stolen jewelry and the, um, the people she stole it from called the police and Dad. Dad allowed them to search the house. They found everything that she hadn't fenced, but many of the items were already gone and never recovered. Some of them were heirlooms. Irreplaceable. Cherished."

"I'm sorry, Ivy." This came from Zane, who now knelt in front of her. "But did you help her steal anything?"

Ivy's back straightened, and her pale cheeks flamed. "Of course not."

Zane's smile was gentle. "Then why are you so embarrassed? Your *mom* made horrible decisions. You didn't. We won't judge you for your mother's behavior. Please don't judge yourself either."

"So." Luke spoke in a way that made it very obvious he was bringing them back to the point. "Your mom went on a crime spree and was sent to jail. Wade took her back even after she got out, but I'm guessing that's when he made some significant changes to his will?"

"He did. Despite everything she did, the will stipulated that Mom got everything of his, including a hefty life insurance policy and some investments. He left her well provided for, but he didn't leave Mom the settlement money."

"Did your mom know he left it to you?"

"No one knew."

"How tight is the will?"

"Indisputable."

Zane cleared his throat, and his annoyance was thinly veiled. "Can you lay it out for us?"

"At the time of his death, the total amount was a little over twenty-five million dollars. Estate taxes took over half of it, and I've used some of it for my business, but mostly it sits there and grows."

Anyone who thought money could make you happy would only need to take one look at Ivy Collins's face to know that it wasn't true.

"He didn't leave it to me outright. There were restrictions. It was to be used for college and for my future business pursuits. Dad made some very specific stipulations, including that I wasn't to give the money away—to a person or a charity or anything—for a minimum of thirty years."

"Wow."

Ivy glanced around the room, then focused on Gil. "I need a break." The whispered words cut through him.

"Of course."

She stood, and Gil and Luke jumped to their feet. Gil pulled her chair away. "I remember where the restroom is. I'll be right back."

He considered following her, but she shouldn't be able to get into trouble between here and the restroom. No one spoke as she left the conference room.

In the stillness of the office, they heard her walk down the hall, then open the restroom door. When it closed, Zane and Luke turned to Gil. Zane went first. "You sure know how to pick 'em. She needs some serious protection. Life insurance. Ransom and hostage protection. Key man coverage for her business."

"She may have all of that."

"Unlikely." Zane spoke and Luke nodded.

"You need to talk to her about it." Luke spoke and Zane nodded.

Great. They were tag-teaming him. "Why me?"

Zane and Luke shared a look that clearly indicated they thought he was being ridiculous and they were annoyed by it. Gil might have found them to be ridiculous and annoying, but he wasn't sorry they were assuming he would be the one to take the lead. "Fine."

Emily leaned toward him. "Do you think her mom could be after her for the money?"

Gil wouldn't lie to her. "I think anything is possible."

No one spoke for several minutes. Then Zane rapped his knuckles on the table as if he were bringing a courtroom to order. "It's not really any of our business, but what did Ivy's mom steal from y'all?"

Gil didn't try to hide his frustration. "Not talking about this, Zane."

"It must have been big." Luke directed his remark to Emily and Emily, the traitor, nodded, eyes wide in confirmation.

"What happened?" Luke kept pushing.

Emily didn't come to his aid. "Gil, you might as well tell them."

"There's nothing to tell."

"Seems like there's a lot to tell," Zane chimed in. "Her mom stole something of value. Then went to jail over it."

Luke picked up the thread. "The same summer that happened was the last time you saw Ivy. So that means something happened that y'all had not gotten over. So spill."

"You're right, but we don't know what happened on her end." Emily spoke before Gil could tell them to drop it. "She and Gil were ridiculously in love. It was kind of gross but mostly sweet. I was thrilled. When Ivy and her mom left to go back to Oregon, Ivy and Gil were going to do the long-distance relationship thing and wait to see where he went to play ball before they made any decisions about the future."

Zane and Luke wore matching expressions of surprise and sympathy.

"Why didn't you tell us?" Zane's question was more of a demand than a real question, and it scraped Gil's nerves raw.

Gil pointed at Zane. "*You* cannot talk to me about keeping my relationships to myself. Unless you're prepared to tell us what's going on with Tess?"

Luke smirked. "He's got you there."

Gil turned his attention to Luke. "And you danced around Faith for years. If she hadn't been assigned to your case, you never would have pulled the trigger."

It was Zane's turn to smirk.

"How about all three of you hush?" Emily stood and leaned over the table, shooting her death glare at each man in turn. "Her mom stole jewelry that had been handed down for four generations. The diamond ring that Gil was supposed to someday give his bride. The diamond earrings and necklace that I should have worn at my own wedding. And two bracelets—one sapphire, one ruby—that Mom intended to hand down to her grandchildren. They were insured, but their real value was that they were family heirlooms. They were some of the first pieces Ivy's mom sold. We haven't seen them since."

She paused and looked at him, a question in her eyes. He knew what she was asking, and he gave in with a nod. "Gil" —Emily pointed to him—"was so in love with Ivy that even if she had personally stolen all of it, I'm not sure he would have cared. Unfortunately, Ivy cared. Ivy cared a lot. She cut off all communication. She changed her cell phone number. Gil wrote to her. I wrote to her. Mom wrote to her. She refused to write back. We were seniors in high school in Tennessee. Ivy was in college in California and refused to communicate."

Gil braced for what was coming.

"Then Gil got hurt. Everything just . . . stopped. He was so sad. So withdrawn. It was terrifying. Then Mom and Dad told us we had to stop trying to communicate with Ivy until after her mom's trial. They were sure that when it was over, Ivy would reach out. She never did."

"That . . . doesn't make sense." Luke was shaking his head. "Ivy Collins is smart, put together, and not a criminal. Why wouldn't she—"

"She's ashamed." Zane spoke with certainty. "And shame does weird things to people. It can make it impossible for them to see the truth, to see love, to see a way out. She was young and obviously couldn't talk to her mom about it. She may not have told Wade what she was doing, so he wouldn't have known to try to talk some sense into her. Sounds like she was alone and floundering."

"Gil, have you talked to Ivy about it?" Luke asked.

"Yeah. In our spare time this weekend." His sarcasm was off the charts, but no one called him on it.

Zane ran a hand through his hair. "I'm sorry, man. I didn't know. I shouldn't have brought it up."

"Actually, I'm glad you did," Luke said. "Gil might never have explained." He gave Zane a pointed look. "Maybe we could all learn something from this experience and be more open."

Zane glared at Luke but didn't say anything further.

Gil caught Emily's eye, and she gave him a look that said "you'd better forgive him or I'm going to be ticked" combined with "don't be mad at me" for good measure. He rubbed both hands through the hair at his temples. "Zane, don't worry about it. You would have known eventually. I was just hoping to talk to Ivy first."

"When do you plan to do that?" Luke asked.

"Maybe when she's recovered. Maybe when she offers the information first. Maybe never."

He could tell no one liked his answer. He really didn't care.

"Can I ask one more question?" Luke gave him a dangerous grin.

"No."

"I'll ask Emily. She'll tell me."

"Maybe." Emily waggled her eyebrows. "Depends on what you ask."

"Why does Gil call her Buttercup?"

Gil relaxed. Emily chuckled. "Do you want to tell it?"

"Fine. Emily was named after Emily Starr, and I was named after Gilbert Blythe, both fictional characters created by L. M. Montgomery. Ivy said she wished she had a literary name, but we all agreed that Ivy suited her. She wouldn't let up about it, so we tossed around names for months. Some of them were okay. Some of them were ridiculous. Buttercup, from *The Princess Bride*, was my favorite, so that's what I called her. She didn't love it at first, but it grew on her."

"Ha." Emily rolled her eyes. "It only grew on her because it was your pet name for her."

"So"—Zane drawled the word—"if I wanted to call her Butter—"

"Don't."

Luke, Zane, and Emily all burst into laughter. Gil did not join in.

IVY HID IN THE BATHROOM, listening to the sound of laughter coming from the conference room.

Lord, I think I'm in big trouble.

She didn't know for sure, but she suspected the Lord was nodding.

I know you have everything under control, but it doesn't feel that way to me. I can tell by the way Gil and the others are looking at me that they think I've been stupid. Or at least very naive. Maybe I have been? How much have I messed things up? And how do I fix it?

The Lord did not answer audibly. She knew he heard her, but she didn't feel better. In fact, she felt awful. Her stomach was messed up, probably from the pain meds she'd popped with breakfast. Her entire right arm was throbbing. She wanted to cry.

She took several slow breaths, concentrating on the way her lungs expanded, then intentionally dropping her shoulders on the exhale.

Lord, I need you. I always need you. But if you don't help me, I won't make it to supper.

Feminine voices in the hall captured her attention. Faith and Tessa had arrived. She leaned against the wall. Was it cowardly to hide in the bathroom until the guys could fill them in on everything?

Maybe.

Did she care?

Not at the moment.

Ten minutes later, she forced herself to leave the room and walk down the hall. She braced for the onslaught of opinions and comments sure to be coming her way. With one final deep breath, she pushed through the conference room door.

And froze. The room was empty except for Gil. "Where is everyone?"

"Working." Gil waved in the general direction of the cubicles.

"Emily?"

"Working on something different." Gil approached her and reached for her left arm. "Let's go somewhere more comfortable."

She wasn't sure how it happened, but seconds later she was walking down the hall, hand tucked in Gil's arm, his hand holding hers in place as he guided them away from the cubicles, past the reception area, and into the office the sign said was for the assistant agent in charge—a position that remained unfilled since Jacob's promotion.

He opened the door and directed her to a seating area that included two plush chairs. "I decided you needed a break."

There were so many things she could say to that. Most of them snarky and revolving around him being bossier than she remembered. She said none of them. Instead, she sat in the chair, rested her head against the back, closed her eyes, and asked, "How did you know?"

"There were several clues, but your fifteen-minute trip to the restroom was what sealed the deal."

She flicked a quick glance at him and then closed her eyes against the look she saw on his face. There was amusement, tenderness, and an underlying protectiveness she wasn't sure . . . no, she knew for sure she wasn't ready for.

Even though she couldn't allow herself to take in any more than that one brief glimpse, she couldn't stop the warmth of what she saw from cocooning her. How long had it been since she'd faced anything with someone by her side? She knew the answer, but she forced it from her thoughts. "I'm okay, Gil."

"I know you are." His response surprised her enough that she opened her eyes again. As soon as her eyes met his, he continued. "And I also know you most definitely are not."

She didn't have a response to either of his assertions, but he didn't seem to need her to say anything.

"You're strong. Smart. Independent. Resilient."

"You don't know that."

"I do."

"Gil, it's been years—"

"I'm not basing this on my memories of you. I'm basing it on what I know about you right now. You couldn't have gone through what you've been through and succeeded in the way you have unless everything I said was true."

"I'm not . . ."

He didn't interrupt her this time. And he also didn't seem to expect a response. He settled back into his chair. A full minute passed. She knew because she counted to sixty.

Maybe because he decided she wasn't going to finish her thought, he pulled his phone from his pocket, swiped at the screen, then settled in to read something.

Another minute passed.

"Ivy, I can feel your tension from here. Try to relax."

"I can't."

"Any particular reason?"

"I'm waiting for you to interrogate me." Surely he was ready for her to explain her behavior.

He frowned. "I didn't bring you in here to interrogate you. I brought you in here so you could have some peace and quiet."

He didn't elaborate. He seemed to be trying to speak as little as possible. She closed her eyes again, but she couldn't let it go. "I thought it might be some kind of reverse psychology technique." She didn't know why, but she spoke softly. "Instead of bright lights and steel tables and chairs, you settle the suspect into a cozy chair, dim the lights, and lull them into complacency until they spill their guts."

Gil's response wasn't much above a low hum. "I'll keep that idea in mind if I ever have a suspect who would benefit from that treatment. Maybe I'll see if Leslie can get me a few scented candles and some massage music."

"That would definitely tip me over the edge."

"You aren't a suspect, Ivy." There was an edge to Gil's voice. "You haven't done anything wrong. Your world has been upended, and you're being forced to share personal information with people who are little more than strangers instead of doing what you should be doing."

"What should I be doing?"

"You should be at home, tucked under a fuzzy blanket, reading a good book, sleeping anytime you want. You should have someone making sure you have something good to eat, access to your pain meds, and space to process. But I can't give you any of that, so what you're getting is the most comfortable chair in the building and a few minutes to breathe."

She opened her eyes and discovered he wasn't looking at his

phone. His phone was on the table beside him. He had his elbows on his knees and his hands in his hair.

"Thank you."

At her words, he straightened. "Not sure you were listening, Buttercup. I just laid out all the reasons you have for hating me right now."

"I could never hate you."

Something that looked a lot like hope flashed in his eyes and in the quiet room, she heard him swallow. "Ivy, you don't really know me anymore."

"I'm not talking about the nine-year-old Gil I left behind." Or the seventeen-year-old whose heart she broke. The words, unspoken, hung between them. "I'm talking about the Gil who walked into my nightmare and could have wished me luck and went on his merry way but instead is walking through it with me. The Gil who slept on his couch last night and who I suspect got very little sleep. The Gil who is protecting me from everyone, including himself."

He stared into her eyes, and no matter how hard she tried, she couldn't tell if what he was thinking was good or bad.

A low "Yo!" came from somewhere down the hall and sliced through the web that had spun between them.

Gil stood and offered her his hand. She took it, and when he tugged her to her feet, she expected him to step back, but he pulled until she was leaning against him. He tipped her chin up and she could feel his breath against her cheek. "Don't count on me protecting you from me for long, Buttercup."

—13—

HE SHOULD HAVE KEPT his big mouth shut.

Ivy had all but bolted from the room after he made that stupid remark, and she hadn't been alone with him since. Faith, Tessa, and Emily had banded together and insisted that what Ivy needed was a girls' night in.

Gil had been kicked out of his own house. Emily told him she'd text him when he could come home.

So instead of spending Saturday night with Ivy, talking about things that absolutely needed to be discussed, he was back at the office with Zane and Luke. They'd ordered pizza. Talked about Ivy's mess, divvied up the investigative tasks, and then returned to their desks.

If it were anyone but Ivy, someone they knew mattered to him, Luke and Zane would not have been at work on a Saturday night. None of them would have. They worked hard and working weekends was hardly a novel concept to any of them, but their caseload was fairly light at the moment and their weekends had been mostly free for the past few months.

He'd always gotten along well with his fellow agents, but after they lost three of them in the space of a few weeks last spring, their bond had solidified. So while it wasn't normal for them to be working on a Saturday night, it wasn't unusual for them to be together.

Three weeks ago, their entire team spent the weekend on the Outer Banks. Emily drove down from DC, and Faith's sister, Hope, joined them. They made the most of the last weekend of summer and had a blast. And two weekends ago, they all worked a protective detail when the vice president came to town to make a speech.

Then last Saturday, Gil, Zane, and Luke went to Carrington to dive with their sheriff's office dive team. Tessa and Faith were learning to dive but weren't as experienced, so they hung out with Leigh Parker and Sabrina Campbell. When the official training session was over, Faith, Tessa, Sabrina, and Leigh joined the others for some fun diving in Lake Porter.

Would Ivy want to learn to dive? She might. But if she didn't, she probably wouldn't mind hanging out with Sabrina and Leigh.

Gil grabbed a baseball, one of several on his desk, and walked the hall. He had to stop thinking of all the ways Ivy could seamlessly slide into his life when everything went back to normal and focus on why someone wanted into her office computers.

Ransomware.

The idea was lodged in his mind, and he couldn't shake it. The other thing he couldn't shake was that he'd never seen a ransomware case like this one. And he'd seen a lot of ransomware.

Ransomware wasn't typically a personal crime. Anyone—all the way from an individual to a nation-state—could perpetrate it. But with the exception of nation-states, who might have more nefarious reasons, the goal was to score the ransom, and it was rare for anyone to resort to physical violence.

Due to the crime's digital nature, the bad actors who set the ransoms might not even be located on the same continent as their victims. They didn't usually have a personal vendetta against the businesses they attacked. They simply wanted the money.

But this was personal. It was as personal as you could get. These people had broken into Ivy's home and tortured her for access to her computer. They must have known that breaking into the office wouldn't be enough. That her system was too secure and the only way they could get in was to have the passwords.

So why not pressure an employee? Luke had volunteered to look into Ivy's employees, but Gil didn't think that would pan out. It was possible the people behind the attack had already tried, and maybe they'd already been successful in getting something from an employee, but even if they had, it wouldn't have worked. They needed Ivy's passwords and the level of access to the system that only she had.

Except she wasn't the only one who had access.

He went back to his cubicle, dropped the baseball in its basket, and pulled his phone from his pocket.

A few clicks later the phone rang, and he waited.

"Campbell."

Wherever he was, it was loud. "Adam. Gil Dixon. Got a minute?"

"Sure. Hang on a sec." Gil heard a whoop and a groan and the dull roar of a football game on a TV, then silence. "Sorry about that. What's up?" Adam was all business, and Gil could imagine why. They were friends, but Gil had never made a habit out of calling Sabrina's husband to shoot the breeze.

Luke and Zane had both come around the corners of their cubicles and stood at his doorway, not trying to hide their eavesdropping.

"Need to put a bug in your ear." With broad strokes, he explained the situation with Ivy. "She told us Sabrina set up her system, and Sabrina sometimes tries to hack into it. I don't have any reason to think anyone knows about Sabrina's involvement, but I didn't want to leave her hanging out there without someone keeping an eye on things."

"Appreciate it." Adam didn't sound grateful. He sounded ticked. "You got a handle on who these guys are yet?"

"Not even close. This case is barely twenty-four hours old, and it's already a mess. We've got counterfeit money deposited into her account that makes no sense. People torturing her for her computer password, which also makes no sense. Today someone tried to snatch her from a Mexican restaurant. I can't prove anything, and I need you to understand I don't have any verifiable reason to think Sabrina could be in danger."

"Don't need one. I'll take your gut instinct any day."

"Thanks."

"How much can I tell Bri?" Nobody except Adam called her anything other than Sabrina or Dr. Fleming-Campbell.

Had anyone besides him ever given Ivy a nickname?

"I'm sure Ivy isn't planning to keep it a secret, but it's all pretty fresh. Let me talk to her tonight and find out if she's said anything to Sabrina and what she's comfortable with me sharing. I'll get back to you before I crash."

"You aren't with her?" Adam's concern was obvious.

"Would love to be, but I got kicked out of my own house by a couple of female agents who didn't appreciate the perceived insinuation that they couldn't provide adequate security for a girls' night in." He knew they would die before they let anything happen to Ivy. It had nothing to do with them being women, and they knew it, but that didn't stop them from messing with him about it. Mainly because he couldn't say the truth. He didn't want to leave Ivy. He wanted to be wherever she was. Full stop.

Adam laughed. "So she's with Faith and Tessa."

"And my sister."

At that, Adam howled. "Hope you weren't planning on going home before midnight."

"They promised me ten."

"Don't hold your breath. When Bri gets together with Leigh, Anissa, and Sharon, there's no telling when she'll finally get home. Last time, Ryan texted me and Gabe at midnight and begged us to do something. We tried. Bri told me to leave her alone. Anissa told Chavez to go jump in the lake. Bri didn't get home until 1:30."

"Not making me feel better."

"Not trying to." Adam's laughter faded. "But seriously, thanks for the heads-up."

They chatted for a few more minutes, then Adam disconnected the call.

"Good move to give Campbell a heads-up." Zane frowned. "But it may get you in trouble with Ivy if he shares with Sabrina before she does."

"I'm on it." He dialed her number.

She answered on the first ring. "I can't believe it's you."

Something was very wrong in her voice. "Are you okay?" When she didn't respond after ten seconds, he prompted, "Ivy?"

"Do you have any idea how long I've wanted to see 'Gil Dixon' pop up on my phone?"

He had no idea what to say to that.

Fortunately, she kept talking. "Sorry. I probably should have just said hello."

Was she embarrassed? Her discomfort loosened his tongue. "I'd say you handled that perfectly."

"Good." She didn't try to hide her relief. "I'm not usually so . . . er . . . awkward."

"I would never use that word to describe you."

"Give it time. You'll change your mind."

"Not likely." Luke cleared his throat, and Gil looked up to see Zane spinning his finger in the universal symbol for "get on with it."

"Leave her alone, Gil! It's girls' night in. No boys allowed." Emily yelled from somewhere, loud enough for him to hear it clearly through Ivy's phone.

"Are you having fun? Or is Emily driving you insane?"

Zane turned and made a show of banging his head against the wall. Luke laughed.

"I'm having fun. Emily, well, you know Emily is awesome. Faith has a surprising sense of humor. And Tessa is hilarious. I've laughed more tonight than I have in, well, I honestly don't remember."

"That's great." Gil made a mental note to buy Tessa a gift card to her favorite coffee shop. And then to stop by the store for a six-pack of Cherry Coke for Faith.

"Yeah." Her voice was soft. "But I'm sorry Emily kicked you out of your house. Where did y'all wind up?"

"The office."

"You went to work?" She sounded horrified.

"Yeah." Gil forced the next words out. "And I had a thought and I acted on it, and now I need to run it past you. I hate to mess with your girls'-night vibe, but I need to know if you've shared anything with Sabrina yet."

"Not yet. Why?"

Tell her. Quick. Like ripping off a Band-Aid. Then she can get back—

"Oh no." She'd figured it out before he could tell her. "She knows my computer system, and she can hack into anything. Do you think she's in danger?"

"I think the risk is small, but if it were me, I'd want a heads-up."

"You said you had a thought and you'd acted on it. What did you do?"

"I called her husband and told him what happened. I didn't go into a lot of detail, but I did want him to know that someone is desperate to get into your computer systems."

"Do you think he can keep her safe?" There was a definite edge of panic in her words.

"I don't think. I know." Gil poured all his certainty into his words in an effort to lower Ivy's anxiety. "He has a lot of experience. She had some drama a few years ago, and when it was over, he put a ring on her finger."

"Then I guess it worked out."

"You could say that. Adam won't share anything with Sabrina that you don't want him to share, but I think it's only fair that she knows what's going on. Mostly because she's your friend, and she'll want to know. But also because she's brilliant, and if she's aware of what's going on, she can be on her guard."

And she might solve the entire case in her head and hand it to them with a color-coded PowerPoint presentation by morning, but Gil didn't mention that.

"I don't mind her knowing, Gil, but I'm not sure I can tell—" Her voice broke.

"You don't have to." He hurried to reassure her. "I didn't go into detail, but I gave Adam enough that he can share with Sabrina, and she'll know what she needs to know. Then, whenever you're ready, you can talk to her about it. If she needs more detail than you're ready to share, you can have her call me, Faith, or Tessa."

"That's a good plan."

"I'm sorry to have messed up your girls'-night-in fun."

"I wouldn't put that above Sabrina's safety."

"I know you wouldn't, and that's why I messed it up, even though I didn't want to."

"I don't want anyone else hurt. Should I contact my employees?"

"No. Not tonight." He said what he had to say as gently as he could. "Right now, your employees are suspects. I hate that, but it's true."

"I don't want to believe any of them could have been behind this."

"I know you don't. And they probably aren't. For now, I'd say the best policy is to hold the information close and think carefully before sharing it."

"I like that plan too."

"Good."

"Gil Dixon!" Emily's teasing angry voice pierced through their quiet conversation. She wasn't standing right beside Ivy, but she couldn't have been too far away. "I'm going to use your fancy-pants knives on the hard plastic cutting boards if you don't leave Ivy alone."

"You tell her if she touches my knives, I'll tell Mom and Dad about the time she lied about spending the night with a friend and was pulled over by the police for TP'ing her teacher's house."

Ivy laughed.

"What did he say?" Emily growled. Ivy told her.

"You don't want to go there, Gil." This time, Emily's voice was right at the phone. She must have been standing close. And there was a hint of devilry in her tone. "You start telling tales, and I'll be forced to respond in kind. But I won't tell Mom and Dad. I'll tell Ivy. Maybe I should start with that away game where you—"

"I'm hanging up. Back to girls' night."

Ivy told him bye, and she was laughing when she did it.

He fired off a message to Adam, giving him the all clear, and Sabrina called three minutes later.

Once greetings were exchanged, he filled her in on what had happened to Ivy. "How secure is everything? Is it even possible to make a system truly impervious to a ransomware attack?"

"Not completely. Malware is sneaky. There are so many vectors, it's difficult to block them all. Short of not allowing your employees to access the internet or ever open an attachment."

"If you know a system is at risk, under threat, is it possible to create a backup of the system so that if it gets infected, you can reboot everything?"

"Clone the system?"

"Sure."

"Yes." Sabrina sounded pleased. "That's a good idea. It's unrealistic, under normal circumstances, to maintain a cloned system. But I could clone what she has, keep it offline, and then if they successfully attack . . . yes. Good idea, Gil. I'll work on that."

"Thanks. I owe you."

"I take payment in cake." She wasn't kidding. "The red velvet with the chocolate chips and the cream cheese icing, please."

"Deal."

— 14 —

IVY WASN'T SURE how she'd wound up at this church on Sunday morning.

Last Sunday, she'd gone to the church she typically attended. She slipped in, found a seat near the rear. Worshiped. Left.

This Sunday, she was flanked on both sides by Secret Service agents. Luke was on one side. Tessa on the other. Zane was beside Tessa, and Faith beside Luke, with Emily rounding out their party beside Faith.

Ivy had fallen down the most ridiculous rabbit hole in the history of rabbit holes. One where long-lost childhood friends grew up to be federal agents and then showed up to rescue bioengineers in distress.

In this same rabbit hole, the Secret Service agent who stole her heart when she was four years old was now on the platform at the front of the church playing the guitar and singing about God's faithfulness.

She knew the words. She'd always gone to churches where they sang hymns, and this one was a favorite. But in this moment, she doubted God would approve of her thoughts. There was probably something extra sinful about ogling someone leading worship.

She tried to stop, but she couldn't. The moment she'd found

her seat, she'd seen Gil in a black button-up shirt—untucked—and dark-washed jeans, holding an electric guitar. And she hadn't been able to tear her eyes away from him.

He caught her staring and winked.

That wink sent a shock wave through her system. One she didn't quite know how to process. Nothing in her previous experience had prepared her for the swirl of emotions that engulfed her now. Her dating resume was sparsely populated. She'd had her share of first dates over coffee or dinner, but she rarely said yes to the second date. She'd had two boyfriends, but she hadn't dated anyone exclusively since grad school.

She'd never realized she had a type. But sitting in a megachurch auditorium, it was clear she definitely had a type, and her type was Gil Dixon. It didn't matter if he was holding a guitar or a gun or a Ginsu knife, he exuded confidence and competence. You couldn't see him and not know he knew how to handle himself and whatever he held in his hands.

And when he held her hand? Yeah, she was pretty sure he knew how to handle her too.

She forced her thoughts back to the song. The words. The deep theology. She needed this. To be reminded God was faithful, especially right now with everything in her world gone mad. Of course, God also designed men and women to enjoy each other. Was it part of God's faithfulness that he'd brought Gil back to her?

Because overall, she couldn't say she was enthusiastic about God's current plan for her life, with one big exception—and that exception was Gil. And Emily, of course, but mostly Gil.

When the music ended and the pastor stepped behind the podium, Gil disappeared to the back of the stage, and she assumed he would reappear at the end of the service. She did not expect him to show up a few minutes later at the end of their row, or for

Zane and Tessa to immediately shift a seat down, leaving Gil the seat beside her. Or for him to settle in to her left and throw his arm over her shoulders, pulling her against his side, with his hand coming to rest well away from her burn.

It was a protective gesture. A claiming gesture. And she didn't expect to like it.

But she did.

It took more than a few minutes for her to settle her thoughts and her heart rate, but eventually she relaxed, not all the way into Gil, but close enough. The sermon was from John. "In this world you will have trouble. But take heart! I have overcome the world."

Wow. Talk about on the nose. Were the others sitting there thinking, *Yep, this is exactly what Ivy needs today*? She couldn't blame them if they were.

The pastor closed in prayer, and as he spoke, Gil's lips brushed her ear and he whispered, "Be right back."

Ivy kept her eyes closed, but she didn't need them to know that Tessa and Zane had slid back into their original seats. She was surrounded on all sides by churchgoers, and Luke was mere inches from her on the right. But they couldn't allow the presence of an empty twenty-four-inch-wide chair on her left? Did they realize how overprotective they were being? Or was this so much a part of their training that they did it subconsciously?

When the closing song came to an end, she leaned behind Luke and Faith to speak to Emily.

And four rows back, she looked straight into the dark eyes of Abott Percy. "Ab?"

Luke placed a hand on her back. "Ivy?"

"It's okay, Luke." She turned back to Abott. "I saw—" He was gone.

She craned her neck, looking through the throng, trying to

find him. Abott Percy was tall. Built. Very good looking. She'd thought she might be falling in love with him once.

He wasn't her type. She knew that now. But once, she'd cared about him. She still did.

"Ivy?" This came from Tessa. "What did you see?"

Tessa had her agent face on. Tessa was always intimidating in the way anyone who looked like her was. She was the kind of beautiful you didn't expect to see in real life. In a magazine? Sure. On a red carpet? Absolutely. Thirty feet tall on a big screen? Take my money.

She was the kind of gorgeous that made women jealous and men lose all sense—and bless her heart, she knew it. But what Ivy had learned last night was that Tessa wasn't conceited or vain.

She knew she was stunning, and she also knew it meant nothing. She didn't want the approval of people who only appreciated her for her looks, and she was baffled by the envy of people who assumed being physically beautiful meant everything else about her life was perfect.

Tessa, Ivy had come to see, spent most of her energy trying to prove she was worth being loved on her own merits. On what she did. On how good she was at her job. On her skills. Her kindness. Her generosity. Her intellect.

All of this made Tessa Reed a formidable woman. But there was nothing frightening about Tessa. She was sweet to the core.

Or Ivy had thought so until this moment. Because Tessa Reed with her agent face on sent a surge of terror through Ivy. Not because she was afraid of Tessa, but because she was afraid of whatever had generated that level of intensity in her new friend.

"Ivy. Talk to me now. Who did you see?"

Ivy sank back into her seat and answered immediately. "I'm sure it was nothing. I thought I saw Ab."

"Who is Ab?" Luke and Zane asked in unison.

Faith, Tessa, and Emily, who had slipped around the end of their row and were now standing in the row ahead of them in front of Ivy's seat, all nodded with understanding.

"Want to clue us in, babe?" Luke directed the question to Faith.

"Her ex."

"Whose ex?" Gil asked as he joined Emily in front of Ivy.

"Ivy's," Tessa answered.

Gil propped his knees in the chair and draped his arms on the back of it and settled his gaze on Ivy. "Ivy's ex?"

"Long-gone ex," Emily jumped in. "Over for years."

"Does he live in Raleigh?" Gil still hadn't broken eye contact. It wasn't a staring contest. He wasn't glaring. He didn't look mad. It took Ivy a few seconds to realize she knew that look.

Gil was gearing up to fight.

"Ivy? Your ex? Where does he live?" Gil asked again.

"Atlanta."

"Any idea why he's in Raleigh?" Hundreds of people continued to leave the auditorium. They were surrounded by friends. But it was as if there was no one else there. Just him. Just her.

"He was guest lecturing at NC State this past week, and he's making a pitch for a grant this coming week."

"So, not so much of an ex that he doesn't call you when he comes to town." It wasn't a question.

"No. He emailed. Told me what he was doing. We . . . we had dinner." Why did she feel guilty for having an innocent dinner with her ex-boyfriend? She hadn't done anything wrong.

"When?"

"Thursday."

Gil frowned and finally released her from his gaze. Well, it had turned into more of a glare than a gaze by this point. A glare that he turned on Tessa. "You didn't think it was relevant?"

What did that mean? Why was he being snippy with Tessa?

"I didn't know about it until last night." Tessa's response was calm. Not soothing, but like she didn't have any problem with Gil's snippiness.

Interestingly enough, Zane did. "Gil. Chill." Zane's low voice rumbled, and he stepped closer to Tessa.

"Let's get out of here." Luke grabbed Faith's hand. Zane and Tessa followed his lead, effectively herding Ivy out of their row and into the aisle.

Emily came to her left side and bumped her arm. "How sure are you it was Abott?"

Ivy shrugged. "I'm not. I mean, I was, but there's no reason for him to be here. And if it had been him, he would have talked to me."

"Maybe," Tessa said from behind her.

"Why wouldn't he?" Ivy twisted her head around so she could see Tessa. Tessa didn't answer, but she cut her eyes with a meaningful glance toward Gil. "Oh."

She and Gil had sat close the entire sermon. Anyone watching would assume they were together. Had Abott seen them and made a similar assumption? She shook her head. "I don't think—"

Before she could finish the thought, Gil bumped Emily over and took her place at Ivy's side. Once there, he rested his hand at her lower back and leaned toward her. "I'm looking forward to hearing all about Abott."

Great. Something to look forward to.

NOTHING WAS GOING AS PLANNED.

He watched from his car as Ivy's entourage left the building. What were the odds that Ivy would wind up in the protective embrace of not one but four Secret Service agents? He'd seen

123

enough documentaries to know they'd created a bubble around her. Similar to the way they would protect the president.

The dark-headed agent who went into her house Friday night opened a car door and Ivy disappeared inside. A dark-haired girl who looked a lot like the agent slipped into the back seat. He expected them to pull out immediately, but they sat still. The blond agent showed up with a telescoping rod and made quick work of checking under the car. Only then did they drive away.

They were checking under the cars for bombs. Smart of them—but not too smart for them to be so obvious about it. He would avoid that option now.

The other agents had paired off, and the three-car caravan pulled out of the parking lot. And then a fourth car pulled in two cars back. He might have assumed it was a random church member, but he'd seen that guy watching Ivy.

How many people were keeping tabs on her?

And how would he know if anyone was keeping tabs on him?

There was always a chance this was going to be complicated. But he'd hoped it would be easy.

So much for that.

ABOTT PERCY THE FIFTH. That was her ex's name? Gil fought hard against the urge to roll his eyes. His mother had taught him manners. Part of that had included intensive training on never teasing someone for anything beyond their control. This included physical features, family of origin, athletic ability (or lack thereof), socioeconomic status, and names.

Names were important to his mom. It was no accident she'd named her children Gil and Emily. An English teacher by training and book addict by lifestyle, she'd given her twins the names of two of her favorite fictional characters. She thought that would guarantee they would always make her smile. Although at different times, they both tested that concept.

But not everyone had a name to be proud of. Whether that was because a family member had committed a heinous crime or had a bad reputation, or because their name had a negative connotation for some other reason. Regardless, his mom's training included never mocking someone about their name because you thought it was weird, dumb, or pompous.

And Abott Percy the Fifth was about as pompous a name as Gil could imagine. He knew he shouldn't think it, but the guy even looked like an arrogant—

"Gil?" Ivy tapped the doorframe. "Mind if I join you?"

At his nod, she opened the door all the way and entered his screened-in porch. She didn't hide her study of the space. "Your kitchen is fantastic, but I think this might be my favorite room in your house."

He pointed to the twin-sized swinging bed across from him, indicating she should sit there. "I've had my eye on this swing. I spotted it earlier today." She eased onto the swing, kicked off her shoes, and settled against the pillows. "Oh yeah. This is perfect. I think I'd be out here all the time."

"It's my favorite too. I like being able to be outside but without the annoyance of mosquitos and gnats."

She pointed to the ceiling. "And with a few fans."

"Definitely." Even when the weather was hot, heavy, and humid, the fans kept the air moving. With the help of some large shade trees on both sides, the porch was comfortable on all but the hottest days. Today the September air was thick and heavy, but the porch was pleasant.

Gil had a million questions. Only a few of them about Abott

Percy. But like he'd told Ivy yesterday, whenever possible, he wanted to give her space to just be. And his screened-in porch was the perfect place to be.

Two minutes later, Ivy settled deeper into a reclined position on the swing. Five minutes later, she was asleep.

The afternoon wore on. Ivy slept on. Gil left the porch long enough to help Emily pack her car and tell her goodbye. Then he returned with his laptop, settled into his favorite chair, and went to work.

He was missing something important. He usually enjoyed this part of an investigation. He didn't mind a certain amount of ambiguity or chaos, because in his experience, rogue leads eventually turned into real ones. The more convoluted a case was, the more likely it was that the guilty parties had either already messed up or were about to.

And when they did, Gil would be ready to capitalize on their mistakes.

But this case was different, because it wasn't a case. Gil didn't believe in victimless crimes. When someone committed a crime, somewhere, someone was paying for it. But with the exception of last spring, when all of their lives were on the line, none of the crimes he'd investigated since joining the Secret Service had commanded the level of urgency that Ivy's case did.

There was a reason they'd come after her this weekend. And if he could figure out what that was, it would break everything open.

He made notes. He researched Hedera, Inc. and was amazed, again, at the phenomenal body of work the beauty sleeping ten feet away from him had amassed in her short life. She was too smart for him, that was for sure. Too beautiful. Too accomplished. She could do a lot better than him in every way except one.

No one would ever love her the way he could.

He wasn't an idiot. It was way too soon to be talking about love. Too much. Too fast. And way too many questions were still unanswered. But Gil Dixon knew his own mind. After Ivy left him and his baseball career ended, he came far too close to ending his life. Then he spent the next five years in therapy. He wasn't ashamed of it. It was life saving, life altering, and life affirming. It also made him willing to give words to deep emotions most people never voiced.

Sometimes Luke and Zane teased him about being way too in touch with his feelings for their comfort level. Would Ivy feel the same way? Maybe. Especially if he did something stupid, like profess his undying love tomorrow or ask her to marry him by the end of the year.

Then again . . . she might not think those things were stupid at all.

— 15 —

WHERE WAS SHE? What was happening to her? Why was she hurting?

"Ivy, you're at my house. You're safe."

Gil's voice tugged at her consciousness. When she finally pulled herself awake, she was sitting upright on the swing. Gil was perched on the edge, in the curve of her body. One hand wrapped around her calf, his thumb moving up and down in a slow, steady sweep. "I've got you, Buttercup."

She slumped back onto the pillows. Gil reached toward her and pressed his thumb to a tear that had escaped from her eyes and was traveling toward her ear. It was followed by another. She couldn't make them stop. And when Gil pulled her all the way into his arms, she stopped trying to plug the dam and all her emotions gushed out of her.

He held her while she cried, and he didn't say a word.

When Ivy pulled her face away from Gil, his shirt was so wet with her tears that it stuck to her cheek.

How much more of a weakling could she be? To wake up,

scared, from a bad dream, and then burst into tears, and then be completely unable to make them stop.

What must he be thinking right now? Probably something along the lines of, *How can I get a break from this girl?*

Emily was brave and strong. Tessa and Faith were phenomenally successful in male-dominated professions. Neither of them had checked their femininity at the door to do it, but she doubted they lost much time crying. Gil spent his professional and personal life with women who did not burst into tears at the drop of a hat.

To be fair, she didn't make a habit out of it. She could get teary easily enough. She felt big, and sometimes her feelings leaked out of her eyes. But a crying jag like the one she still hadn't recovered from? That wasn't normal.

She wouldn't blame Gil if he was trying to figure out how quickly he could dump her at a safe house and get on with his life. But that wasn't what he was doing. His hands moved from around her back to cradle her face. His thumbs pressed gently across her cheeks as he brushed away the wet that clung there. "Want to tell me about it?"

She closed her eyes and shook her head.

Gil didn't press her for more. He dipped his head until his forehead rested against hers, and they sat that way, swaying on the swing, until her breathing leveled with one final sigh. "Gil?"

"Yeah?"

"We need to talk."

"Whenever you're ready. Not before."

"Gil?"

"Right here, Buttercup."

"I'm ready." She leaned back against the fluffy pillows that cushioned the back and side rails of the swing. He scooted across the mattress until his back rested on the opposite side, mirroring her position. She sat cross-legged. He stretched his legs, one foot on the floor to keep the swing moving, the other leg stretched out beside her.

Gil nudged her leg with his foot. "We used to sit like this in the window seat and read. Remember?"

She remembered. She remembered everything. This cozy companionship was what they should have had for the past fifteen years. But they didn't, because of her. "I'm so sorry, Gil."

Once those words left her mouth, it all came out.

"I didn't know what Mom was doing, Gil. I promise I didn't. I never would have dreamed she could be so cold and heartless. Not to anyone, but especially not to your family. When we left your house, we went straight back home to Oregon, and even though we were going to be separated again, I was so happy. Our reunion had been more than I'd ever dared to dream it would be." How was she going to get through this? How could she ever explain?

"Ivy, I know you didn't know. And I never blamed you. None of us did."

"I was so embarrassed."

He didn't comment on that.

"I didn't answer your phone calls because Mom's attorney said we couldn't be in contact. And when I didn't get any more letters from you, I thought you were too angry—"

Gil sat straight up. "What do you mean you didn't get any letters? I wrote to you. Every day. For weeks." There was so much raw pain in his words, she felt them slice through her heart.

"Mom stole those too."

Gil's mouth moved, but nothing came out.

"I found them, after Dad died. When I went home for the funeral, I went with a plan. I cleaned out everything of mine that was in the house. Books, photo albums, pictures, dolls, and stuffed animals. Everything. When I got it all unpacked in my apartment, I found them stuck in a copy of *Anne of Green Gables*. I don't think Dad knew they were there. And it was the kind of thing Mom would do. She wouldn't have destroyed them, but she wasn't about to give them to me either. She was on house arrest while she was waiting for trial, and she was so angry. I should have reached out to you, but it had been so long . . ."

She dropped her head into her hands. "Gil, I couldn't face you. Or Emily. Or your parents. I spent five years thinking you'd cut me out of your life. I left for college thinking that you wanted nothing to do with me. Then I read the letters and realized what had happened, but by then I knew you assumed *I* had cut *you* off. I've thought about calling you, or Emily. So many times. When you were shot in the spring, it was all I could do not to show up at the hospital. But what could I have said? I have no claim on you. No right to insert myself into your life. Not anymore."

Gil scooted toward her, but she kept talking. She had to get this out now or she never would. "Every year I almost sent a Christmas card. But what would I say? 'I'm sorry my mom was a thief'? 'I'm sorry I didn't fight harder for us'? 'I'm sorry I believed you didn't want anything to do with me' when there was nothing in our entire history that should have made me think that?"

"Buttercup." Gil pulled her toward him until his forehead pressed to hers and his hands caressed her face.

"I'm so, so sorry." What else could she say?

"I can forgive you for thinking I'd turned my back on you, if you can forgive me for thinking the same. We should have fought harder. Come after you. Insisted on talking it out. We didn't. You are hardly the only one to blame here."

"But *my* mom was the one who precipitated the situation. Not yours."

"So that means it's all on you?"

"Well, yeah."

"Want to know what you're wrong about?"

She wasn't sure if she did or not. "Maybe?"

"We were both young, both immature, both dealing with heavy things, and we both made the stupid decision to assume the worst in each other rather than the best."

They sat in silence for several minutes. Gil broke it. "I have all your letters from when we were kids. I kept them."

"I have all yours too. From when we were kids and the ones I didn't see until it was far too late."

"I also have letters that I never sent you."

She pulled back so she could see his face. "What?"

"My therapist thought I should write out what I was feeling and thinking. He told me to pick someone I could write to and be honest with, but that I would never actually send the letters. I chose you."

Ivy had rarely been rendered speechless, but that did it. She could not form a single word.

Gil's hands hadn't left her face, and his thumbs continued to stroke her cheeks. "What if we bought plane tickets and left town for a month? We could hide on a beach, or maybe in a mountain cabin with a fireplace? Do you think anyone would notice?"

He spoke so seriously, it took her a few seconds longer than it should have to realize he was joking. No. That wasn't right. He wasn't joking. He did want that. He also knew they couldn't have it.

"I like the mountain and fireplace idea the best." She was still whispering. "Although, I've never lived in a house with a fireplace. Do you know how to start a fire?"

"I do."

"Oh." Why did she think they might not be talking about fireplaces anymore?

Gil's hands slid from her face and down her left shoulder but carefully jumped over her injured right shoulder, and now his right hand was tangled with her left fingers while his left hand was pressed into the swing at her side. "You slept for a while. Are you hungry?"

She recognized this for what it was. Gil was pulling them out of the deep mire of their complicated past. The conversation was over. The truth was out. They now knew what had happened that broke them apart, but what they were going to be in the future was uncertain. And that wasn't going to change tonight. They both needed time to process the past and think through what they wanted for the future.

Once she gave the idea a few seconds of brain activity, she had to admit she was hungry. She nodded, and Gil's face relaxed into a smile that had been cute when he was little but had grown into something breath stealing and heart racing in its beauty.

"Finally. Something I can fix." He stood and pulled her up beside him. "How do you feel about pasta?"

"I love pasta."

"Excellent." He led them back into the house. She went to freshen up while he proceeded to the kitchen, and that's where she found him twenty minutes and a full refresh on her makeup later.

"What are you making?" She slid onto the stool she'd occupied at breakfast.

"Baked ziti. That work for you?" The room smelled of garlic, basil, and oregano. Two mason jars rested in the sink with the remains of what might have been homemade tomato sauce clinging to the glass walls.

"Sounds great."

Their conversation was stilted at first, but it didn't take long for it to slide into the easy rapport they had always shared. Gil prepped the ziti and slid it into the oven, then whipped up a vinaigrette, tossed a salad, and made garlic bread from the loaves they'd used at breakfast. Gil wasn't giving her intense looks. There were no heavy pauses filled with deep meaning. It was casual. Easy. Two old friends reconnecting over dinner.

It was exactly what she needed. Two hours later, Ivy finally got up the nerve to ask the other questions she needed answers to. "Gil?"

"Hmm?" he asked from the opposite end of the sofa where they were sitting.

"I think we need to talk."

His eyes widened. "Again?"

She tried to reassure him with a smile. "Not about that."

He waved a hand in her direction, indicating she should proceed. It looked casual, but the way his face hardened and his eyes narrowed, she knew he wasn't nearly as relaxed as he was trying to appear.

"I need to know what's happening." Once she started talking, all her questions from the weekend tumbled out of her. "I need to know if I can go to work tomorrow. When I can go home. If I need to do something different with my security system or hire a bodyguard. I don't want to put my staff at risk, but this is a big week for us. I'm making a pitch on Wednesday for an enormous grant. The pitch session is by invitation, and only six of us were invited. It's a big deal, and I need to be on my A game. And I'm not sure what's happening with my case."

Gil didn't make any effort to stop the words, and she couldn't rein them in. They kept coming.

"This weekend, you, Emily, your friends—I appreciate it more than you'll ever know, but it feels like I've been in a bubble since you walked into my house on Friday night. Your idea of leaving town is appealing, but since it isn't an option, I need to make decisions about tomorrow and the rest of the week. In order for me to do that, I need you to explain everything to me so I can choose wisely."

She blew out a long breath. "I have to get my head in the game." Gil didn't respond. He barely moved. His eyes held hers. "What are you thinking?"

"That you're remarkable."

Whoa.

Before she could process that, he continued, "And if you're ready to talk about what's going on, I can answer most of your questions."

He'd been waiting for her to be ready to talk. He'd given her the space to process. Was it possible the real Gil Dixon might be every bit as awesome as she'd hoped he would be? Maybe she didn't need to be afraid anymore that the dream wouldn't match the reality. "I'm as ready as I'm going to be."

His expression held something beautiful. Like he was proud of her. "Okay, Dr. Collins. Let's do this."

GIL WAITED WHILE IVY SITUATED herself at the end of the sofa. Her cute little feet tucked under her. Her left hand wrapped around her drink, some fruity-smelling decaf herbal tea he kept on hand because Faith liked it. Her shoulders straight. Her eyes wary.

"Should I get a pen and paper?"

"If it makes you feel better, I'll get it for you."

She considered this, then shook her head. "No. Give it to me in one go. I'll write my thoughts out when we're done, condense them, and synthesize them."

Did she realize she bit down on her lower lip when she was concentrating? Probably not. And it would be best if he didn't look at her biting down on her lip while he talked. *Concentrate, you idiot.* "First, I need to ask you a few questions."

"Shoot."

"Tell me more about this grant proposal. I'm not trying to be obtuse, but you told us you have access to twenty million dollars. Why are you applying for a grant?"

She shifted deeper into the sofa. "First, because it's smart business. Twenty million seems like a large sum until you start thinking about manufacturing a prosthetic. Manufacturing equipment, even small scale, is exorbitantly expensive. And while, sadly, there is always a need for prosthetics, in the early days we'll be making each one custom. At least that's the plan. Sinking a large sum of cash into the business is a given. In the meantime, we still have other research ongoing. I employ six PhD bioengineers who have a strong predilection for receiving their paychecks without delay."

Gil could barely fight back the laughter. "Can't say I blame them."

"Indeed. It's crucial I keep many income sources flowing into my business while I'm preparing for a significant outlay of resources. It's true you have to spend money to make money, but while I would be willing to live on beans and rice again, my staff would not."

"Again?"

"In grad school, I was broke. I spent my stipend on supplies to build a prototype of the prosthetic we're ready to run trials on. I ate a lot of ramen, beans and rice, and lentil soup that year."

"But what about—?"

She raised a hand and cut him off. "I started college at sixteen. Finished undergrad in three years. I was nineteen when I started grad school. Dad was still alive. He helped with school. Paid my rent, tuition, books, etc. But the settlement money was socked away, and I had no reason to ever believe I would have access to any of it for my work."

Ivy pulled a throw pillow onto her lap. "I was excited. Passionate. I was taking an enormous class load working on my MBA and my master's in bioengineering at the time. I had this concept for the prosthetic, and I finally had the skills and access to the equipment needed to make it. I devoted hours to working on it." She grinned at him. "I'm letting my nerd flag fly, aren't I?"

"Buttercup, you can let whatever you want fly whenever you want to. It's adorable."

She blushed from her neck to her hairline, but she didn't stop talking. "I can become rather animated when I talk about my work."

"Is that a problem?"

"It's not always professional to be so ebullient."

At that, Gil lost his hold on his humor and laughed. "Ebullient?"

She flushed again, even deeper scarlet than before. "Yes, it means—"

"Over the top enthusiasm. I know, Buttercup. But I'm not sure I've heard anyone use it in conversation before."

Her eyes dropped to the pillow.

"That's not a bad thing." He gentled his tone. "I like it. You're very specific about your word choices. I imagine you're also very specific about your work and your plans. Those are admirable qualities."

"I'm a nerd."

"You're a successful businesswoman. You're passionate about what you do. You're changing lives. None of that sounds nerdy to me, but even if it did, it wouldn't matter."

"Why not?"

"I like nerds."

Her eyes widened.

"A lot."

She blinked a few times.

"How could you not remember this?" Gil gave her a mock exasperated glare. "You were there. You saw Mom, always with her nose in a book and expecting all of us to do the same. And Dad. How many times did the two of you get so lost in a conversation about the physics of the curveball that Emily and I would leave the room until you finished? And let's not leave Emily out of the mix. You weren't around for this, but she made every assignment look like child's play and grew up to know more about human anatomy than most doctors. By the time we were teenagers, our dinner conversations varied from sports to politics to science to journalism to literature, and there was no room for slacking. You said something stupid at the table, you'd get called out for it. Not in a mean way, but there was no room for weak arguments or logical fallacies."

Her mouth had closed, and her eyes were filled with humor.

"Bottom line. I like nerds. I like brains. I like people who know what they're talking about and know how to think through a problem to reach the right solution. I'm looking forward to you showing me around your office and explaining what you do, and I can't wait to see this prototype of yours in production. I'll also add that it's okay if you call yourself a nerd, because there's nothing wrong with being a nerd. But it's not okay if you say it in a way that makes me think you're embarrassed by it, or you think it somehow makes you weird. Because there's nothing wrong with having a brain and knowing how to use it. And if anyone ever made you feel like being smart was a liability, feel free to point them out to me. I'll be happy to enlighten them regarding their idiocy."

Ivy was full-on grinning now. "Gil, I really think you need to learn to open up and express how you feel." They both laughed. Ivy wiped at her eyes and got control before she added, "Anyway, I didn't know Dad planned to give me the money. And I'm glad I didn't. I sacrificed a lot for a few years, and it helped me focus on what I wanted to do and how I wanted to do it. If it had been handed to me on a silver platter? Maybe I would be where I am now, but maybe not. And that's partly why I'm still going for grants, because that money won't last forever. The other reason, specific to the pitch this week, is that the company offering the grant has some technology that could be critical to another prosthetic we're developing. Winning the grant isn't about the money. It's also about access to the tech. That's why we're all going after it."

"Who is we?"

"Everyone invited to the pitch."

"Who, specifically, are you competing against?"

"There are two companies similar to mine. One out of New York, the other out of Texas. The other three are all professors at universities. Ab's here to pitch for the bioengineering department at Georgia. Clemson and Texas A&M were also invited."

"Ab?"

"Yes. That's why he's in town. He did some guest lectures this past week at NC State, and then he's pitching on Tuesday."

"Does he come to town often?"

"No."

— **16** —

"INSISTED?" GIL'S EXPRESSION had gone from open and de-lightedly curious to confused to something that resembled a thunderhead. "How did he insist?"

"He wouldn't let it go. I said yes because it's been a while since I've seen him in person, and I didn't have a legitimate reason to say no."

"Ab knows about the money."

He didn't phrase it as a question, but she confirmed. "Yes."

"You were with him when your dad died?"

"No. We'd already broken up."

"Then how does he know about it?"

"He came to me a while back, and we were discussing busi-ness. He knows better than most how much it takes to run a place like Hedera. The start-up cost for a private venture is prohibitive, which is why a lot of research is done at universities."

"So he asked you about the money?" Gil was looking at her like her answer could be the secret to world peace, immortality, and ending poverty—all with one word.

"Not specifically. He was asking for advice. There was no way for me to give him what he needed without being honest about my financial situation. He swore he wouldn't share that information, and I trusted him not to."

"I would think he would have had to back you into a corner to make you give that info up." Gil ran a hand through his hair, and it stood up all over his head like a porcupine. It would have been funny if the conversation hadn't been so serious.

"He didn't back me into a corner. Ab's a nice guy. Gentle. Sweet. He's funny and smart. And he cares about me. He's not pushy or bossy, and he's not intimidating or unkind."

Gil's expression shifted from one of hostility to one of speculation. "Sounds like a great guy."

"He is." Ab was great. Although it did bother her to think he might have been at church today and didn't speak to her. That wasn't like Ab.

"If he's so great, why aren't you still together?"

Ivy found this question enlightening on several levels. One, Gil wasn't hiding that he didn't like Ab, but he had no reason for his dislike, which had already made her consider the possibility that Gil was jealous. Two, the way the question was worded left it clear that Gil didn't know who had ended the relationship. Which led her to the third, and possibly most fascinating, scenario—that Gil was worried she might still be into Ab.

"He's a nice guy. That doesn't mean we made a good couple."

"That's a partial answer. How about you give me the full one?"

"Have I mentioned you can be bossy and intimidating?"

"No, although I did notice you mentioned that *Ab*"—he put heavy emphasis on the name—"wasn't."

Definitely jealous. She couldn't stop herself from grinning.

"I'm not sure there's much funny about this, Buttercup."

"No. I wouldn't think you would see the humor," Ivy fired back. "But I think it's hilarious."

He quirked an eyebrow. "Why?"

She wasn't about to answer that question, but she could give him a more complete explanation. Ivy waved a hand to indicate her body. "People look at me and think I'm a pushover. I've fought that my entire academic career. I'm a blonde female with a PhD in engineering. We aren't unicorn rare, but we aren't as common as pennies either. I worked hard to get where I am, and along the way I met Ab. He wasn't intimidated by me. He also didn't patronize me. We were compatible in every imaginable way. He understood my work. I understood his. We had similar tastes in almost everything, even the stuff that shouldn't be a deal breaker. Music, vacation destinations, food, houses. But there was one thing about which we were not on equal footing. And that one thing was enough for me to end it."

She could still see Ab's face the night she broke up with him. It still seared through her, the pain she'd caused. "He was more into me than I was into him. It wasn't fair to him."

Gil rubbed his hands over his thighs. "I'm guessing he didn't appreciate you making that decision for him. A guy might be willing to be more into a girl than she is into him. Especially if she's the right girl."

"Ab made that argument."

"Why didn't it work?"

"Because it wasn't fair to me either." She lowered her voice. "I'm not interested in settling. I'm a realist in almost every part of my life, Gil. Logical. Practical. Careful. But when it comes to my heart, that's a different story. My heart got a taste of something pure and beautiful when I was young, and it has refused to settle for anything less."

"Buttercup." The name wrenched out of Gil, but Ivy had gone as far as she was willing to go. For tonight at least. So she retreated and left no room for Gil to do anything but follow her where she was leading their conversation. Away from the heart and her dreams. Back toward the mind and the painful realities they had to deal with before they could be free to explore whatever was happening between them.

"Ab is a good man. I don't believe he would harm me or attempt to get the money for himself. I can appreciate that you won't see it that way, but you should know if you want to change my mind, you'll need to provide hard facts."

Gil still hadn't recovered. She wasn't even sure if he'd heard what she said. She pressed on. "As for this week, I need to know what the plan is. I cancelled the painters, but unless I get on the phone and tell them to take the day off, my team will be back at work bright and early tomorrow. I need to know what to tell them. I also need to know if I should look into hiring security or if I can go about my business. And finally, I can't thank you enough for your hospitality and kindness, but at some point, I'm going to have to go home, and I'd like to know when that is happening."

To his credit, Gil had pulled it together. Mostly. He rubbed his temples with his fingertips before muttering, "Don't hold back, Buttercup."

"I usually don't."

GIL DIDN'T TRY TO HIDE his amusement. "Fine as china. Tough as nails."

Ivy narrowed her eyes at him, probably trying to decide if he meant that to be a compliment or not. He did. But he wouldn't get into it with her at the moment.

There were more pressing issues for tonight. "Faith is on her way here."

"What? Why?"

"Two reasons. The main one is that Emily ran her mouth at church and told Tessa, who told Zane, who told Luke, who told Faith . . ." He shook his head in clear exasperation. "This makes us sound like we're in middle school. Good grief."

"What did Emily tell them?"

"That I haven't slept much the last two nights, and they decided that needs to change. Faith won't be here to crash. She'll be up all night on the couch."

"They're worried about your sleep?"

"Yeah. It's ridiculous. Faith is crazy protective, and you wouldn't know it to look at her, but Tessa's a mother hen. When we all got banged up last spring, she took it hard. She's working that out, and part of the way she's doing that is by being all up in our business. Emily knew if she told Tessa, she'd make sure I had some backup tonight."

"You seem frustrated, but that's beautiful, Gil. To have friends who care that much and who know you that well. That's a gift."

He didn't disagree. He also didn't comment. "But why Faith?"

"They picked a number."

"What?"

"I know. More middle school. Faith won. The way I heard it, they all wanted to volunteer, and the number system was employed to keep them from fighting about it. Emily thought it was hilarious."

"You don't?"

"No. But I get it. If the roles were reversed, I'd do the same. Bottom line, you're here again tonight. We should be able to get back into your house tomorrow, but if it's all the same to you, I'd rather you didn't go over there alone."

She shuddered.

"I can take you to work in the morning, then pick you up at the end of the day and take you home. In the meantime, police officers will be around. Morris called this afternoon while you were asleep. He's got some buddies who plan to make it their mission to show up. They may park in the parking lot. On the street. Might come inside and get eyes on you. That kind of thing."

Ivy's eyes had gone huge. "That seems like overkill."

"That's the point. Anyone watching will see it. Will know there's no rhyme or reason to it. No schedule."

"Do you think someone might come after me at work?"

"I think it's telling that they didn't try to get to you inside your building. I was impressed with the security you have. The fact that they wanted your passwords and computer info makes me think they want you alive and they want your business operational, meaning they're unlikely to shoot up the place to get everyone out."

Ivy's porcelain skin paled.

"I'm not trying to frighten you." That wasn't true. He was trying to scare her. Not enough to give her nightmares, but enough to keep her vigilant. "If we have a law enforcement presence, you should be safe inside. If you need to leave the office for any reason, I would appreciate it very much if you would call me first."

"I appreciate the way you asked instead of telling me I would be calling you."

"I appreciate that you noticed. I'll be talking to Morris again in the morning. I'll also be diving into the law firm that did your dad's will, and I'm sorry to have to say this, but your mom and the new husband are also on my radar."

Ivy flinched but didn't comment.

"It would also help if you could give us permission to see your dad's will."

"Anything you need."

"And then, finally, we'll be checking the video footage you have from your fundraiser."

"What?"

"The reason I showed up at your door Friday night was counterfeit money. I still need to figure out what's going on there."

"Right."

"Now, the next thing we need to discuss is your schedule for the week. When is your pitch? Where is it? What are your evenings like?"

She gaped at him for a few seconds before she responded. "In reverse order, I don't have plans for my evenings. I usually work. The pitch is at a hotel conference center in one of the ballrooms. I can get the address tomorrow. Or tonight, if you need it. Our pitch is scheduled for Wednesday."

"You probably won't like this either."

Ivy's body went straight and still.

"I know you're used to doing your own thing, but you need to have people around you anytime you're not in your office."

"Okay." Instant agreement.

"All the time."

"Okay." No drama.

"By people, I mean mostly me."

"Okay."

Time to push his luck. "Every night this week."

"Okay." Soft. Sweet.

"Okay."

Gil's phone buzzed. He pulled it from his back pocket and tapped the screen.

I'm in your driveway. I can drive around for a bit
if I'm interrupting anything.

You're fine. Come on in.

Gil waved the phone toward Ivy. "Faith's here."

"She's going to sit up all night? Awake?"

"Yes."

"I'm surprised you agreed."

"Did you not hear what I said earlier? I was set up by Emily. Then ambushed by the rest of them. Honestly, we're getting off easy."

Ivy seemed willing to accept everything he'd told her. Then she cocked her head, her brow furrowed. "What's the other reason?"

"What?"

"You said there were two reasons."

"For what?"

"Faith is coming so you can sleep. I get that. What's the other reason?"

Gil slid his phone into his pocket before he answered. "I just thought, with Emily gone, it would be better if someone else was here."

Ivy's laughter held an edge to it. "We're adults, Gil. I've known you my entire life. I don't think we need a chaperone."

Gil leaned closer. "We're adults. We've known each other our entire lives. And if you don't think we need a chaperone, then you haven't been paying attention."

— 17 —

HE CHECKED HIS WATCH as the police cruiser slid past him.

4:00 a.m.

He'd been in this car—a car he did not own but which was conveniently sitting in a neighbor's driveway while that neighbor was on vacation—for eight hours.

Everything was quiet, and he'd started planning what it would take to get inside. But then one of the two girl agents who'd been at the church, and the restaurant, walked in.

And didn't walk out.

The police cars started an hour later. This most recent was the seventh time tonight. All random. All different. No pattern for him to work with.

And there were the other cars. Three of them. All sedans. All with government plates. One made a pass around midnight and then came back by around three. One showed around two. One came by thirty minutes ago.

He hit the steering wheel and cursed.

Years of making nice. Years of smiling and pretending everything was fine. Years of waiting.

And time was running out.

He ran through his options. Her office was a no-go. He'd ruled it out a year ago and then again two weeks ago. Too many people. Too well secured.

He had no plans to become a murderer.

But they couldn't keep watch on her 24/7. Could they?

No. They could try, but they couldn't keep her locked down indefinitely.

She had her pitch coming up on Wednesday. There was no way she would miss that. Ivy was smart, but she was also a crusader. The kind of crusader who would refuse to miss an opportunity like that pitch.

He knew how much it meant to her.

And he knew that was his best shot.

If he failed?

He slipped from the car and loped into the dark night. If he failed on Wednesday, things were going to get messy.

—18—

GIL'S PHONE VIBRATING under his shoulder dragged him from the depths of sleep. His first conscious thought was of Ivy, and he bolted to a sitting position and searched for the phone. His sleep-fogged mind registered the time and the caller, and his body relaxed.

4:30 a.m.

Faith.

He climbed from the bed and answered. "You heading out?"

"Yes."

"Anything I need to know?"

"Other than that everyone made at least one drive-by during the night?"

"Seriously?" He grabbed a T-shirt, pulled it over his head, and eased from his room.

"They care."

"They're over-the-top."

"So are you." She wasn't wrong. "I've already made coffee so you can start the caffeine infusion immediately."

Gil hit End on the call, entered the kitchen, and made a show of eyeing the coffee pot with skepticism. "You know how to make coffee?"

151

Faith slid her own phone into her pocket. "I learned."

"Is it any good?" Now he was poking the bear, and he knew it. Faith Malone didn't do anything unless she did it well.

"I haven't had any complaints."

Gil kept pestering. "Luke wouldn't complain."

"Zane would."

She had him there. Zane had moved in with Luke this spring and was a frequent, but not unwelcome, third wheel in Faith and Luke's relationship. He would have had ample opportunity to comment on Faith's coffee. And he wouldn't hesitate.

Gil grabbed a mug from the counter. "When this is over, we need to talk about Zane."

Faith's brow wrinkled, and she traced a pattern on the kitchen counter. "Luke says he's bottled up tight."

"Tessa?"

"She's bottled up tight too. I've tried." Faith's eyes softened in a way that was unusual for her, and he knew she was going to say something about Luke, because that was the only time she got that dreamy look on her face. "I never imagined I could be as happy as I am right now, Gil. And they could make each other happy if they would get over whatever their hang-up is."

"He's leaving soon, Faith."

"I know."

He poured a cup of coffee. "That may be the hang-up, and if it is, there's no getting around it."

"I don't think that's it. It's big, but I don't think it's about the job."

He took a sip. "When things settle, we'll figure it out. And this coffee is great. Thank you." That earned him a shoulder nudge as she walked past him.

"I'm outta here."

152

"Faith?" She paused at the door. "I owe you."

"Not keeping score, Gil."

He followed her to the door, watched as she checked under her car, then climbed in. He held his breath for a few seconds until the car engine turned over. He continued his vigil until she was out of sight. Then he reset the security alarm and went about making the morning as calm and easy as he could for Ivy.

GIL PULLED INTO his office's parking lot at 8:30.

There was more to do than he had hours to do it. But his first order of business this morning was to learn everything he could about Ivy's ex.

Abott Percy.

Initial searches revealed exactly what Ivy had communicated, but with added nuance. Abott Percy was six years older than Ivy. Hardly a deal breaker in the relationship department. And not all that interesting, considering she began her academic career early and set a blistering pace on her path to earning multiple degrees.

But what was interesting, and not in a good way, was that Abott Percy had a military background. The guy was a Marine. An officer. Did four years after college. Then left to get his master's and eventually his PhD in bioengineering.

He did a tour in Afghanistan. Saw some combat.

Gil stared at the photo of Dr. Abott Percy from his University of Georgia website and compared it to the military records. Same guy. Same intensity in his eyes.

Somehow, listening to Ivy talk about Abott, calling him sweet and kind, Gil had created a visual that did not match the real man. He didn't want to admit it, but hearing about Abott Percy hadn't tweaked him nearly as much as *seeing* Abott Percy did.

Gil didn't claim to understand women, but he'd always prided himself on having a better handle on the feminine psyche than most of his brethren. He grew up with a girl. Emily was a constant in his life. The girl he protected, fought with, played with, and, bottom line, loved with every cell of his DNA. She felt the same way about him, and they could, and did, talk about anything and everything.

And one thing he knew from those heart-to-hearts was that a lot of women, and Emily would include herself in that demographic, were suckers for a guy in a uniform. Put a smart guy, a guy Gil could objectively acknowledge was good looking and physically impressive, in a uniform? Abott Percy probably had his pick of dating partners.

And he'd picked Ivy.

But she'd eventually turned him loose because she didn't love him enough.

That was a tough one. The kind of thing that could mess with your mind.

Was it enough for Abott to snap? Was it enough for him to come after her money? To attempt something that would crush her? Could he want to ruin everything so he could be the one to swoop in and save the day?

It was twisted, but Gil had seen a lot of twisted things in his career. He'd been on the receiving end of twisted, and so had Ivy. If there was any way he could stop it, Ivy would never be touched by it again.

Gil paused around 11:00 when Tessa came in, set a coffee on his desk, and said, "Ivy's good. Working. Cool office."

He hadn't known she was going over there. Typical Tessa. "Thanks, Tessa."

She squeezed his shoulder. "I'm busy until two thirty. After that, I can devote some time to anything you need for Ivy."

"I'll let you know."

He focused until 11:30, when he lost his hold on his stress levels. He needed to see her. For himself. It was irrational. He should leave her alone. She was fine.

Didn't matter.

Can I bring lunch?

A pause.

Sure.

No emojis or exuberant punctuation. She could be thrilled. She could be annoyed that he wouldn't leave her alone. Either way, he was going.

"I'm taking Ivy some lunch." He spoke to no one in particular and received two deep grunts and one soft "good idea" before he left.

Forty-five minutes later, the receptionist buzzed him through, and he made his way to Ivy's office. Her smile told him his presence wasn't unwelcome. She directed him to a small table, and two minutes later, the food was blessed, and they dove in.

"You didn't have to do this." She took a bite of her sandwich and immediately reached for a napkin to dab at her lips.

"Sure I did. I made you promise not to leave the building, then left you here with no food."

She cut her eyes to him. "Did you do that on purpose?"

Was she flirting with him?

"Maybe."

"I could have ordered takeout."

"True. But then I wouldn't have been able to check on you myself."

"Tessa came by."

"She told me."

"Did you ask her to?"

"No."

"Really?"

Gil swallowed before he responded. "You shouldn't be surprised to see Luke, Faith, Zane, or Tessa. At any time."

"But . . . why?"

"Why?"

"They don't know me."

"They like what they know."

She didn't respond for several bites and a sip of the half-cut sweet tea he'd ordered for her. "They're doing it for you." She didn't say it in a whiny way or like she was fishing for a compliment or angling to get him to disagree.

"They're doing it for us." He modified her assumption. And when he said *us*, he didn't mind one bit the way her eyes widened and flicked to him before returning with overdone concentration to her sandwich. "They like you for you. They like you whether I'm around or not, as evidenced by girls' night in and your plans for going to the movies and having lunch with Faith and Tessa during the week. That's all about you, Buttercup."

He set his sandwich back into the takeout box. "With that said, we're tight. We take care of each other. And that means they want to help me take care of you, because they know it would gut me if anything happened to you. They know I'll do whatever I have to do to protect you, and they want to be sure we both come out of this without any holes."

"It would gut you?" Her voice broke, and he couldn't look away from the questions in her eyes.

Before he could answer, an intercom buzzed. "Dr. Collins, Dr. Percy is here to see you."

IVY CLOSED HER EYES. When she opened them, Gil hadn't moved. But his expression, which had been open, slightly teasing, and achingly gentle, was now closed, hard, and possibly furious.

"Were you expecting him?"

"No." Why was she whispering? "But he was here last week. Twice. And he's in town. It makes sense that he would stop by."

Gil frowned. "I don't like this."

"What do you think he's going to do? Throw me over his shoulder and haul me out of here with you sitting three feet away?"

"I'm considering going with that move myself, so I wouldn't put it past him."

"Can you be nice?"

His eyebrows flew up at that. "What?"

"Be nice." What was confusing about that?

"You want me to stay here while you see him?"

"Of course. He's heard about you. He'll be thrilled we've reconnected."

"I wouldn't hold my breath, Buttercup." He stood and leaned over the small table between them, pinning her in place with his look. "If anything weird happens, you promise you'll do whatever I tell you?"

She nodded.

"If I tell you to run? To get under your desk?"

"Gil, you're scaring me."

"I'm trying to."

He wasn't kidding. "Gil, Ab is not dangerous."

"Ab is a Marine with a PhD in bioengineering. He is the very definition of dangerous."

"How do you know that?"

"I looked into him."

"You look—"

"Dr. Collins?" Tina's voice interrupted. "Should I send him back?"

Ivy held Gil's gaze. He gave the barest hint of a nod, then resumed his seat.

"Yes, Tina. That's fine." She stood and waited. While she waited, she tried to figure out what had happened. She wasn't used to being bossed around by anyone. She did the bossing. And Gil had no right—

A movement out of the corner of her eye arrested that thought. Gil had shifted so his weapon and badge were in full view. He'd also grabbed his phone and was texting someone. She'd guess Luke, Zane, and Tessa. Maybe Faith too.

His gaze caught hers and held, then softened. "It's covered."

Gah. He was so protective. It was almost smothering. Almost. But then a spike of pain shot through her right arm, and she remembered that it was Gil who had appeared in the middle of her nightmare. Gil who had protected her since. Gil who had never given her any reason not to trust him. His protectiveness might be over the top, but she didn't feel smothered.

She felt safe.

He was being unreasonable about Ab, but he didn't know him. After he met him, it would be fine.

Gil hadn't moved from his seat, but she could sense the tension coming from him. "It would probably be best for you to choose your words carefully when you explain what happened. Do you follow me?"

"You want me to lie?" She could hear her disgust at the thought.

"No. But you don't have to go into detail. Please."

"Okay."

He closed his eyes, the relief palpable, and leaned forward. He almost looked like he was relaxed.

"Ivy?"

She looked from Gil to the door. Ab stood there, eyes raking over her, heavy on her right arm and hand, lingering at the bruising on her cheek she hadn't been able to completely hide with makeup, and landing on the split at the corner of her lip.

"What on earth happened?" Ab was in her space before she could respond. One hand on her right elbow. One at her hairline. "What's going on, baby?"

She'd always liked the way he called her "baby." It was sweet. Tender. Especially coming from a mountain of a man like Ab. But with Gil sitting ten feet away, she wished he would drop the "baby" and also let her go. She stepped back, and his hands dropped from her and landed on his waist. "Ab—"

"I want to know what happened to you."

"If you'll stop being bossy, I'll tell you." She took another step back. "But first, I'd like to introduce you to someone."

She turned and indicated Gil. When she did, he stood, approached, and extended his hand. "Gil Dixon."

Ab took Gil's hand and what commenced was a handshake showdown that, until that moment, Ivy thought happened only in books. She'd never imagined two people she cared about could take such an instantaneous dislike to each other.

"Why don't we sit?" Ivy motioned to the table.

Both of them frowned but moved toward the chairs. If they hadn't, she might have been forced to call Luke or Zane to come rescue her, and Gil probably wouldn't like that. No, she'd call Tessa. One look at her and Ab would fall at Tessa's feet in immediate adoration, and the crisis would be averted.

Both men remained standing until she sat. Then Gil returned to the seat he'd had earlier and resumed eating his sandwich. Ab took the seat she indicated and sat, but barely. He looked ready to spring from his seat at the first sign of trouble. Between Ab and Gil, Ab was the one who looked like he thought she was in immediate danger. If she hadn't had to talk Gil off the ledge five minutes earlier, she wouldn't have had a clue how tight he was strung.

"Ivy?" Ab's question rumbled out of him—deep, serious, and insistent. "You were fine on Thursday. Today you're banged up and bruised."

"I'm fine."

Both Gil and Ab bristled at her words, and she looked at them in turn. "I am fine." She enunciated each word. "The situation is . . . complicated."

"I'm not blind, Ivy. I can see the splints."

"I have two broken fingers."

"How did you break them?"

"I had the misfortune of running into someone who wanted information I was unwilling to provide and—"

"Someone did this to you?" Ab exploded, then glared at Gil. "Was it him?"

"Of course not," Ivy snapped. "Ab, this is Gil. *My* Gil. He would never hurt me. He's taking care of me." Ivy stopped talking as the two men reacted in completely different ways to her statement.

Ab looked like someone had sucker punched him.

Gil looked like he'd won the lottery.

She retraced her words. *My* Gil. She'd said that out loud. She couldn't take it back, and she wouldn't if she could. Although maybe she wouldn't have been quite so blunt in front of Ab. She knew he still cared about her, and she tried to be sensitive to that. But after days of fear and fatigue, her filter had failed her.

Ab recovered and grumbled, "Did you catch the guy who broke your fingers?"

Ivy wasn't sure if Ab was asking her or Gil. Gil nodded at her in what she assumed was his way of saying she should answer Ab's question however she saw fit.

She went with the simplest and most honest answer. "Yes."

Ab made a show of checking out Gil's badge and gun. "You the one who caught him?"

"After Ivy shot him, it didn't require much effort." Gil delivered the line as if Ivy went around shooting people every day.

Ab didn't try to hide his shock and returned his full attention to Ivy. "You shot him?"

"Yes." There was no way she was going to volunteer the information that her attacker had been approaching Gil and she didn't know if Gil knew he was there or not, so she had to shoot him to save Gil.

"You shot him," Ab repeated, no question in his voice. "Well, then I assume he's in jail?"

"No."

"Did he escape?" Again, Ab looked at Gil as if this was all his fault.

Ivy glanced at Gil's badge. Not being an expert on all things law enforcement, if she hadn't already known he was with the Secret Service, she probably would see the badge and assume he was a detective. Maybe Ab assumed the same?

"I don't make a habit out of putting dead people in jail, Ab." Gil's accent—which was typically subtle, hinting at his Southern roots but not screaming them—had thickened and the words came out in full drawl.

What was Gil doing? Why was he doing it?

Ab glared at him. "Dead?"

"Heart attack in the hospital."

"So what happens now?"

"Raleigh PD is working the case."

"You aren't Raleigh PD." Ab stated this as fact. Maybe he did know the difference in badges.

"I am not," Gil confirmed without detail.

"What's the Secret Service got to do with Ivy?" Ab recognized the badge.

"The Secret Service is investigating an unrelated matter involving Hedera, Inc."

"And that investigation requires around-the-clock protection?"

"No."

"Then what are you doing here?"

Gil nudged the takeout box still holding half of his BLT. "Lunch."

At any moment, Ivy's head was going to explode. She knew without having to ask that there was a zero percent chance Gil would go away and leave her alone with Ab. Her only hope was to talk Ab down and get him to leave. All without bloodshed. "Ab. Bottom line, I'm fine. I'm covered. I'm at work, prepping for the pitch. I wasn't expecting to see you today. I assumed you'd be working on your pitch."

Ab frowned. "Had a couple of hours. One of my coworkers had an appointment. We're back at it around three. I thought I'd pop by and see if you're free for dinner?"

"Sorry. No way I can do it until after the pitch." And probably not after.

"Fine. I'll call you Thursday. Set something up." With that pronouncement, he stood. "Gil." He acknowledged Gil with a grimace. Ivy scrambled to her feet, swayed slightly, and Gil was there behind her with a hand at her waist to steady her. And, undoubtedly, to prevent Ab from going in for the hug he usually left her with.

Ab ignored Gil and focused entirely on Ivy. "Thursday." He spun on his heel and left the room.

Gil squeezed her waist and pushed down with enough pressure for her to get the point that he wanted her to sit. She settled into her chair, waited for Gil to resume his, then leaned forward. "What was that?" Her question had a definite hiss to it, and she didn't care.

He ignored her frustration. "You handled that beautifully."

"What?"

"Told the truth. No lies. No details. Thank you."

"Are you kidding me?"

He winked. "Nope."

"If my head spins around and flies off into the other room, you should take it as fact that it's your fault."

He chuckled. "You should finish your sandwich before it gets soggy."

"You're back to being bossy."

"It was a suggestion. Not an order."

"How am I supposed to tell the difference?"

"Buttercup."

"'Buttercup' is not an answer."

He leaned forward then, setting his sandwich back on the take-out container, all humor gone. "There are a lot of things I'd like to be to you, Ivy. 'Boss' is not one of them. I have no desire to control you. The only time I will ever expect you to do what I say without hesitation is if your life is in danger. If that happens, you can rest assured I will order you around like you're a private in my own personal army. Otherwise, you can assume anything I say is a suggestion, which you are free to follow or ignore at your discretion."

There was a lot to unpack in that, but she didn't get a chance to say anything. Gil's phone rang. He glanced at the screen, then answered. "Dixon." A pause. "We're good." Another pause, then a chuckle, another pause. "Don't think I'll be hitting the batting cages with him anytime soon."

What?

"Thanks." His eyes flicked to the clock over her desk. "Leaving in ten. Yep. Later."

He slid the phone into his pocket and took another bite of his sandwich.

"Do I even want to know?"

"I don't know. Do you?"

"Would you tell me if I said yes?"

"Sure."

"Then yes."

Gil wiped his hand on a napkin, swallowed the last bite of his sandwich, took a sip of his drink, and focused on her. "That was Luke. He's following Percy. He saw him leave the building and observed that Dr. Percy was . . ." He searched for the right word. "Unhappy. Luke surmised that my presence was responsible for Dr. Percy's discontent. I confirmed this."

"Luke's following Ab?"

"Yes."

"Why?"

"He's a suspect. Especially after rolling in here acting like he didn't know you were injured, like he was surprised to see me, and not mentioning he was at church yesterday where he saw you were injured so he couldn't have been that surprised to see me today."

"What?"

"Security footage." His voice gentled. "A buddy of mine monitors the camera feeds during the services. I called this morning and asked him to take a look. He confirmed Dr. Percy was at church yesterday." Gil wasn't gloating, but he didn't hold back either. "It wasn't your imagination, and he doesn't have a doppelgänger. You did see him. I'm sorry he didn't speak to you, and I'm sorry he didn't mention it when he was here."

Ivy slumped back into her seat. This made no sense. No sense at all.

"I'm not sure what his game is, but you have to understand that until I know, he's high on my suspect list."

Ivy stared at the door where she'd last seen Ab. "He would never hurt me."

She didn't think it was possible for Gil's voice to get any softer, but she was wrong. "Buttercup, he just did."

— 19 —

IVY WASN'T PAYING ATTENTION until Gil swiveled their seats so that they faced each other, with his knees brushing hers. "I hope I'm wrong. His record, his accomplishments, his service to our country, the fact that you care about him all combines to make me hope he's as good of a guy as you believe him to be."

She nodded but didn't make eye contact. She was too close to crying. Again.

His fingers brushed across hers. "I have to get back to work. I'll pick you up tonight."

She nodded, still not looking at him.

When she refocused on the room, the only trace of Gil's presence or their lunch was her tea, which now sat on a coaster on her desk.

Her phone buzzed, and the text was from Ab.

Baby, don't be mad. I didn't handle that well. I know who he is to you, and I've hated the very idea of him for a long time. Can't say I'm happy he's sitting in your office in real life. I promise

to be on my best behavior next time. Good luck
with your pitch. We'll talk Thursday.

Ivy dropped the phone onto her desk. She'd give anything to
be able to call her dad. To hear his voice. To tell him what had
happened, and that she was scared and tired.

"I miss you, Dad." She whispered the words in the hope that
maybe, somehow, he could hear her. Then she dug deep, finding a
depth she didn't even know she possessed, and went back to work.

She shouldn't have been surprised when her receptionist buzzed
her office and said, "Luke Powell to see you."

She glanced at her watch. 3:00 p.m. Good grief. Had they set
up a rotation so she wouldn't be alone for more than two hours
at a time? "Send him in."

Luke strolled in. "You good?"

"Did you follow Ab?"

"I did."

"And?"

"He went to his hotel. Then to his room. As far as I know, he's
still there."

A horrible thought occurred to her. "Are you tracking him?"

"No." Luke was all innocence and sweetness, but she didn't buy
it for a second. "That would be illegal without a warrant. Which
we don't have." Now he sounded regretful.

"Do you think he's behind this?"

"I don't know."

"Gil thinks he is."

"Gil thinks he could be. He's a suspect, so we're keeping tabs
on him."

"He doesn't know Ab."

"You're right, but it doesn't matter. Gil would do the same thing even if he did know him. We have to follow the evidence, even if we don't like where it's leading. Why do you think Gil showed up at your door Friday afternoon? Do you think he suspected you of wrongdoing? Because he didn't. And it had very little to do with your personal connection. It was because you have a reputation in this town. He didn't believe you knew anything about that money. He still followed the leads, regardless of his personal opinion. That's what he's doing now."

"I guess that makes sense."

He waved a hand around her office. "Now, do you have time to show me around? Not the detailed tour, just broad strokes. Gil wouldn't shut up about it earlier today. Said it's some of the coolest stuff he's ever seen."

She gave Luke the tour, and by the time he left, she'd decided Luke Powell was the kind of friend anyone would be lucky to have—and she was glad Gil had him. And she was glad Faith was marrying him. And maybe someday soon, she would be able to say he was her friend too.

GIL WAS BACK AT FIVE. He didn't bother her. Or he tried not to anyway. He sat in the lobby with a laptop. She didn't know he was there until her receptionist tipped her off to the presence of "that hot Secret Service agent who brought you lunch, not the hot one who came by later" on the sofa in the corner.

Ivy tried to finish quickly, but it was still after six before she wrapped up.

Gil drove her home, walked in with her, and held her hand as they wandered through the kitchen. "Who cleaned up?"

Gil dropped his head.

"Gil?"

"Please don't be mad." For the first time since she'd seen him on Friday night, she could see the little boy she remembered. His eyes were wide and earnest, and it was clear he did not want her to be upset and was worried she would be. "Tessa and I came over this afternoon. I didn't want you to come home to a mess. You've had a tough few days, and this is your home. I want you to feel safe here, and I know you probably won't, at least not right away. But I didn't want you to have to come in and clean up fingerprint powder and blood." His eyes swept through the living area. "I doubt everything is exactly the way you had it, but Tessa gave it her seal of approval. Which, in case you're wondering, means right now you could safely eat off the bathroom floor."

That remark caught her so off guard that a giggle escaped, and the tension eased. "I'll pass, but good to know."

After the heavy conversations of the day, Ivy braced for more emotional overload. But Gil kept things light. Friendly. He was a little bit bossy, but only in good ways. He refused to let her help with dinner and told her to go change into something comfy and let him take care of it. He also refused to let her clean up, making the argument that she had broken fingers and therefore had a solid case for not doing dishes.

He was cool about everything. Kind. Gentle. She couldn't miss the way he watched her, but he didn't hover. When they settled on the sofa, she was prepared for him to launch into a heart-to-heart. He didn't. They chatted about music and books and, at his request, looked through some photo albums.

It was all going well, and part of her, a big part, wanted him to reopen the discussion about their relationship. Of course, it was fast. Too soon. Too quick. But if Gil Dixon asked her out on a date, she was going to say yes.

But he didn't do . . . anything. When they looked at the photo albums, he sat close, his knee and thigh brushing against hers, but aside from that, nothing. He didn't hold her hand. He didn't put his arm around her. He made no moves at all.

Around 8:30, Gil sat back on the sofa, pulled the album from her hand and closed it, then tucked a strand of hair behind her ear. "Buttercup, you're about to fall asleep sitting up. Why don't you go ahead and go to bed?"

"It's early."

"You're running on fumes. Take your pain medicine. Go to bed. Don't worry about anything. I'll be here all night. Luke's coming later, and we're taking shifts. You can rest easy."

She wanted to argue. If she had any manners at all, she would have. She couldn't let him and Luke stay up half the night while she slept.

Then his hand curled around her cheek, and he whispered, "Please?"

When she nodded, he stood, helped her to her feet, and squeezed her arm. "Good night."

She walked to her room, turned at the door, and found him watching her with an expression she couldn't decipher. "Good night, Gil."

There was a lot to think about. A lot to process. She'd had the best night she'd had in a long time, and it had lasted only two hours. Still, she could get used to nights like tonight, and not because Gil cooked and cleaned. But because he was easy to talk to, she liked being around him, and he made her feel very safe.

Even with the added headache of going through her nighttime routine without the full use of her right hand and arm, she was in bed and had the lights out before 9:00 p.m. When was the last time she'd gone to bed before 9:00? She had no idea. High school?

She heard Gil getting ice from the freezer, and there was something comforting about knowing she wasn't alone. She closed her eyes, and even with the half dose of pain medicine she'd taken, she was fully expecting to toss and turn for a while before sleep claimed her.

She was surprised when the next sound she heard was the grinding of coffee beans.

—20—

IVY WAS SERIOUSLY CUTE first thing in the morning. She'd shuffled out of her room and into the kitchen, looking around the space as if she'd never seen it before. Unlike the previous three mornings, her hair and makeup weren't done, and Gil suspected she'd rolled out of bed and come straight to the kitchen like she would have done had she been home alone. Probably to get a cup of coffee before she did anything else.

"Good morning." He kept his voice soft. "Coffee?"

"Please." The word was followed by a yawn.

He poured coffee into a huge mug and left a ridiculous amount of room for cream. He grabbed the hazelnut creamer from the fridge, a spoon from the drawer, and set both by the coffee as she slid onto the barstool. He watched as she poured a healthy glug of creamer into the coffee, stirred it, then took a small sip. "Thanks."

"You're welcome." She was still a bit fuzzy and confused, two words he could already tell were rarely applicable to her. He had no way to know if this was how she was every morning or if it was a direct result of waking up after taking pain medicine the night before. Either way, it was endearing.

"I hope you still like blueberry pancakes."

Her answering smile held on to her morning muzziness, but there was also surprise mingled with what he suspected, and hoped, was delight. It sent something warm and comfortable straight through him. This was the fourth morning in a row he'd made her breakfast, and he was in no hurry to hand in his spatula. When she was safe, if she would let him, he'd come over every morning for the privilege of fixing her breakfast—and the fun of seeing her first thing before all her synapses started firing at their normal genius-level pace.

"Blueberries?" Her brow was wrinkled, her eyes blinking a bit faster than normal. The mental cobwebs were making a hasty retreat. She must have known she didn't have blueberries in her fridge, so how was he making blueberry pancakes?

"Luke brought them last night."

She turned on the stool, looking toward her sofa.

"He left about thirty minutes ago."

"Oh." She didn't say more, and he didn't push her.

He'd had a long talk with Luke yesterday. Then another with Emily as he drove to Ivy's office. He'd lost his mind when it came to Ivy. It was ridiculous. He couldn't, shouldn't, expect her to fall in love with him in three days. He shouldn't even expect her to have considered the possibility that he might want to be more than a friend. Not yet. It was too soon. He was going too fast. So he'd slammed on the brakes and done everything in his power to pull back from the edge.

Not that he hadn't thrown himself over it already. He was gone. He knew it. He was good with it. Well, maybe not good. Truth be told, if he thought about it too much, it scared him. He wasn't a masochist, and like he'd told Emily before, he wasn't sure how he'd survive losing Ivy a second time. But what was done was done. And while no one would believe it, he was pretty sure he'd handed his heart to Ivy in elementary school, definitely in high school. And even after she walked away, he never made any serious effort to give it to someone else. It was hers. Always would be.

It was nuts, but that's how he felt. He was lucid enough—especially after Luke told him he was scaring her and Emily told him no girl who'd been through what Ivy had been through on Friday needed a man messing with her head or her heart—to know that if he wanted to have a future with Ivy, he needed to back off.

So that's what he was doing—he was backing off. Not out of sight. Not even out of reach. But hopefully far enough that she wouldn't panic and bolt at the first opportunity.

He made pancakes, she sipped coffee, and Gil waited, letting her set the direction of the conversation. She didn't offer a word until he slid a plate with two blueberry pancakes in front of her, then pushed the syrup in her direction. "Thanks."

"You're welcome." He turned back to the griddle and flipped two more pancakes onto a plate for himself, then joined her at the bar. "Mind if I bless the food?"

"Please."

He offered a brief prayer and watched as she lifted her fork and took a bite. Her eyes closed, and she turned to him. "Amazing."

Did she realize she was speaking in one-word sentences only?

She took three more bites before she turned to him and asked, "What should I expect today?"

"What do you mean?"

"I mean I'm not accustomed to having friends popping by at seemingly, but not"—she gave him a pointed look—"random intervals. I'm not used to having anyone bring me a lunch I didn't order for myself. I'm also not in the habit of being chauffeured around as if I've lost the ability to drive. And when I get home, I'm definitely not used to having someone cook my dinner, clean it up, then send me to sleep deeply while being guarded by men who—and this is something not lost on me—protect the president of the United States. So, if it's all the same to you, I'd like to know what to expect today."

Wow. She went from one-word responses to fully formed arguments in the space of half a cup of coffee and four bites of pancakes. In the future, if he wanted to stand a chance, he'd need to slip in his most ridiculous requests first thing. As it was, he answered truthfully. "I would imagine today will be similar to yesterday."

She studied him for a beat. Then turned back to her pancakes and said, "Okay."

IT WAS CLEAR TO GIL that Ivy had a lot on her mind, and he walked her into her office wishing he had the right to insist that she share. Instead, he squeezed her elbow, promised to bring lunch at 1:00 p.m., and went to work. Tessa rolled in right after he did, armed with a massive coffee for him, which he accepted gratefully. Then Leslie, their office manager, sent a message that chocolate cake was in the conference room and would they please not eat all of it before Jacob, the special agent in charge, had a chance to get a piece.

Jacob rarely arrived as early as the rest of them during the school year because he took carpool duty three or four days a week. This was something he pretended not to like but in fact loved because it gave him quality time with his kids, and he adored his kids. It was also a tangible way he could help his wife, and he was a happily married man who enjoyed doing things to make his wife's life easier.

Zane and Luke arrived ten minutes later, and at 9:00 they convened in Jacob's office for a morning meeting.

175

"Two things to cover this morning." Jacob's mouth quirked in a weird way and Gil braced for what was coming. "First, I got a phone call late yesterday from an agent in Tennessee. Gil, I've given him your info. Looks like that counterfeit currency is spreading around."

Gil nodded. This was neither good nor bad news. It was simply news.

"Second." Jacob hesitated, then looked straight at Zane. "We have received a request. An agent is rotating off the president's protective detail, and he's asked to be assigned to our office."

Gil looked around the room. They all knew what this meant. They were down three agents at the moment. There was no way Zane was going to move to the protective detail until they got at least one agent, maybe two. A new agent was good news for Zane.

It also stunk. They all liked Zane, and while he was overdue for his shot at a protective detail, it was still going to be a wrench to have to say goodbye. Gil could tell Luke was thinking similar thoughts to his. Happy for his friend. Bummed for himself.

Tessa's expression had gone completely blank. He didn't think it was possible for Tessa to show no emotion. She was usually expressive, especially with her eyes. But at this moment? Nothing.

And that nothing spoke volumes.

Jacob kept talking. "In the request, he mentions he's worked with us on a case, in a tangential fashion. His name is Benjamin North."

At the name, Gil relaxed. So did Luke. Tessa was still blank. But Zane muttered, "I knew it."

"I'm not surprised Benjamin wants a North Carolina office for his Phase 3," Luke said. "He's got it bad for Carrington's medical examiner."

"No kidding?" Jacob took a sip of his coffee.

"Already put a ring on her finger. If he doesn't move in this direction, she'll move wherever he goes. I thought he might go for Greensboro or Charlotte, especially with all our drama."

Luke wasn't wrong about that. Lately, no one wanted to work in the Raleigh office. After what happened earlier in the year, he couldn't blame them much. But it kind of hurt to have a tarnished reputation that had nothing to do with their ability to solve cases and everything to do with the unfortunate fact that Raleigh agents had a bad habit of winding up dead, shot, or blown up.

"The Carrington guys like him a lot. We should get him down here for an interview. See if he's a good fit. I'm thinking he will be." Luke turned his attention to Zane. "Gonna miss you. Don't want to see you leave, not at all. But wouldn't want to hold you back. Not even for a second. We get Benjamin here, you're closer to DC."

Zane nodded. "I know."

"Well," Jacob said as he stood, "I'll work on getting North in for a visit. I'll let you know when he's coming. In the meantime, I'm going to get cake. And then, Gil, I want an update on Hedera and Ivy Collins."

"Yes, sir."

Gil didn't bother leaving Jacob's office but instead settled in to wait for him to return. When Gil's phone buzzed with a text from Faith telling him she was on her way to see Ivy, he relaxed into his seat, closed his eyes, and took the few minutes he had to redirect his thoughts.

Lord, please protect her. Help me make the connections I need to make to figure this out. To keep her safe. And, Lord, if she's not the one for me, I may need a heart transplant, because I already can't stand to be away from her for more than a few hours at a time.

He let his thoughts wander, something he frequently found to be a useful technique. A lot could be said for concentrated effort. He hadn't been a serious athlete in over a decade, but he knew how to focus his mind and body on one goal. He didn't direct such energy at perfecting his fastball anymore, but that didn't mean he didn't call on that single-mindedness when he needed it.

But sometimes, giving his thoughts room to flow without forcing them into any preconceived path helped him see connections he might have missed otherwise. It was no surprise to him that given free rein, his mind turned to Ivy. He allowed himself a few moments to consider how beautiful she was, how soft her skin was, how perfect she felt in his arms, but when he did that, he remembered why she'd been in his arms in the first place. Then his brain tugged at snippets of conversations and random pieces of info he'd gleaned while researching Hedera and looking into Ivy's friends and family.

Given what he knew her mom was capable of, he'd already initiated a search into records that went back to before Ivy was born. He'd also requested information on the new husband, Preston. Ivy didn't like him. Why? Was it because she was never going to like anyone except the man she called her dad? Or because knowing what she knew about her mom, she suspected anyone who was attracted to her must not be all right?

And that's when Gil had a thought he didn't want to have, because Ivy adored Wade Collins. Loved him. Had not one bad thing to say about him. But what if . . .

Gil dropped his head in his hands and sat that way until he heard Jacob come in and settle into his chair.

"You okay?"

Gil lifted his face. "Have you ever had to investigate a dead guy?"

—21—

ON WEDNESDAY MORNING, Ivy woke praying the same prayer she'd been praying when she fell asleep.

Lord, I don't know what to do, so my eyes are on you.

She was capable of eloquence. She appreciated beautiful liturgies and ancient creeds. But God didn't need flowery speech to hear her prayers. And she didn't have it in her to do more than breathe in and out the same words over and over. *My eyes are on you. My eyes are on you. My eyes are on you.*

Her week had been . . . surreal. She'd been dropped right into a Salvador Dali painting, where everything she knew was still there but distorted in new and mostly disturbing ways.

Tuesday was a repeat of Monday, except Faith had shown up with coffee at ten instead of Tessa, and Zane had shown up mid-afternoon instead of Luke.

Zane was quiet. Reflective. He didn't get into her business the way Luke had. But he also dropped a few bombs into her world, including the fact that Gil was investigating everyone she'd ever known but was focused on her mom, Preston, and Ab.

When she later questioned Gil about it, and she did this as he cranked the engine of his car after he picked her up from work,

Gil didn't deny it. But he didn't tell her anything more than what Zane had told her.

Then he asked her a question about her favorite ice cream flavors, which led to a discussion about the merits, or lack thereof, of vanilla ice cream, with her arguing in defense of vanilla and Gil pointing out the superior qualities of every other flavor. She was laughing when they pulled into her driveway, and for a little while, she forgot about the chaos swirling around her.

It was like he was on a mission to keep her distracted so she wouldn't ask too many questions, and while she let him distract her, and even enjoyed the break from reality, she wasn't fooled.

No matter how hard Gil worked to keep her mind occupied, his continued presence, the way agents kept showing up at her office and police cars continued to drive through her parking lot, shouted at her that she was in danger. To make the situation worse, she had no idea how to get out of being in danger. And the scariest part was that nobody else knew either.

When they got to her house, Gil let her help in the kitchen—if pulling out plates and silverware and then unloading three mugs from the dishwasher counted as helping. He not only served her crab cakes and a homemade remoulade sauce that rivaled the best she'd had anywhere, including Maryland, he also proceeded to prep something in her Crock-Pot for the next day. And instead of calling it good, he pulled out a roll of cookie dough, homemade by him and apparently mixed up the night before after she went to bed, and made the most amazing chocolate chip cookies that had ever been dipped in milk.

While he did this, she sat at the bar and they reminisced, the conversation focused on her college days. As much as she enjoyed spending time with him and the way he kept her mind from cartwheeling down a twisted and terrifying path, when he started dropping hints about her needing sleep, she wasn't hard to convince. Had she ever been this drained? Mentally, physically, emotionally, spiritually—she had nothing left to draw from.

In the quiet and aloneness of her room, the fear she'd been able to beat back when she was in Gil's presence climbed on her back and threatened to strangle her. She could have gone to Gil. Told him she was scared. He would have held her. But he had enough on his mind. Her personal terror would only add to the burden he already shouldered. She crawled into bed and fell asleep, praying with every exhale.

Now it was morning. She'd survived another night. And her house smelled amazing. Coffee and something nutty and buttery. The low murmur of deep voices told her either Zane or Luke had joined Gil last night and had stayed for breakfast.

Gil had to stop doing all the cooking. She'd told him that on Monday and again last night. He'd ignored her. But she was having a hard time complaining. Gil was amazing in the kitchen, and while her left hand was fully functional, the broken fingers on her right hand and her still-aching right shoulder made everything she did take longer. Not having to fix her own breakfast was something she could get used to.

Yesterday morning she'd been out of it thanks to that stupid pain pill, and she'd walked right to the kitchen in her pajamas. Last night she'd skipped the pain pill in favor of over-the-counter medicine, and this morning she had the good sense to stay in her room until she tamed her hair. She hurried through her morning routine and thirty minutes later walked to her kitchen. Gil was the only one in view. "Good morning."

"Morning, Buttercup. How did you sleep?" Gil handed her a cup of coffee.

It had so much cream, it was almost white. She took a sip. Perfection. "Did it cause you physical pain to make this for me?"

"I powered through." He winked. "Yours isn't as bad as Emily's." He nodded to the counter. "Hungry?"

"Starving." At her remark, he set a plate with two muffins, a healthy portion of scrambled eggs, and a bowl of sliced strawberries in front of her. "And spoiled."

He brushed her hand with his and said, "Not possible." He took a sip of his own coffee and then waited for her to take a bite. "Luke and Zane are en route to the hotel."

She almost choked. "What?"

"Tessa is going to be your shadow today."

"What?"

"I'll be around, but not as obvious as Tessa. Tessa looks less threatening, so we decided she was the best option for the overt presence."

"Excuse me?"

"Of course"—Gil got a wicked glint in his eyes—"looks can be deceiving, and that makes her one of the most dangerous agents we have."

"Gil! What are you talking about?"

"Protection for your pitch today," Gil said as calmly as if he'd commented on the weather and not on the fact that a Secret Service agent planned to hang out with her all day. Whether he was oblivious to her mental drama or simply choosing to ignore it, he continued. "You'll be out of the office, in public, lots of people. If I were trying to nab you, that's where I'd do it."

Ivy set her fork on the plate. "You would?" Did that squeaky sound come from her?

Gil leaned toward her, eyes holding hers. "He won't succeed." There was no mistaking the confidence in his remark.

Confidence Ivy didn't share. So many things could go wrong. The terror from last night slithered through her chest. This must be why Gil had been acting different this week. After two solid days of what she thought was intense flirting, he'd backed off. Sort of. He drove her to work. He brought her lunch. He picked her up. He slept in her guest room. He made her breakfast and supper.

But he was different. If anyone had questioned her on Monday morning about their relationship status, she would have said she thought Gil would ask her out on a date at any time, or that he might kiss her first, then see if she would go out with him.

Now? He was still with her, still focused on keeping her safe. But less focused on, well, whatever he'd been focused on before.

She was confused, and scared. "Gil, we need to talk."

"About what?" Could he be that clueless? She'd heard the snap in her statement. There was no way Gil could have missed it.

"Maybe about how you've set me up with a protective detail but failed to inform me you were doing it? I'm not eight years old anymore, and even if I was, I would still expect you to involve me in the conversation. What if I don't want a protective detail? Did you ever think of that?"

"We've been protecting you for several days without any complaint. How is this different?"

"You've been at my house. At night. And you've shown up to my office a few times. This isn't the same thing. You're talking about shadowing me all day, in public."

She did want protection, but he should have asked and not assumed. She pulled in a slow breath and forced herself to speak slowly, and what was probably a full octave lower. "I'm not stupid, Gil. I know I'm up to my neck in something that has 'nightmare' written all over it. I've already been tortured for my computer password, and I'm not interested in meeting the mastermind behind that experience."

She couldn't stop the shudder that started at her neck and trembled all the way over her back and down her legs. "I'm thankful, beyond thankful, that you were the one who came to my rescue. But saving my life didn't give you the right to make decisions *for* me. And knowing me for our whole lives doesn't mean you have tacit permission to orchestrate every hour of my day without clueing me in to the plan."

Gil's tanned skin had a definite rosy undertone now. She didn't know him well enough, not anymore, to know if he was embarrassed or angry, but if she had to guess, she'd say it was a bit of both.

"For today, I'll go with your plan, whatever it is, because, as previously noted, I'm not an idiot and I prefer to survive the day unscathed. Also because I do trust you, despite the fact that you're infuriating, and I do appreciate the effort you've gone to in the past few days to keep me safe and happy. But after today, we sit down and discuss the rest of the week. This will involve you asking me what *I* think and what *I* want before you set any grand plans into motion that affect *me*. Are we clear?"

Gil stared at her a long moment. He swallowed hard, nodded twice. Then he leaned toward her. "We're clear. You're right. I'm sorry. You have no idea how sorry. We'll talk tonight." Gil's soft, repentant words came with another brush of his fingers on her hand. "Now eat. Your eggs will get cold."

He left the kitchen, and when the snick of the bathroom door closing reached her, she picked up her fork and tried to slow her racing heart. She could have handled that better. Why had she yelled at Gil? Sure, he'd overstepped by a light-year, and she wasn't sorry for what she said. But it would have been better if they'd had a conversation instead of her delivering a rant and him standing there and taking it.

Rants felt good in the moment, but the second they were over, the guilt and recriminations flooded in. Gil didn't deserve her anger. His motives were honorable. And he undoubtedly thought he was making her life easier by planning everything on her behalf.

He was probably in the bathroom texting Emily about how Ivy was a loose cannon and asking if she remembered Ivy having such a bad temper.

She didn't, normally. But she'd had no practice with how to cope with being held captive, tortured, forced to shoot a man, rescued by her lifelong crush, reunited with said crush, nearly snatched out of a Mexican restaurant, and thrown into a world of uber protective special agents. Not to mention all the weirdness with Ab. Oh, and how could she forget that her own mother and attorney were now being investigated for their possible involvement in this situation or that someone had passed counterfeit bills and her company had deposited them?

Sheesh. She'd been overdue an explosion, but regret crept through every thought. She should apologize for yelling and for losing her temper. If Gil had done that to her, she would have been livid. He should be furious, but he seemed more upset with himself than with her.

She took a bite of her eggs and then stared at her hand where he'd brushed against it. Would he have done that if he was angry? Gah! It was too early to solve the mysteries of Gil Dixon. She took a bite of the muffin and tried to get her mind focused on something else. Given that the last thing she wanted to think about was her impending kidnapping that included potential dismemberment, she chose to focus on her pitch.

Hedera had an excellent chance of winning this grant. But Ab's team also had a solid proposal. They'd talked about it on Thursday at dinner. He'd shared. She hadn't. Despite what Gil thought, it wasn't that she didn't trust Ab, but when it came to business, she was all business. The only people who knew the details of her pitch were her researchers and her assistant. Once the pitch was over, she'd be happy to share with Ab what she'd proposed. But not before.

Those thoughts carried her through finishing breakfast, putting her dishes in the dishwasher, returning to her room, and completing her morning routine.

When she stepped into her living room, Gil was standing by the door. "Ready?" He delivered the question without any apparent malice, but she could almost feel the wall, a wall she built, that now stood between them.

They drove to her office in silence. As he had all week, Gil walked her into her office, did a walk-through of her building, then returned to tell her goodbye.

"Gil—"

He held up a hand. "We'll talk tonight." Ivy could almost see the wall between them grow another three feet. "Tessa will be here in a little while. It would be helpful if you could do whatever she asks. She's an excellent agent, and her only mission today is to make sure you're back here tonight in one piece."

"Gil, I—"

"You probably won't see me, but I'll be around. Good luck with the pitch."

Then he was gone. Ivy sat behind her desk and dropped her head against the high back of her seat. *Lord, I don't know what to do. I don't know what to do.* It took her several minutes before she managed to whisper, "But my eyes are on you."

— 22 —

SIX HOURS AFTER LEAVING Ivy at her office, Gil stood with his back to a column at the far end of a long hotel corridor. He could hear what was going on in the ballroom, but he couldn't see Ivy. There was comfort in knowing Tessa was in there, but he still wished he had eyes in that room.

He had seen her on her way in but had stayed out of her line of sight. She looked great. Calm. Confident. Focused. She looked like what she was. The CEO of Hedera, Inc., prepared to make a pitch for a grant and fully intent on getting it.

She did not look at all like she had this morning. Eyes wide and burning. Voice trembling with rage and a full octave higher than normal. A few times, two octaves higher. Face tight with her fury at him.

A fury he deserved.

He'd been treating her like she was fragile and it was his job to cocoon her in Bubble Wrap.

She might look delicate, but she was brilliant and capable. He should have known by the way she'd endured torture and then made a phenomenal shot that she wasn't the kind of woman who needed to be handled. She needed to be included and consulted.

What had he done? The exact opposite. He'd made decisions

on her behalf about issues that directly impacted her, and he'd done it without asking her.

The truth was, he didn't feel as bad about it as maybe he should. If she'd tried to refuse the protection, he would have arranged for it anyway. There was a zero percent chance that she was going to be in this hotel today without her friends having her back. But he still should have talked to her, asked her, and given her the opportunity to express her concerns and make suggestions about how to handle it smoothly with minimal disruption to her routine and plans. As she'd forcefully expressed this morning, she wasn't an idiot. She would have agreed to the protection.

He pressed into the column at his back. Why was this so hard? He didn't want to alienate her. He wanted to date her. But after this morning, he wasn't sure if she'd be receptive to being texting buddies, much less to spending time with him.

He refocused on the door to the ballroom. By the sounds of things, they were wrapping up.

"It was a pleasure to meet you as well." Tessa's soft alto came through the earwig. She'd walked into the ballroom at Ivy's side, introduced herself as Ivy's intern, and then chatted with them about prosthetics and some of the unique challenges faced by amputees in a way that left Gil stunned. Had she given herself a crash course in bioengineering over the past forty-eight hours?

After the introductions were made, Zane had muttered, "Killing it, Tess" in a low voice that indicated no surprise, only pride. And maybe something else. Yeah. When they sorted Ivy's mess, Gil was going to have to sort out the Zane and Tessa situation.

Although it might be too late for Zane and Tessa. If Benjamin North moved quickly—and all indications were that he was highly motivated to make Raleigh his home base for the next few years—Zane could be gone by Christmas.

At the end of the hall, Luke, in a navy suit and power tie, strode to an elevator, phone to his ear. To an observer, he would appear to be a businessman focused on a phone call, not a Secret Service agent focused on the hallway. The jacket hid the shoulder holster he wore, and Gil wouldn't be surprised if Luke had an ankle holster as well.

Faith was also in the building. Unlike Luke, Faith was dressed down. Way down. Sitting casually in the lobby in yoga pants and tennis shoes, with her hair in a messy bun and a phone in her hand, looking for all the world like she was waiting for someone to show and not like she was watching the feed from the camera Tessa had in her glasses. Glasses that weren't helping Tessa see but were making it much easier for Faith to follow the activities in the ballroom.

Gil still didn't like it. They'd only had a few days to plan, and they were doing it on their own. Not that they'd gone rogue. Their boss knew what they were up to. So did Faith's. But that didn't mean this protective detail was sanctioned by the Secret Service, the FBI, or the Raleigh PD.

As much as it had irked him to do it, Gil had made a phone call to Detective Morris, who, upon hearing what was going on, had a lot to say about Gil, Gil's friends, Gil's ability to do his job, Gil's manhood, and Gil's parentage. He ended his rant with, "I'll be around," and hung up.

Did "I'll be around" mean he would be in the hotel if they needed him or he'd be around if they all got arrested so he could watch them get booked? With Morris, it was impossible to know. His moods made no sense.

The massive clock on the far wall said it was 4:00 p.m. Ivy had been in there for two hours. He could hear Tessa when she spoke, but he didn't have clear audio for Ivy. Technically, he didn't need it, not with Tessa in the room. And as much as he'd been tempted to, he wasn't watching the video—Faith had that covered. Gil watched everything else. Doors, people, luggage, deliveries, room service carts—anything that moved. And for the most part, while there were numerous opportunities for him to marvel at the diversity of God's creation, both in appearance and temperament, he'd only had two hits on his personal radar. He'd taken care of them, and no matter what else happened today, he'd done some good work this afternoon.

Gil rested his head against the wall. Would he be able to tell Ivy about this at dinner tonight? If she was still speaking to him, he'd love to share it all with her. He wouldn't allow himself to dwell on the possibility of a future with Ivy anymore. If he did, he'd start wondering what it would be like to come home every night to a house they shared and tell her about his day, then hear about her day, then make some memories of their own for her to add to her photo albums, and then wake up the next day and do it again.

The future had to wait. In the present, he assessed the men and women in the space around him, any one of whom could be here with the intent to capture and torture Ivy until she gave them what they wanted.

A clicking in his ear drew his attention to the ballroom doors. Tessa emerged, followed by Ivy and three men, all of whom looked like they might be prepared to donate a kidney if it meant they could continue to bask in the presence of the two beautiful women they'd spent the afternoon talking to.

"Dr. Collins, you and Ms. Reed should join us tonight. We're not your typical science geeks."

As much as he hated to admit it, the guy had a point. Unless science geeks had changed dramatically in the decade since he'd been in college, the three men walking toward him were atypical of the breed. He'd researched the company Ivy was pitching to, and as soon as they knew who was on-site this week for the meetings, he'd done a quick check on all of them.

To keep them straight, Gil had given each man a nickname—GQ, Surfer Dude, and Brutus. GQ was the one who'd just asked Tessa and Ivy out. He was tall, dark-skinned, with a shaved head. And even after a full day of meetings, his dress slacks and dress shirt held no wrinkles. He was the kind of guy who knew how to dress, knew he was good looking, and knew everyone else knew it too.

"He's right." This from Surfer Dude, a tanned white guy who looked more like someone had kidnapped him off a beach and crammed him into a suit than what Gil knew him to be—a genius with a gift for designing computer code that mimicked the way nerve endings fired and sent signals to the brain.

"Come on, ladies." This from Brutus. He looked like he could be a walk-on with the Carolina Panthers and immediately start as a defensive end. He was massive. His neck was probably the same size as Gil's thighs. But that bulk was pure muscle. He had the look of a man who knew how to use his body, and right now, his body was very, very close to Tessa. As in, his hand was about to land on her lower back.

"We'll have a blast. You can show us your favorite haunts in Raleigh." Brutus leaned forward, his hand resting on Tessa's back as he stage-whispered, "We can regale you with tales of our latest adventure, which I should go ahead and tell you ended with that one"—he pointed to Surfer Dude—"in jail."

Gil heard a low rumble in his earwig, and he didn't have to see Zane to know that he was holding on by a thread. Gil could see Luke, and he looked as furious as Gil currently felt as he watched Brutus press closer to Tessa.

Tessa remained cool and didn't drop the guy like Gil wanted

her to, and like she could if she'd been so inclined. Instead, she linked her arm through Ivy's, and in doing so, twisted her body so Brutus was no longer able to touch her. "No can do, gentlemen. Dr. Collins has a previous dinner engagement with a smoking-hot guy who would not take kindly to being stood up. And I don't want you to be too jealous, but I'm afraid my plans for the evening include a command performance on a family-wide Zoom call. Acceptable excuses for missing this call include death and incarceration, but, sadly, don't include dinner with a band of hottie science nerds."

Brutus mimed being stabbed in the heart. Surfer Dude dropped his head and shook it in overdone sadness. But it was GQ who stretched his hand to Ivy. When she shook his, he gave her a smile that, even from twenty feet away, Gil knew wasn't the kind of smile he bestowed on just anyone. "Dr. Collins. Another night."

Was Ivy blushing?

"Dr. Stillman." She acknowledged his remark with a nod. What she did not do was agree to a date. She turned to the other men. "Gentlemen."

From his spot, he couldn't tell who was in the bigger hurry to get out of there, but Tessa and Ivy weren't letting the grass grow as they quick-marched through the lobby.

Luke would reach the door before they did. Zane was on an intercept from their right side, Faith from the left, with Gil bringing up the rear. By the time they reached the outside, Ivy would be back in the bubble until they had her in the car. To the casual observer, it would appear they were doing the dance any group did when they exited a building. But unlike the frequently awkward interactions when three strangers paused to wait for the others to leave, this dance was choreographed to go off without a hitch.

The automatic doors opened on Luke's approach, and he stopped just outside and scanned the area. He gave a small signal that they were clear and moved completely out of the door area. Faith and Zane reached Ivy and Tessa, and Gil was five feet behind them. They were ten feet from the door when the air was pierced by the unmistakable sound of a burst of machine gunfire, followed by the screams of the hotel patrons.

— 23 —

FAR TO THE RIGHT OF THE LOBBY, a tall figure tackled the shooter. Gil didn't have time to think. All he could do was react. He put a hand on Ivy's back and shoved. Zane was at her right side. Tessa at her left.

Luke was visible through the glass doors. He stood by the open door of a taxi, and they went straight to him. Luke jumped in and then reached across the seat toward the door. Tessa released Ivy and took up a defensive position at the back of the cab. Faith was already at the front of the cab in a similar posture.

Gil shoved Ivy toward Luke, then turned his back to them, his weapon drawn, shielding her from whatever was happening in the lobby. Zane followed her into the cab, the door slammed, and the taxi peeled out of the circular drive.

Once it was gone, Faith, Gil, and Tessa huddled behind a brick post, well away from the glass doors.

"Where did he come from?" Faith hissed in frustration.

"No idea. Once we started our exit procedure, we couldn't watch the entrances anymore. Not enough manpower." Tessa's usually gentle voice had a sharp edge now.

"I hate being outside instead of inside." Faith voiced Gil's own thoughts.

They'd made the right call. Getting Ivy out of the building was the priority, and not just because he cared about her. It was likely that Ivy had been the intended target, and getting her out of the building not only saved her but also ultimately saved the people now lying with their faces to the floor inside the hotel.

But that left him, Faith, and Tessa outside while the people inside were terrified and waiting to see what would happen.

"Do we have any idea who tackled the shooter?" Tessa asked. "I was focused on Ivy, but I saw him go down."

"It was Morris." Gil closed his eyes and could picture it. "Not sure that was the right move, but I haven't heard any more shots. Hopefully he has him contained."

The circular drive soon filled with police, ambulance, and fire vehicles. Morris emerged from the hotel and barked, "Dixon. Reed. Malone. Get over here."

Gil moved. Tess and Faith flanked him. "Guess Morris has earned our cooperation." Tessa sighed heavily. "Forever."

Faith groaned. "Tackling an armed shooter? We're in eternal debt."

They weren't wrong, but in this moment, Gil couldn't drum up any frustration about owing Morris. Ivy was alive. Safe. He'd deal with whatever Morris dished out.

Tessa dropped back and accepted a call. When she caught up, she bumped his shoulder. "They went to my apartment."

Good call. Tessa lived in a secure high-rise. Ritzier than anything most single Secret Service agents could swing. But Tessa wasn't most Secret Service agents.

"How are they getting in?" Faith asked a valid question. Maybe if they flashed their badges, the security guard would let them up. Or maybe Tessa had already talked to the guard and given her permission.

Tessa whispered something Gil didn't catch. Faith did though. "Zane has a key?" Faith managed to pack shock, excitement, humor, and something else into a few words.

All Tessa said was, "Yes," but her expression and tone in that one word left no invitation for further comment.

Faith widened her eyes at Gil. "Okay, then."

They reached Morris and he barked, "Tell me you've got her locked down."

"We do." Gil didn't know for sure when it had happened, but at some point during his questioning of her, Ivy had caught Morris in her web.

"How locked down?" Morris pushed for more.

"Very." This came from Tessa, and Gil appreciated that she gave Morris more, but not all. If he thought they were going to give him the address of Ivy's current location in a public place where any bystander could be involved in whatever was swirling around her, he was nuts.

Morris narrowed his eyes at Gil. "Thought you'd be with her."

"I want this to end, so I need to be here." Gil didn't add that Ivy might not want him around. Morris didn't need that kind of ammunition.

Morris grunted and fixed a glare on Gil. "Shooter may be a dead end, but you can come to the station and sit in on the questioning if you want. And before you ask, no, he doesn't match the description of any of the guys who held Ivy hostage."

"I'm there." No brainer. "What makes you think he could be a dead end?"

"The guy's high as a kite."

Great.

"Didn't ask for a lawyer. Told me he was given two hundred bucks and some, and I'm quoting now, 'quality product' to enjoy before he came in. Keeps rambling about a game, but he's going to have to come back to earth before we'll get anything useful from him. He told me he was supposed to grab the blonde and go out the back."

Great. Whoever had been waiting in the back would be long gone by now.

"We'll have hotel security share their video footage, but I don't know what they have." Morris didn't look hopeful.

"The hotel has cameras back there. We might get something useful."

"How sure are you about the cameras?"

"Talked to hotel security yesterday. Scouted it yesterday. They're there, and they were still functional as of early this afternoon."

Morris grunted. "I'll get a deputy on that. Can you meet me at the station in thirty minutes?"

"Yes," Gil responded without hesitation.

Morris nodded toward Faith, then Tessa. "Nice work today, agents. Next time I find myself in an active shooter situation, I'd count myself lucky to have you at my back."

Faith and Tessa acknowledged the comment with nods. Gil tried not to vomit. Grumpy Morris was annoying, but charming Morris? He didn't even know what to do with that.

"Morris, you know you've got us wrapped around your little finger now. Don't push it." Faith's warning held no punch.

"It'd be a privilege to have you at my back, Morris. And an honor to take yours again in the future." Tessa backed up her comment with a squeeze to his arm, and Gil saw something he didn't think Morris had intended to give away. What Faith and Tessa said meant a lot to the normally surly detective.

Of course, Morris had to ruin the moment. "You two"—he pointed to Faith and Tessa—"anytime." He pointed to Gil. "Gonna have to see about a probationary period for this one."

Gil refused to take the bait. "You can't make me mad, Morris. Not today."

"You got it bad for our girl, don't you?"

"You're claiming her now?"

"You gonna dispute my claim?"

"Guess it depends on what you're trying to claim."

Morris slapped Gil's back. "Just some of the responsibility for keeping her alive. And the name of your firstborn."

Faith and Tessa burst into laughter.

Gil couldn't stop his own grin. "You got any name other than Morris?"

Morris had a definite twinkle in his eye now. "Daniel."

Crap. Daniel was a great name. "We get to that point, I'll keep it in mind."

"All I can ask."

— 24 —

NOT FIREWORKS! When her brain finally registered that the loud cracks echoing through the lobby were coming not from fireworks but from a gun, Ivy's gut reaction had been to drop to the floor. And she would have, if she hadn't been grabbed from three sides and literally shoved out the door and into the open air of the hotel drive and then into a taxi, where she found herself sandwiched between Luke and Zane.

"Go!" They both barked the order at the driver, Luke shoving credentials toward him. The driver took one look, put the cab in drive, and floored it.

Ivy pulled in three quick breaths. Partly because she wasn't sure she'd taken a breath since she heard the gunshots, but mostly because in the chaos, someone, she assumed Zane, had not been gentle with her right hand and arm. Pain ricocheted through her hand, fingers, shoulder, and even up through her neck and into her face. When the worst wave had settled, she twisted in her seat. There were no cars racing along behind them. "Where are they?"

"Who?"

"Who?" Was Luke crazy? "Gil! Tessa! Faith!" She glanced between the men with her and the cars behind them as the hotel fell farther away. "We have to go back. We left them. They were right there with us. I assumed they would get into the next cab. What happened?"

Zane and Luke shared a look, and Ivy did not like what that look said. Because even though she didn't speak special agent, she did speak friend, and she could tell they were worried for their friends. And her special agent translation skills were coming along, because she also knew without them telling her that there was no way they were turning around.

"Um, agents or officers or whatever I hope you are since if I find out you've kidnapped this lady, I'm not gonna like that"—the driver sucked in a breath—"where to?"

Luke and Zane shared another look. Zane gave an address and followed it with, "We're Secret Service. She"—he dipped his head toward Ivy—"is a friend."

Luke squeezed Ivy's left arm. "Ivy, it might help if you could assure our driver here. Otherwise, he's going to drive us to the police station, and once we're there, Morris may throw you in a cell to keep you safe."

Hmm . . . that idea didn't sound as bad as Luke probably thought it did. Safe? Without endangering everyone else?

"Don't even think about it." Zane shook his head at her like she'd been caught doing something naughty. "They're fine. Gil's fine. He will not be fine if he can't get to you when he's done at the hotel. And you don't want to be in a jail cell for any reason, even if it's to keep you safe."

"But maybe—"

"No." Luke and Zane both spoke simultaneously. Again. Were they twins separated at birth? There was no flexibility in their faces, and upon further reflection, she could see their point.

She angled her head until she could meet the taxi driver's eye in the rearview mirror. "My name is Ivy Collins. I'm the CEO of Hedera, Inc. You can google it if it will help you feel better." She pointed to Luke. "This is Special Agent Luke Powell. And this"— she pointed to Zane—"is Special Agent Zane Thacker. They're with the Secret Service, and they're friends of my childhood best friend, Special Agent Gil Dixon, who is still at the hotel and hopefully isn't full of bullet holes."

They stopped at a red light and the driver met her gaze again in the mirror, so she continued. "I trust them, and I would greatly appreciate it if you'd drive us to the address Zane gave you. And then, someday when you're free, please swing by my office. The address is on the website, and you can see for yourself I'm alive and well, and I can thank you, and you'll rest easy."

The taxi driver nodded at her in the rearview mirror. "My name is Eli."

"Hi, Eli," Ivy said in a whisper. "Thanks for getting us out of there."

"Sure thing, ma'am."

When she sat back in her seat, Luke and Zane were both talking on their phones and scanning the road on their respective sides of the car. She thought she'd get mental whiplash from trying to keep up with both conversations.

Luke, she gathered, was talking to their boss, Jacob. "Don't know, Jacob. Heard the gunfire, got her out. As far as I know, Faith, Gil, and Tessa are still on the scene."

At that, Zane reached across her and bumped Luke. When Luke turned to him, he mouthed, "Still on scene." Zane glanced at Ivy. "No bullet holes in anybody, so you can get that look out of your eyes." He turned his gaze back to the road and continued his conversation. "Yeah. I have the key. Yeah. When the scene is secure, we'll regroup." A pause. "Tessa?" Another pause. "Stay safe." He disconnected the call and stared out the window.

Ten minutes later, they pulled up to a swanky apartment building. Fairly new. Not cheap. "This the spot, agents?" Eli asked.

"It is." Zane climbed from the car, then reached toward Ivy, but she pulled her arm back against her body and tried to slide out without letting him touch her. If he yanked her arm one more time, she might scream a little. He frowned and then stretched his arm toward her. "Hang on, and I'll help you."

It wasn't a perfect solution, because with her splinted fingers, she couldn't wrap her hand entirely around his forearm, but she held on as best she could and he pulled her toward the door, then up and out. When she was on her feet, his mouth contorted and he grumbled, "Gil's gonna kill me."

"Why?"

"I hurt you, didn't I?"

Luke joined them and kept them moving until they were inside at the elevators. "How did you hurt her?"

"I'm fine." It wasn't true, but it popped out.

"Grabbed her arm." Zane reached for her right arm, and it was then that she realized she was cradling it to her chest again. His fingers closed around her forearm, and he pulled it away from her chest with a gentleness she hadn't known he possessed. He eased it straight, then returned it to a bend. She couldn't stop the wince. "I'm sorry, Ivy. Can you move it on your own for me? Let me see if we need to take you to the hospital?"

"I'm not going to the hospital." She flexed her arm at the elbow to prove to Zane she could, even though it made the burn on her shoulder pull and twist. "See?" She used her left hand to tug on Zane's shirt until he pulled his eyes away from her arm and met her gaze. "You look like you ran over a puppy. Let it go. I'm fine."

"You're hurt."

"I was already hurt. And I think I should point out that hurting means I'm not dead. Given the option, I'll take the one that involves pain and not the absence of it."

The elevator dinged. They climbed on. Zane reached into his wallet and pulled out a keycard that he used to unlock the elevator, then pressed seven. The doors closed, and Zane's attention refocused on her. She needed a distraction of some kind, so she asked, "Can you tell me where we're going?"

"Tessa's apartment."

Zane had a key to Tessa's apartment? *That* was distracting enough to ease the pain. Zane stared straight ahead and didn't make eye contact with anyone. Luke was staring at his feet, but his lips were twitching. He clearly thought there was something amusing about this, while Zane did not. Either way, Tessa had some explaining to do.

Two minutes later they entered the apartment, and Luke stood between her and the door while Zane prowled through the apartment.

From where she stood in the entryway, Ivy could see the living area and the floor-to-ceiling windows that opened onto a balcony. An irregular but roughly rectangular ottoman was flanked on one side by a cream sofa. The throws and pillows were eclectic and colorful. The rug on the floor was a splash of blue and teal. Two chairs and three floor pillows rounded out the seating.

Zane returned and gave them a quick chin lift. "Clear."

At that, Luke grabbed his phone. Zane pulled the curtains, hiding the stunning city views, then returned to where she stood studying her new surroundings and herded her to a cushy chair on the opposite side of the room from the windows. He stalked to the kitchen and returned with a bottle of water, which he opened and handed to her.

"Thanks." She took a sip. Then turned the bottle up and drank half of it in one go. Then went back for more until she'd drained it.

"Want another one?" Zane removed the empty bottle from her hand.

"No. I think I'm good now. Thanks."

He ignored that, and a few seconds later he was back in front of her with another bottle. "Can I get you some meds?"

"No. I'm fine." Another lie, but there was no way she was going to break down in front of Zane and Luke. She had to hold it together.

Luke joined Zane, and they both made no effort to conceal their study of her. "You've had a busy day, you're in physical pain, and in a few minutes your adrenaline is going to crash, if it hasn't already." Luke grabbed a throw blanket from the back of Tessa's couch, flipped it out, and settled it over her. "Try to relax."

"Right." Did he have any idea how ridiculous that suggestion was?

"Did you ever hear the details about what happened last spring?" Luke flopped onto the sofa and propped his feet on the ottoman.

"No."

"It's a thrilling tale, made better by the fact that you already know we survived." Zane settled onto one of the floor pillows and leaned against the wall. They were trying to distract her. Maybe they were also trying to distract themselves. She didn't call them on it. She snuggled deeper into the chair and said, "Let's hear it."

— 25 —

THE HOTEL LOBBY was still a buzz of activity, but when Jacob arrived on the scene, Gil and Tessa found a quiet corner of the lobby to give him an update. Faith joined them a few minutes later when her boss, Dale, arrived, and the joint update continued. When they were done, Dale directed a question at Gil. "You think they were coming after your friend?"

"It's the most likely scenario."

"Will Detective Morris take the case? Because I think it would be best if we kept any hint of Secret Service or FBI involvement out of it." Jacob gave Gil and Tessa a pointed look.

"Agreed." Dale took in Faith's appearance. "Although Faith certainly doesn't look like an agent in that getup."

"I'll communicate our desire to be kept out of the press conference," Gil offered, and Jacob and Dale both nodded. A few minutes later, both special agents in charge left the premises.

Faith watched them leave. "It's a good thing they get along."

"That's true." Their agencies had been on friendly terms ever since Gil had come to Raleigh, but that was because Dale and their former SAIC, Michael Weaver, had been friends for decades. Fortunately, when Jacob took Michael's position, the open communication and sense of camaraderie had continued. "I'm going to head to the police station. What are you two going to do?"

Faith pointed to the building. "I think we need to make sure everything's settled in there. Then head to Tessa's."

Tessa nodded her agreement.

"I'll catch up to you when I'm done with Morris." Gil turned toward the parking garage.

Tessa fell into step with Gil and called over her shoulder, "Faith, I'll be back in a minute. I'll have Gil drop me back at the door."

Faith responded with a nod and disappeared inside the building.

"I don't need an escort to the car, Tessa."

"Yes, you do. None of us needs to be wandering around parking garages alone right now."

She had a point, and she stayed close as they walked to his car. His phone buzzed, but he didn't pull it from his pocket until they were in the car and he had backed from the parking space and moved into a less confined part of the garage. Then he pulled it out of his pocket. After a quick glance, he dropped his chin to his chest, then took another, longer look. Luke had sent him a photo of Ivy asleep in a chair in Tessa's apartment. Safe. Resting.

"You okay?" Tessa placed a hand on his arm.

He turned the phone in her direction. She saw the photo and grinned. "You're okay." She squeezed his arm and released it. Then her expression grew speculative. "What happened this morning?"

"What?" He might have been able to pull off the innocent and confused act if his voice hadn't cracked.

As it was, Tessa wasn't buying it. "Ivy's worried."

"She's worried? Why?"

"I gathered the two of you had a heated conversation this morning."

"What did she tell you?"

"That you'd had a disagreement. She said she lost her temper and the situation hadn't been resolved before you dropped her off at work."

Gil groaned. "I overstepped."

"Did you try to kiss her?"

"Not that kind of overstepping. Although, in the future, if I screw up and she starts yelling at me, kissing her might be a good way to short-circuit the argument. Couldn't hurt to try."

Tessa gave him a withering glance. "I wouldn't recommend that."

"What would you recommend?"

"Groveling."

Gil couldn't stop the snort that Tessa's matter-of-fact response shocked out of him. "Pretty sure that's a given."

"She's crazy about you. You don't need to worry about it. You messed up. Apologize. Ask for understanding. Seek to understand. Then move forward."

"I'll keep that in mind."

"She's under an overwhelming amount of stress, and she's mostly alone. The only people who are in the know are people she met less than a week ago."

"She's known me her whole life."

"Yeah, with a fifteen-year gap that ended only five days ago." She paused, and when he didn't argue her point, she continued. "It has to be disconcerting. You know we're trustworthy and only have her best interests at heart. She wants to believe that, but under the circumstances, you can hardly blame her for having doubts. We're asking her to trust strangers while simultaneously telling her everyone who knows her is a suspect. That's a mind game no one should ever be asked to play."

Gil counted the cars ahead of them. Four more until they could pay and leave. He hated parking garages, and he'd never wanted out of one so badly in his life.

Tessa didn't speak as they inched forward while two more cars cleared the gate. "I don't like this. Who shoots up a hotel lobby in an effort to get to her? I don't know how we stop them from doing whatever they might do next when I can't make any sense of it."

Gil grabbed his credit card and slipped it into the reader. "I still think it has to be the money, but there's an edge of desperation to their actions this week that I don't understand. It's not like the money is going anywhere."

"It all makes sense from their perspective. We have to figure out where they, whoever they are, are coming from." Tessa kept her gaze to the window.

Gil exited the garage and drove back to the front of the hotel. Tessa opened her door, and Gil stopped her from climbing out by grabbing her arm. "Stay in contact. I may not be able to respond for a while, but I want updates."

"You got it."

"And Tessa?"

"Yeah?"

"Thank you for protecting Ivy today."

Tessa flashed her full-wattage smile. "Anytime, Gil."

TWENTY MINUTES LATER, he stood against the wall of the in-terrogation room while Morris scooted his chair close to their shooter. "Billy, you and I have already chatted." Morris had a gruff voice, and it didn't have a soft setting, but he wasn't barking at this guy. It was a good call, because with the way Billy Rice was twitching and scratching, he had to be desperate for a fix, and yelling at him wouldn't be the key to unlocking his lips.

"Yeah. We chatted when you jumped on me and messed up my game."

"Your game?"

"I already told you. It wasn't real. The gun. The bullets. Fake. I was supposed to go in, shoot into the air, get the girl, and go out the back. Then I'd get my blow and my cash. And the girl would get, well, whatever it was she was supposed to get out of that."

What was this guy implying? Gil pressed his palms into the wall, his heels into the floor.

Morris cocked his head to one side. "I'm not following you."

"It's a game. They do this stuff all the time."

"What stuff?"

"Role-play." Billy looked at Gil, then back to Morris. "These rich people get a kick out of it. They stage a kidnapping, then the boyfriend gets to play the hero and rescue her. They all live happily ever after. It's not my thing, but it's not the weirdest stuff I've ever heard of."

"In this role-play game, does the girl know she's going to be kidnapped?"

"Yep. They said all I had to say when I grabbed her was, 'You want to be sure no one gets killed, you come willingly.' That was the code. He made me memorize it. Said when she heard that, she'd realize it was part of the game."

"What were you supposed to do if she didn't come willingly?"

"They told me she would pretend to put up a fight because that's what you do when you get kidnapped, but she wouldn't fight too hard."

Billy's eyes narrowed as something occurred to him, penetrating the fog of his addiction, and he whispered, "You don't think I would have hurt her, do you? I wouldn't have hurt her. She's pretty. Nice clothes. Looks like the type who would take care of kittens and stuff. I like my blow, but not enough to hurt a girl. I'm not that far gone."

That was debatable.

"So you were supposed to grab her, take her out back, put her in a car, get your payoff, and that was the end of it?"

"Yeah."

Morris frowned. "What about all the other people?"

"What do you mean?"

"The other people. The fifty people you scared half to death and who spent some time with their faces pressed into the filthy floor of the hotel while you played this game. A game, by the way, *they* didn't know you were playing."

"Didn't think about that."

"While you weren't thinking this through, did it not occur to you that the police would arrest you?"

Billy brightened like a kid whose favorite teacher asked a question he knew the answer to. "I asked about that, but they said once I told you it was part of the game and showed you how the gun was fake, that it would be cool."

This guy was an idiot.

"I hate to have to tell you this, but that was a real gun filled with real bullets being used to really kidnap that pretty lady."

"No." Billy looked from Morris to Gil, then back to Morris. "No. No. No." Each word was softer than the one before, until he was mouthing the word, his head shaking back and forth, tears streaking down his face.

Morris had a look on his face that made Gil suspect he was questioning all the decisions he'd made in his life that had led to him sitting in this room interrogating this moron. "Can you give me a description of the man who hired you?"

Now Billy's nose was running. Gil grabbed a box of tissues from a small desk in the corner and slid it across the table.

Once the snot situation had been resolved, he sniffled out a muted, "He was a Marine."

"What?" The word escaped Gil's lips, and he clamped his mouth shut.

"Yeah. Had the tattoo on his arm. You know the kind the Marines get?"

Gil knew the tattoo.

"Big guy. Not fat big. Strong. Muscles. Dark hair cut short, like a Marine."

A strong, muscular Marine? Gil pulled his phone from his pocket and sent Faith and Tessa a text.

> See if you can get a lock on Abott Percy's current location.

Morris continued to interrogate Billy, but he couldn't give them much else to go on. An officer came in and took Billy to a sketch artist.

"I'm gonna have to lock him down for his own safety," Morris said after Billy left the room. "They must have had a plan for neutralizing him before he could do any damage."

"They probably planned to drop him as soon as he delivered her to the car. Either that, or they were going to give him some polluted drugs and he would be dead—another overdose. He's lucky to be alive, and he doesn't have a clue."

"What's got you tweaked about this guy being a Marine? I'm a Marine. Hate to think of a Marine being behind this, but it does happen. We aren't all angels."

Gil ignored the bizarre vision that flitted through his brain of Morris with a halo. "Ivy's ex is a Marine. He's also built and has dark hair he still wears in a high and tight even though I'm guessing he's been out for close to a decade. Long enough to get a PhD in bioengineering and become a professor at Georgia."

Morris pulled out his notebook. "You got a name?"

"Abott Percy."

"Any reason to believe he's in town?"

"Every reason. She had dinner with him on Thursday. He was at church on Sunday but didn't approach her. Came to her office yesterday while I was there."

Morris cut his eyes to him. "Bet that went well."

"About as well as you would imagine."

"What's his motive?"

"The money? Jealousy? He made a pitch yesterday to the same company Ivy talked to today. They're competitors for the grant."

Morris rubbed his shiny head. "Think he's infatuated with her and is trying to create a situation where she has to come to him, see him as the hero, in an effort to restore their relationship?"

"I've considered that. She doesn't think he's a threat, but he keeps showing up, and I don't get a good feeling."

Morris chuckled.

"What?"

Morris's chuckle morphed into a snort. "You aren't ever going to get a good feeling about any of her exes. You've got it bad, and I hope you don't think you're hiding it. You might as well be holding your heart in your hands and following her around with it while singing love songs and promising her a future where you spend your life adoring her and making beautiful babies with her."

Gil was rendered temporarily mute by Morris's declaration.

"That's what I thought." Morris clapped him on the back. "I'm not saying you're wrong about the ex. He sounds sketchy. I'll do some digging. But no one's ever gonna believe you aren't biased. Not when it comes to this."

What was he supposed to say to that? Thanks? You're right? Shut up? All he wanted was to get out of this conversation. Away from Morris. Away from everyone.

Except Ivy.

"Go on." Morris was flat-out laughing now. "Find our girl. Make sure she's okay. Maybe hold off on telling her you have to name your firstborn after me. Might be too soon."

Morris was still chuckling when he left Gil standing in the hall outside the interrogation room.

Now what?

— 26 —

IVY OPENED HER EYES and straightened in the chair. How long had she been asleep?

Her hand went to her mouth and encountered a little bit of wet at the corners. Her heart rate spiked. Had she drooled on Tessa's squashy chair? She ran her hand over the fabric. Dry. She'd woken up before she slobbered on the furniture. Well, there was one thing that went right today.

She leaned forward and rested her head in her left hand. Her entire right arm throbbed. She hadn't had any pain meds, prescription or over the counter, all day, and that had been a mistake. Huge.

But after she lost it on Gil, she was so discombobulated, she forgot to take them. Then she was in full-blown pitch mode and forgot again. Then she got caught in a shooting in the middle of a hotel lobby, and no one could be expected to remember anything after an experience like that.

Right?

She lifted her shoulders, dropped them, and repeated the movement until some of the stiffness left. As she worked her shoulders, she listened to the murmurs from the kitchen. She could make out four voices. Luke, Zane, Tessa, and Faith.

But not Gil. If he was in there, he wasn't making a sound.

Her bag was at her feet. She rummaged through it until she found her phone. Sixteen text messages from colleagues at work, all asking how the pitch went and if she'd already left the hotel before the gunman shot up the place. The answer to the first was simple. The pitch went great. They had an excellent chance of winning the grant, and not because the lead researcher wanted her to go out with him.

The answer to the second was more complicated. She doubted her new friends would be thrilled if she spread it around that she'd been in the building but they had hurried her out the door. Not that anyone would fault her for leaving the scene of an active shooter situation. Given the option, most people would get out of there.

Lord, why is this so hard? I want to make people's lives better. I want to help, and I want to do a good job, and I don't want to be afraid all the time. Will I ever not be afraid again?

Although, if she was honest, at the moment she wasn't afraid for herself. At least not that she would get shot or blown up. She was afraid to face Gil, and that wasn't anyone's fault. Well, except Gil's. Mostly Gil, and a little bit her. She was still frustrated with his high-handed treatment. That was over. Period. End of discussion.

But the yelling. Her skin flamed at the memory.

"You're awake." Tessa came around the low corner. "How's the arm? Need some meds?"

Zane must have told Tessa he'd grabbed her arm. "Zane isn't still worried, is he?"

Tessa lifted her hands in a "what can you do?" gesture.

"I'm fine. I think I'd rather wait and take the strong stuff before bed."

Faith joined them and sat on the sofa across from her. "Where do you want to go tonight? Back home?"

"Do I have a choice?" Ivy wasn't trying to be a brat, but she hadn't had much choice about anything since Friday night.

Faith and Tessa shared a look. The kind of look that told her Gil had spilled the tea. Faith dove into the fray. "Gil made it clear that you were to be free to decide where you sleep and who is with you."

Tessa made a pitiful effort to fight a smile but lost the battle. "You made your point, Ivy. And you aren't wrong. But"—she glanced at Faith, then back to Ivy—"Gil's intentions were good. He's protective of everyone he cares about. He can't help it. It's who he is. I'm not saying his feelings for you are similar to his feelings for me, or Faith, but he's protective of us. He's also protective of Zane and Luke. And he's crazy protective of Emily. Not that he should have taken over your life and started running it. But I'm just saying that if you can't handle a protective guy, then you aren't going to be able to handle Gil."

Faith nodded her agreement. "At all."

"I don't mind protective." Why was she whispering? She cleared her throat. "But there's a difference between protective and smothering."

"Yeah. Pretty sure you'll spend the rest of your life explaining that difference to Gil. Good luck." Tessa glanced at her watch. "But for now, the question is, do you want Gil at your house tonight or would you rather have one of us?"

"We're happy to hang with you if you need some distance." Faith glanced toward the kitchen, then leaned closer. "But I have to say, distance isn't all it's cracked up to be."

"I don't want distance." Ivy slumped in her seat. "I'm . . . I . . . Where is he now? Why isn't he already here? Is something else wrong?"

Tessa blew out a breath, and unless Ivy was very much mistaken, there was relief in her tone when she spoke. "He's been at the station with Morris, interrogating the shooter. If you want him here, he'll be here soon. And he'll take you home whenever you're ready to go home."

Could she open up to these women? They'd done nothing but had her back, protected her, and now, taken her side even though Gil was their friend. They weren't throwing him under the bus. They clearly loved him and thought highly of him, but they weren't condoning his behavior either.

Before Ivy could stop herself, she blurted out, "That's what I want. I want Gil to take me home."

Faith and Tessa had their phones out before she'd finished her sentence. "That's great." Tessa didn't look away from her device. "Because he's pulling into the parking lot now."

Thumbs flying, they fired off simultaneous texts, and then Faith called out, "Coast is clear! You can come back in here!"

The scraping of chairs preceded Luke and Zane joining them in the living area. Luke pulled Faith against him and pressed a kiss to her neck. "What's the plan?"

Faith settled deeper into Luke. "Gil's coming up. We'll figure out the rotation. He'll take Ivy home. You'll take me to get dinner, and then you'll take me home, and then you'll go home."

He grabbed her chin and pulled it around so he could kiss her lips. It was far from inappropriate, but the tenderness in Luke's expression made Ivy feel like she should look away and give them some privacy.

Tessa looked at her phone. "Gil's in the elevator."

GIL KNOCKED ON THE DOOR to Tessa's apartment.

Tessa opened the door but didn't let him inside. "Did you get my text?"

"I did."

"Are you going to be nice to her? Because she's a wreck. And if you aren't prepared to be nice, you can turn around and go home alone."

"Of course I'm going to be nice. Whose side are you on, anyway?"

She moved to the side and whispered, "I'm on the side of both of you getting past this and moving forward."

He walked into Tessa's den and caught his first glimpse of Ivy, curled up into a tight ball in a chair. This morning's anger was long gone from her face. In its place was a combination of fear and relief.

Faith and Tessa had both texted him that if he approached with an apology and the promise of open communication in the future, the road to Ivy was clear. Tessa had indicated that if he didn't make a move, a real move, and soon, then he was an idiot. Faith had suggested that when he got her home, he should go ahead and propose and save them all a lot of time.

He waved a hand to indicate everyone but Ivy. "How about if y'all clear out for a few minutes."

Tessa had turned her second bedroom into an office space, and they all moved in that direction. He knelt in front of Ivy's chair and squeezed her knee. "Hey."

"Hey."

"Are you okay?"

"Am I okay? I didn't stay behind with a maniac holding a machine gun. How are you?"

"Physically? Fine. Still not sure about the rest. I acted like an idiot and hurt you. I'm sorry."

"I overreacted."

"You weren't wrong."

"I could have handled it better."

"I could have treated you like the brilliant, capable, savvy woman you are instead of acting like you need me to swoop in and save the day."

"I still could have been nicer." She leaned toward him and didn't stop until her forehead rested against his. "But I'm tired. I hurt all the time. And . . . I'm scared."

He gave himself a few seconds to relish the way she'd handed him all of that, accepting it for the gift it was, even while hating that she was in this situation. He lifted his hand from her knee, found her hand, and laced his fingers with hers. "I'm scared too, which is why I was an idiot."

He gave her a chance to agree or disagree. She said nothing, and he took that as a good sign. She probably agreed with his assessment, but she also didn't seem to need to make him feel any worse. "I'm a quick learner. I should have asked you what you wanted and kept you informed. I'll do better. Promise."

Her head moved against his.

"Is that an 'I forgive you and will never use this against you in the future' nod, or am I reading too much into it?"

The laugh that answered his question succeeded in doing what nothing else had been able to do all day, and the wall between them crumbled. He brushed his nose against hers. "Ready to go home?"

"Yes."

He sat back and looked into big blue eyes, lashes damp with unshed tears that she blinked away before they escaped. He stood, and since their fingers were still entwined, she stood with him. He kept her hand in his and maneuvered them around Tessa's coffee table and into the doorway to Tessa's office.

Four sets of eyes met his, flickered to the spot where his hand still clasped Ivy's, then hit Ivy's face, before landing back on him.

Before anyone could comment, Gil jumped in. "Ivy wants to go home. What's our best strategy for making that happen?"

He had a strategy, but if he was going to keep Ivy in the loop as promised, then she needed to hear all the scenarios and be part of the decision-making process.

"Call Morris. See if he can have some officers present when you get there. It's either that, or we follow you home and clear the house before you enter. Oh, and we call Morris either way." Zane didn't have to get Ivy's opinion and clearly didn't care whether she wanted this or not.

Ivy's hand tightened on his. "Do we need to do all that? It seems a bit excessive. I have a security system and—"

"It's the smart play." Tessa gave Ivy an encouraging smile. "They made a move this afternoon. It didn't work. We don't know what the next move will be, but we need to be ready for whatever it is."

"I get that. But—"

"Gil will step in front of a bullet for you, Ivy." Faith didn't seem to be making any effort to soften her words. "If he has to do that and there's no one else around, not only do they take Gil out of the picture, but they also get you—and ultimately, they get whatever they want."

Ivy jolted against him at Faith's response. "Wow, Faith. Don't sugarcoat it for me."

"Oh, I'm not done. Because I know what it feels like to watch Gil get shot." Faith's voice broke, and she cleared her throat. "I'd like to make sure you and I don't share that nightmare." Her eyes glistened, but her voice firmed. "I like you. A lot. I think you were right to call Gil out for not clueing you in to what's going down, and I support you being part of the decision-making process. But I will not be quiet if you try to refuse to allow us to protect you in a way that not only protects you but ensures we all live to fight another day."

Ivy pressed into his arm. "That seems fair."

"Good." Faith caught his eye. "And don't you get grouchy with me for laying it out for her. Someone needed to, and we all knew it wouldn't be you."

"Hey—"

"Let it go, Gil" Luke put an arm around Faith. "You know she's right."

Zane's low voice broke through the stalemate. "Tessa, call Morris. Gil, take your time getting Ivy home. Don't go straight there. Hit a drive-through. Backtrack a few times. Make it look like you're headed to Faith's or Luke's or even your place."

Zane jerked his head toward Luke. "You and Faith head out with Gil and Ivy. Make sure they get to the car and out safe. Then take your time getting home. I'll wait here for a few minutes, and then I'll go straight to Ivy's and cruise the neighborhood. If I see anything I don't like, I'll holler."

"I'll come with you." Tessa fixed a look on Zane that did not invite argument or dissent. "None of us needs to be alone."

He accepted that with a brisk nod. "Once everyone is back in their respective homes, we'll touch base via text. I'll hit the sack and come back to Ivy's around two so Gil can get some sleep. Agreed?"

Everyone murmured their assent.

"Good." Zane winked at Ivy. "Sorry, Ivy, but this crowd can talk a situation to death. At some point, someone has to make a decision."

"Bossy," Tessa said on a cough.

"So bossy." Faith mimicked Tessa.

Zane's glare lacked heat. Luke wasn't even attempting to pretend he didn't think this was hilarious.

Gil wasn't amused or annoyed. Zane was right, and they had

a plan and Ivy had agreed to it, so it was time to get Ivy home. "We're headed out. Luke and Faith, you coming?"

They didn't talk on the elevator, but when they stepped out and split off to their respective cars, Faith pulled away from Luke and walked straight to Gil. Without making eye contact, she put her arms around him and squeezed him tight. "Don't get shot."

He squeezed her back. "I'll do my best."

"Promise?"

"Promise."

She released him and, still without looking at him, walked to Luke, who tucked her against his side, pressed a kiss to her forehead, and directed her to his car.

Ivy didn't comment on the exchange until they were in his car and on the road. "Did she really see you get shot?"

"Yep."

Ivy chewed on her lip before whispering, "She can be a little scary."

"Faith sometimes comes across as brusque, but there's a lot of depth to her and lots of emotion she rarely shows. The more emotion she's feeling, the more likely she is to come across as tough and unfeeling. And clearly, there's a lot of emotion wrapped up in this."

"Did you know she has nightmares about it?"

"Didn't have a clue. She probably wouldn't have ever mentioned it if she hadn't believed I was in danger."

"I'm sure that's part of it, but I'm guessing you've been in danger since then and it hasn't come up." Ivy reached for his hand. "I think it's more that she wouldn't have said that if she hadn't believed I was in danger of seeing the same thing."

Gil let that settle around him. It made sense. Faith knew what he did. Knew what dangers he regularly accepted. Anyone in law enforcement had to accept that getting shot was a possibility.

But Ivy seeing him get shot? No. That wasn't something Faith would want for her.

"She's a good friend to you."

"She is. And she's trying to be a good friend to you too."

"I used to think friends were always nice to you, but these days, I think the best friends will see you doing something stupid, call you on it, and still like you."

"I would agree with that assessment." He squeezed her hand and opened her car door. She slipped into the seat with a grimace.

When he'd joined her in the car and pulled out onto the road, he asked, "Are you hurting? Zane told me he grabbed you too hard."

"Oh, good grief." He could hear the exasperation in her voice. "Do they inject you with an overprotectiveness serum when you take your oath to be a Secret Service agent?"

"What?"

"Zane treats me like I'm glass."

"He knows you aren't glass. Zane's default is to treat women with a great deal of deference. And it isn't because he thinks women are weak or inferior. It's the exact opposite. He firmly believes that the more you value someone, the more carefully you should treat them. He had to hurt you in order to protect you. And he did it because he's well trained and highly motivated and capable of putting aside his aversion to putting his hands on a woman when it's necessary to preserve her life. But that doesn't mean that when it's over, he doesn't struggle with it."

"Well, then, that's good, I guess."

Time to get them into safer territory. "What do you have on your calendar for tomorrow night?"

In his peripheral vision, her head snapped in his direction. "Tomorrow night?"

"Yeah. I know you didn't have 'run from shooter' penciled in on your calendar for today, but if all this wasn't happening, what would you be doing tomorrow night?"

"Tomorrow's Thursday?"

"Yeah."

"I usually go to hot yoga on Thursdays, but I don't imagine sweating would be a fun experience with this charbroiled arm of mine, and these broken fingers wouldn't be a fan of some of the poses. I'll have to table my yoga for a few weeks."

She leaned back in the car seat and looked out her window. "I guess that means I'm free. Why?"

"Well, prior to our conversation this morning, I had arranged for Faith and Tessa to hang out with you tomorrow evening."

"Seriously?"

"Yes." He hadn't lied to her about anything yet, and he wouldn't start now. "I made the assumption that you'd be tired and would prefer to be at home. But, obviously, that was idiotic. Let me try to make it right."

"Okay." There was a lot of hesitancy in that word, but he'd take caution over fury any day.

"I help coach a Little League baseball team with a buddy from church. He's the head coach, and there's no drama if I can't be there. In fact, the boys think it's cool when I'm not there because they dream up all kinds of crazy stuff."

He cut his eyes at her. "That may be partly because I got shot in the middle of the season last year and missed a couple of weeks because of it."

"That would make an impression."

"Yeah. Anyway, we have a game tomorrow night. Six o'clock. It's a fourth-grade team. This is their first season where the kids are pitching and catching."

"I used to love going to your games. Those kids are lucky to have you helping coach." Her voice held the soft edge of memory mingled with something that sounded a lot like pride.

"I don't know how lucky they are. I'm lucky to get to be involved again. I missed the game, and this is a good group of kids."

"I'm sure they are."

He took a deep breath and plunged ahead. "I know you want to be involved in the security decisions, but there's no way I'm leaving you alone tomorrow night. It isn't safe."

"So what are my options?"

"You can have another girls' night in with Tessa and Faith. Or Zane and Luke will go with you if you want to go out."

"Hmm."

"Or—"

"There's a door number three?"

"There is. You could come to the ball game with me and sit in the dugout with a bunch of crazy nine- and ten-year-old boys. And when the game's over, we could pick up some takeout." He risked a glance in her direction. "I have to be honest with you. It's not what I had envisioned for our first date. I would have preferred something with less dirt and significantly fewer children."

"This would be a date?" There was a tremor in her voice. Was it excitement? Trepidation?

It was time to hit that fly ball to her and see if she caught it or let it drop. "It doesn't have to be a date, but I would like it to be."

— 27 —

THE LAST DATE she and Gil had gone on, they'd driven to Atlanta for a Braves game. They held hands, ate peanuts and hot dogs, and daydreamed about what it would be like when Gil played for a major league team.

Two days later, she left for Oregon.

Gil cleared his throat, and there was no mistaking his discomfort. He'd taken a risk, and she'd left him hanging. "I'd love to." The words tumbled over each other in her hurry to accept and reassure him. "It sounds fun. I haven't been to a baseball game in years. And I like kids."

Gil's relief was palpable. "Then it's a date."

"It's a date."

Gil's hand reached for hers, and after she laced her fingers through his, he pulled their hands until they rested on his thigh and brushed his thumb across the back of her hand in a slow, soothing sweep.

He stopped at a red light and turned to her. "There's food in your Crock-Pot, but we can set it in the fridge. It's a stew, and stews always taste better a few days later anyway. And we need to kill a little bit more time. Where would you like to pick up something for dinner?"

Dinner? Who could think about dinner? He'd asked her out. There was no room for dinner in her stomach.

"I'm not super hungry, but I wouldn't turn down an iced tea from wherever you want to go."

Gil frowned. "Why aren't you hungry? You haven't eaten in hours."

"I don't know. If I get hungry later, we have a ton of food in the fridge because you cook for ten and not two."

He laughed. "You don't have as much left over as you think you do. I cook for the people who are raiding your fridge at two a.m. They come hungry."

"Really?"

"I've spoiled them. I cook, bring in the leftovers, and they eat them for lunches. That's when they don't show up at my house for dinner. Zane and Luke do that a lot. Now I'm stuck with them. You should see my grocery bill."

He pulled up to a drive-through, ordered a Coke for himself and a half-cut tea for her, then pulled back onto the highway. "Why didn't you get anything?"

"I'll wait and eat with you." He reached for her hand again and settled it back against his thigh. "You can have this hand when you need to take a drink, as long as you give it back when you're done."

"Deal."

They drove around for another ten minutes. Gil's phone rang, and he answered it through the Bluetooth. "Dixon."

"Where are you?" Zane did not sound happy.

Gil's entire body went stiff. "Ten minutes from Ivy's. Why?"

"Make it five."

Click.

"Did he hang up on you?"

"Yeah." Gil didn't release her hand, but he did increase his speed.

"Should I be worried?"

"I wish I could say no, Buttercup."

Lord, please let my house still be standing when I get there.

Seven minutes later, they pulled into her driveway. Zane stood in front of her open garage door, hands on his hips, giving his best impression of the grumpy cat. Tessa stood beside him, and it would have been obvious to someone watching from a high-altitude satellite feed that she was furious.

"Crap." Gil put the car in park and turned to her. "Will you give me one minute to talk to Zane and Tessa before you get out of the car? Please?"

She wasn't sure she wanted to hear what they had to say, so she nodded.

He pulled their linked hands to his mouth and pressed a kiss on her knuckles. "Be right back."

He climbed out and jogged to the garage. Zane's gaze landed on hers, and he held her eyes. She could be wrong, but she sensed he was trying to share some of his strength with her, and while she appreciated it, it also scared her.

They talked for less than twenty seconds before Gil dropped his head, shook it slowly, and came to her side of the car. He opened her door. She swung her legs out, but before she could stand, he knelt beside her.

Ivy braced herself for whatever was coming. "Tell me."

"It's bad."

"I guessed that by the way Zane is standing in the driveway like some kind of avenging angel and Tessa looks like she could make cement catch fire with her gaze."

"Well, your avenging angel and human flamethrower got here after the police checked the perimeter. The police left, and they decided to peek in the windows."

"And?"

"Then they called Morris. He's on his way."

"Why?"

Gil reached for her left hand with his right. He wrapped his left hand around her right calf, physically bracing her for what he was about to say. "There's a body in there."

She must have misheard. She unlocked her tongue and gasped out a rough, "What?"

"They couldn't determine through the window if he was alive, so they went in through the garage door. They should have waited on more backup. But if he was alive, they wanted to provide medical assistance."

"I'm assuming since they're out here, there wasn't anything they could do."

"Once they got inside and had the lights on, it was clear there was nothing to be done. They never touched the body, but . . ." Gil hesitated and then plunged on. "Based on the amount of blood, there's a good bet the guy died here."

Ivy had never understood people who threw up after receiving bad news, but right now she was relieved nothing was in her stomach but a few sips of tea.

Gil's hand flexed on her calf. "I'm so sorry."

"Did they recognize him?"

"No, but . . . he has red hair."

Red hair? "Is he tall?"

Gil nodded.

"It could be the guy who stunned me."

"Could be."

"Why would someone kill him in my house?"

"I don't know. Someone's sending a message, but until we check everything out, it's impossible to know exactly what they're trying to tell us."

"Where's the body?" Gil clearly didn't want to answer. She could sense the reluctance all over him. "Gil?"

"Your bedroom."

"WHAT!"

The grip he had on her calf tightened. "Buttercup, take a slow breath. Not deep. Not fast. Count four in. Four out."

She did as he said, with Gil muttering the count in a low voice. When she regained some control, she asked, "Do I have to go in there?"

"No."

"Ever?"

"Do you want to move?"

"Yes. I'll put it on the market tomorrow. I don't think I ever want to go back in there. Ever."

Gil's hands flexed. "Maybe we could agree that you aren't going in there tonight and leave the future on the table?"

"I'll consider it."

Cars were pulling in around them. Based on the flickering lights that danced across her garage, at least some of them were police cars. She dropped her head onto Gil's shoulder, and his arms wrapped around her waist. His head turned and his lips whispered across her cheek. "I've got you."

Voices filtered through the evening air. Most were deep. Some higher. All crisp and efficient. Morris's bark was distinguishable not only because it was Morris—at this point, she'd recognize his raspy voice anywhere—but because there was rage in his tone. Barely contained, simmering, and ready to boil over.

She didn't know why no one interrupted her and Gil, but she couldn't make herself care. She let Gil hold her. She tried to pray for the investigators. For the dead man in her bedroom. For herself and her family and her business and her clients. But she couldn't find words, so she rested her head against Gil and let her mind go blank.

GIL STRAINED TO HEAR every conversation taking place around him. Luke and Faith were on scene. They'd joined Zane and Tessa, and the four of them maintained a bubble around him and Ivy that no one dared to breach.

At the moment, he was thankful for the years he spent alternating between being a pitcher and a catcher, because most people couldn't hold the squat he was sitting in for long. It helped that he was leaning against the car frame and that Ivy was hanging on to him like he held her future in his hands.

Lord, please let me hold it safely for her forever.

He didn't want this moment to end.

I want to protect her from everything, Lord. I don't understand why so much evil is touching her world. Help me to trust that you love her more than I do.

Love. Did he love her? That was the wrong question. Had he ever *not* loved her might be the more appropriate question. And he knew the answer to that.

She blew out a long breath that tickled his neck. Then she pulled back and settled herself deeper in the seat of the car. She reached for his face and brushed her thumb across his cheek. "I would love to stay right here and pretend all of that"—she jerked her head toward her house—"isn't happening. But I don't guess we can."

"No. But I wish we could too."

231

She dropped her hand. "What should I do now?"

"If you want, you could stay where you are while I go check in with Morris and the others. Then I'll let you know what our options are."

She nodded. "Unless I can find some courage I don't currently seem to possess, I'm guessing you're going to need to pack another bag for me."

"No one enjoys seeing a dead body. And it isn't weak to want to avoid having that memory."

She sagged against the back of the seat, twisted at an odd angle, probably trying to avoid putting any pressure on her burned shoulder. He gave her knee a squeeze. "I'll be right back."

He stretched to his full height and gave his legs a second for the blood flow to normalize. Luke stood directly across from him, back to him, phone to his ear.

Gil turned and spotted Tessa twenty feet behind him, giving off an aura that screamed "do not approach." Faith took a sip of a Cherry Coke and met his gaze. Hmm. Definitely a toss-up between who was angrier right now.

Zane and Morris were talking to a forensic tech, and Zane waved him over. Gil turned back to Faith and Tessa and tilted his head in Ivy's direction. In response, both women moved closer to the car. No one would get to Ivy while he was gone.

He was still fifteen feet from Morris when he growled, "She okay?"

"She's not whistling show tunes, but yes. Can we get inside?"

"Yeah, but you aren't gonna like it." Morris turned on his heel and marched to the house.

Zane fell into step beside Gil. Moments later, Luke jogged up from behind them. "Have either of you been inside yet?"

"No. Morris doesn't have a great relationship with the lead forensic tech, so he wanted us to give them some space," Zane said.

"Why does that not surprise me?"

They followed Morris inside, scanning the kitchen and living areas. "They didn't trash the house," Luke observed.

"No. But how did they get in? She has a security system, and I watched her set it this morning."

"We're working on getting info from the alarm company." Zane pointed to the box on the wall. "The alarm was set. When we walked in, I had to disarm it before we went to the body."

After camping out at Ivy's for the past couple of nights, Luke, Zane, Tessa, and Faith all knew Ivy's alarm code. But how many others knew it? Gil added that to the mental list of questions he was going to have to ask Ivy.

They entered Ivy's bedroom and paused at the door.

Her room was destroyed. Clothes everywhere. Mattress on the floor and sliced up. Box spring open and gaping.

"Someone was looking for something." Morris waved a hand around the room. "And they focused in here."

"No kidding." Gil couldn't stop the sarcasm from slipping out.

"We're going to need her to tell us if anything is missing." Morris frowned at the mess. "Although I'm not sure if she can even tell."

"She doesn't want to come in here."

"I'm not saying she needs to come in now." Morris put his hands on his hips and jerked his head toward the body. "Don't want her to have this in her head."

At least they were on the same page.

Gil gave the mirror over her dresser a long glance. The picture he'd noticed that first night was still there. Should he tell her he had the same one in his office? Or wait for her to find it. Maybe he'd wait.

He scanned the rest of the room, and his eyes caught on a decorative box tipped on its side on her nightstand. Letters and note cards spilled from it.

He knew those letters.

He'd written those letters.

His fingers twitched as he fought the compulsion to scoop the letters from the floor and settle them safely back where they belonged.

"You okay, man?"

Gil turned his attention away from the mess and to Zane. "No. Let's get this done."

They picked their way through the path forensics had made and went into Ivy's bathroom. Makeup and all the random stuff women somehow managed to find time to use every day lay everywhere. "What was this guy looking for? Did he think she'd keep something in her makeup bag?"

Ivy legitimately might put the house on the market when she saw this. It might be easier to sell the whole house "as is" than to restore order.

They walked back through the bedroom and paused in the hallway. Morris waved a hand in the direction of the other rooms. "As far as we can tell, nothing was touched in the rest of the house."

Luke and Zane shared a look, and Gil was pretty sure he knew what they were thinking. "Either he had a specific reason to expect her to have something hidden in her private space, or he found whatever he was looking for."

Zane paced away from them and into Ivy's living area, and they followed him. "What if he wasn't alone. There's a lot of chaos in that room. It could have been done by one man with some time or by a team moving quickly. Either way, someone besides our dead guy was here."

Luke jerked his head toward the bedroom. "That's a lot of blood in there. Any thoughts on what killed him?"

"The only obvious injury is the slice through his neck." Morris didn't elaborate. A knife used in the right—or from the victim's point of view, wrong—place could sever both the jugular and the carotid. Their bad guy turned victim would have bled out quickly.

"The victim's a big guy. It would take either some serious strength or someone very fast to get a knife to the guy's neck. And there are no obvious signs of struggle." Gil closed his eyes and forced his mind to recreate Ivy's bedroom. "The damage looks intentional. Sliced mattress and box spring. Clearly done with a knife. Maybe even done with the murder weapon. Drawers pulled open and dumped. But the lamps are intact. The mirror isn't cracked. Whatever happened in that room was methodical. Not the actions of a tall guy flailing around trying to keep someone from slicing his neck."

Morris nodded. "The ME may be able to give us something preliminary, but we won't get an autopsy report until tomorrow, and even then, we won't get tox back for at least a week or two. DNA takes longer. There was no ID on the guy, and his fingertips have all been sliced off."

That explained the extra blood around the victim's hands.

"He's a redhead—red hair on his arms, red eyelashes—and the size matches. He could be the big guy who stunned Ivy."

"If so, someone's cleaning house." Zane looked out the front windows. "I stand by what I said earlier today. She can't be left alone, Gil. Not for a second."

"I agree."

"But will she agree?" Zane pressed.

"I don't anticipate much argument. Especially not now."

"Then get her out of here." Morris jabbed a finger toward the door. "I'll get you a picture of our dead guy. Preferably one that disguises the neck."

Gil dreaded this for Ivy. "She won't be able to place him as one of her kidnappers. He had on a mask."

"But she might recognize him from somewhere else."

"True." Morris was right. At least the photo would be better than the in-person experience they'd all been subjected to.

"What are you waiting for?" Morris asked.

"She wanted me to pack her a bag."

"Forensics won't be done until tomorrow. And they don't want us to remove anything from her room."

"She's going to need a few things, Morris. It's not like she keeps a bag packed in her car."

"Got it covered." Luke held his phone for Gil to see the text thread. He scanned it. Faith and Tessa would get enough for Ivy to get through the night. If forensics released her room, they'd come over in the morning and get clothes. If that wasn't possible, they'd take her shopping.

They wrapped up everything with Morris, and Gil headed to the car. His legs felt like he'd strapped fifty-pound weights to each ankle. He didn't want to be the one to give her the bad news. He walked to the driver's side and climbed in.

She turned to him, and he reached for her hand. "I will tell you everything, but can you wait until we get to my house?"

In the light from the overhead lights in the car, he watched with no small amount of fascination as she studied him. He didn't know what she was looking for or what she found, but she nodded.

"Let's get you home."

—28—

GIL DIDN'T TALK to her on the drive to his house. He held her hand, his thumb sweeping across the back of hers in a soothing circle. He'd climbed into his car without the bag she requested and without giving her any information.

And she was okay with that.

No. That wasn't quite right. She wasn't okay with what was happening. What she was okay with was the way Gil was treating her. He was asking, not assuming. And he'd given her no reason not to trust him. If he wanted to wait until they were at his house to explain, then she'd trust him.

He pulled into his garage, parked, and escorted her inside. He disabled his security system, cleared the house, then reset the security system before he returned to where she waited in the kitchen.

He opened the refrigerator, stared into its depths for a moment, then pulled back and cocked his head at her. "How do you feel about sandwiches?"

She slid onto a stool. "As a rule, I'm pro-sandwich as long as there's no mustard involved. Or lettuce."

Gil faked being distraught at her declaration, and while he made her sandwich, he hassled her about her refusal to try any of the six—yes, six—varieties of mustard he had on hand. Twenty minutes later, she'd had a sandwich, a few chips, and a slice of pie.

What she didn't have was a clue about what was going on.

She told Gil about the pitch. They laughed about the guys who had tried to get Tessa and Ivy to go out with them tonight and speculated about the situation with Tessa and Zane while Gil cleaned up the kitchen. He tossed a towel over the handle of the dishwasher, leaned a hip against the counter, and studied her for a long moment. "Are you ready?"

She knew what he was asking. "Yes."

He told her, and while she had no previous experience with discovering murdered men in her bedroom, she was pretty sure he didn't sugarcoat anything. When he was done, he leaned across the counter and reached for her hands, taking extra care to avoid the splints on her right hand. "Talk to me, Buttercup."

"Someone was killed in my bedroom today. I don't know what to do with that."

"That's understandable."

"I don't know anyone who could kill someone like that."

Gil pinched his lips together, and he didn't have to say a word for her to know what he was thinking.

"Ab did not kill him!"

"I didn't say he did."

"You think he did."

"I think he's capable of it. He's a Marine. He's physically powerful. He's in Raleigh when he's normally in Georgia. He—"

"He loves me."

That shut him up. But not for long. "I know. It's obvious."

"I don't love him."

"I believe you, but I'm not sure you've convinced him." He studied their hands for a beat. "Does he know your alarm code?"

How could she explain this? "He might."

Gil's response was a quirked eyebrow, and she had a strong urge to trace it with her finger. *Focus, Ivy. Focus.*

"I'm not naive. I don't use my birthdate or anything. The numbers appear to be random."

"But they aren't?"

"No." She tried to pull her hand from his, but he held on. "It's the date of my dad's accident." She couldn't look at him. "Does that make me morbid? Maybe it does. But it's a significant date for me. I don't know that I would have become what I am today if I hadn't watched him learn how to do life without his arm. I might have been some type of engineer or entrepreneur, but I don't think I would have been so driven to succeed, and I'm not sure this field would have been on my radar. For me, that was a pivotal day. It's the day everything changed."

"That makes complete sense."

She couldn't look at him. He said it made sense, but that didn't mean he didn't think she was bonkers.

Gil released her hands and tipped her chin up. "Hey." He didn't continue until she lifted her eyes and met his gaze. "It makes sense." He emphasized each word. "It is not weird." He didn't let go of her chin until she nodded.

She studied the counter. "I've used some variation of that date for years. My garage, my ATM pin. Anytime I have to provide a four-digit code, I use it. Sometimes in the American order, sometimes in the European. But it's the same few numbers. If you already know I do that, it wouldn't be hard to guess the code."

"I'm assuming Ab knew your code from when you dated. And he knew the significance of the numbers and might consider the possibility that you would use the same numbers in a different order. Is that accurate?"

"Yes."

"Who else would know?"

"It's unlikely, but Mom might."

"I thought you didn't talk to your mom anymore?"

"I don't. After I went to college and she went to jail, I only went home to see Dad."

"So what makes you think she might know?"

She traced the patterns in the grain of the countertop. "That summer, after we got home but before I left for college, she took a thousand dollars from my checking account."

"Your mom stole from you."

"Yeah."

"I didn't know it was her at the time. Three separate withdrawals were made over the space of a week at three different ATMs. All three happened while I was working in Dad's shop on my prototype. I didn't know the money was missing until my bank statement came the first week of classes. I knew I hadn't withdrawn the money."

Ivy fought the urge to hide her face in her hands. "There's never been any doubt in my mind that Mom took my ATM card and stole that money. She knew my PIN because we'd talked about it when I set up the account. At the time I never considered that she would steal from her own daughter."

The familiar stab of grief pierced her chest. "By the time I realized what she'd done, my world had already imploded. Mom was in jail. She had hurt so many people. *I* had hurt so many people. I couldn't deal with it. So I never mentioned it to Dad or anyone else."

"I wish you could have told me."

Gil said it with no rancor. There was nothing but sympathy in his expression, and it soothed a place that had burned with shame every time she'd thought of it.

"Me too. I was so stupid."

"You were sixteen."

She couldn't accept the absolution so easily. "I wasn't your average sixteen-year-old."

That earned her a grin. "You've never been average at anything. But you were in uncharted territory. It's understandable that you got lost."

What could she say to that? She had been lost. Then Gil had found her. And if she had anything to do with it, she would never be lost again.

Gil pulled the conversation back to the earlier topic. "Did you change your PIN after you found out what she'd done?"

"I did. But I just reversed the numbers."

"If your mom knew your pin, she could have shared it with her husband."

Ivy appreciated that he didn't call him her stepdad.

"I'm investigating both of them. And the lawyers. And Ab. Everyone who knows the details of the money. Preston's whereabouts are currently unknown. Your mom is on a cruise in the Caribbean. When we find them, we'll be questioning them both."

Ivy pressed the heels of her palms into her temples. "I almost can't believe this is happening."

Gil walked around the counter and stood beside her. He reached for her hands and pulled her to her feet. Then he wrapped her arms around his waist and slid his arms around her. She couldn't stop herself from snuggling into his embrace. "I'm not going to let anyone hurt you." His lips moved against her hair. "Or take your business from you. Or steal your money."

She wanted to believe that. But she didn't. "You can't promise that."

"Fine. I promise I'll do everything in my power to stop anything

241

bad from happening. I'll keep digging until I figure out who is behind this. I won't stop until you're safe. I can promise you that."

She heard the sincerity and could feel the intensity that fueled his words.

"Now, a few more things."

She braced her mind and her body. He must have sensed her tension, because one hand swept up and down her spine in a slow, calming rhythm. "Your bedroom is currently off-limits, so I couldn't pack a bag. Tessa and Faith are going to show up here soon. They said they would take care of it, and I trust them to do that."

"Okay."

"You can't go home tonight. That's not me saying that. That's the Raleigh PD. I'm sure you could argue with Morris, but I don't think he would listen."

"He doesn't seem the type, no."

"If you want to stay here, you can."

"I want to stay here."

"Are you sure? Tessa has a secure apartment. Faith's home isn't as secure, but we can get units to patrol, same as here. Luke and Zane have a spare bedroom and lots of firepower. You'd be safe there too."

She leaned back so she could see his face. He relaxed his hold enough for her to move a few inches, but not enough for her to pull out of his arms. "Do you want me to go to Tessa's?"

"No."

"Do you want me to stay with Luke and Zane?"

"No." Gil's response was quick and gruff. "I want you to stay here with me."

"Good. Because I want to stay here."

His lips quirked. "Good."

She stared at him. He stared back. He was holding her. Maybe, if she tried, she could talk herself into the idea that everything Gil had done for her since Friday night had been because of their childhood friendship and not because of anything else. If she put forth a reasonable amount of effort, she could even make a case that there'd been nothing romantic about any of their interactions, although she doubted that case would stand up to a trial of her peers, because she had to admit that every woman she knew would take one look at the events of the past few days and tell her Gil was into her. And more than as a friend, what with the hand-holding and protectiveness and general presence he'd been in her life.

But this? There was no mistaking this. This wasn't a friendly hug. This wasn't a brotherly embrace. Gil was affectionate, especially with Emily, but he didn't hold Emily like this. This was a declaration. It should be awkward. Shouldn't it? But nothing had ever been awkward with Gil, at least not until she made it that way.

He'd been her friend. Her childhood crush. Her first love. Her first kiss. He'd held her this way lots of times that summer when life stretched out before them beautiful and full of promise.

But for him to hold her this way. Now. After all that had happened and all they'd been through. This was a grown-up statement. If she pulled away, he would let her go. She knew it. And she probably should pull away. Things were moving fast.

If they started this and it ended badly, it would crush her. Because this was Gil. *Her* Gil. Nothing could be casual between them. After over a decade of her missing him, he was standing right here. They should take this slowly and make sure they didn't mess anything up. And if she explained it right, he would understand that she wasn't telling him no. Just suggesting they be careful with what they had.

Gil moved one hand and brushed her hair behind her ear. He

— 29 —

GIL HOPED HIS DISAPPOINTMENT wasn't evident on his face as he released Ivy and walked back around the counter. He needed to put some space between them. He'd done it again. Pushed too hard, too fast, and at the worst possible time. He rolled his neck from one side to the other and opened the fridge. "Faith and Tessa should be here soon, and then you can get some rest."

"Right."

Was it his imagination, or did Ivy sound disappointed? He grabbed a bottle of water and pointed it toward her. "Want one?"

She shook her head.

He twisted the cap and took a long drink. When he lowered the bottle, Ivy had walked around the counter and was coming straight to him.

"Gil." She whispered his name. Then she leaned into him, and her body moved against him as she came up on her toes, and her face came closer.

It was like watching a movie when the action is slowed, and the viewer sees it frame by frame. He saw her coming toward him, and then her lips brushed his. She didn't step back, but her body moved down as she came off her toes. Her face was now several inches lower than it had been a moment before, her cheeks flamed, and she blinked several times in a way that made Gil almost certain she was as surprised as he was. She tipped her chin down so all he could see was the top of her head. With one arm, he kept her close. He pulled his other arm around and rested his hand on the side of her neck. "Ivy." He didn't recognize his own voice. It was rough and low, and he cleared his throat but didn't try to speak again. He kissed the top of her head, and then she responded to the light pressure he placed on her chin and lifted her face to his.

What he saw on her face now gave him hope. There was still some fear, maybe some questions. But there was also the emotion he'd been looking for, and he knew he wasn't imagining it.

He bent his head to hers and her eyes fluttered closed, even as her face moved toward him.

The doorbell chimed, followed by two quick, then three longer knocks.

Ivy leapt away from him, her face scarlet. Eyes to the door, the floor, the wall. Everywhere but him.

What on earth?

"You'd better get that," she said. "I'm going to, uh . . ." She mumbled a few incoherent comments and all but ran into his room.

He wanted to chase after her, but he couldn't leave Tessa and Faith standing at his door. They were sitting ducks out there. He pulled in two deep breaths and went to the door.

"We hope we got everything you need." Tessa was talking before he'd even pulled the door all the way open. She stepped inside and scanned the room. "Where's Ivy?"

"Bedroom." Gil tried to keep his voice casual. "She'll be out in a minute." He hoped.

Tessa dropped her bags on the sofa.

Faith followed Tessa in. "Did she decide to stay here?"

"Yes." She had, and at this point all Gil could do was pray she didn't change her mind.

"Excellent. There's been a change of plans for tonight. Zane's still at Ivy's. Tessa's going to run me back to my house so I can get a few things. Luke and I will be back for the first shift. Luke said you would get up at four and hold down the fort until daylight. It doesn't get any of us much sleep, but maybe enough to keep functioning."

"Sounds like a plan."

Ivy emerged from his bedroom and didn't make eye contact. Was she regretting what had happened? He knew she was scared. That's why he hadn't tried to kiss her in the first place. But then she'd kissed him. Maybe it had been a rare moment of spontaneity, and once she had gotten away from him, she had a chance to remind herself of whatever she was afraid of.

Who could understand women? He had no clue what was going on with her. She wasn't sending him mixed signals. No, that would be too easy. Normal women sent mixed signals.

Ivy was sending him signals in encrypted code. She let him hold her hand, let him hug her, said yes to a date, but wasn't ready to be kissed. Then she kissed him. And she was going to let him kiss her, he was sure of it. Until Faith and Tessa showed and Ivy retreated like a turtle, back into her shell, and all signs were that she wasn't coming out anytime soon.

But she seemed to be her normal self with Tessa and Faith. They chatted about the stuff they had purchased for her, and Gil gathered they'd raided a clothing store and a pharmacy. He made himself scarce in the kitchen, but he heard Ivy exclaim over a cute dress and some leggings and a T-shirt.

"If we can't get permission for you to go into your bedroom, we'll get Morris to let someone in there tomorrow." Tessa sounded like she was ready to take Morris on if he didn't come around to her way of thinking. "We'll make sure you can get your own things, so we didn't go crazy at the store. Just the necessities for tonight."

Gil bit back a chuckle. If the number of bags they brought was them not going crazy, he'd hate to see what would happen if they let loose.

"Thanks, y'all. I can't tell you how much I appreciate this." There was a tremor in Ivy's voice, and Gil forced his feet to stay planted in the kitchen.

"You're going to be fine." Faith spoke like she was taking the oath of office. "I know it's been a long, confusing day. Don't let Gil keep you up late. Take a shower, put on these comfy jammies, and go to sleep. Luke and I will be back in an hour, and we'll keep watch."

"Thank you."

"What is it?" Tessa must have seen something from Ivy that Gil couldn't see from his position in the kitchen.

"I'm worried about him." Ivy had pitched her voice low, but he could still hear her. "Gil needs more than four hours of sleep. It's been almost a week since he's had a full night's sleep."

"He's tough, and he's used to running on inadequate sleep. If it makes you feel better, I'll mention it to Luke, and Tessa can tell Marty."

"Marty?"

"Leslie Martin. She's their office manager/den mother."

Tessa laughed at that. "True. If I tell Leslie that Gil needs sleep, she'll nag him until he takes a nap."

"Would he be able to take a nap?" Ivy asked the question with a mixture of skepticism and hope.

"Oh yeah. We keep weird hours." Tessa wasn't wrong about that. "If we're busy, it's not unusual for us to catch an hour or two of shut-eye in the middle of the day on a sofa in the office. Takes less time than going home. And, weirdly, we can sometimes rest better in the office because we know we're right there and can be back in the game immediately if we're needed."

"Thanks."

"Is something else bothering you? We don't have to hurry away. If you need to talk . . ."

"There's a dead man in my bedroom, Faith. A lot of other things are bothering me. I haven't been this overwhelmed since my dad died. If someone had told me one week ago that I would be held against my will, have a man snap my fingers with his bare hands, then burn me repeatedly, that I would be rescued by my childhood best friend, shoot the man who tortured me only for him to have a heart attack later and die . . ."

She paused for a breath but kept going immediately. "That I would be reunited with Gil and Emily, something I've both wanted and been terrified of, only to have someone try to snatch me in broad daylight out of a restaurant. Oh, and let's not forget I've now spent time in a jail and a US Secret Service office, neither of which I'd ever stepped foot in before, so that's not weird at all. Not to mention my new, er, um, well . . . that Gil would be ready to have a throw down with Ab, and my family is being investigated as possibly being behind these attacks, all of which has driven Gil into what I can only hope is not typical, overly possessive behavior, leading me to have a fight with him. A fight! Over him trying to keep me safe. Seriously? How ridiculous is that anyway?"

No one responded to her obviously rhetorical question, not that she gave them time to. "And I made him so mad, he stayed away all day until the moment a lunatic decided to open fire in a hotel lobby in an effort to kidnap me, again. All of which led to you"—at this point, she must have been indicating Tessa and Faith—"throwing me into a car with your men, who whisked me away to your apartment where they kept me safe while you sorted out the mess at the hotel. Then, when we finally agree I can go home, I can't because there's a dead man in my bedroom!"

Ivy's voice had gotten higher and higher as she spoke. She reined it in enough to modulate her pitch before she carried on. "And let's not forget the whole reason Gil and Zane walked into my house in the first place was because somehow my company deposited counterfeit money, and no one is even talking about that. If someone walked in and told me Martians had made contact and wanted me to help them design prosthetics for their alien army, I wouldn't be surprised. In fact, I would be relieved, because at least that might make some kind of weird sense. And sense is something currently in very short supply."

No one spoke. Gil eased toward the end of the counter and peeked around the corner. From his position, Ivy's back was to him. Faith and Tessa were sitting across from her, and he could see their faces. They were staring at Ivy with identical worried expressions.

Ivy's shoulders slumped, and her face fell forward into her hands. "I'm sorry. That was—"

Faith and Tessa moved fast, and they huddled around Ivy. "That was brilliant." Tessa patted Ivy's back.

"It was," Faith agreed. "We're all idiots for not being more sensitive to how much you've been through in the past few days. It's more than anyone should have to handle."

The three women sat in a huddle for a solid minute before Tessa spoke. "Are you sure you're okay here with Gil? If you've been fighting—"

"I want to be here." Ivy's words were garbled, probably because she was still leaning forward with her face in her hands. "There's nowhere else I want to be. Gil . . ."

Faith lifted her head, and her gaze locked onto Gil's. She frowned but didn't give away his presence.

"Gil's the only good thing . . ." Ivy sat up. "Not that I'm not thrilled to have gotten to know you and Luke and Zane. And of course I'm ecstatic to have reconnected with Emily. But Gil . . ."

Her voice dropped to a whisper, and Gil couldn't hear what she said next. Whatever it was, both Tessa and Faith leaned closer and gave her a hug.

Faith took charge. "Here's what we're going to do. We're going to leave you with Gil. Luke and I will be back in an hour, and when we get back, I expect you to be in bed. I promise I'll send Gil to bed immediately after we arrive. Luke and I will stay until five. That will give Gil a little bit more time to sleep. Sound good?"

Ivy nodded.

Faith stood and came to the kitchen. Gil backed up, and then he kept backing up until she cornered him against his pantry door. "What did you do?" The words were low and hissed and might have been scary if he hadn't known her well enough to see the humor in her eyes.

"None of your business." He mouthed the words.

Her eyes flared and she leaned closer. "Whatever it was, don't let her push you away. She's scared, and the timing is terrible." She pointed toward the living room. "But she has it bad for you, and if you don't make sure she knows—tonight—that you have it worse for her, you might lose your chance."

"I'm trying, and I was doing a pretty good job of it until you showed up and interrupted me."

Faith waggled her eyebrows at him. "Then I suggest you make sure you finish the job before she goes to bed. She's brilliant, but she's also a woman on the brink, and she's hitting her breaking point. You need to be the one to catch her, not shove her over the edge."

With that, Faith stomped out of the kitchen. He followed her. Tessa gave him a fierce look, and Ivy didn't look at him at all.

Gil had no idea how it was that he'd done exactly what Faith had wanted him to do, and apparently what Ivy had wanted him to do, and probably what Tessa had wanted him to do, but he was in trouble with all of them now. How did that make any sense?

— 30 —

IVY HUGGED FAITH AND TESSA, then stood back from the door as Gil watched them climb into Faith's car. He closed the door, reset the security system, and turned to her.

When she'd run from him earlier this evening, she'd closed the door of the bedroom and leaned against it until her heart rate settled. What she'd wanted to do was jump up and down and squeal. Alternately, she was considering jumping out a window and accepting her fate, because there was no way she could face him again.

She'd kissed Gil. And unless her brain was playing tricks on her, he'd been about to kiss her when Tessa and Faith showed up. It had taken her a few minutes to pull herself together and return to the living room. She'd sensed him watching her, and she knew he wasn't happy about the way she'd escaped his arms and fled.

Why had she bolted? What must he be thinking?

Gil walked past her and into the kitchen and pulled the pie plate out of the refrigerator. "I'm going to have another slice of pie. Care for one?"

His voice was casual and easy. That's how this was going to

go? He was going to pretend it hadn't happened and everything was back to normal?

"No. Thank you. It was delicious, but one slice is plenty for me."

He didn't say anything else. He didn't push her to have pie, to go to bed, to come over and kiss him. Nothing.

"It's been a long day. I think I'll get ready for bed."

He settled his piece on a small plate and turned his back to her as he returned the pie to the fridge. "Let me know if you need anything."

His head was still in the fridge. Now he was rearranging some dishes. "Thanks, Gil."

"Anything." The word was a whisper, but she'd heard it.

She didn't respond. Fifteen minutes later, she'd changed into the comfy pajamas Faith and Tessa had brought, washed her face, brushed her teeth, and given up on falling asleep. Gil had insisted she take his bedroom again since it had its own bathroom. He was sleeping in what he referred to as Emily's room and using the hall bathroom.

She paced the room. She should go out and talk to him. Tell him she was interested in him, romantically. That she'd always been interested romantically, but she was also terrified. What they had, their friendship, was precious to her. What if they messed it up? She didn't know if she could bear to lose him again.

But could she bear to be around him with this—whatever this was—between them?

No.

She couldn't.

She was going to talk to him. They were intelligent adults with years of history and a future that included each other in some form or fashion. They had to clear the air. She took a deep breath, marched to the door, and before she could talk herself out of it, yanked it open.

Gil stood two feet away, his expression one she'd never seen but knew she would never forget. She couldn't stop her forward momentum, or maybe she could have, but Gil reached for her and pulled her close. Either way, she'd barely processed that her body had slammed into his when his lips found hers.

She didn't lose track of where she was. Her brain didn't disconnect. Instead, she was hyperaware of every sensation. The softness of his lips, the way his arms had wrapped around her and how he was being careful not to bump her right shoulder, the sense that this was where she was meant to be—and she never wanted it to end.

What she did lose track of was time. It could have been thirty seconds or thirty minutes when Gil broke the kiss. He didn't release her but slid his face until his lips brushed her ear. "You had two more minutes, and then I was knocking. Or maybe breaking the door down. I'm not sure."

His voice was husky and intense. He pulled back and studied her face. "I know we need to talk, but tonight probably isn't the best time. So let me put this out there. I know you're worried about the future and what might happen if things don't work out between us. I understand that. But I'm not worried. We're going to be amazing together." He squeezed her closer. "Now, perhaps I should ask why you came out of the bedroom?"

Her cheeks burned and she tried to drop her head, but he caught her face in his hands.

"Ivy?"

"We've already done what I came out for."

At that, Gil's eyes widened, and he was laughing when he lowered his face to hers again.

Then he wasn't laughing.

And Ivy lost all track of time. Again.

THE GARAGE DOOR CREAKED OPEN, and a car pulled inside. This time, Ivy didn't race to her room but stayed in her spot curled against Gil on the sofa. She probably would have shifted and put a little bit of space between them, but Gil met her gaze. "They can let themselves in."

"Did you give them your garage code?"

"Luke has my garage code programmed into his car."

"What?"

Gil shrugged. "While I was recovering last spring, we were paranoid about parking on the street and walking across the yard. But I didn't have a bunch of extra garage door openers lying around, so they would call, I would open the garage door, and then they'd park in the driveway and come in. But it was a pain. When Luke and Zane got their cars replaced after the attack, they had the capability of holding three different garage codes, and we programmed my garage in. It's easier. And safer. You open the garage door, park in the driveway, and dash inside. You're exposed for a few seconds at most."

"Makes sense."

"I can get into their garage the same way. Faith can get in the house too. And we can all get into Faith's place. The only person whose home isn't accessible is Tessa's. But she lives in those swanky apartments with a doorman and secured elevators."

"Yeah. I saw that today. Zane has a card he scanned at the elevator and then at her door."

Luke and Faith hit the living room, and Gil launched in. "So, Zane has a keycard to Tessa's apartment?"

Faith grinned. Luke shrugged. "Apparently. And he knows how to use it. Waltzed right in like he owned the place."

"I've kept my mouth shut, but if you two"—Faith pointed to Luke and Gil—"don't find out what's going on with them, I will."

"Maybe we could get past Ivy's drama first?" Luke's suggestion didn't have much conviction behind it.

"Yeah. Last spring you said to wait until we were past that drama. And now Benjamin's coming for an interview, and you know he'll hit it off with Jacob, and he'll move here, and Zane's going to move to DC, and he and Tessa won't ever get together."

"After we get Ivy squared away." This time, Luke sounded like he meant it.

Gil nodded. "Agreed."

Faith glared at both of them. "I'm holding you to it." Then she focused on Gil, and there was a teasing gleam in her eye. "At least one part of the situation with Ivy is sorted, or I'm assuming it is, based on the cozy cuddle you have going on."

Luke nodded with mock solemnity. "She's not kidding. This is all I heard the whole way here. So, thank you." Then he turned and gave Ivy a slow smile and a wink.

After that, Faith and Luke settled in for the evening. It was the first time Ivy had seen them do this. She'd always been in bed when they arrived. Tonight, she was struck by how comfortable they were in Gil's home. Faith emptied the contents of a bag, which turned out to be an alarming combination of firearms, chocolate, and two decks of cards.

Luke went to the fridge. "Faith, baby, want some Key lime pie?"

"Sure."

Gil leaned in to Ivy and whispered, "This is why I had another slice. There probably won't be any left by morning. If you want a piece, speak now."

Luke puttered in the kitchen and returned to the living room with two large slices of pie, a cup of coffee, and a Cherry Coke.

More confirmation that Luke and Faith were regulars in Gil's home. Unlike the way Luke had been at Tessa's. But Zane had known where everything was at Tessa's and had been completely at ease. Ivy tucked this away for future consideration.

Faith made a show of checking her watch. "I hate to be the mother hen, but the whole point of us being here is so you can sleep. Ivy, I told you I expected you to be in the bed when we arrived. I'm going to give you a pass since I can see you've been putting your time to good use." She smirked. "But I also promised I would send Gil straight to bed when we arrived, and even with the extenuating circumstances of the two of you being all snuggly on the sofa and looking adorable, I don't like to break my promises. Off to bed. Both of you."

"Yes, Mom." Gil stood and pulled Ivy with him. "Good night."

Luke followed them out of the room, and Ivy was trying not to be annoyed. She wouldn't mind some privacy before she told Gil good night. "Ivy?"

"Yes?"

"I have something for you."

"What is it?"

Luke pulled a small box from the assortment of items Faith had dumped out earlier. "Gil told me you like to shoot a .38. This is Faith's personal firearm, and it's usually in her closet. She doesn't fire it often. We got it out and checked it tonight. You have a concealed carry permit, right?"

"Yes."

He handed her the box, which she now realized was a gun case. "I don't know how long it will be before we get your weapon back from the Raleigh PD. I think it would be wise if you kept this on you until things settle down."

Gil didn't comment, but she could tell from his body language that he approved. He also took the box of ammunition Luke handed him. "Good idea. Thanks."

"No problem. Get some sleep. We'll see you sometime tomorrow." Then Luke shocked her by stepping close and squeezing her good shoulder. "Sleep, Ivy. We've got this."

She nodded and hoped Luke could read the gratitude in her eyes.

Gil walked all the way into her room—well, it was his room—and set the ammunition on the nightstand, then reached for the gun case. "I know you can do this on your own, but it might be hard to load with your right hand. Do you mind if I do it?"

"That would be helpful. Thanks."

Gil made short work of loading the weapon. He placed it in the drawer of the nightstand. "Be right back." He disappeared into his bathroom, and she realized he hadn't had a chance to grab any of his toiletries or personal items before she'd escaped into his room earlier in the evening.

He was back in minutes, wearing a pair of athletic shorts and an ancient Atlanta Braves T-shirt. "Do you need anything?"

"I'm good."

He reached for her hand, and she didn't need any prodding to snuggle close to him. A tremor shuddered through her at the thought of what she currently had with him—and how fragile it was. He placed a feather-light kiss to her lips, then her nose, then her forehead, and finally, her hair, with a whispered, "Good night, Buttercup."

When Gil left the room, Ivy crawled into bed and closed her eyes. She could hear murmurs of conversation in the living room. Probably Luke hassling Gil, or maybe Faith giving him the third degree about what was going on between them.

She closed her eyes and whispered into the dark, "Father, protect them. Protect us all. And please, if you could help us figure out who's after me? That would be amazing. Especially since we seem to be spinning our wheels."

So much was on her mind and in her heart, she'd expected sleep to be elusive. But the next thing she knew, the sun was streaming in through the transom windows of Gil's room.

She'd survived another night.

Now to see if she could survive another day.

GIL SIPPED HIS COFFEE, his third cup already, and made another lap through his house. Even with all the caffeine in his system, if he sat down, he'd fall asleep. It was almost 8:00 a.m., and as much as he hated to do it, he was going to have to wake Ivy. Sooner rather than later. She needed to get to work, and so did he.

Not that he was going to give her all the gory details, but he had a game plan for today and was ready to put it into motion. Unless something came up with the body found in Ivy's bedroom, Gil was looking at a full day in the office, so he was going to do a very deep dive into Ivy's Marine, PhD, around-too-much ex, Abott Percy, and Preston Johnson, Ivy's mom's husband. And the lawyer, although that would be trickier. His gut told him the answers to Ivy's problems were held by one of those three. Which one remained to be seen.

He'd checked them all out, and there'd been no red flags. But something was there. He would go back through everything until he found it.

His bedroom door opened, and Ivy walked out dressed and ready to take on the day. He grabbed the mug he'd already prepped with her hazelnut creamer and filled it the rest of the way with coffee. "How'd you sleep?" Gil slid the mug across the counter toward her.

"Surprisingly well. I thought I'd wake up when Faith and Luke left, but I didn't hear them. I feel guilty about it." She took a taste of the coffee and her face morphed into that "first sip" expression most coffee drinkers had right after their first hit in the morning. She took another sip and slid onto the barstool. "What's on the agenda for today?"

He could get used to this. Fixing her coffee. Talking about their day. Knowing whatever it held, they would be together at the end of it. "Work. Then play."

"Hmm."

He pulled the breakfast casserole from the oven, where it had been staying warm for the past hour. He cut a generous slice and settled it on a plate already holding fresh fruit and a muffin. He grabbed a fork from the drawer and set the plate in front of her.

She'd watched him the whole time but hadn't said a word. She murmured a quiet "Thank you," bowed her head in silent blessing, then lifted the muffin and took a bite. "Delicious." One word, and she meant it. But she still didn't offer to start a conversation.

He fixed himself another slice of the breakfast casserole and settled across from her, and they ate in silence. It was comfortable enough, but something wasn't right. He couldn't take it anymore. "I'm sure they're worth about a million bucks, so I won't insult you by offering a penny." Gil had a hip to the counter and a fork full of eggs headed toward his mouth. "But I'd love to know what thoughts are zipping around in your head right now."

"You're a sweet talker, Gil Dixon."

"You deserve all the sweet in the world, Ivy Collins."

She dropped her gaze, but not before he caught the flicker of surprise, and maybe pleasure, but also maybe terror, in her eyes. Even after what had happened last night, maybe he still needed to take things slow. "Do you want more of anything? I'm going to clean this up and get us both to work."

Gil got a great view of the top of her head. "I'm good. The food is amazing. Thank you."

Ivy polished off her final bite. "Mom was never much of a cook. That's probably why I'm not either. But Preston's a good cook."

"So he has at least one redeeming quality?"

"Yeah. Not enough to explain why he married Mom."

"Wade married your mom, and you adored him."

"Mom tricked Dad. Pure and simple. He was a good man. She met him, made him think she was something she wasn't. Saw the opportunity to hitch her star to a man who could provide for her, and for me, and never looked back. Knowing what I know now? I think her marriage to Dad was her longest-running scam. I assumed her marriage to Preston was a similar scam, but now I'm not so sure."

He hadn't been expecting that. "What do you mean?"

"I was thinking this morning, with you being so sweet, making my breakfast, taking care of me, paying attention to me, treating me like I'm the most amazing creature in the known universe—"

"Because you are." Gil reached for her left hand and squeezed.

"You've made my point. This is so nice, I don't even know how to handle it. I've never had this. Never felt this . . . this . . ." She waved a hand between them.

Gil hoped he knew what she meant, but he didn't want to presume. He also didn't want to push her.

"I've dated, and I've even had a couple of longish relationships, but"—she blew out a breath—"not to put too much pressure on the situation, Gil, but no one has ever made me feel the way you do."

Gil didn't feel any pressure. None. If anything, her words made him feel lighter.

She looked up at him. "It's almost addictive. I can see how any woman who'd ever had this would want to have it again. Until Mom showed her true colors, Dad treated her like gold. Even after she left no doubt as to her motivations, he still treated her with kindness. Far more than she deserved. Now she has Preston, and from what I can tell, Preston dotes on her."

She squeezed his hand. "I've only been around them a few times, and he's so sweet it's almost gross. But now that I've had a taste of what it's like to have someone who wants to make everything easy for me, I kind of understand why Mom might have been quick to find someone new."

Gil took her coffee cup and refilled it, complete with the ridiculous amount of creamer, then slid it back to her.

Ivy took a sip and grinned at him. "Eventually you'll get tired of waiting on me hand and foot. It will happen. I'll have to pour my own coffee and make my own breakfast, and I'll be bereft." She sighed in overdone drama and wiped away fake tears.

"Tell you what. I'll let you do it on your own every now and then so you won't forget how." Gil winked at her. "But I wouldn't hold your breath on me getting tired of it."

"Totally addictive." Her expression shifted from teasing to contemplative. "I tried to warn Preston about Mom before they got married. They showed up for a visit. He was all, 'I have to meet Patty's girl' and acting like we could be one big happy family. We went to lunch. I was blunt. Asked him if he knew about Mom's past, her jail time, her crimes, her husband. He knew it all. I was actually stunned that Mom had told him. He said he didn't care and he loved her. What can you do in the face of that?"

Ivy continued, talking in a way that made Gil wonder if she even realized she was sharing her thoughts out loud. "His life hasn't been smooth and easy. He lost his job when the company he worked for went under. He took any jobs he could find but ended up having to declare bankruptcy. It wasn't until a few months before he met Mom that he found a job he enjoyed. Although, he probably doesn't realize that if he hadn't had that job, Mom wouldn't have given him a second look."

Ivy believed Preston had lost his job and declared bankruptcy?

Bankruptcy, even from years earlier, would have shown up in the background check Gil had run. But there'd been no bankruptcy.

Preston had lied to Ivy's mom.

Why?

It might be nothing. It might be something, but unrelated to what was happening to Ivy now. Either way, Preston was now at the top of Gil's list of suspects. Which meant he needed to get Ivy out the door so he could find out the truth about Preston. "I hate to ruin our tranquil morning, but we both need to get to work."

Ivy sighed. "True. My team will want the scoop on how things went yesterday." She stood. "Is it crazy that with the huge exception of finding you, I miss the way my life was this time last week?"

"It's normal to crave normal. Our brains want it. They don't have to work hard when they already know what to expect. When every day is new and different, and in your case, dangerous, it's stressful for the brain and the body."

Ivy grinned. "I didn't know you were an expert in neuroscience."

"I'm not, Ms. I-Have-So-Many-Degrees-I-Don't-Have-Enough-Wall-Space-to-Hold-Them-All."

She laughed at his joke, but she didn't move toward the bedroom.

"Did any of your classes cover the fact that we can't alter the time-space continuum and therefore should have left ten minutes ago?"

She scrunched her face at him, but there was nothing but humor in her eyes. "Fine. I'll be ready in five minutes."

Was it the way the skin wrinkled over her nose or the way her eyes squinted or maybe the way she tilted her head as she attempted to glare at him? Maybe. Maybe not. Regardless, Gil wasn't in a hurry anymore. "Ivy."

She turned around but kept walking, backward, toward his room. "What? You rush me, now you're holding me up."

He came around the counter, and she must have seen his intention because she spun and ran toward his room.

He caught her left wrist and twirled her into his arms. Her hands landed on his chest, and she was laughing. "This is not helping us get to work on time, Special Agent Dixon."

No. It wasn't. And he was fine with that. "You forgot something this morning."

Her laughter died, replaced with wide-eyed anticipation. "What did I forget?"

"This."

He leaned toward her, and she met him halfway. Their first good-morning kiss was soft and sweet and held the hope of thousands of future mornings spent together.

GIL WAS STILL THINKING about that kiss when he settled behind his desk an hour later. He opened the file he'd started on Preston. Then opened a search on his computer. Time to find out why Preston had lied to his wife about his bankruptcy.

Sylvester Electronics had made a variety of products used in industrial processes all over the world. Had there been a big advance in technology they'd failed to capitalize on?

He kept digging. Ten minutes later, he stared long and hard at his screen.

He'd gone as far as he could with the searches available to him. But he would need more before he jumped to conclusions.

He picked up the phone and waited for it to connect. "Sabrina. I need some help."

— 31 —

EVEN IF SHE'D HAD AN INFINITE NUMBER of choices, Ivy never would have imagined that "look at a photo of a dead red-head" would be on her agenda for the day.

But that's what she was doing.

Gil had driven to her office because he didn't want her to be alone when she saw the photo, which was sweet and so like Gil. Especially because she could tell he was crazy busy and needed to be back at work.

She stared at the man's face, paying close attention to his, thankfully, closed eyes.

"It could be him. The lashes match." She handed the first photo back to Gil and picked up the second, which showed nothing but what seemed to her to be a very random section of the dead man's arms.

She closed her eyes and forced herself to remember every detail she could about the man who had participated in her capture. He'd been covered from head to toe, but once he scratched at a spot on his left wrist. She refocused on the left wrist. "This also could be him. He had a scab—a thin, straight one above his watchband. There's a fine white line in this photo, and that could be from the scab coming off." She handed it to Gil. "I don't imagine that would stand up in court, but that's the best I can do."

"It's great." Gil squeezed her left elbow. "We aren't going to assume it's him, but we'll keep it as a possibility."

"That's not much."

"Sure it is. We never rule out the importance of any evidence, no matter how minor. You never know how it might come into play. On the one hand, we don't want to assume this guy is one of the men who held you, but it makes more sense that he would be than it does that someone would kill a random redhead and leave him in your bedroom."

"True." She relaxed as he removed the photos from the table.

"Sorry to interrupt your morning with this." Gil reached toward her and tucked her hair behind her ear. "And I hate it even more because I have to get back to the office and can't stay and take you to lunch and distract you until you forget those images."

"I'll be fine."

"I still wish I could stay."

"Me too. But we'll hang out tonight. I get to watch you play baseball. It will be fun."

Gil frowned. "You do realize I won't be playing."

"You call it coaching, but I see it for what it is. You get to play ball. And you love it. Some parts of childhood are too good to leave there. Baseball is that for you."

Gil leaned closer. "Not just baseball. Not anymore." He pressed a kiss to her forehead and stood. "I'll see you in a little while." He paused at the door. "By the way, Morris has a patrol unit in your parking lot and an officer in your lobby. No one goes in or out unless they use the front door, and anyone who comes in who isn't supposed to be here will be stopped."

"What?"

"You'll have to take it up with Morris."

"Oh, I'll take it up with Morris."

Gil raised both hands in mock surrender. "I'm not saying I wouldn't have asked, but I didn't have to. He already had it covered. He's gotten very attached to you."

"Who would have thought?"

"Morris is a good detective. He's crusty and cantankerous, but I think it covers a mostly good heart."

"I think if I call him on it, he'll tell me he's a selfish jerk who wants to avoid the paperwork and publicity if someone offs me."

Gil stared at her for a few long beats and then burst out laughing. "Please promise me you'll test this theory sometime today." He pulled it together. "I'm out of here. Be good."

"I try."

His laughter floated back to her, and she allowed it to settle into her soul before she shoved the image of the dead man from her mind, again, and went back to work.

She pulled off an hour of work before her phone buzzed. She hit the speaker button. "Yes?"

"Dr. Collins, Dr. Percy is here."

Ab? Ivy didn't believe he was behind any of the attacks. But that didn't stop her from texting Gil.

Ab is in my office.

There. She'd let him know. "Send him back."

Ab strode in a few moments later. "Baby, please tell me you weren't in the building when that madman opened fire." He was talking as he entered her office, and he kept moving until he was leaning over her desk.

"Lovely to see you too, Ab."

"Ivy?" Ab growled his question.

Should she tell him the truth? That she'd been inside but had been hustled to safety by a phalanx of four Secret Service agents and one FBI agent?

Why had Gil put these questions in her mind? Ab was a friend. A good friend. He'd never harm her. Or allow her to be harmed.

Ab pushed back from her desk, hands on his hips. "It's not a difficult question, Ivy. Either you were or you weren't."

"Excuse me? I am not one of your grad students, Dr. Percy."

She held his eyes and refused to back down. Ab's jaw tightened and his nostrils flared. When he spoke, it was with a refined and formal tone. "Fine. Dr. Collins, would you be so kind as to tell me where you were when the shooting started?"

"Since you asked so nicely, I'd be happy to." She went with the truth, but not the whole truth. "I was on my way out when the shooting began. Our group hopped in a cab and vacated the area."

Relief washed over Ab, and he sank into the nearest chair. "I heard what happened, and I knew it was close. All I could think of was you lying facedown on the floor while someone made threats and fired a weapon."

"They caught the guy." She used the same tone she would use to speak to a lost child. "And no one was injured."

"Doesn't mean the people who lived through it weren't traumatized."

He had a point. The argument could be made that she'd been traumatized. She'd barely had time to process what was happening before she was safely away from the chaos. She didn't think Ab would appreciate her telling him that Gil had her covered, so she kept it simple. "I'm good, Ab."

Ab ran a hand through his hair and shifted in his seat. "I guess I'll have to take your word for it. Although I have to tell you, the heavy police presence in your lobby and parking lot doesn't give me a great deal of confidence in your honesty."

"It's a precaution." She didn't suspect Ab of any wrongdoing, but based on his reaction to the shooter at the hotel, there was no way she was going to mention the body in her bedroom. He'd lose his mind.

Ab stood and pulled his keys from his pocket. "I have to get on the road. I'd love to stay and make you give away all your secrets, but I'm trying to get home before the weather completely locks everything down. I just couldn't leave town without seeing for myself that you were all right. And, of course, I wanted to say goodbye."

He was such a good guy. She stood and walked around her desk. When she reached him, she gave him a quick side hug. "Thanks. It's been great to see you this week."

He gave her a look that sent a ripple of pain through her chest. "Not quite like old times." He pulled her in for another hug. This one longer and probably not quite appropriate.

Okay. Not appropriate at all, given that if Gil walked in, she would jump about ten feet away from Ab. She disengaged and stepped back, trying to be gentle physically and emotionally. One look at his face told her she hadn't succeeded in either.

"If things don't work out with your Secret Service agent, give me a call. I'll always be here for you. Always."

"Ab."

"Sorry." He didn't look sorry at all. Resigned, maybe. Sorry? No. "But I couldn't leave without saying that either."

What was she supposed to say? She couldn't give him any sort of hope. Gil or no Gil, Ab wasn't the one for her. She'd moved on from him long ago.

He let the silence hang for a few seconds past awkward, but then he turned to the door. "Stay out of trouble and stay in touch."

This she could respond to honestly. "I'll do my best. On both counts."

He gave her a small salute, and then was gone.

She sat at her desk and pressed the heels of her hands into her temples, then took several slow, even breaths. When she opened her eyes, she picked up her phone and sent another text to Gil.

> Ab's gone. I haven't been abducted or threatened. Thought you should know.

Three dots blinked back at her.

Good. You okay?

> Yes.

Did he make a pass at you?

How did he know?

> Yes. But I didn't even try to catch it.

Can't say I'm sorry he's gone, but I am sorry if he made you uncomfortable.

> I'm okay. What time is the game tonight?

6 p.m., if we don't get rained out. League says we're going to try to get the game in, so you'll probably want to dress for wet weather.

> Any word on whether or not I have access to my closet?

Sorry. No. I'll call Morris.

> Thanks.

Anything. Anytime.

Ivy stared at those two words, and the heaviness in her chest eased. She would always care about Ab and always want him to be happy. But she'd found the one she'd been looking for.

Her office phone rang and pulled her back to her work and her obligations. For the next few hours, she operated in the headspace she most enjoyed. Total focus. Minimal distraction. Items checked off her to-do list. Successful interactions. It was all-consuming in the best possible way.

At three, she checked her phone and found a message from Tessa.

Tessa apologized for failing to convince Morris to allow Ivy to reenter her home, but the good news was that the crime scene techs had agreed to allow Tessa to enter, under their supervision, and she was prepared to get whatever Ivy needed. Ivy gave her a detailed list, and Tessa promised to make it happen.

An hour later, Tessa arrived at the office, stayed long enough to drop off the bags, told her she'd see her later, and then was gone.

Tessa was friendly. Compassionate. Thoughtful. She wasn't the type to drop a week's worth of clothes and toiletries at the office and not even ask if she'd gotten everything.

Alarm bells blared in Ivy's brain. She picked up her phone and called Gil.

No answer.

No need to panic. He was working. He had an important job. If she was going to be with him, she needed to get used to the idea that he wouldn't be instantaneously accessible every time she had the impulse to speak with him.

But . . . he hadn't responded to her initial text about Ab showing up. That should have generated an acknowledgment of some type.

She tried to focus on a spreadsheet. A couple of minutes later, she gave up and grabbed her phone.

> Hey. Everything good?

That didn't sound too desperate. Did it?

She tried to refocus on the spreadsheet, but when her phone dinged three minutes later, she reached for it so fast, she bobbled the phone and dropped it on the floor.

> Hope you're having a good day. I'll pick you up
> at 5. Is that okay?

Ugh. That was . . . annoyingly normal.

Shake it off, Ivy. She'd turned into a paranoid skeptic. She tried to work, but the flow she'd found earlier in the day was gone.

Something was wrong. She didn't know what was happening, but she couldn't deny the tension in her shoulders, the queasiness in her stomach, and the heaviness in her arms—all physical manifestations of the anxiety weighing on her mind.

She dropped her head back and looked at the ceiling. "Lord, this is getting old." She shouldn't complain. She'd been held and cared for throughout this entire nightmare. She could see God's hand and love in everything. She should be able to trust him with this. She wanted to. But still . . .

She pulled in a breath. "Lord, help my unbelief. And whatever Gil Dixon is up to right now, protect him. Because I don't think I can bear to lose him again."

HE WAS DONE. Nothing he'd tried had worked. This shouldn't have been difficult. But he had her now. Ivy had a weakness, he knew it, and he was going to exploit it.

He should have done it this way from the beginning. Force her hand, take the money, disappear.

But he'd held out hope. Hope that he could have it all.

And it burned him up that he couldn't.

The only bright side was there was no way anyone could trace this back to him. He'd spent years covering his tracks, and he'd kept his hands clean over the past few weeks. There was no DNA, no fingerprints, not even a footprint that could be used to place him anywhere near her. Once the money was in the account, he'd move it immediately, and then he'd be gone.

He'd even planned that to throw them off the scent. He didn't care if they figured it out eventually, as long as he had time to get away. It wasn't hard to hide in this big, bad world—at least not when you were willing to walk away from your former life completely.

And he was.

A few quick searches had given him the information he needed to make this happen tonight. A few hours of reconnaissance, a couple of phone calls, and he'd be ready.

Ivy Collins would give him everything he wanted.

He had no doubt.

—32—

HUNTING DOWN CRIMINALS on television was so much more interesting than it was in real life.

Gil spun his chair away from his computer, stood, and worked through the three-minute stretching routine he tried to do several times a day but usually only remembered to do a few times a week. At most.

His phone rang, and the caller ID told him he needed to answer. "Dixon."

"Got an ID on the body."

That had been a lot faster than expected. "Care to share?"

"Oliver Teague. Thirty-four."

"He looked twenty-five. Tops."

"Yeah, but he's a ginger. They always look younger than they are." Morris said this like it personally offended him. "Family in South Georgia reported him missing a week ago. I'll send you what I have. Check your email."

Morris disconnected the call without any additional commentary.

Gil checked his email and then plugged in all known facts about Oliver Teague into the spreadsheet he'd created earlier that morning. He was looking for connections, and he was going to find them.

An hour later, he was once again staring at his computer. After this morning, he'd put Preston at the top of his suspect list. But Oliver Teague had served in the Marines with Abott Percy. Then he wound up very dead in Ivy's bedroom. There was no way that could be a coincidence.

He called Morris.

Luke and Zane walked up while he was talking to Morris. He held up one finger and indicated that they should hang on, so they hovered in the entry to his cubicle. When he disconnected the call, Luke said, "Update. You first."

Gil filled them in on what he'd found out earlier about Preston. And what he'd learned about Oliver Teague and Abott Percy.

"I still don't see it." Luke tapped his closed fist along the edge of the cubicle. "This Abott guy is in love with her."

"Or his desire to keep Ivy close could be an act." Zane loved to dissect a motive. "By being nice and charming, he can stay close to her, keep tabs, etc."

"Maybe." Gil could see a few holes in both of their theories.

"But what about her mom's new husband? Where does he fit into this?" Luke asked.

"I've got Sabrina digging into it," Gil said. "She knows how to run searches that will get us what we need without crossing any legal lines."

"He doesn't have to be in North Carolina to be masterminding the attacks. In fact"—Zane's eyes lit as he shared his idea—"it would be genius to stay in Oregon. Makes it a lot harder to pin anything on him if he can claim he was on the opposite side of the country when she was taken."

"True. But"—Luke dragged out the word—"the more people

he involves, the more likely someone will get caught. And besides, what's the endgame?"

"It has to be the money." Gil had a lot of questions, but this wasn't one of them. "There's no other explanation. There may be other motives we can't see. Maybe Preston hates Ivy because she doesn't like him. Maybe Ab never loved Ivy at all. Or maybe he loves her so much that he's got some twisted notion that if he destroys her, she'll come crawling back to him. And of course he'll be magnanimous and welcome her back with open arms. Or maybe it's pure jealousy. I don't know."

"Because it might not be any of them." Gil didn't hold back his glare, and Luke took a step back. "Don't shoot the messenger."

"Have you made any progress on the attorney?"

"I punted what I had over to Faith after lunch."

"Luke Powell? Coordinating with the FBI? What's next? You going to marry an agent?"

Luke didn't acknowledge the teasing remark. "She has a contact at the Oregon State Bar from some case she worked early in her career. She volunteered, and it freed me to help Zane go over the security footage from the fundraiser where the counterfeit cash came from."

"Tell me you found something."

"We found something."

They moved to the conference room, and Zane mirrored his screen so the video appeared on the large television mounted on the wall across from the framed photos of the president, secretary of homeland security, and the director of the Secret Service.

Luke pointed to the screen. "I talked to Tina, Ivy's assistant, yesterday. She did a lot of the planning for the fundraiser, and she was a big help." He grabbed a laser pointer from the cabinet under the TV, and the red dot traced a line from the parking lot into the road. "They had booths all over the parking lot. Ivy managed to sweet-talk the city into allowing her to block off the street, and they set up a few carnival rides. I had someone in DC take a look, and they estimated between seven hundred and a thousand unique individuals were on the property throughout the course of the day."

Great.

"The good news is that money changed hands in only three locations." Luke pointed to a booth at one end of the parking lot, then another booth on the opposite side. Finally, he hovered over a large tent. "The actual flow of cash is hard to see at the ticket booths. The cameras are for the security of the building and weren't placed the way we would have needed them for the security of the event." Luke hovered over the tent. "Except for inside the food tent. There were two extra cameras installed, both near the vendors."

"Why?" Gil asked.

"Tina spent thirty minutes explaining it, but I'll give you the short version. Last year, near the end of the night, a food fight broke out when some students from UNC, NC State, and Duke got into an argument. They destroyed the tent and made a huge mess. Ivy"—Luke grinned at Zane, then turned the grin to Gil—"and, brother, this does not bode well for you, but Ivy lost her mind."

"I'm well aware that she has a temper."

"She waded into the melee, took tons of photos with her phone, and told them they either pulled it together and cleaned up the mess, or she'd give the photos to the press and their pictures would be splashed all over the news."

"Smart play."

"It was, especially since a reporter was still on scene, and she grabbed the photojournalist who was with her and had them come in and take video."

"The guilty parties cleaned up the mess, but Ivy insisted on cameras in the tent this year."

"This was the short version of the story?"

"It was. If you don't like it, we can ask Tina to give you the long version the next time you see her."

"I'll pass."

Zane froze the video. A teenage boy, maybe fifteen or sixteen, handed two twenties to the attendant at the counter. "Most people paid with credit cards, which made it easier for us to narrow it down."

Gil wasn't fooled. Nothing was easy about narrowing this down. There were hundreds of people in and out of that tent. Luke and Zane had spent days staring at tiny clips of video and then looking for any sort of pattern they could find.

"We've narrowed it down to five suspects, but this is our number one."

"He's a kid."

"Yep."

"What makes you think it's him?"

Zane forwarded the video frame by frame. The boy reached into one of his pockets and pulled out cash. The bills were folded in half, and based on their thickness, Gil would estimate he had a hundred dollars in that stack. He'd probably already spent the rest of the cash before he was captured on video.

The counterfeit bills that had been deposited had been folded at one time. But not folded individually. The crease was wide, like the entire stack of bills had been folded in half. What he was seeing now matched the evidence.

Zane stopped the video. "We're going to go back through and look for him, but we've already caught one shot of him coming in. He walked in, and he was alone."

"Thanks, guys." The words were inadequate, but he meant them.

"It doesn't answer the question of why, or where he got the bills, but at surface level, it looks like a kid who got some cash and spent it." Luke traced the kid's face with the pointer. "He certainly doesn't look like a threat to national security."

Gil agreed. "He doesn't look nervous either. If he'd had any idea he was spending counterfeit currency, he might have been a bit more fidgety."

Luke slid the laser pointer back into the drawer. "Do you need us at the ball field tonight? If you don't, we're going to stay here and work on the video."

"No. I'm going to ask Ivy to consider going home with Faith or Tessa until I'm done with the game."

Zane crossed his hands behind his head and leaned back in his seat. "Didn't that get you into big trouble before?"

Gil couldn't argue. It had. "I didn't ask before. I assumed. I'm done assuming. But given what I've uncovered about Preston and Abott Percy, I—"

"You don't want her anywhere near your kids, do you?" Zane, as usual, didn't miss a thing.

"I can't risk it. Whoever is responsible, they hired someone to snatch her out of a hotel filled with innocent people—mostly men and women, but several children were there. The fields will be crawling with families tonight. Even if his focus is on Ivy, I can't presume the presence of children would be a deterrent."

"You're not wrong."

"I've got Sabrina doing a deeper dive on Preston. Tessa is on Abott. You have the video. Faith has the lawyers. And I've done the unthinkable."

Zane exchanged a look with Luke and asked, "Which is?"

"Put in a call to my mom."

"Why?" Luke sounded confused. Understandably so. Calling your mom for advice on a case? It just wasn't done.

"I need her take on Ivy's mom."

Zane grimaced. "Based on what you've told us, I bet that will be a fun conversation. What do you think your mom will be able to tell you about Ivy's mom that you don't already know?"

"I don't know of anything specific. When Patricia stole from us that summer, and Mom and Dad pressed charges, they didn't keep it a secret or hide anything from us. Emily and I were seventeen. Plenty old enough to understand what was happening. And, of course, with Ivy in the mix, our parents thought it was crucial that everything be aboveboard. They had no idea Ivy would disappear. Mom and Dad both expected Ivy to be part of our family, and they thought the best way to handle it was to be transparent about what they were doing, the legal action they were taking against Patricia, etcetera."

"But you think they held something back?" Zane stretched one leg, then another, then stood.

"Not intentionally. No. I think they told us everything. But, again, I was seventeen. I was in love with Ivy and she'd disappeared. Her mom had stolen priceless heirlooms and was going to jail, and my baseball career had ended before it started. I wasn't in a good place mentally or emotionally. So my memories of that time, and of what happened, could be skewed, or even completely wrong. I want to get Mom's take on Patricia Draper Collins Johnson. Obviously, I know she was a thief. But would she be willing to put Ivy's life at risk to get to that money?"

"That would be rough." Sometimes Luke had a real knack for understatement.

"Agreed. We've all met hardened criminals who were devoted

family men. They wouldn't think twice about ordering a hit, but then they'd go home and read bedtime stories to their kids at night. I've always assumed Patricia fell into that category. Not a great mom, but not a mom who would endanger her daughter. With everything that's happened, I need to rethink that."

The fact that neither Zane nor Luke contradicted him was a testament to what they'd all experienced in their careers—never assume innocence. That was for the courts. Not for the investigators.

"I'm surprised your mom didn't take your call." Luke frowned. "I would think she'd be dying to talk to you."

She was. She'd texted him ten times over the past few days. He wasn't avoiding her. Much. But she wanted details about Ivy, and he wasn't prepared to give her what she wanted. The details were his. His and Ivy's. No one else's.

"I called this morning during her planning period. But she texted that she doesn't have a free period today because she's helping cover another teacher's classroom so the woman can go to the dentist. She'll call when school lets out."

Zane rapped his knuckles on the table. "I always love talking to Mama Dixon. Have her call you on your office line and put it on speakerphone so Luke and I can chime in. We'll make sure she knows about Buttercup and how she's stolen her little Gilly's heart."

Zane was a dead man.

"Princess Buttercup. I guess that means it's 'wuv, twu wuv.'" Luke's imitation of the line from *The Princess Bride* was spot on. So was Gil's aim.

The marker hit Luke right in the sternum. "Ow." Luke rubbed the spot as he retrieved the marker and tossed it onto the table. Gil put the marker back in its assigned location. Leslie had a strict dry-erase marker policy, and no one broke the conference room rules.

"Come on." Zane nodded toward Luke. "Let's go find out why Gil's girl got a bunch of funny money. Maybe if we solve that piece of the puzzle, he'll invite us to the wedding."

Both men were out of sight by the time Luke landed his parting shot. "At the rate Gil's going, he'll be married before I am."

"Don't give me any ideas," Gil yelled out the door. Their laughter was the only response.

GIL LEFT HIS OFFICE AT 4:45.

His normal attire for a ball game was shorts, T-shirt, tennis shoes, and a ball cap.

For tonight, he'd gone with hiking pants and added a waterproof rain jacket. If anyone asked, he'd say it was because of the impending deluge. A hurricane was expected to approach the coast but stay offshore. Damage should be minimal, but it promised to dump a lot of rain over eastern North Carolina for the next few days.

He didn't make a habit of dressing for the weather. But he also didn't make a habit of being armed when he was around the kids. Tonight would be an exception. He had an ankle holster and a shoulder holster, and both were in use. His pants had lots of pockets, and he'd put them to good use as well.

He'd considered skipping the game tonight, but despite a promising start to the morning, every lead he thought he'd found had gone cold.

Now he was going to do the next hardest thing.

Try to convince Ivy to stay away.

He drove to her office, and she appeared in the door before

he even got the car in park. She was at the car by the time he got her door open, and then she slid into the passenger seat with a murmured, "Thanks."

As soon as he returned to his seat, she asked, "What's happened?"

— 33 —

GIL DIDN'T ANSWER IVY'S QUESTION. He didn't even speak until he'd put the car in drive and exited the parking lot.

"Spit it out, Gil."

"Nothing specific, but I need to ask you something."

"Then ask."

"Would you consider going to Tessa's this evening while I'm at the game?" Gil didn't give her a chance to respond. "I talked to Morris, and you still can't go home."

The last thing she wanted to do was spend an evening at home, alone. She wasn't sure if she'd ever want to spend another evening in that house alone. Or even not alone. But she did want to spend the evening with Gil. She'd been looking forward to it all day. It took effort, but she didn't say any of that out loud.

If Gil noticed that she wasn't arguing or agreeing with him, he gave no indication of it. "I want you to come to the game with me. I want to introduce you to my kids and see you sitting in the dugout." He looked left and right before turning left onto the highway. He didn't look at her but kept his focus on the road. A road that led directly to Tessa's apartment. "I don't know what's happening, Ivy. I don't know why you're being targeted or who's behind it. You could be completely safe, or you could be in immediate danger. I don't want to leave you alone tonight. I don't want to leave you, period. But . . ."

She should probably tell him that she appreciated him asking, and since the whole dead-body-in-the-bedroom situation, she'd had a change of heart about insisting on spending any time out from under the protective care of Gil or his fellow agents.

She should probably mention how she'd been tense and edgy all afternoon and how she kind of missed the way people had popped in earlier in the week.

She didn't, and Gil continued on in his quest to convince her to do something she was already prepared to do. "The thing is, I can't put my kids at risk. Or their families. I keep thinking that whoever is after you hired a guy to kidnap you in broad daylight out of a crowd of people. Twice. That makes me think a family oriented event like a ball game wouldn't stop them. In fact, they might think it would be an ideal scenario."

"You're right."

"I realize I overstepped before. I promise I'm not trying to handle you or micromanage your life. But Tessa will be home anyway, her apartment complex is secure, and it's unlikely that whoever is after you knows where she lives. They might be able to follow you, or her, to the building, but once inside, which apartment? It makes it pointless for anyone to come after you there."

"Okay."

"I realize this may make me seem indecisive, and I don't want you to think I'm going back on my word. If you want to go to the game, I can take you. But I hope— Wait." Gil's expression shifted from earnest to confused. "You're good with going to Tessa's?"

"I am."

"Why?"

"You made a convincing argument. I would never put anyone at risk, much less children. I don't love the idea of putting Tessa at risk, but she's equipped to handle it, and my guess is that if I go to Tessa's, Zane will show up at some point claiming to be there to keep me company but will actually be there to back Tessa up should everything go sideways."

Gil pulled the car into a gas station and parked in a spot along the edge.

"What are we doing?"

"We're stopping."

"Why?"

"Because kissing while driving is dangerous."

Gil drew her toward him and kissed her long enough to get them a few honks from passing motorists but not long enough to suit her. Not even close. He kissed her eyelids, then her nose, then settled back into his seat and smoothly pulled them back into traffic.

"As I was saying"—Ivy cleared her throat and attempted to regain the ability to form rational thoughts—"I'm fine with going to Tessa's. But I *was* looking forward to this evening, so you'll have to issue a rain check."

"Done." He grabbed her hand and squeezed. "We have one or two games a week from now until the end of October. You'll have ample opportunity to cash that in."

They would, wouldn't they? They had time to get to know each other as adults. Time to fall in love, although she had a funny feeling that was going to be a very short trip. Time to fit into each other's lives the way they used to—but better. How had this happened? Not that she was complaining.

"I'm looking forward to it. And thank you for keeping me in the loop and asking for my opinion. Although I did notice you were already headed to Tessa's before I agreed to anything, so . . ."

Gil chuckled. "I was counting on being able to talk you into it. I was prepared to beg."

"That might have been fun."

"For you, maybe."

They settled into comfortable silence, her hand snuggled in his, and for a few moments she forgot about all the chaos in her world. Then Gil parked in a parking space near the entrance and pulled her fingers to his lips. "Wait for me to open your door, please. I would love it if you always allowed me to open doors, close doors, hold chairs, jackets, and, when absolutely necessary, your purse."

He *was* a sweet talker.

"But right now, I need you to do this because I don't want you exposed any longer than necessary."

He was also brutally honest. Her little bubble of calm burst, and she couldn't find any words. Her mind whirled, her insides churned, her respirations lost their mind and alternated between quick and almost nonexistent.

"Be right back." Gil exited the car, jogged to her door, opened it, and even though his hurry was palpable, he was still gentle as he reached for her arm, dodging burns and bandages, and helped her out of her seat. As soon as she gained her feet, he swung her into his side, wrapping her injured right arm behind his back.

She wasn't so foggy that she didn't recognize this for what it was. Until now, he'd always kept her left side to him in an effort to keep from hurting her. But right now, with his right hand resting on the weapon at his waist, she knew he'd sacrificed her comfort in order to keep his right hand and arm free.

He hustled them into Tessa's building, flashed his badge, and spoke to the doorman, who sent them to the elevator and up to Tessa's floor without delay.

Tessa was waiting at her door when they stepped into her hall. "Get in here before Gil loses his mind."

They followed her inside and were met with the unmistakable aroma of chocolate chip cookies. Ivy's mouth watered, and even though her world was completely bonkers, she relaxed. Who didn't love a hot cookie straight from the oven? Gil held her close and stopped inside the door.

"I'll give you some privacy." Tessa didn't turn around but kept walking to her kitchen. "I'll lock up after you leave, Gil."

"Tessa makes great cookies. You're in for a treat."

"I doubt she's better than you."

"We'll call it a tie. These cookies are fabulous. A friend in Carrington gave us the recipe. Chocolate chips, toffee, you're going to love them." His expression shifted. "Do you have your weapon in your purse?"

She nodded.

"Good. Keep your purse with you, even here in the apartment. Take it into the kitchen, take it into the bathroom. I'm not kidding."

"Okay."

"I wouldn't leave if I didn't think you'd be completely safe while I'm gone. But if things go sideways, do whatever Tessa tells you to do. She'll take care of you."

"Got it." He didn't move to go. "Gil, the sooner you leave, the sooner you get back."

"True." He pressed a kiss to her forehead. "Be good, Buttercup."
He looked over her shoulder. "I'm leaving, Tessa."

Tessa came around the corner and followed him to the door,
locking it and setting her security system before she turned back
to Ivy. "Cookies first. Then supper. Then I'll give you all the dirt
I can think of on Gil."

Excellent.

-34-

BASEBALL ALWAYS MADE THINGS BETTER.

Tez, a fourth grader who still had a little bit of a Gerber baby face behind his round glasses, had pitched a great game. Carlos had settled in to the catcher's position like he'd been born to do it. He played first base last season and had lots of practice catching balls coming at him from all directions. Elementary ball players weren't known for their accuracy.

Gil glanced at Max, the shortstop. His gray pants were filthy on the front from the diving catch he'd made in the third inning, and on the back from sliding into second, then third, and then home in the fourth inning. The kid was a beast at the bat and a vacuum in the infield. Any ball hit near him wound up in his glove.

His gaze flicked to his outfielders, who were bored stiff but trying to stay engaged, then rolled back through the infield. Then out to the families and friends in the stands and seated around the fence. This was a great team. Good kids, good families. No drama in the stands, no one yelling at their kids for dropping balls or striking out.

It had been a perfect night for baseball, but for the first time, possibly ever, Gil couldn't wait to get off the field. The rain had held off most of the evening, but fat drops were randomly pocking the infield dirt and pinging off the dugout's tin roof. This was the last at-bat, and unless the opposing team found a miracle in their lineup, the game would end with a victory for his team.

He scanned the stands. Moms, dads, grandparents, and siblings were on their feet scrambling for rain jackets and umbrellas.

He saw a few unfamiliar faces, but that was to be expected. All eight fourth-grade teams in this league were playing at this complex tonight. And they'd only played tonight's opponent once before. It was impossible to know if the new faces were friends and parents who hadn't been able to make it last time or if they were there looking for Ivy.

Gil had a firm "no phone in the dugout" rule for himself. He wanted the kids to know they had his complete attention. He wanted to show them it was important to focus fully without the distractions of texts and notifications.

He'd broken that rule tonight. Every inning. Sabrina hadn't gotten back to him before he left the office, but she'd promised an update as soon as she had one.

Tessa had sent three messages. All of them pictures of food. None of them of Ivy. But at least he knew she was okay and that he had authentic butter chicken and naan waiting for him after the game. And he would need it, because he was in for a long night. Gil had sent a fellow Secret Service agent on what he'd expected to be a wild-goose chase this afternoon, but based on the email sitting in his inbox, he may have hit the jackpot. He'd only scanned the message, but the company Preston had worked for until it shuttered its doors was the same company that designed, produced, and installed the safety mechanism that failed and cost Wade Collins his arm.

Gil hadn't thought it would be possible, but Preston had leap-frogged over Abott and now held the top spot again as his lead suspect.

A crack of lightning split the air. Followed fast by thunder that rumbled in Gil's chest.

Ball game.

The sky opened, and the smattering of raindrops turned into a downpour.

Pandemonium.

Parents from all four baseball games opened umbrellas. The players ran off the field to the dugout, got shouted congratulations on a great game, and then dashed to their parents. The walkways were filled as everyone hustled to the parking lot and to the safety of their minivans and SUVs.

Gil helped his fellow coaches gather the water bottles, sweat-shirts, and batting gloves left behind and then set out at a slow jog to his car. He stripped off his now-soaked rain jacket and tossed it into the back seat, hopped in the car, cranked the engine, and waited for the parking lot to clear.

On a typical weeknight, the games ended at slightly different times, with each coach taking more or less time after the game to talk to their team. This meant the departure from the ballpark was staggered and congestion was minimal.

Not tonight. The parking lot was gridlocked. No one was moving, and they wouldn't for a while.

He texted Ivy that he'd get there soon.

He texted Emily to tell her, again, not to come down this week-end. He could barely keep Ivy alive. He didn't need to add Emily to the list of people he was responsible for.

His phone rang. "Hey, Mom."

"I'm sorry to be quick, Gil. I want to hear all about Ivy and what's going on with her and you and everything. I want to hear about your game tonight, and I would love to hear about that shooting at the hotel you're going to try to tell me you had nothing to do with, but I saw the news footage and recognized you from the back, so don't even try to tell me you weren't there."

Gil didn't try to squeeze in a word. Best to let Mom continue to vent.

"But, lucky for you, unlucky for me, I have a meeting in a few minutes with a young single mom who is studying for her GED, so we don't have enough time for me to get into all of that. What did you need to know?"

"First, I love you, Mom."

"Oh, Gil." She didn't sound frustrated anymore. "I love you too."

"Second, I need to know if there was anything about Patricia that worried you that you didn't share with us. I know it's been a long time ago, Mom, and I promise I'll explain this later."

"Define worry."

Gil blew out a breath. His mom loved words, literature, and stories, and she had a vocabulary to rival the dictionary. She insisted that choosing the correct word mattered. He didn't have time to get into the finer points of worry versus anxiety versus concern. "Mom, was there anything about Patricia that would make you think that if she had a shot at millions of dollars, it would be enough to tempt her to hurt Ivy?"

Her gasp was no surprise. He'd been blunt, and he'd done it on purpose.

"Anyone could be tempted by millions." Also no surprise. His mom could see all sides to any situation. "But I'm sorry to say that I believe Patricia would be particularly susceptible."

That *was* a surprise.

"Don't misunderstand me. Patricia loved Ivy in her own way, but not in a selfless way. She was always scheming how to make some cash, and if it meant Ivy had to be left alone or, say, with us, Patricia was fine with that. She cared more about getting more than she did about Ivy."

"Can you elaborate?"

"I don't like this, Gil. I've always been honest with you about Patricia, but this feels like gossip and slander."

"Mom, I respect that about you. Always have. But that's not what this is. I'm not asking you to bad-mouth Patricia. I'm asking you to tell me everything you can because I need to know for an investigation. It's important, or I wouldn't ask."

She blew out a long sigh, then asked, "How much do you remember about Ivy's situation when you were kids?"

"That she spent the night with us a lot when Patricia worked. And sometimes you sent home food."

"I've been thinking about all this since Emily called and told me everything she learned last weekend. The more I ponder it, I wonder if I handled it correctly."

"What do you mean?"

"I don't think you realize how difficult their situation was when we met them. They had nothing. At the time, we believed Patricia was doing everything she could, but it was never enough. We helped financially, with food, and of course by taking care of Ivy. We were very invested in their success, so as you can imagine, your dad and I weren't happy about the move to Oregon. I lost sleep worrying about Ivy and how long it would take before Patricia fell in love with some wretch who wanted her to work while he partied and drank all her money."

"She did that?"

"Several times when y'all were little. To her credit, she kept those men away from Ivy, but she and I had words more than once over her relationship choices. She loved Ivy, but not enough to make better choices in men. At least not until Wade Collins showed up. I didn't believe he was as good as she claimed, but he won me over at the wedding."

"I didn't know you went to their wedding."

"That's because I never told you. We could barely afford for me to go alone. There was no way we could afford for you and Emily to join me, but I wanted to see for myself that everything was okay. I was thrilled to see how happy they seemed. Wade was a good provider, and it was obvious he doted on Patricia and Ivy. And they returned the affection. At least Ivy did."

"Patricia didn't?"

"I have no proof, but in my opinion, what she felt for Wade wasn't love. She liked him. She liked having a roof over her head, money in the bank, enough to eat, and more. She was willing to be the doting wife if she got that, plus someone to help with Ivy, in the mix. I know the sun rises and sets with Ivy for you, sweetheart, but Ivy was a challenging child."

"She was not."

His mom's chuckle floated through the speaker. "She was wonderful. But precocious. So smart that at five years old she thought she knew better than any adult. Her mind is fascinating. Oh, I cannot wait to talk to her again."

Gil could see where this was going. He kept his voice gentle but serious. "Focus, Mom."

She let out a small huff but didn't argue. "Right. As Ivy got older, her abilities, her memory, her intelligence required a great deal of activity and stimulation to keep her occupied. Ivy was a reader, just like you and Emily, but when she finished a book, she wanted to build replicas of the castles or weapons or airplanes that had been in the story. She could be quite persistent, and she nearly drove Patricia nuts. Wade, with his engineering background, was a perfect fit for Ivy's ever-increasing need for mental challenges."

"So you think she married him so her life would be easier on every level."

"It's harsh, but yes. I do. And if I'd had any doubt, the way she handled him losing his arm only confirmed it. I'm afraid from all I knew of the situation, Patricia didn't give Wade any of the love and support that a devoted spouse would give. I always suspected that the only reason she stayed with him was because she anticipated a big settlement to come from it."

Gil forced himself not to interrupt. Was it possible that more people knew about the money than Ivy realized?

"Of course, the settlement, whatever it was, was never disclosed. And even during her trial, the details weren't mentioned. I assumed it wasn't that much money. If she'd had access to millions, there's no way she would have left him. Or gone on the crime spree she went on with Ivy that summer. She would have become the perfect doting wife if it meant she had that kind of cash."

His mom gave a little hum that he knew indicated her extreme disapproval. "Patricia is a deeply selfish soul, Gil. It isn't kind to say it, but it's true. I couldn't imagine why Wade stayed with her after her jail sentence, but I had hoped she would repent and recognize what kind of man she had. But there's no reason to suspect she ever did. Especially with what Emily told me. Remarrying so soon after Wade's death? It doesn't look good, but at the same time, it isn't surprising. Patricia never could stand not to have a man in her life."

A door opened, then closed, and some muffled greetings were exchanged. "Sorry, honey. I have to go. Bottom line, if you're asking me about the woman I knew? I would say it's possible, and I would look very carefully at the new husband. Patricia may have found a good one with Wade Collins, but her track record with men would make me question her decision-making."

"Thanks, Mom."

"I want a full debrief this weekend. And as soon as she's safe, you're bringing Ivy home to me, is that clear?"

"Yes, ma'am."

"Love you, baby."

"Love you too, Mom."

The parking lot had finally cleared, but the exit road was still backed up. Gil connected his phone to the charger, backed out of his space, and eased into traffic.

His phone rang again. He didn't recognize the number, and normally he'd let it go to voice mail, but under the circumstances, dealing with a spam phone call was less worrisome than missing something important. "Dixon."

"Gil. Rex Jones. Tez's dad." The man sounded like something was wrong.

"Yeah, Rex. Everything okay?"

"I can't believe this, but in the rain, Stacey and I got our wires crossed. I thought she had Tez. She thought I had him." Gil whipped his car out of the line and turned around, heading back to the parking lot while Rex continued. "We got home, and neither of us have Tez."

"I'm still at the complex. I'm headed back to the field. I'll check all the fields, bathrooms, covered areas. Anywhere he might go to stay dry. I sat in the parking lot for a while and didn't see him, so he may be hunkered down."

"I'm headed back too." Rex was frantic.

"Be careful. It will take you longer if you have a wreck. I'll call you back."

Gil parked sideways across three spaces. He grabbed his phone and rain jacket, mainly to cover up his weapons, and ran for the ball fields.

Ten minutes later, he stood at the gate with Rex as they waited for the police. Gil had teamed up with some of the facility workers, and they'd searched every space a nine-year-old could hide.

There was nothing for it but to accept that Tez was missing. There was still a possibility he'd caught a ride with a teammate, but Gil didn't hold out much hope for that. Any of the parents would have made sure Tez's family knew he was safe.

He texted Ivy.

> Situation at the ballpark. Missing kid. Not sure when I'll be there. Will update when I can.

Then he did the only thing he could do, and the one thing he knew for sure mattered in this moment. He prayed.

— 35 —

IVY HAD CURLED HERSELF into the same chair she'd been in the day before. Tessa had poured short glasses of milk, perfect for dunking, and set the plate of cookies on the ottoman between them.

She told Ivy story after story about Gil, Luke, and Zane. She made them sound more like the Three Amigos than the Three Musketeers, always up to some kind of prank or mischief. But Ivy sensed the respect and camaraderie Tessa felt toward all three men. She was funny, she could tell a great story, she knew how to deliver a punch line, and like most class clowns, she was lonely and scared and hurting.

Ivy could see it, and she suspected Faith did too. She wasn't sure if any of the guys realized how deeply Tessa experienced everything. She'd been around Tessa quite a bit over the past few days, but it was only tonight that she'd realized that Tessa didn't feel sad, she plummeted into despair. She didn't feel happy, she catapulted into delight. She didn't love Jesus, she, quite literally, adored him.

Tessa brimmed with intense emotion, but depending on the circumstances, she hid it behind a professional demeanor or a dazzling smile or witty banter. Was it because she worked in a male-dominated profession and didn't believe emotion had any place in law enforcement? Or was it because she had always kept that part of herself locked down?

All Ivy could do at this point was hope she could stick around long enough to find out. Her phone buzzed, and she pulled it from her back pocket. She read the text, then read it out loud to Tessa.

Tessa went from friendly and funny to ferocious and frightening. She grabbed her own phone, shot from the couch, and moved across the living room. She tapped a few buttons on the phone, then flipped on a police scanner before returning to the sofa. Not to sit but to pace behind it with the phone to her ear. "Hey. Gil says there's a situation with a missing kid at the ballpark and he's running late. You heard anything?"

A male voice, maybe Zane's, responded in the negative.

Ivy's phone buzzed again, and she reached for it, her focus on Tessa's conversation. She glanced at the phone.

Then she stared at it.

Then she screamed. "No!"

Tessa whirled on her. "What?"

Ivy couldn't answer. All she could do was hand her the phone, then drop to her knees. "Christ, have mercy." She murmured the words over and over. Ancient. True. And never had she needed Jesus to be merciful the way she did now.

"Christ, have mercy." Tessa's voice joined hers once—holy, passionate, pleading. Then her tone shifted. Ivy only caught pieces of what Tessa was saying to Zane.

"Call Gil . . . Get Morris in the loop . . . Jacob can . . ." A longer pause. "The office?" and finally, "Sabrina."

At Sabrina's name, Ivy focused in time to hear, "Yes. We'll wait." Then, "I said we'd wait. We'll wait." The last said with a hefty amount of attitude. Tessa slid her phone into her back pocket but kept Ivy's and set it on the ottoman before she slid to her knees in front of it. Tessa bowed her head, and while she didn't speak out loud, Ivy saw her lips moving and knew she was praying.

Ivy joined her. As she knelt by the ottoman, the photo captured her attention. It was a boy. Young. Baseball uniform. Dirty, like he'd finished a game. Wet like he'd been caught in the rain. Behind his round glasses, his eyes were closed and there were no obvious injuries.

But the text made it clear that he was in big trouble.

> Tez would love to see his family again. Stay by your phone. We'll be in touch.

Ivy didn't try to stop the tears that rolled down her face. "Please. I'll give up anything. Please don't let him harm that child. Please." At some point, her prayer devolved into wordless petition. God could make sense of it. He would have to. She was officially out of ideas.

GIL STARED AT THE PHOTO Tessa had forwarded from Ivy's phone.

Tez. Probably drugged. Snatched in the postgame chaos. An incoming call notification popped onto his screen, and Gil walked twenty-five feet away from Rex Jones, who was on the phone with Tez's mom.

"Dixon."

Luke didn't bother with a greeting. "Morris talked to Jacob. We're setting up a command center at our office. It's secure, less chaotic than the PD, and we can control the situation better from there. Morris will be at the PD, and he'll be our liaison. Also, Sabrina Fleming-Campbell is on her way from Carrington, and she's bringing friends."

"Good."

"Leslie is on her way to the office. Faith is en route. She's also bringing friends."

"I don't want the FBI to—"

"They aren't." Gil heard the "not yet" even though Luke hadn't said it. "Faith's boss has been made aware of the situation and has offered their full cooperation and support, but Zane's running this."

"I—"

"*You* are too close to this, and you know it. Zane runs it. We all work it with him. You hold it together and you get to participate. You don't, Zane will hand you and Ivy over to Morris and let him sit on you until this is over. None of us wants that."

No matter how he worked it, he couldn't find a way around Luke's plan.

"Gil. You with me? And clue in—the only correct answer here is yes, and you need to give it to me and mean it."

"Fine. Yes."

"I know you hate it, but you made the right call. Now, Tessa has Ivy at her apartment. Morris is sending uniforms to escort them here. She promised Zane she'd wait for the escort."

Ivy must be completely freaking out by now.

"We'll get him back. I doubt they want to hurt that boy."

"What makes you say that?"

"Because he's asleep and unmarked. If they were going to hurt him, or even wanted to cause more stress to the family, we'd get hysterical video. And because so far, the only person they've physically harmed has been Ivy or the people who were used to threaten her. No one else. I'm not a profiler, but kidnapping a kid? That's a desperation play."

"I pray you're right."

"We're all praying, brother. Hard."

Gil disconnected, then jogged back to Rex Jones. "Rex, I need you to go with the officers. They'll take your statement, get you home, and wait with you. I would stay with you, but I can do more for Tez if I work the case."

Rex nodded, but Gil had no idea if anything he'd said penetrated. Gil ran to his car, flashed his badge several times to get out of the parking lot and onto the main road, then floored it. His government-issued sedan wasn't known for speed, but that didn't stop him from pushing the car to the limit.

Fifteen minutes later, he was running into the Secret Service building, his bag at his side. He didn't pause to speak to anyone, but went straight to their locker room, stripped off his soaked clothes, and left them in a pile sure to make Leslie's head spin if she found it before he could do something with it. Dry and still in bare feet, he left the locker room at a jog and went straight to the conference room.

Tessa was there. So was Ivy. Her eyes were red and puffy, but they were dry. She must have been crying earlier, but now she looked ready to annihilate anything and anyone that stood between her and rescuing Tez.

Gil went straight to the chair beside her but didn't have time to do anything more than squeeze her knee, because the second he landed in the seat, Zane spoke.

"Here's what we know. Tez Jones was taken during the confusion after the ball game tonight. A photo of Tez was sent to Ivy indicating that Tez would be returned when Ivy does what she's told. They indicated that further instructions would be forthcoming."

Zane glanced at the computer and then back at the group around the conference table. A group, Gil noted, that included a man and a woman who he recognized were FBI agents, but he couldn't remember their names. They must be the friends that came with Faith. Faith's boss, Dale, had also joined the party, and they were all seated at the end of the table with Jacob.

Faith had her omnipresent iPad and Apple pencil. Luke stood by the whiteboard, an array of dry-erase markers at the ready. Zane nodded toward Gil. "We also know Tez Jones is nine years old, throws a wicked curveball for a fourth grader, and pitched a great game tonight. He's the son of Rex and Stacey Jones."

He tossed a glance at Jacob and Dale. "What happened tonight could have happened to anyone. They have four kids, they split up in the rain, they each assumed the other had Tez. As soon as they discovered Tez wasn't with them, they called Gil and a host of others. They're at their home. Morris has Raleigh PD officers with them. Raleigh PD will follow all their standard protocols for a kidnapping, but in this room, we know what's going on. Rex and Stacey are not suspects."

Gil squeezed Ivy's knee again. He hated that she would hear it this way, but saving Tez was more important than sparing her feelings. "That photo was sent to Ivy. Based on our investigation into her situation, we have a few suspects and, as of today, some insight into motive."

— 36 —

IVY COULDN'T LOOK AWAY FROM GIL. He knew what was going on? He had a suspect and a motive? Had he been keeping this from her? What was happening?

"I found something questionable this morning and made a phone call to an agent I know in Iowa," Gil said. "We trained together a few years ago, and he's solid. He was happy to do some digging."

From the corner of her eye, she saw Zane shift from one foot to the other. "And?"

Gil dropped his head and addressed her, not the group. "I'm sorry, Buttercup. But Preston worked for Sylvester Industries until they . . ."

He continued speaking. His mouth was moving, but she wasn't hearing it. Sylvester Industries? That couldn't be.

"He said he'd worked in textiles someplace on the East Coast that closed when they moved production to their plant in Mexico."

Gil's sympathetic expression told her he understood, but he was confident in his findings.

"Would one of you please explain the significance of Sylvester Industries?" Zane wasn't harsh, but he wasn't messing around either. His question hit like someone had doused her in cold water, and it yanked Ivy from the edge of the abyss she was teetering over. There would be time later to analyze what had happened and how. Right now, they needed to stop Preston and make sure Tez spent tonight in his bed.

"Sylvester Industries was a family owned company out of Iowa. They designed safety systems for industrial-sized equipment used in manufacturing facilities. Specifically, they wrote and designed the system that was supposed to prevent the accident that took my dad's arm."

Ivy glanced around the table and saw understanding dawn on the faces of everyone except the three people who'd come in with Faith. She looked at them. "My dad lost his arm in an industrial accident. Sylvester Industries was found to be negligent. They knew there was a design flaw, and they didn't do anything to fix it. My dad didn't want the money, but he did want the faulty equipment fixed so no one else would be in danger of experiencing what he went through."

Gil's arm slid around her shoulders, but she kept her attention on the strangers. "The judge wanted to make a point. He awarded my dad millions. Sylvester Industries not only couldn't take the financial hit from the lawsuit, but they also couldn't afford the repairs that were needed to their equipment, which was installed in manufacturing facilities all over the country. They went out of business. Several hundred people lost their jobs. Dad always felt bad about that." She twisted toward Gil. "Do you think Preston's behind this? And if he is, is my mom in on it?"

"I have no way to know if your mom is in on it or not."

It still hurt, that her mom loved her in an "I'm glad you exist, but you cramp my style" way, but if she found out that her mom was part of this? She had no idea what she would do with that. She certainly couldn't deal with it right now. "You didn't answer my first question."

"He's at the top of my list."

Ivy's phone chimed, and everyone in the room turned to her. Gil pulled her close. "Do you want me to look first?"

She couldn't bear it if anything was wrong with Tez. She handed the phone to Gil. He opened the message, and she felt his weird combination of relief and tension.

"They want Ivy to go to Hedera tonight. They want her in her office and on her computer within the hour. They'll send further instructions to her private email account."

"I can access that email from anywhere. Why do I need to be in my office?"

Gil didn't answer but continued reading. "They're claiming Tez is fine, and if you do this quickly, he'll be left in a safe location and we can get him back."

"I'll do it."

"There's no guarantee they'll spare Tez. You could lose the money, lose the ability to help thousands of people live better lives, and still not get Tez back."

"I appreciate the risk, but if they want to ruin my business, they can. If they want the money, they can have it. Whatever they want. I can't not try." Ivy swiped at a rogue tear. She would not cry. "Tez is nine." An image of nine-year-old Gil flashed through her mind. "You know he's old enough that something like this will impact him for the rest of his life. We give them what they want and get him back tonight. When he's home and safe, I'll deal with the consequences. I can start over."

Zane leaned toward her, both of his hands on the table. "Ivy, I appreciate what you're willing to sacrifice—"

"What I'm *going* to do." He gave her a look, and it crawled all over her. "Zane Thacker, don't patronize me."

"Ivy, I wouldn't do that. But you need to understand that we don't have time to protect you completely. If you go to Hedera, you're risking your own life."

Before Ivy could respond, the conference room door opened and Sabrina entered. She was dressed to kill in a floor-length evening gown. She was followed by a petite Asian woman in similar attire. "Sorry it took us so long."

"SABRINA. LEIGH?"

Leigh Weston Parker grinned at Gil. "I was with Sabrina when we got the call." She said this as if that explained everything.

Sabrina didn't even say hello. "Tessa, please send me the photograph of the child."

"Sure thing." Tessa grabbed her phone.

Sabrina took in the room, and her eyes narrowed when she hit the strangers in the back. "Who are they?"

Faith answered the question. "FBI colleagues." At Sabrina's quirked eyebrow, Faith continued. "They're trustworthy."

That must have satisfied her, because she didn't ask any other questions as she pulled her laptop from her bag.

Gil caught Leigh's eye. "I'm thrilled that you're here, but how—"

"We were together when Sabrina got the call. Our husbands dropped us off here and are headed to check in with Raleigh PD to offer their services."

"No time for lengthy explanations." Sabrina pointed to Ivy as she took a seat in a chair along the wall. "You're going to ignore FBI protocol and give these people what they want."

The FBI agents sat straighter in their seats. Zane crossed his arms over his chest.

Sabrina barely spared Zane a glance before she continued. "To be more precise, we're going to make them think you have. Gil had the idea days ago, and I can implement it from here. Although, if you can get me into the Hedera offices without too much drama, that would be better."

"You cloned the system?" Ivy asked.

"I did. And assuming this is a ransomware issue and they're going to ask for the money, I wrote code we can use to handle the money transfer."

Of course she did.

"Are you Dr. Sabrina Fleming?" One of the FBI agents at the end of the table had his eyes narrowed on Sabrina.

She didn't look up from whatever she was doing on the laptop. "Yes."

He sat back in his seat and turned to the agent beside him. "Whatever she wants to do, I say do it."

"Agreed." No hesitation from the other FBI agent. Obviously Sabrina's reputation was good enough for them.

Zane cleared his throat. "Sabrina, I'm thrilled you're here and that you have a plan for protecting Ivy's business and assets. Getting into Hedera isn't going to be a problem." He filled her in on the most recent request. "But we also have to figure out what's going on with Preston—"

"I have that information as well." She pulled a flash drive from her pocket and tossed it to Gil. "You're even smarter than you are handsome."

Leigh coughed out an embarrassed laugh. "I'm not sure that was an appropriate compliment." She turned to Gil. "For what it's worth, coming from Sabrina, that's high praise."

"He doesn't care," Sabrina said. "He's focused. So am I. Plug that in."

"Yes, ma'am." Zane slid a laptop toward him, and Gil inserted the flash drive.

Sabrina, still working on the computer, asked, "Ivy, are you close to Preston?"

"No."

"Good."

"Why is that good?"

Now Sabrina looked up. "He's a con man on a mission to get your money. If you liked him, that would make it harder for you to believe the facts."

"I like facts."

Sabrina returned her focus to the screen. "You aren't going to like these. Gil, I typed up my findings on the way here. I'll clean it up if we need it for court."

Gil stared at his own screen and the report Sabrina had prepared. He scanned through the bullet list of facts, and it was worse than he'd suspected.

"Tell me." Ivy placed her hand on his arm.

"From the beginning, Preston and Abott have been my top two suspects. Abott has been open about his desire to have another shot with you. I can hardly blame him. But my concern was that he could have been using that as a ruse, to keep tabs on you so he could get what he was after—your money, and possibly your business."

"I still don't think he's behind this." Ivy gave a small shrug.

"I don't either," Gil said, "especially now. But you should prepare for the possibility that he might have been used."

Ivy's brow furrowed at that. "What?"

"We need more evidence, and we need to talk to Abott again, but I suspect Preston encouraged Abott to make an effort to win you back so he could keep tabs on you through Abott and not raise any suspicions."

Ivy frowned. "That's convoluted conjecture. What would make you think Preston has had anything to do with Abott?"

"You told me he and Preston got along. If Preston maintained contact with Abott, that could also explain how he connected with Oliver Teague. Oliver Teague and Abott served in the same unit. Preston may have used Abott to recruit Teague, and then he may have been afraid Teague would tell Abott the truth, so he killed Teague to keep him quiet."

Ivy's expression was a mixture of disbelief and horror, but she didn't push back at his assertions.

"First things first. We need to find Preston. Two of the men who held you are dead—Larry Briscoe and Oliver Teague. We have Leon Parish from the restaurant and Billy from the hotel attempt. Both of them are in police custody. But since neither of them match your description of the third man, there's a possibility he's with Preston. Although, if that guy has any sense at all, he'll get as far away from Preston as he can, because Preston is cleaning house." Gil squeezed Ivy's knee. "Regardless, when we find Preston, we can ask him about Oliver, Abott, the money, and everything else we need to know."

"I'm with you on that, but can you tell me why you're sure Preston is behind this?" Ivy's body was rigid, clearly braced for whatever Gil was going to tell her.

He had no way to make this any easier, so he plunged ahead. "Preston is his middle name. His first name is Cornelius." Ivy made a strangled sound at the mention of Cornelius. "I'm guessing the name Cornelius Johnson rings a bell?"

Her mouth tightened. "He was one of the designers of the equipment that failed. The one that cost Dad his arm."

"Yes." Gil had expected her to recognize the name. "When Sylvester Industries closed, Cornelius Johnson couldn't get another job in his field because as soon as a company would call for a reference, it was all over. He was vilified in his community to the point that he moved away. From this"—he pointed to the screen—"it looks like when he moved, he stopped going by Cornelius and started going by Preston. Based on the photographs, it looks like he had some minor plastic surgery. He doesn't look like the same guy unless you look closely."

"Which I did," Sabrina chimed in with a grim nod.

"While the motive remains cloudy, what's clear is he decided to come after your mom and you. Maybe it was some sort of twisted revenge. He wanted the money but figured if he could make your mom fall for him at the same time, it would make his payback even sweeter. Who knows?" Gil said. "With what Sabrina has given us, we'll get warrants and then we'll get the police in Oregon to raid the house and look for evidence."

"If he has a computer, he's mine." Sabrina spoke with quiet confidence, and a hint of malice.

— 37 —

IVY CAUGHT THE UNDERTONES in Sabrina's comment. Sabrina wasn't one for lavish displays of emotion, but endangered children were one of her hot buttons. Preston had made an enemy fiercer than he could have imagined. An enemy who was currently working on something with so much ferocity that it wouldn't have surprised Ivy if the computer had burst into flames.

But Sabrina wasn't ready to share what she was doing, and Ivy turned her attention back to Gil. "I don't want to sound ungrateful, but I don't care why he did it or how he did it. As long as we get Tez back unharmed, I don't even care if we catch him before he flees to Argentina, where he lives out his days sipping cocktails on a beach."

Okay. She cared, but she could deal with it. "What I want to know is, how are we going to find him? He doesn't live here. I don't have a clue where he might hide a child."

"Do you have any way to mirror my screen to that TV?" Sabrina asked no one in particular.

"Sure." Luke tossed a remote to Zane. Moments later, the TV screen filled with an image. It was Tez, but what took up most of the screen was a super close-up of his glasses.

Sabrina stood and walked to the TV. "I caught a hint of something in the reflection. I don't know why the bad guys don't watch more television, but as long as they forget about the reflective properties of glass, it will continue to make my job easier."

She looked around the room, then bounced her focus between Gil and Zane. "Do you see it?"

Ivy wasn't sure what she was supposed to be seeing. In her peripheral vision, Gil leaned toward the table. "Is that a crane?"

"I believe so." Sabrina traced an image on the screen. "I was intrigued by this." Only Sabrina would say a picture of a kidnapped child was intriguing, but then again, she volunteered a lot of hours to searching for human trafficking victims, so she had unique expertise in this area. "The abductor has made an effort to disguise the location. A hotel room gives away more than most people realize. Bedding, carpet, wall decor all can be used to determine location. This photograph has none of that. They've propped up Tez against a nondescript brick wall. There are no distinguishing features around him, so he could be almost anywhere. But the crane will help."

Ivy reached for the hope that flickered just out of her grasp. "There can't be many cranes currently in use in Raleigh."

"Probably not. But based on the timing of the abduction and the sending of the photograph, we don't need to know where all of them are, just how many are within a five-to-ten-minute drive from the ball field."

Ivy found herself abandoned on both sides as Gil and Tessa jumped to their feet and went to a tall cabinet along the side wall. Together, they pulled out a large map of Raleigh and propped it across the arms of two chairs.

The map turned out to be multiple maps in a thick stack, bound at the top. Tessa and Gil stood on either side and flipped the first map over, studied the map beneath it, then flipped that one over. This happened three times before Gil indicated a location in the left quadrant. "There's the ball field."

Faith, Luke, and Zane converged on the map and blocked her view. They pointed out various locations approximately ten minutes from the ballpark. Two minutes later, they pulled back slightly. Ivy peered in between Tessa and Faith. The map now had a large shape, hand-drawn in red ink. It wasn't a rectangle or an oval but something in between, with irregular and wavy lines.

Zane studied the photo. "Where is the crane?"

The five agents stared at the map.

Sabrina pulled her phone from her pocket, wedged herself between Luke and Faith, and snapped a photo of the map. She returned to the table and tapped the screen a few times. A male voice answered through the speaker. "Bri?"

"Would you please give the locals the picture I sent you. Tez is somewhere in that space—or to be precise, he was when the photograph was taken—and that location is somewhere near a crane." She rolled her eyes at Ivy. "Federal agents sometimes forget the local officers know exactly where that crane is."

Before anyone could respond, the voice, Ivy assumed it was Adam Campbell, came back through the speaker. "New subdivision. Million-dollar homes. Two miles from the ballpark. A crane is being used to set trusses."

"Are the houses occupied?" That question came from Tessa.

A garble of unintelligible voices rose, then faded. Then Adam was back. "They say not yet, but some are far enough along to have power and water, maybe even HVAC, but probably no appliances."

"They would be easy to get into, especially in the middle of a storm. No one around at night and the house is dry, warm. Location makes sense. Brick could be on the side of the house. Crane in view," Gil said. "Adam, is Morris around?"

"Here." The grumbly voice of Detective Morris came through the line. "We'll work on locating Tez. You get Dr. Collins covered. They'll send the details of what they want from Ivy soon, and we need to be ready."

— 38 —

FIVE MINUTES LATER, Ivy's phone buzzed on the table in front of her.

Gil stood and leaned over Ivy's shoulder. A string of individual texts and photographs filled the page.

Ticktock. Tez is going to wake up soon.

Be a shame for him to be scared.

The photo that filled the screen was of an electric hacksaw.

Be an even bigger shame for him to lose an arm.

Follow my instructions to the letter.

I'll know if you don't. And Tez will lose an arm.

I was going to let you decide which one, but after watching him pitch tonight, I think you know which arm I'll choose.

Ivy trembled, and Gil wrapped his arm around her and pulled her against his chest. "It's a risk to go to the office."

"I'm willing to take it."

Gil pressed a kiss to her temple. "Then let's go."

People around the room moved at his words.

After a brief discussion about who should stay and who should go, Gil, Ivy, Tessa, Sabrina, and Leigh huddled under umbrellas and made a mad dash to the parking lot. He and Ivy climbed into his car, and Tessa rode with the others.

Gil's phone rang. Luke was calling.

"Dixon."

"Morris sent a patrol unit to Hedera with instructions to block access to the area immediately around the building. He's not thrilled with this play, but he quit fighting it when the Carrington team volunteered to come to Hedera to be extra eyes and ears. You'll have a Raleigh PD unit and four Carrington investigators within the next ten minutes. Zane's calling Tessa to let her know."

This was all good news. "Thanks."

"Once everything is coordinated, Zane and I will leave Jacob with the FBI agents and head your way."

"Thanks."

"Be safe."

He ended the call. *Thank you, Lord. Please protect Tez. Protect Ivy. Show us the way.*

"The Carrington team?" Ivy's voice was steadier than it had been before. He reached for her hand.

"Two of them are Ryan Parker and Adam. Ryan is Leigh's husband. Not sure about the other two."

"But they don't know me."

"Sabrina knows you. That would be enough for them. For that matter, a missing kid would be enough for them. But our office has a good relationship with them too. We worked together on a case earlier this year, got to know them, and now we go diving with them."

Ivy leaned her head against the window. "How will they find Tez? They could have moved him after they took the photo."

"Raleigh SWAT has several former special forces guys, and they know their business. They'll send a small team in, quiet and careful, to check the houses until they either clear them, or locate him. Then they'll regroup and plan what to do next."

"If he's there, will they try to rescue him? Isn't that dangerous?"

"They won't try unless they're sure they can do it safely. And I wouldn't be surprised to learn that those two FBI agents sitting in our office have some hostage rescue expertise."

"Will they take over?"

"Unlikely. But if asked, they'll assist. Faith wouldn't have let them in if she didn't trust them. And if Faith thinks they can help, she can smooth the way with Morris. Which is probably why she chose to stay behind rather than come with us."

"I'm glad she stayed." She looked out the window. "The focus needs to be on Tez."

"Ivy, I know you're scared for Tez. I am too. But even when"—he refused to say *if*—"we get Tez back, no one is safe until we stop Preston. As hard as it is, we have to let the others focus on Tez while we focus on keeping you safe and blocking the plays Preston is making."

TEN MINUTES LATER, Ivy sat in her office at Hedera. Sabrina was behind her desk, fingers flying over the keyboard. Leigh was curled into the corner of a sofa, flipping through a book on anatomy.

Leigh's husband, Ryan, and Sabrina's husband, Adam, both wore expressions that could melt diamonds. Now that introductions had been made, she knew they were the investigators from Cárrington County that Morris had mentioned. They had been at a formal event raising money to combat human trafficking, which explained why the Carrington contingent was in formal attire. Ryan and Adam were huddled with Gil, Tessa, and two other Carrington investigators who Ivy had learned were a newly married couple, Gabe and Anissa Chavez.

Gil had given them the two-minute version of the story. Tessa had shown them photographs of Preston, Abott, and Tez. Then she pulled up photos of the two guys currently in jail for attempting to kidnap Ivy—Leon Parish and Billy Rice. She followed that with images of the dead guys, Oliver Teague and Larry Briscoe.

None of the Carrington team recognized any of the parties, but they studied the photos, especially the photos of Preston Johnson.

"I'd love to change and get my weapon on my hip instead of where it currently is." Anissa's voice carried from the corner. Anissa wore a glittery silver gown, and if she had a gun anywhere under that dress, she had to be extremely uncomfortable. "We'll take turns getting out of these monkey suits and then we can help maintain the perimeter."

The huddle broke. Gabe and Ryan jogged outside and returned with four bags. Ivy directed them to the offices off the main work area and pointed out the location of the restrooms, then returned to her office.

Gil stood, hands on his hips, talking with Tessa, who was glaring at the floor.

She didn't care if it was a private conversation. She walked right up to them. "Is there news? Has something happened?"

Gil shook his head. "No news. Luke, Zane, and Faith are en route."

"Is it my imagination, or are y'all being a bit overprotective?

Tez is nowhere near here. Assuming the culprit is Preston, all he wants is the money. Which he's going to get."

"No, he isn't," Sabrina said from behind Ivy's desk.

"Excuse me?"

"I've got that covered. Well, I can't take credit." Sabrina peered over the monitor. "I know you're a genius, Dr. Collins, but I hope you understand that your man is crazy smart. He's considered possibilities, made contingencies, and—"

"I didn't expect him to kidnap one of my kids," Gil cut in, his face a mask of regret.

"No one can predict everything, Special Agent Dixon." Sabrina had pulled out her professor voice. "You aren't God, so don't give yourself more credit than you deserve. What you did is going to make the ramifications of tonight's events far less costly than they might have been. Detective Morris will get Tez, and Ivy will be safe. You won't ever forget this week, the good and the bad. But eventually the bad will fade, and your memories will focus on Ivy and all the good that has come from having her in your life."

Her gaze flicked to a spot behind Gil. Ivy turned, and Adam Campbell—now in khakis, a polo shirt, and a light jacket that didn't hide the weapon and badge on his belt—went straight to his wife and planted a kiss on the top of her head. He said something too low for Ivy to catch and left the room.

Sabrina's expression was tender, and she watched until Adam was out of sight, then turned back to Gil. "Trust me on that."

The dreamy expression lifted, and Sabrina's normal intensity returned. "Dr. Collins, your system has been completely cloned and backed up to remote servers. We could be wrong, but we're assuming the email will come with ransomware attached. You'll have to open the attachment to get the directions, which will launch the ransomware. You won't lose anything, and it will only take me a couple of days to rebuild—less if you'll allow me to bring in a few of my grad students. This will make a fabulous real-world case study for them."

Ivy sagged against Gil. She knew Sabrina could do stuff like this, but knowing it was done and her systems were safe? Her relief was intense.

"Maybe we should hold off on the grad students until we're sure everything is resolved." Gil squeezed her elbow, and Ivy wasn't quite sure if he was talking to her, Sabrina, or both.

"Point taken." Sabrina frowned at the screen. "You're up, Dr. Collins."

Gil squeezed her elbow again, and her legs propelled her forward. Sabrina relinquished her position behind the computer but didn't go far, her eyes focused on the monitor.

Ivy took her seat and moved the mouse from the right side of the keyboard to the left. Her hands trembled, but she clicked on the email. The message was blank except for an attachment. *Lord, please let what Sabrina did work.* She opened the attachment.

Nothing happened.

She'd expected flashing images on the monitors and squawking from the speakers. She couldn't tear her eyes away from the normal-looking screen. "Is it happening?"

Gil knelt beside her. "Right now, malware is attaching itself to the files in your system that will enable it to lock you out. When it's finished, you'll get a message."

"How long will that take?"

"It can happen fast, but you have a secure system, with multiple firewalls."

"Will the malware be able to get around them?"

"It wouldn't have," Sabrina said, "but I created openings. It will find them."

"You seem sure."

"I didn't open the doors, but I cracked more than a few windows. Honestly, I'll be disappointed if it doesn't make it through."

"Why would you say that?" Ivy tore her eyes from the monitor to look at Sabrina.

"I want Tez back. I want you safe. But I also want the Secret Service to apprehend the bad actor who designed this malware."

"We do too." Gil stood. "It's too much to hope that Preston designed it."

"He has computer skills, but I'm not sure he can handle this." She drummed her fingers on the desk. "Although, it could happen."

Another minute passed. Then the screen changed.

Ivy read the message. Then read it again. It was on the third read that she realized her mouth was open and her eyebrows felt like they had permanently taken up residence at the top of her head.

Could this really be happening?

— 39 —

GIL STOOD BEHIND IVY and read the message once. Twice. It didn't change the third time.

The first part was expected. The system had been encrypted. The encryption code would be made available upon the transfer of $10 million, $2 million to five separate accounts.

It was the final part of the message that was the curveball no one had seen coming.

> We don't condone physical violence, so we'll be keeping the money. If you haven't figured it out already, Cornelius Preston Johnson is behind this. When you find him, put him in jail for the rest of his life with our blessings.
>
> Dr. Collins, check your personal email.

Ivy reached for her phone.

Gil snatched the phone from her hand. "Maybe we should get Sabrina's thoughts before we open an email from the people who are holding your system hostage for $10 million."

"But they aren't holding it hostage. Sabrina has it secured."

"Yes, but they don't know that." Ivy didn't argue further, and Gil waited for Sabrina to weigh in.

"Opening the email won't cause a problem. Your email is also backed up to servers. The malware is usually in the links and in the attachments. I say let's see what they sent us."

Gil handed the phone to Ivy. She held it up and waited for the facial recognition to unlock it. She opened her mail application, and then the email in question.

Her eyes met his, wide and confused. "Who are these people?"

IVY READ THE EMAIL AGAIN. There were no attachments or links. What it did have was a narrative summary of Preston's attempts to get the money—first from her mother, then from her. It detailed his involvement in her kidnapping, the torture, the hotel shooting, Oliver Teague's murder, and then Tez's kidnapping.

"What's going on?" The question came from Luke, but when Ivy looked up, she found Tessa, Luke, and Faith on the other side of her desk waiting for the answer.

"The ransomware developers are double-crossing Preston." Gil filled them in on the email's contents.

Ivy spun in her chair so she was facing Gil. "What does this mean for Tez? If there's no leverage, what will happen?"

"We'll get Tez back. We have to." If Gil had any doubts, they didn't leak into his voice. "Then we'll find Preston."

"Do you think Mom knows about it?"

"No way to know, Buttercup. Either Preston sent her on the cruise to get her out of the country so he could make his play without worrying about any interference from her, or . . ."

"She went on the cruise before he made his play so she would have plausible deniability."

"I'm sorry, but yes. Those seem like the most reasonable scenarios. Regardless, her ship will be in port tomorrow at five a.m.

She'll be met by some very nice officers who will hold her until we know what we're dealing with. This will serve two purposes. If she's innocent, it will protect her from any last-ditch efforts Preston might attempt. If she's guilty, then we'll have her in custody with no difficulty."

Ivy's emotions made no sense. Part of her was afraid for her mother. Part of her was sad. Part of her was angry at her mom for putting herself in this position. Part of her just wished her mom cared enough not to be a jerk.

Gil leaned closer and spoke in an almost whisper. "Buttercup, you may not believe me, but I really hope your mom doesn't have a clue and gets out of this with nothing worse than a broken heart and wounded pride."

His words were a cozy blanket wrapped around her soul. "Thank you." She rolled her neck in a circle, first one way, then the other. Then intentionally pulled her thoughts from her mother and back to the issue at hand. "What happens now? What do we do? There's no time frame given. No demand made."

"The money in most of your accounts could be transferred within minutes during normal business hours. The money tied up in bonds would take a few days. But none of it is going anywhere at midnight, and these guys"—Gil pointed to the screen—"know that. I doubt they expect to hear from you until you've contacted the FBI or the Secret Service, although most people start with their local sheriff's office or police department."

"So they aren't trying to hide it?"

"No. I doubt this is their first rodeo. Ten million is a steep ransom for a business the size of Hedera. The bad actors who perpetrate crimes like this want to get paid. They typically set ransoms that hurt but don't cripple a business."

"Because if the ransom destroys the business, why bother paying it? But if the ransom hurts but allows you to get back to work, it makes paying seem like the reasonable alternative."

"Exactly."

"Savvy criminals."

"Sometimes. Yes."

"Nonviolent."

"We see it as a violent crime to the business. But yes, they often see themselves as nonviolent."

Zane's phone rang, and everyone turned to where Zane paced in a small circle in the middle of her office. He didn't seem to be capable of being still. "Thacker." As he listened, his steps slowed, then stopped. He gave the okay sign to Gil. "You've got him?"

A collective sigh of relief was the only response from the room as everyone focused on Zane.

"No injuries. Not even awake?" Zane listened a few more minutes. "Great. Any sign of—?" Ivy assumed Zane had been planning to ask about Preston but had been cut off. "Best news ever. Yeah." A pause. "Here? Ivy's system has been attacked by ransomware, and they're demanding ten million dollars in exchange for the encryption key, but Dr. Campbell has that well in hand." Another pause. "But Morris, you aren't going to believe what they did."

PRESTON REPLAYED the video message on his phone.

Then he threw the phone against the wall of the hotel. It bounced off and landed on the floor. Unbroken. He couldn't even manage to break a phone when he tried.

Nothing had gone right.

He'd gone after Patricia Collins with one goal in mind. Take the money and run.

He was playing her, but then he fell in love with her. He didn't mean to. Didn't want to. But she wasn't like anyone he'd ever known, and he couldn't help it. By the time he discovered the truth, that the money was in Ivy's name and she had full control, he was already so far gone for Patricia that he convinced himself the money didn't matter.

But it ate at him. That money had ruined his life. Destroyed his career. He worked as a janitor for a large industrial complex now. A place where, fifteen years ago, he would have had an office with a computer and his hard hat perched on a cabinet that held his engineering textbooks, plus four weeks of vacation and enough money to enjoy a nice one.

Wade Collins had hardly left Patty destitute. They had more than enough to live on, but even living off a dead man's money didn't satisfy him. There had to be a way to get the money and keep Patty in the dark. He spent two years considering his options, mentally trying out various scenarios, before he landed on the perfect solution.

Ransomware.

Take Ivy's systems hostage, force her to pay the ransom to get them back, then invest the money. Wait another year or two and have a long-lost cousin die and leave him a windfall. Not too much, but enough. Patty would be thrilled, and she would never connect his windfall to the money that had been stolen from Ivy.

The plan was perfect. But Ivy still managed to mess everything up. First, she had some hotshot computer-geek friend who created an impenetrable system. And Ivy had already trained her employees in computer security to the point that every time they sent malware, it was deleted. They'd tried for weeks before he'd resorted to plan B.

He'd had to. Without Ivy paying the ransom money, he had no way to pay the malware developers, and they were getting impatient. So he'd come up with a new plan. One guaranteed to get him what he wanted. And once it was his, he would leave the country and live out his days in ease. Patty loved him, and she'd always wanted to travel. She'd be willing to go with him. He could make it work.

The fundraiser and tour of Hedera had been the perfect opportunity to get the intel he'd needed. He'd considered talking Patricia into going to see Ivy and doing the legwork himself but ultimately decided to keep his hands squeaky clean. There would be no fingerprints, no DNA, no trail back to him.

He'd given that kid the money, told him to have a great time. And the kid had come through. He'd used his phone to record every accessible inch of the Hedera property and most of the employees and had even managed to get a tiny glimpse of Ivy's office. He'd planted the listening devices as requested, not that he knew they were listening devices, but they'd done exactly what Preston had needed them to do. That part of the plan had gone off as planned. The kid didn't live in Raleigh. He lived in Tennessee but had been visiting family for the weekend. Even if they got the kid on security footage, he'd be hard to locate.

A few days later, Preston heard Ivy and her assistant talking about the painting and the scheduled downtime, and he knew that was when he would strike.

Abott had been helpful, the schmuck. So in love with Ivy. So clueless that she didn't want him and never would. So focused on her that he didn't notice he'd gotten sloppy drunk off a couple of beers, thanks to the drug Preston had slipped into his drink. He probably had no memory of the night. It hadn't been hard to get him to talk about Ivy. Abott shared all kinds of information that Preston used to try to guess her passwords. The only thing that paid off was the tidbit that the date of Wade's accident was important to Ivy. After he'd learned all he could about Ivy, they swapped war stories and details about their buddies. Abott told Preston about Teague, who had a serious gambling problem and needed cash. A man who could be convinced to look the other way if it kept him alive. From there, it hadn't been too difficult to find the people Preston needed to flesh out his plan.

But that's when everything went wrong.

He never dreamed that the night he made his play to get the money would be the night the Secret Service waltzed through Ivy's door. He'd been behind the eight ball for a week.

It was over.

By now, the police had probably located the kid. His bargaining chip was gone. His money was gone. His wife would never speak to him again, and Ivy would marry Gil Dixon and live happily ever after. She probably wouldn't even care that the money was gone as long as she had Gil back in her life.

No.

He couldn't allow it.

If he couldn't have the money, fine.

But if he was going to lose everything that mattered, Ivy would too.

— 40 —

GIL USHERED IVY into his house at 1:33 a.m.

Ivy had been amazing. She was so strong. She'd shed more than a few tears tonight, but for his part, he'd never bought into the idea that crying made someone weak.

He tucked Ivy close to his side. She was still on her feet through sheer force of will. She clutched her purse with the good fingers of her right hand. Her left she raised and brushed his cheek with it. He gave her a nudge toward his bedroom. "Go. Shower. Change. Get ready for bed. But come tell me good night so I know you didn't fall asleep in the bathroom."

She gave him a bleary nod. "Today was awful."

"Most of it was."

"Tomorrow, or, well, later today, will be awful."

"Some of it will be."

"I'll have to talk to my mom."

"You will."

Ivy swayed. Maybe he'd walk her all the way to the bathroom door.

"But Tez will be fine?"

"He will." The last report from the hospital was that Tez had been given a strong dose of a medication with highly amnesiac properties. Tez remembered pitching, and he remembered the rain starting, and that was it. He had no memory of being taken, no memory of any of the time he was kidnapped, and, unfortunately—or fortunately, depending on who you talked to—no memory of who abducted him. He also had no memory of the SWAT team that rescued him. He was currently sitting in a hospital bed with his parents and siblings surrounding him, and Gil suspected it would be a long time before he saw Tez without his entire family present.

"How worried should I be about Preston?"

"That's the ten-million-dollar question." Ivy had the energy to roll her eyes at his remark. "I'm serious. That kind of money makes people do stupid things. We don't know if he knows they played him. If he's smart, he'll walk away. Tonight. Every hour he stays nearby, he risks being caught."

"Do you think he knows that we know he was behind it?"

"Hard to say. It's possible they didn't tell him. He could be under the delusion that he can still get out of it. But there's nothing more we can do tonight. Sabrina will be back tomorrow with her grad students, and they'll have your systems up and running in no time. Then they'll analyze them, and I wouldn't be surprised if Sabrina winds up writing a scholarly paper on malware from this. Now that Tez is safe, Sabrina will be like a geek at Comic-Con."

That earned him a lip twitch but nothing more. Fair enough. Ivy was in no mood for any kind of humor. He couldn't blame her. "Go to bed, Buttercup. Tomorrow we'll sleep in a little. You'll work with Sabrina to rebuild your systems. I'll work with the FBI, the Raleigh PD, and anyone else I need to help me find Preston—and that includes the Tooth Fairy."

There it was. Finally. The tension left her body. She put her left hand around his waist, her right hand with her purse rested against his chest, and she smiled at him. A real smile that, even with her fatigue and sadness, carried a hint of teasing. "You always thought the Tooth Fairy was creepy. Would you really work with him for me?"

"For you? Anything. Always."

He pressed a kiss to her forehead. Then her nose.

GIL'S LIPS BRUSHED hers with the barest hint of contact before he pulled back.

Her disappointment must have shown on her face because he grinned at her before coming closer and speaking against her lips. "Go to sleep. We've got time."

She wanted to argue, but she couldn't. Her body ached everywhere, and sleep had never been more appealing. Still in his arms, she released his waist and twisted toward the bedroom door.

The sound of shattering glass and the alarm system blaring pierced her fog. Gil shoved her toward the bedroom. "Close the door. Call 911!"

For some reason, instead of following her, he crouched low and ran toward the living room. She froze in the doorway and watched as he snatched up a small object from the floor and hurled it out the window. The instant he released it, he was back down, then his arm whipped out again. A second object—she realized too late that it was a grenade—flew through the now-broken window.

Based on the explosions that followed, Gil had pitched them through his living room, out the shattered front windows, over the yard, and into the street. Then he dashed to the wall and hit the light switches, plunging them into darkness.

"Gil?"

"Ivy! Get in the bedroom and call 911. Then stay there. Don't walk through the house."

She kept her eyes on him as he moved along the edges of the walls and did something that silenced the alarm. In the quiet, she heard Gil whisper. "Yeah. It's Dixon. Two grenades just detonated in the street outside my house." A pause. "I know they were grenades because before they were in the street, they were in my living room." He was closer now, returning to where she waited. Another pause. "Yeah, we're good."

Gil continued to talk, but Ivy's focus was now entirely on the red dot dancing around on Gil's chest. Without pausing to scream or even think, she reached into her purse and retrieved the gun she'd been carrying for the past few days.

She followed the direction of the beam. It was coming from the back deck. She pointed the gun at the back windows and broke one of the cardinal rules of discharging a weapon.

She fired blind.

— 41 —

GIL TACKLED IVY and covered her body with his own. He pressed his lips to her ear. "What was that?"

"Red dot." She gasped the words. "Your chest."

She'd unloaded her weapon into his back windows, but Gil had no way to know if she'd hit anything. Sirens wailed far in the distance, but hopefully the knowledge that help was on the way would be enough to keep their attacker from trying again.

"We're going to stay on the floor and move into the hall. You with me?"

Ivy's head moved up and down. "Let's go." Gil rolled off Ivy but kept her hand tight in his. It took a long minute to army crawl to the hall, but once they made it, there was nothing more they could do but wait.

The sirens grew closer, then stopped and everything was quiet.

"They'll check the perimeter of the house before they come in," Gil whispered to Ivy. "Won't be long now."

She didn't speak, but her hand clenched around his and she didn't relax her grip while they waited.

The garage door opened. Then he heard a soft snick that indicated the door that led from the garage to the house had opened.

"Dixon? Ivy? Talk to me!" Morris, or someone who sounded a lot like Morris might if he were scared to death, called out.

"We're in here! We're fine." At least Gil hoped they were. He was fine, but Ivy might be worse for wear after he'd landed on her.

Then Zane's and Luke's voices carried from the yard, repeatedly, with the same basic theme of, "Let us in there now!" Morris had probably refused to allow them to come in until he'd cleared everything.

"Talk to me." Morris approached.

"Did you get the shooter?" Gil asked as he ran a hand over Ivy's cheek.

"I didn't. You did though." Morris was back to his disgruntled normal.

Ivy froze under Gil's touch. "What?"

"Found Preston laid out on the street. Two wounds."

Gil, not looking at Morris, pressed his palm against Ivy's face. "How bad?"

"Depends on your perspective. Do you want him to live?"

"Yes," Ivy answered immediately.

Morris grumbled something that sounded a lot like "women" before he said, "He'll probably pull through. One was to the leg. One hit him in the shoulder. Found a weapon on the deck. Won't be surprised to find his prints. Paramedics are hustling him to Wake Med."

He looked from Gil to Ivy then back to Gil before landing on Ivy, who was still holding the weapon in her left hand. His eyes went wide. "*You* shot him?"

"Gil threw the grenades. I fired the weapon. Do you need to arrest me?"

"Are you kidding? You'll probably get a medal. But give me that gun. I need to enter it into evidence." She handed it over and

Morris stomped off, muttering to no one in particular and practically growling at Luke, Faith, Tessa, and Zane as they rushed past him.

Gil stood and helped Ivy to her feet. "It's over, Buttercup."

OVER DIDN'T MEAN what Ivy had always thought it meant. The immediate danger was over. The repercussions of that week never would be.

Ivy and Gil had given their statements. Sometime that morning, they'd fallen into beds at Luke's house, and when Ivy woke, it was midafternoon. Voices downstairs pulled her fully into wakefulness. There were still so many questions that didn't have answers, and she needed answers.

Before she'd made it down four stairs, Gil was at her side. "Are you okay? You should sleep more."

"I'll sleep tonight. I want to know what's going on."

Gil fixed her a cup of coffee—complete with hazelnut creamer, which she was too tired to ask about—then sat beside her at the kitchen counter and alternated between twirling her hair and tracing patterns on her back as she called her mom. She might never know for sure, but her mom insisted she'd known nothing about what Preston was doing and declared that if she didn't kill Preston in the hospital, she would file for divorce due to irreconcilable differences. Ivy didn't expect any judge in the land would quibble.

Tessa, Faith, Luke, and Zane were waiting in the den when she got off the phone. "You don't have to go in there." Gil looked ready to protect her from all enemies, foreign and domestic, but she had nothing to hide. Not from these people. It was crazy, given that she'd only known them for about a week, but she needed the support and encouragement.

She and Gil settled into an oversize chair in Luke's den. It was a comfy space, and for the moment everyone was there.

"We've been talking," Luke said from where he sat with Faith. "Our first order of business will be to replace all of Gil's windows."

Gil lifted his hands. "You were right. I should have replaced them a long time ago."

"Let the record show that Gil has come to his senses." Luke made eye contact with everyone in the room.

"I'm not sure I understand," Ivy said. "Why *all* the windows?"

"Because." Luke huffed out an exasperated and overdone sigh. "New windows are double-paned. That means they save a ton on energy bills. But, more important to the current situation, while you can shoot through them, it's actually very hard to *throw a grenade* through them."

"Ah. That makes sense." Ivy could see Luke's point. She turned to Gil. "The air pocket between the glass means—"

"I know. I know." Gil rolled his eyes. "Double-paned windows everywhere. First thing."

Zane spoke up from where he paced behind the sofa. "Good. Now that we've settled that, let me bring you up to speed, then we have to get back to work."

Everyone nodded. "Preston pulled through. He's awake but not talking yet. Morris is itching to get a hold of him, but the doctors are adamant that no one can question him yet."

"Tez is fine." Tessa's smile could illuminate a small town. "I talked to his parents, who, of course, are completely freaked out, but Tez is outside playing with his brother."

Beside her, Ivy could almost see the worry leaving Gil's body. He kissed the tip of her nose, apparently unconcerned with the presence of four other people.

"I talked to Abott this morning," Luke said. "He's a wreck.

Worried about you, Ivy, and also worried that he might have given Preston the tools he needed for the attack. He knew Teague and saw him a few months ago. He said the guy had a serious gambling addiction and was in way over his head with the kind of people you don't get in over your head with. Preston probably offered him a lot of money for his services. Leon Parish and Billy Rice both identified Oliver Teague as the person who hired them to kidnap Ivy. We still don't know where the third guy who held you hostage is, but we have alerts sent to the local morgues."

Luke's expression said he thought the guy was long gone, and not in the trip-around-the-world sense. "Right now, the theory is that Preston left Teague in your bedroom in hopes that it would point a finger at Abott and buy him the time he needed to get the ransomware installed on your systems."

Zane continued to pace behind the sofa. "We think he expected you to be at the ballpark, and he planned to grab you there. Forensics found three syringes at the house where Tez was located. We're guessing he planned to drug you, get you to talk, and then leave you with no memory of what had happened. Taking a child probably wasn't in the plan, but when you didn't show at the ballpark, he adjusted on the fly."

Faith tilted a bottle of Cherry Coke in Gil's direction. "You almost got shot again last night. I've told you. I'm done with that. Now, stop it."

Gil blew her a kiss. "Yes, ma'am."

She narrowed her eyes at him, then shocked Ivy to her core when she jumped up, came straight at Gil, and threw her arms around him. "I mean it," she said into his neck. "Don't do that to me again." Gil hugged her close and whispered something Ivy didn't catch. Faith squeezed him tighter, then released him and turned the full force of her presence on Ivy.

"As for you, I don't know if we should take your weapon away or hire you. You never, ever shoot blind. Never." Ivy didn't know how to respond to that, but Faith didn't give her a chance. "Nice shooting. Tessa and I will take you to a range we like out in the country. We shoot scarecrows and bales of hay. It's awesome."

Ivy had no idea how to respond to that either, but there was no way she was going to disagree with Faith Malone when she was clearly fired up about a lot of things, including Gil getting almost shot. "That sounds great."

Luke, Zane, and Gil all huffed and looked to the ceiling, then to each other.

"What?" Ivy asked.

"The last time they went there, they picked up two new boyfriends." Zane glared at Tessa.

"Each." Luke glared at Faith.

Gil glared at Ivy. She glared back. "Don't look at me that way. I haven't even been there."

"Don't get any ideas." Gil wasn't joking. "I had to threaten one of them with jail time before they backed off."

Faith and Tessa grinned. Zane and Luke groaned.

Gil squeezed Ivy closer and whispered, "Welcome to the family."

— 42 —

THREE MONTHS LATER

Gil's alarm went off at 6:10 a.m. It was time. He pulled on clothes, checked his pockets, and left his childhood bedroom. Two steps down the hall, he opened Emily's door. Two twin beds held the two women he loved beyond all reason. His sister's dark head lifted from the pillow, and there was a definite hint of merriment in her eyes.

"Good luck," she mouthed, then rolled toward the wall, very obviously giving him privacy.

He crept to the other bed and knelt beside it. He brushed a blonde strand from Ivy's cheek and tucked it behind her ear. "Buttercup? Wake up for me, baby."

"What's going on?" Her voice was thick with sleep, and her words were garbled.

"Come with me."

"What time is it?" Her brow furrowed in confusion, but she sat and moved toward him. "Is everything okay?"

"Everything's great, but I need to show you something."

"Can I get dressed first?"

He kissed her forehead. "Yes, but don't take too long. I'll meet you in the kitchen."

He left her sitting on the side of the bed and went to the kitchen. The coffeepot was full and waiting, and he poured a glug of hazelnut creamer into an insulated mug, topped it with coffee, then fixed his own cup.

She didn't make him wait long. As soon as she entered the kitchen, he handed her the coffee, then took her fully healed right hand in his left and pulled her to the door, bundled her into her heavy jacket, and walked out through the backyard.

She sipped her coffee and joined him without any argument but also without any conversation. Good. The only way this plan had any hope of working was if he could get her to their spot before she became fully awake. Once the coffee kicked in, her curiosity would overtake everything.

They walked through a pasture along a narrow path until they hit the creek that was the back edge of his parents' land. He turned left, and they walked another fifty yards until they reached a large, flat boulder that jutted over the creek.

"Gil." Her hand clenched in his. She was catching on.

"Here." He handed her his coffee and climbed to the top of the boulder. Then he reached down, and she handed him both coffees before she scrambled up beside him. He sat down and crossed his legs, and without him saying anything, she did the same, sitting so they were facing each other, their knees touching.

The last time they'd sat this way had been at 6:30 a.m., exactly twenty-four years ago. He'd been nine. She'd been eight. She'd said goodbye and ran back to the house in tears. He'd followed, slower, because he didn't want anyone to see his own tears.

But before the tears . . .

"You remember?" They'd never talked about it. Not even the

summer when they were together as teens. But Ivy's memory was impressive. He was counting on it now.

Her lips turned upward. "A girl never forgets her first kiss."

"I promised you I'd never tell, and I didn't. Not even Emily."

"Me neither."

He took her hands in his. "Do you remember what I told you?"

She looked from their fingers twisted together between them, then back to his face. "You told me that after you grew up, you'd find me. And you did."

"Do you remember anything else?"

Ivy's cheeks flushed scarlet in the morning haze, but she didn't look away. "Yes." The word was a whisper. He squeezed her hands, and she went on. "You said after you found me, we'd be together forever."

"Yes, I did." He leaned toward her and pressed his lips to hers. It was a brief, gentle kiss, reminiscent of the childish, tentative one they'd shared twenty-four years earlier. He pulled back, but only a few inches. "Would you allow me to keep the second part of my promise by becoming my wife?"

Her answering smile told him everything he needed to know. She threw her arms around his neck, pulled him to her, and kissed him until they were both breathless. Only then did she gasp, "Yes. Yes. Yes. Always yes. It's always been you. It will always be you."

He stopped further conversation by pulling her fully into his arms, and it was quite a while before he remembered that he'd forgotten a key part of his carefully planned proposal. "Ivy?" He murmured her name, his lips brushing hers.

"Hmm?"

"Do you want to see your ring?"

They were both laughing as he slid the diamond onto her finger.

Acknowledgments

No one ever writes a book on their own. My eternal gratitude to:

The experts who wish to remain anonymous but without whom I would never have attempted to write this story.

My extraordinary family—Brian, Emma, James, Drew, Jennifer, Mom, Dad, and Sandra—for your love and patience with me through yet another novel.

Lynette Eason for being there every time I get stuck, but mostly for your friendship.

My sisters of The Light Brigade, for your ever-present support.

Deborah Clack and Debb Hackett, original members of #Team-Gil, for knowing me so well and liking me anyway.

Kelsey Bowen and Amy Ballor for your editorial expertise. You are a gift.

The remarkable team at Revell who make the publishing journey such joy.

Tamela Hancock Murray, my kind and encouraging agent.

Friends who helped along the way—Carrie Stuart Parks, Colleen Coble, Robin Caroll, Pam Hillman, Edie Melson, Emme Gannon, Linda Gilden, Alycia Morales, Tammy Karasek, Erynn

Newman, Michelle Cox, Molly Jo Realy, Lisa Carter, and Alison Hendley.

Most of all, to My Savior, the Ultimate Storyteller, for allowing me to write stories for you.

> Let the words of my mouth and the meditation of my
> heart be acceptable in your sight,
> O LORD, my rock and my redeemer. (Psalm 19:14)

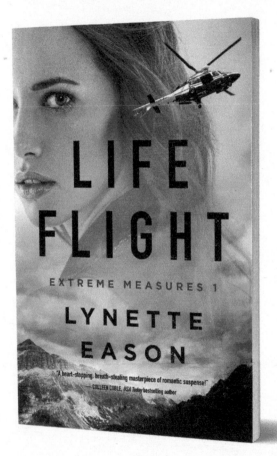

—1—

Today was not going to be the day they died—not if she had anything to say about it. EMS helicopter pilot Penny Carlton tightened her grip on the throttle of the MBB Bo 105 chopper and prayed the wind would calm down long enough to get their patient to Mercy Mission Hospital on the other side of the mountain.

Flying in bad weather was nothing new, and Penny often did it without hesitation, knowing it was a life-or-death situation. But today was exceptionally bad, with rain and ice slashing the windshield, requiring all of her concentration to keep them on course. Not to mention in the air as the potential of icing increased.

"Come on, Betty Sue, you can do this. We've come this far, we're gonna make it, right?" Penny talked to the chopper on occasion—mostly when she was worried.

She'd protested the flight to her supervisor, and he ordered her to do it or find another job. With only a brief thought that she should walk away, her mind went to the person in jeopardy. At the time, the weather hadn't been nearly as violent as it was now, so

351

she'd ignored the weather warnings and agreed, praying they could beat the storm long enough to get in, get the patient, and get out.

Unfortunately, things hadn't worked out that way, and now she battled the weather while fifteen-year-old Claire Gentry fought to live.

Claire had been hiking with friends along one of Mount Mitchell's most rugged trails when a gust of harsh wind had blown her off balance and over the side of the mountain onto a ledge below. Once the rescue team had gotten her back up, it was Penny's turn to make sure Claire lived to see sixteen. "How's she doing back there?"

"Not good," Holly Cooper said into her mic. A nurse practitioner, Holly could handle just about any medical emergency that came up. However, controlling the weather was out of their hands. "Raina, hand me that morphine," she said. "She's hurting. And get pressure back on her side. She's bleeding again."

Raina Price, the critical care transport paramedic, moved to obey. The three of them had been saving lives together for the past twenty months.

Thunder boomed and lightning lit up the sky way too close for comfort. Penny tuned out the familiar beep and whine of the machines behind her, knowing the best way she could help Claire was to get her to the hospital.

A hard slam against the left side of the chopper knocked the cyclic control stick from her grip, sending them sideways. Yells from Raina and Holly echoed in her ears. "Hold on!" Penny grabbed the stick, righted the chopper, and pushed the left antitorque pedal, the helicopter sluggish in response to her attempts to turn it into the wind.

"Penny! What's happening?"

"We got hit with something! I think it damaged the tail rotor. I'm going to have to land it."

"You can't." Holly's calm words helped settle her racing pulse. A fraction. "Claire's most likely going to die if we don't get her to the hospital."

The wind threw them into a rapid descent, sending Penny's stomach with it. The chopper wasn't spinning, so the tail rotor wasn't completely damaged, but something was definitely—desperately—wrong. "I don't have a choice!" They would *all* die if she didn't do something now. She keyed her microphone and advised air traffic control of the emergency and their approximate location.

". . . breaking up . . . please repeat."

Penny did and got silence for her efforts. "Mayday! Mayday. Anyone there?"

Nothing. She was out of time.

The instrument panel flashed and went dark. "No, don't do that! You're not supposed to do that."

"Do what?" Holly yelled.

Penny ignored her and got a grip on her fear while she tried to make out the fast-approaching ground amid flashes of lightning. The last one allowed her to spot a small neighborhood with a row of houses farther down the side of the mountain—at least she thought that's what she saw. The storm was now raging, visibility practically nil.

She would have to go by the memory of the brief glances. The top of the mountain had looked flat with a bare area where she thought she could safely land. Or at least not crash into trees—or homes.

The throttle was set, controlled by the governor. Now all she had to do was point the nose of the chopper downward to keep them from entering an out-of-control spin. "Come on, girl, you can do this," she muttered. "We can do this. Just a little farther."

The trees were somewhere straight ahead. The loose watch on her left wrist bounced against her skin in time with the movement of the chopper.

"Penny!" Holly's tightly held fear bled through her voice. "Tell me what we're doing."

"Just focus on your patient and I'll get us on the ground. We're going to be fine." *Please, God, let us be okay. Please.* She'd trained for this. Over and over, she'd practiced what to do if she lost a tail rotor or had engine issues or whatever. The engine was still good, and a Messerschmitt-Bölkow-Blohm could perform amazing aerobatic maneuvers when called on. For a brief moment, her panel flickered to life and she quickly checked her altitude and airspeed. So far, so good. For now.

"I can do this," she whispered. "Come on, Betty Sue, please don't quit on me now."

They'd *all* trained for situations like this. Mostly, focusing on how to keep the patient stable in the midst of an emergency landing. *Landing, please. Not a crash.*

When her panel fluttered, then went dark once more, she groaned and squinted through the glass. More thunder shook the air around them, but the nonstop lightning was going to be what saved them.

The landing spot she'd picked out wasn't perfect, but it would have to do. At least it was mostly flat—and big. "Brace yourselves," she said. "It's going to be a rough landing, but we *are* going to walk away from this. *All* of us."

The tops of the trees were closer than she'd like, but the small opening just beyond them was within reach. "Almost there!" A gust of wind whipped hard against her and debris crashed into the windshield, spreading the cracks. Penny let out a screech but kept her grip steady. "Come on, come on." She maneuvered the controls, keeping an eye on the trees through the cracked windshield. Okay, the tail rotor was responding somewhat. That would help. "We're going to have a hard bounce! Be ready."

She whooshed past the trees, their tips scraping the underbelly of the chopper, but she cleared them. Her heart pounded in her ears. Down, down . . .

The helicopter tilted, the right landing skid hitting first and sliding across the rocky ground. A scream came from the back and supplies flew through the cabin. Something slammed into the side of Penny's helmet, and she flinched and pushed hard on the collective, angling the rotors, desperate to get both skids on the ground. They bounced, rocked, then settled on the skids. Upright and still breathing.

She'd done it. She was alive. *They* were alive. With shaking hands, she shut down the engine and took off her helmet. *Thank you, Jesus.*

She turned to see Raina and Holly unbuckling their safety harnesses. Holly dropped to her knees next to the patient while Raina dabbed at a cut on her forehead.

"You okay?" she asked Raina.

"Yeah. This is minor compared to what it could have been."

"How's Claire?" Penny asked.

"Hanging in there," Holly said. She pulled the stethoscope from her ears. "Where are we?"

"I don't know, but there's a rescue team on the way. I hope." If they could get through. Even now, the rain and wind whipped at the chopper body. "We just need to stay put until someone comes."

Raina met her eyes. "You did good, Pen. I don't know how you did it, but you did."

Penny wasn't sure either. "God did it. I was praying the whole time, so that's the only explanation I've got."

"Yeah."

She needed to check the chopper and see what the damage was. Not that she could fix it, but . . .

She glanced upward. "Thank you," she whispered.

Holly shot her a quick look. "What?"

"Nothing." Penny eyed Claire and didn't like what she was seeing. She snagged the radio again. "Mayday, Mayday, Mayday. This is Medevac 2646 advising of an emergency landing somewhere on top of Mount Mitchell. Requesting immediate extraction. Four passengers. One critical. Over." Then waited. No reply.

With another glance at her passengers, she tried one more time, all the while knowing it was useless. "Mayday, Mayday!"

No response.

"Okay, that's not good," she muttered. She snagged her cell phone from her pocket. One bar. She dialed 911 and waited. The call dropped. She tried again with the same result. If she had a sat phone, she could use that, but she didn't have one, and she didn't have time to be angry over the reason why.

Think, Penny, think. She turned back to the others, who were monitoring Claire. "Holly, I can't get a signal and nothing's happening with the radio. I'm going to have to try and walk until I get something."

Raina scowled. "Stupid mountains."

"All right, here's the deal," Penny said. "I have no idea if anyone heard my Mayday—or anything else. You guys keep Claire stable. I'll be back as soon as I can get word to someone where to find us. I saw a few houses scattered in the area. I just need to find a road and follow it. Hopefully the closer I get to a neighborhood or house, I'll pick up a cell phone signal."

"Can't they track the ELT?" Holly asked.

The emergency locator transmitter. "They should be able to,

but I don't want to take a chance on it malfunctioning. Something's going on with the electrical. The instrument panel keeps flickering and the radio's not working."

"You can't go out in this," Raina said. "This weather is too dangerous."

"If Claire wasn't in such bad shape, I'd sit it out with you guys, but I've got to try—and when we get back, we're having a fundraiser for a satellite phone." She was going to have it out with her supervisor as soon as she saw him face-to-face. Thanks to his budget cutting, they could very well die out here. If she had a sat phone, she could—

Nope. Not going to think about that.

Penny grabbed the poncho from the bin next to the stretcher. "If I'm not back and help arrives, you get Claire to the hospital. I can wait for the next ride."

"But, Pen—" Holly started to protest, but Penny was already shaking her head.

"I mean it," she said. "You know you can't wait on me to get back."

"Fine," Raina said. "But if you're not back in an hour, I'm coming looking for you."

"Don't you dare. Holly needs your help with Claire. I'll be fine. If I can survive juvie, this little storm is child's play."

"Juvie?" Holly asked. "Why is this the first I've heard of that?"

"Long, boring story. I was a bad girl, they sent me to juvie, and I got my head on straight. End of story."

"Right."

Penny pulled four protein bars and two bottles of water from the small pack she carried on every flight. "Just in case you guys get hungry." She slid the pack with the remaining protein bars and bottles of water over her shoulder and grabbed the emergency flashlight from the box, then opened the door. The rain had slacked off slightly—at least she thought so. She pulled the poncho over her and the pack and hopped to the ground. "Keep her alive! I'll be back!"

Penny shut the door behind her and turned. With her cell phone clutched in her left hand, she darted into the woods.

FBI SPECIAL AGENT Holton Satterfield jerked his feet from the desktop and slammed them to the floor even while he pressed the phone to his ear. He hadn't thought the day could get any worse. First, his conversation with his sister Rachel about their older sibling, Zoe, had gone so far south, it was probably north at this point. And now this. "I know you didn't just tell me that."

"Unfortunately, I did," Gerald Long said. The Special Supervisory Agent didn't sound any happier than Holt. "But Rabor is armed and on the run."

"How?"

"He had help. His loyal girlfriend, Shondra Miller, disguised herself as a nurse and walked right in with a key to the cuffs." Gerald's disgust echoed through the line.

Holt didn't bother asking how she managed to bypass all the security and ID checks to get to the patient. That was someone else's responsibility to investigate, but it had happened and now he needed to deal with the fallout.

"When?" After Darius Rabor had killed a federal judge, the FBI had joined the hunt for him. Holt had been lead on the task force that put Rabor away a year and a half ago. He'd been on death row, his execution date coming up next month.

"Two hours ago," Gerald said. "Rabor was in the hospital for emergency gall bladder surgery. Killed a nurse and the two transport officers. One of the hospital security guards is in surgery. I'm reconvening the original task force, as everyone is already familiar with this guy. I need you and Sands in Asheville, North Carolina, yesterday."

"Asheville. Of course he'd go back there," Holt muttered. Rabor knew the mountains well and had family there. Holt was in the Columbia, South Carolina, field office, and Rabor had been incarcerated at the Broad River Correctional Institution just a few miles away. Where Holt's sister was also an inmate. He grimaced at the unwanted thought. But there was nothing he could do about Zoe. He had a killer to capture again before anyone else died by his hand.

"He had surgery yesterday," Gerald said. "This afternoon, he was in his room, cuffed to the bed. The next time someone checked on him, he was coming out of the bathroom, dressed in street clothes. Before the guard had a chance to pull his weapon, Rabor used a knife to stab the guy three times."

"That's his weapon of choice. A knife slipped to him by his girlfriend, along with the key?"

"No doubt. And the clothes to allow him to blend in. After he killed the guard, he took the man's weapon and, in the ensuing chaos, shot his way out. The two then stole a car from the valet parking attendant and headed out of town with police after them. They made it to Asheville, then crashed at the bottom of Mount Mitchell. He and Shondra took off on foot, going up. I'm sending you the coordinates. Police chased them up the mountain and put out an alert for residents to lock their homes and report anything suspicious. Asheville's RA is expecting you and will be offering support." He paused. "On the ground anyway. Air support is iffy at this point, with the storms getting ready to unleash their worst on the area. But you're going to have to take a chopper to get there. It's standing by. When you land, the RA has a car waiting for you."

Great. "We're on the way." He hung up, took a moment to gather his thoughts and emotions, then shot to his feet.

His partner, Martin Sands, looked up. "What now? More stuff with Zoe? Her kids okay?"

Marty was the one person Holt felt comfortable venting to about his sister and her confession to killing her husband two years ago—and the fact that he'd finally conceded that she did it. He ignored the shame that tried to creep in every time he thought about her. He should be turning over every rock to find evidence to the contrary, but the truth was, his sister was guilty of murder. Why work to prove her innocence when all the evidence and her own words said the effort would be a waste of time?

"No, she's on the back burner for now. Her kids are fine." They lived with his parents for the moment. Twelve-year-old Ellie and eight-year-old Krissy. His precious nieces that he never got to see enough of. "Rabor and his girlfriend are on the loose. You and I are now officially back on the task force to recapture him."

"What? You're kidding me. How?"

"I'll explain on the way."

Martin followed him out the door, muttering his displeasure. Holt let him vent while he concentrated on how best to catch the man. Again. It hadn't been easy the first time.

It would be even harder now, as Rabor wouldn't make the same mistakes twice—and he had his girlfriend helping him this time. However, he was one day out of surgery. How far could he get? Then again, the fact that he'd managed to kill three people in spite of being on drugs and, most likely, in pain, sent dread coursing through him. Holt knew better than anyone just how resourceful the killer was, and he had the scar to prove it. His hand went to the area just below his vest on his left side, but he didn't need to touch the place to know what was there. The nightmares reminded him most nights.

They headed for the chopper while thunder boomed in the distance. It wasn't raining yet, but it was about to start at any moment. The pilot nodded to them and soon they were in the air, headed toward the mountain. Thirty minutes later, Holt slid into the driver's seat of the Bureau's waiting sedan and checked the weather app on his phone. "This is going to be a fun drive. It's cold and icy, and storm warnings are everywhere."

"We've driven through worse. Right?"

True, but he didn't like it any more than Marty did—and Marty *really* hated bad weather. Holt's phone dinged again. "Command center is on the way too. We'll meet them there."

They drove through the blowing wind and rain with Holt fighting to keep the vehicle on the road. Across the street from the base of the mountain, the mobile command center had already been set up in the elementary school parking lot. Holt ducked into the customized motor home and shook the water out of his hair. Marty entered behind him. Seated in front of the first computer to Holt's left was Julianna Jameson. "Jules? What brings you here? He hasn't taken any hostages, has he?"

"Not yet."

Julianna was one of the Bureau's most skilled negotiators with the Crisis Negotiation Unit. She was also one of his favorite people, with her quick wit and dry humor. However, she usually didn't go into the field unless the situation called for it.

"I was in the area doing some training. When I got word about the situation, I hightailed it over here. I'm here as a precaution," she said. "Local cops are swarming the area in spite of the weather. There are six small neighborhoods spaced out along the road that leads to the top of the mountain. Two cop cars are assigned to each one. One at the entrance and one that's driving a constant loop."

"What about the houses that don't have neighborhoods or fences or alarm systems?"

"We've activated the Reverse 911 and officers are going door-to-door and asking residents to phone everyone they can think of to warn them, but it's definitely possible someone will be missed."

"Yeah."

"That's not all. We've gotten word that a medevac chopper made an emergency landing about an hour ago in a clearing on top of the mountain, and Gerald asked me to be on-site just in case Darius manages to get there first."

"Oh no." He took a seat opposite her.

She studied him. "It's Penny and her crew, Holt. They've got a fifteen-year-old patient in pretty serious shape."

Holt raked a hand through his hair. Penny, Holly, and Raina had been the ones to save his life eighteen months ago. He and Penny had hit it off and gone out a few times after he'd recovered. While their relationship was only at a friendship-but-could-possibly-be-more stage—and had been for longer than he liked as he was ready for the "more" part—their schedules hadn't allowed more than brief dinners and short conversations on the phone. But he cared about Penny. A lot.

She and Julianna were tight friends, sharing a past that he still didn't know all the details of. "All right, then we need to head that way and get them down off that mountain. If Rabor or Shondra run into them . . ."

"Yeah. And unfortunately, they're not answering the attempts to contact them. The emergency locator beacon is the only thing they have to go on right now."

"That doesn't sound good."

"This storm is only going to get worse in the next little while,"

Julianna said. "Hopefully, we can get to them before too much longer."

"We?" Julianna wouldn't normally do something like that, but since it was Penny—

"I'm going with you." She narrowed her eyes. "There's a killer up there. And so are Penny and the others. If he manages to grab one of them, it's not going to be good."

"Yeah."

"I need to be there."

"I agree," Holt said. "Rabor knows we're on his tail and is going to be looking for someone he can use as leverage. I don't want to give him that opportunity."

She nodded. "Exactly."

With practiced movements, they gathered their gear, satellite phones, and rain ponchos and headed back out into the storm.

Lynn H. Blackburn is the award-winning author of *Unknown Threat* and the Dive Team Investigations series. She believes in the power of stories, especially those that remind us that true love exists, a gift from the Truest Love. Blackburn is passionate about CrossFit, coffee, and chocolate (don't make her choose) and experimenting with recipes that feed both body and soul. She lives in Simpsonville, South Carolina, with her true love, Brian, and their three children. Learn more at LynnHBlackburn.com.